Sleep in Peace

Melanie Doctors

Text copyright © 2024 by Melanie Doctors

Cover Illustration © Nat Mack
Distributed by Simon & Schuster

ISBN: 978-1-998076-45-1
Ebook: 978-1-998076-47-5

FIC045010 FICTION / Family Life / Marriage & Divorce
FIC044000 FICTION / Women

#SleepInPeace

Follow Rising Action on our socials
Twitter: @RAPubCollective
Instagram: @risingactionpublishingco
Tiktok: @risingactionpublishingco

Please note content warnings: Domestic abuse and manipulation, a scene of marital rape, alcoholism, child sexual abuse

For Ronald Doctors, the ultimate renaissance man and the best dad a girl could be lucky enough to have. You inspire me to walk the infinite and glorious road of my imagination.

Love you forever.

Sleep in Peace

Chapter One

San Francisco, California, May 2007

It was worth cold toes and all-consuming guilt to fold Susan's silvery blanket up, leave it like a *Dear John* letter on her swanky couch, and slink into the darkness. Tonight's "session" had been particularly brutal. My forty-three-year-old empty shell of a soul begged for the curative powers of a particular two-bedroom Craftsman on a tree-lined street: Mom's house. Not a sleepover at Susan's, where she plied me with cocktails, psychoanalyzed me by the numbers, and would no doubt interrogate me over excellent morning coffee.

A chilly mist rose from the bay as I darted barefoot across the crooked street, my scuffed boots and thrift-store-chic knapsack clasped in my arms like a dozing infant. I tossed my stuff in the back seat of my baby blue Mercedes, and slid in. Fuck her.

I fired up my beloved beater—a spluttering, cantankerous geezer rudely woken in what was left of the night. I cringed and prayed that the racket hadn't roused Susan and Brett, the Wonder Husband. Neither of them knew anything about endless, sleepless nights; the perfect couple no doubt dreaming in stereo.

Per the secret clause in our friendship bylaws, I had a few character defects that could be tweaked, and I had offered myself as a willing guinea pig for Susan's latest passion: how to be an unlicensed therapist in sixteen online classes. Why a successful divorce attorney needed to learn the equivalent of psychological warfare—in sixteen classes—I didn't want to know.

After take-out sushi from Akiko's, I burrowed into her plum velvet couch, imagined demons in the flames of the fireplace, and sucked down an Old Fashioned, the cocktail brandished against my chest like a Roman shield. After fourteen weeks of "therapy," Susan was still dead wrong. I'd *never* go back to Scott, another rat bastard *wouldn't* take his place, and I didn't have *daddy* issues. When Daddy had been dead for forty years, the issue were long gone.

I fished a can of Coke out from the mess on the front seat and popped it open with one hand. I never drank water. Since the age of eight, I'd been haunted by Mom's claim that everything is recycled, including Julius Caesar's pee. Perhaps Susan was right, and my childhood wasn't as normal as I liked to believe.

Did Susan deserve an explanation as to why Scott's latest affair hadn't hurt me as much as she thought it should have? She did, not that she'd understand. Comfortably numb was a blessing, not a curse.

"Leanne, you fished a warm, damp, Barbie-pink thong off your bedroom floor. React. What the hell is wrong with you?"

I'd snagged another Old Fashioned from Susan with the hand that wasn't curled into a permanent fist. "What was I supposed to do? Burn it and ruin original oak flooring and torture myself with a permanent scorch mark?"

"Fire seems a little extreme."

"Good thing I was fresh out of lighter fluid."

Susan tossed me the blanket in case therapy rendered me too distraught to drive home. That, and the bourbon. She was a considerate and conscientious tormentor.

"Why aren't you livid, or crying, at the very least? Let's try a little hypnosis. Delve into the misty corners of your subconscious. Hypnosis is an effective modality, and Brett won't let me practice on him."

"Hell, no." I took a long, slow sip of orangey bourbon goodness. "I'm processing. Isn't that what you call it? Letting reality simmer on a low boil while I figure out how I feel?"

I processed while driving across the Bay Bridge, the mist hiding everything except a set of taillights ahead of me. It's lonely at 4 a.m., the hour of the wolf, when most of the world sleeps without hesitation, but never those ruled by an unknown force. *Warm* thong? I snickered and leaned against the cracked leather headrest, exhausted from Susan's relentless desire to save me from myself. With the touch of my finger, *Fool That I Am* blared from the sketchy speakers, breaking the silence.

The streetlights were out when I pulled into the driveway, but a new daisy border glimmered against the dark rectangle of the lawn. What the hell is going on? Mom doesn't garden. I flipped on my high beams. In front of the old oak, a putrid green *For Sale* sign with a picture of real estate agent Sandy Selridge leered in anticipated triumph. I death-gripped my steering wheel and stared. *Oh no you don't, Sandy Selridge—not my mom, not our house. Fuck your cheap-ass daisies.*

With trembling fingers, I rummaged in my purse and found my house key attached to a frayed red ribbon. The thrill of getting my very own key on my tenth birthday still got me. My throat tightened; I crunched a handful of cinnamon Altoids and pulled on my boots, ready for battle. Our home wasn't for sale.

Where in the hell was the gold four-leaf clover that hung over the front door? I poked around the fresh foliage and saw a glint of gold. The real estate tramp had tossed my birthright in her goddamn bushes. I flipped over Sandy Shitridge's hideous flower-filled planter, jumped on top, and hung the talisman on the hook where it belonged.

Once inside, I rested my cheek against the heavy oak door, smooth from a thousand baths of lemon oil. She wouldn't sell. There must be a mistake.

"Mom? What's with the for sale sign?"

I flipped the lights on.

"Mom?"

I tiptoed down the hall and eased her bedroom door open. Not a pillow was out of place on her bed. I rifled through her closet—a handful of her favorite dresses and fake mink coat were gone. Strange. The medicine cabinet in her bathroom was full, but her sequined cosmetic bag and her bottle of Miss Dior, her signature fragrance, were MIA. And the matching bottle of lotion. Interesting priorities. This wasn't a kidnapping.

I hit my number one contact. When she didn't answer, I texted her.

Mom! Where *are you? Call me.*

Cold sweat slithered down my back. My lungs squeezed shut. Should I call Jeffrey, my one and only sibling? Hell, no, he'd give me a hard time for being a baby.

Call me NOW.

The house was creepy, like a cold body had been carried out moments before on a stretcher. The fire in my gut exploded. I headed to the refrigerator, desperate for ginger ale. A bottle of flat Diet Coke and the Chinese takeout I'd brought over three nights ago sat center stage. Three days? How long had she been gone? I reached into a scratched cabinet, grabbed Jeffrey's faded Batman juice glass and a full bottle of Smirnoff from under the sink, and poured a drink.

The Caped Crusader had seen better days. When we were kids, Jeffrey had sent in twenty Rice Krispies Box Tops to win that prize. Neither one of us liked Rice Krispies—we were Lucky Charms people. We choked down those bland pellets until he had enough to win the damn glass.

Daybreak snuck into the backyard as I peered through the kitchen window at the freshly rolled-out sod and another fucking generic daisy border.

"You'll sell this house over my dead body, Ms. *Shitridge.*"

I tossed back the booze to soothe the lump in my throat. I poured another and grabbed the sesame chicken from the fridge, along with a fork. Curled up on the couch with Batman, I conjured memories to fill the painful void in my chest.

Once a month, Jeffrey and I tagged along while Mom gathered the occasional dead cat or dog from between the gravel-strewn road and the dirt on the side of the highway. We didn't think she was weird. She was like the English archeologist in the King Tut movie during rainy-day

5

recess—respectful and quiet, like the roadkill was the fragile remains of a long-dead king.

She'd get us popcorn with fake butter and follow her usual route like Bob the mailman. We'd stay in the car while she placed broken bodies in handmade coffins she made with the tools she got in the Sears after-Christmas sale. I guess everyone needed a hobby.

"Leanne, why is she taking so long?" Jeffrey said, sitting like a monkey, his dirty sneakers on the seat and buttery palms and lips plastered against his window.

"Get your hands off the glass. No one's gonna buy a car with greasy windows." I glared at the brat.

Mom was the secretary at Mr. Benjamin Woods' Used Ford and Chevrolet, the 'Family First' dealership in Lafayette. She said she felt like hired entertainment between the creepy sales guys and a bunch of mechanics.

"I've half a mind to tell those wives what goes on, but they'd never believe me. The world's not fair, Leanne. They don't hire you unless you're pretty, and then don't let you finish your work when you are."

Jeffrey slumped in the back seat, his sweaty boy-hair sticking up like devil horns. I cracked a hard kernel between my back teeth and thought about those stupid men, Mom's movie star sunglasses sheltering my eyes from the bright sunshine.

Jeffrey threw a handful of greasy popcorn at my head. "Leanne, answer me."

We had strict instructions not to make a mess in *this* car, a lilac-scented, baby-blue convertible that would sell in a heartbeat with my pretty mom driving it around town. She slid into the driver's seat, palm outstretched for her sunglasses, her eyes more than a little red.

"Goddammit. What did I tell you about the windows? Mr. Woods could fire me. Leanne, get in the back seat." She snapped open her purse, took out her compact, and fixed her face.

"Better butter on the window than a dead cat in the trunk," Jeffrey said.

I shoved his dirty knee to his side of the car and smacked G.I. Joe off the seat.

"Idiot," I mouthed at him.

Mom shifted the rear-view mirror and gave Jeffrey her best zombie stare; her unblinking, tiger-colored eyes could take your soul hostage for hours.

"I don't know where you bought that smart mouth, mister, but you better return it before it gets you into more trouble."

"Would Mr. Woods fire you for butter on the window?" I asked.

"He could, but he'll never know because Jeffrey will scrub the car spic and span after the funeral."

Jeffrey made G.I. Joe burp in my face.

When we got home, Mom put a boil-in-the-bag Salisbury steak on the stove, and Jeffrey dug a hole in the backyard while I picked yellow marigolds from the neighbor's garden. Mom joined us as Jeffrey filled in the dirt, and I placed the flowers on the newest mound.

"Leanne, please say a prayer," Mom said.

I pressed my hands together and closed my eyes. "Dear God, please bring this precious cat to heaven, and we ask you to curse the rat bastard who ran over him. Amen."

"Leanne! What did I tell you about swearing?"

"Rat bastard doesn't count. You say it all the time."

Mom rolled her eyes and went inside to finish making dinner. Jeffrey and I stayed with the cat for a bit, so it didn't feel lonely.

After dinner, Jeffrey and I watched Mutual of Omaha's *Wild Kingdom* in the living room. We turned it as loud as possible to drown out the buzz of Mom's saw and helped ourselves to a half-thawed coconut cream pie. We rooted for the oldest wildebeest, which Jeffrey had named Bob, like our mailman, but the lions won. Then Mom came in with a fresh coffin. She smelled like burnt wood.

"Come help me with the dishes."

"Why don't you burn RIP on the top instead of SIP? SIP is dumb." Jeffrey followed Mom, licking the last scraps of cream from the aluminum pie plate.

"Sleeping lasts longer than resting, it makes more sense to me. " she said, putting the coffin on the counter.

"Did you put SIP on Daddy's coffin?" Jeffrey asked.

Mom grabbed the Salisbury steak knife and hurled it at the closed kitchen window. I put my hands over my ears, but every shard exploded as it hit the brick patio below the window. Jeffrey's eyes widened as he clamped his hands over his mouth, both of us frozen with fear like Bob the wildebeest. I stared at the butterflies on Mom's apron until they stopped moving and willed myself not to cry. She whispered, "I'm sorry," and reached out to us with the saddest smile I'd ever seen.

"Who wants to get a Frosty?" she asked.

Jeffrey should have known better than to mention Daddy's coffin.

Batman suggested we text Mom again.

Since when don't you come home? Call me ASAP.

As I set aside the last bite of chicken, dread spun my mind like an old-school DJ with a stack of vinyl of songs I didn't want to listen to. *Breathe.* I picked up my favorite photo from the coffee table. Jeffrey clutched a plastic pitchfork in his fat little hand, his devil mask smeared with chocolate. I was in a flowing white dress, angel wings on my back, my face covered by a golden mask, and both of us held Daddy's hands in front of a big old Jack O'Lantern.

I loved Dad's face with his tender smile, his eyes full of warmth. All I had left of him was a mantle of bowling trophies, a closet full of old clothes, and lots of pictures. I kissed his forehead and settled the frame over where Jeffrey had carved a wiener dog named Bob into the soft pine.

Desperate for a distraction, I consulted my phone. Who could I call? Susan? Not after last night. Enough was enough. Was it too early to call Levi? He was my other best friend, the sweet, non-pushy one, who would no doubt be awake, dressed impeccably, and squeezing organic oranges for the kids' breakfast. Reasonable, grounded Levi. He'd talk me off the ledge. I hit contact number three and kept my voice light.

"Did you kidnap my fabulous mother for one of your all-night bridge parties?"

In the background, Eloise begged for chocolate milk, and Paulka told Elliot to grab a light sweater and his *Lord of The Rings* lunchbox.

"No, and it's mahjong now, not bridge. What's wrong?"

Damn. How did he know?

"Mom's not home. She's always home." An apple-sized lump took up residence in my throat to match the ball of terror filling my gut. "She's selling the house." I picked up the photo again and rubbed sesame sauce off the glass with the sleeve of my hoodie.

"Who's selling what house?" Paulka asked with an audible gasp.

"Am I on speakerphone again?"

"We have no secrets. Secrets are the devil's undescended testicles," Paulka said.

Too bad Europe hadn't embraced Paulka as the only pint-sized male model to grace the runways of Prague. It was near impossible to get Levi to myself anymore, let alone his sage-like serenity without a hearty side of drama, courtesy of *the model*. It was bad enough that I had had to share Levi with Mom since he had realized how fabulous she was. I bet they had secret lunches.

"Don't you have kids to get to school?" I asked.

"Why do you think we get up at five?" Levi said.

"It won't take long to unstress you," Paulka added.

I grabbed my drink and made my way down the hall, embracing Paulka's compassion. He loved me like the paparazzi he wished he had. Batman slopped a little vodka on the green shag carpeting. Fuck it. The techie millennials who would undoubtedly buy the place would rip it out anyway.

"There's a *For Sale* sign on the house, and she's disappeared."

"She's probably off on a naughty adventure," Paulka said.

I sniggered. "*My* mom? Mom's *always* home."

"I'm sure there's a reasonable explanation," Levi said.

Silence. Whispering. What did they know?

"I hate to ask, but are you slurring or really tired?" Levi said.

"Come on, kids. Daddy and I need to save Auntie Leanne before school."

"No one needs to save me, Paulka. According to Susan, I can save myself. Levi, I'll call *you* later."

I clutched my silent phone, burrowed into Mom's buttercup-yellow, satin comforter, and closed my eyes. I forced myself into a loose interpretation of namaste calm, my wise mind nowhere to be found, abject panic prying apart what little composure I had left. I dug deeper under the covers and left another text.

Where are you? Come home now. Please.

The Miss Dior lingering on mom's pillow took my panic down a notch. *Breathe.* As a child, I loved lounging on her bed while she lectured Jeffrey on how not to grow up to be a rat bastard.

"When you talk to a woman, look at her face, never at her boobs. Otherwise, it's nothing but a cheap thrill, and nothing cheap lasts longer than a toilet flush."

Jeffrey narrowed his eyes into slits and looked like he understood. I didn't know if he did, being a boy and all, but for the next week, he flushed the toilet enough to wear out the handle.

My phone buzzed against my cramped fingers, and, with it, terror receded to its secret lair. The lump in my throat was back. I swallowed it down and turned on my serious adult voice. Lower pitch, no slurring if possible.

"Where are you? Are you okay?"

"I'm fine, Leanne. Why are you in my house?"

"You mean our house? The one Sandy-Shit-Selridge tricked you into selling?"

"It's *my* house. You have your own house."

"Where are you?"

"If you called before invading at dawn, you'd know that I moved to a condo in the city. It's stunning. You'll love it."

"Bullshit." I punched my fist into her favorite squishy pillow and rolled over. "Three days ago, your big decision was Chow Mein or sesame chicken. You hate the city. You hate apartments, and all those people in tiny boxes. Does Jeffrey know about this?"

"Maybe yes, maybe no. I can't remember, and don't swear. Anyway, I had a dream that I should sell the house."

"A dream? Really? Do tell."

I flipped through the books on her nightstand. *How to Sell Your Home in 30 Days*. *Sex After Sixty*.

What the hell? What else lurked? I yanked open the drawer, which slid to the floor and spilled her bedtime rituals.

"What's that noise? Get out of my nightstand." Mom said.

Little girl guilt washed over me. Mom detested anyone touching her things. Jeffrey and I were banned from her bedroom unless she was in the room. I shoved lotions and potions back in the drawer and headed to the kitchen.

"When are you getting all your stuff?" I asked.

"I took what I wanted."

"Are you kidding me? You left everything. This is weird, even for you. Most people don't move in secret, and when they do, they take their shit with them."

"I mean it, don't swear, or I'll hang up. Sandy said I'd timed the market perfectly."

"You're selling my childhood for a dirty profit. Why do you need to move? We love this house."

I opened the bread drawer, found a box of ancient Oreos, and ripped open a sleeve. The cookies spilled out around my feet.

"And you left all of Daddy's things."

"Have you been drinking?" Mom asked.

Yikes. Again? I channeled my best Meryl Streep and upped my diction. "What about your salute to Vincent Price? I'm sure that you have to disclose there's a pet cemetery in the yard."

Why the hell didn't she have a decent broom? I put the phone on speaker and propped it against the toaster oven.

"It's a non-issue because I haven't buried anything in years. What's that noise? What are you doing, Leanne? You need to leave now."

I shoved a cookie in my mouth and dumped the rest into a trash bag along with the stack of Shitridge's business cards and her glossy brochures.

"Don't touch anything, and go home."

"I won't let you sell our house."

"You're forty-three years old, for God's sake. Time to let some things go. I'll talk to you later. It's *my* house."

She hung up on me. Unbelievable.

She's not leaving our stuff or selling our house. *Why would she move with no notice? Am I ridiculous?* She had sounded agitated and edgy, and *didn't answer my question.* Something was wrong. I shivered like someone walked over my grave, drank down to Batman's utility belt, and shoved my phone into the back pocket of my jeans.

Leave? Oh, no. I wasn't going anywhere, and since she wouldn't explain the madness, I'd figure it out for myself. I refilled the glass to Batman's pointy ears and sauntered back to her bedroom. Sunrise cast an almost biblical ray of light onto her maple dresser. Susan was right; the universe provided definite signs.

I slid the forbidden bottom drawer open, where turquoise beads glistened like the coins Jeffrey and I counted out on the Sears jewelry counter, hoping we had enough for a Mother's Day present. I draped the six strands of sparkling plastic around my neck. *Too valuable*, she insisted when we begged her to wear them to Antonio's, the fancy place we went for manners practice.

I pushed aside a paper turkey with faded orange and yellow Popsicle sticks for a tail. Under the turkey, a pink bag with paper-lace hearts hid a dusty J.C. Penney box. She'd kept every Valentine Jeffrey and I made for her, and now none of this mattered? *What is going on?* The brittle hearts scattered like autumn leaves as I pulled the box out and set it on her bed.

An emerald satin dress. A cheesy ring set with a scratched, yellow stone. A faded black-and-white photo in a peeling metal frame. A slick-looking man in a pinstripe suit, a cigarette dangling from his lips, a drink in one hand, and a noticeably young Mom in a low-cut cocktail dress, ropes of pearls around her neck and wrists, perched on his lap like a voluptuous marionette.

What the hell? Mom had to be about sixteen. This guy was what, twenty-six? I didn't like how he wrapped around her like a hot, well-dressed cobra. Mr. Slick looked like the guys I was addicted to. No wonder she'd stashed the photo. She'd never mentioned any man except Daddy, and married at eighteen. I pried the frame open and took out the picture.

On the back, in Mom's dramatic scrawl: *Good Times at Taffy's San Francisco with Vivi and Verin.*

Daddy? He didn't smoke or drink. Since when did Mom call herself Vivi?

I scrutinized the photo more closely. Mr. Slick looked nothing like Daddy.

My phone buzzed against my ass. This better be Mom. Nope. A text from my soon-to-be-fired intern, Candy Mackenzie.

You won't believe this, but Venice is sinking. Not kidding. Got to see it while I can. Ciao.

What happened to ask the boss first? We had a critical order to get out. I couldn't get the mousse order done by tonight even if I mainlined French roast and ate the grounds.

I texted Susan.

ME: Candy's gone to Venice. HELP!

Susan: That's what you get for hiring cooks with stripper names. When is she coming back?

ME: She's in Italy. I don't want her back, and I'm begging.

SUSAN: Two more sessions?

ME: Seriously? I told you no more. I'm fixed.

SUSAN: Sounds like you're a neutered cat.

ME: Not funny. And if I was a cat, I would be spayed.

SUSAN: Yes, funny, and do you want help or not?

ME: 8 a.m.?

SUSAN: You owe me.

I shoved Mom's buried treasures into the box, finished off the vodka, and threw in Batman to keep an eyes on the mysterious Mr. Slick. Vivi had some explaining to do.

Chapter Two

S usan hovered over the professional, ten-burner range in white jeans, a pale blue button-down shirt, and a blue gingham apron tied with a crisp bow. After studying the state health and safety chart pinned to the wall, her hair was scraped into a high ponytail to avoid any legal infringement she deemed crucial. Once a lawyer, always a lawyer.

I'd thrown on a black T-shirt and jeans after a hasty shower at my place. At Kook's, with a white chef's apron tied around my waist, I was the professional. My family crisis stowed, for now.

"The chocolate's taking forever to melt," Susan said. "I'm turning the heat up."

"Don't you dare. Chocolate likes gentle heat, like me."

"Is that why you left last night? Did I hit a nerve? Too intense?"

"I didn't want you to hound me over breakfast about the guy you want to set me up with." I kicked the fridge door shut.

"His name is David."

I tumbled the contents of a case of key limes into the triple-wide, stainless-steel sink, my head pounding from lack of sleep and hydration. Mr. Slick was still slithering around in my brain.

"Shhhhh. Please, stir until I tell you to stop and leave the heat alone."

Cool water ran over the fruit, and several lucky baby spiders escaped the deluge. Could Susan get the truth out of Mom? It would take more than a questionable online class to break the ultimate mistress of sketchy silence.

"I'm helping since you won't help yourself," Susan said.

"Setting me up is not helpful."

"You deserve someone plug-and-play." Susan gestured at me with her chocolate-coated spoon.

The need to confide in her about Mr. Slick and Mom's suspicious behavior became overwhelming. Had she secretly hypnotized me over the Volcano Roll? I wouldn't be surprised.

I motioned to her to keep stirring. "Alright, I'll indulge your silly notion. Who is he?"

"Brett's new running buddy."

"I don't run." I lifted limes onto a clean towel and rubbed the little orbs dry.

"His wife died two years ago. Brett says he's ready to date. He's a doctor for older people. What's not to love?"

"Scott left another message. He misses me."

"Scott's a serial cheater, and last night you swore you'd never go back. Consider David, would you?"

Susan plunged her dripping spoon into a cup of coffee I'd forgotten on the counter yesterday. The cream had separated like gasoline on water, the smell like old cigars. She held out her phone, showing me a photo of Brett the Wonder Husband and Dr. David.

"Gimme that." I peered closer—dark brown, hair almost black, and cobalt blue eyes. Warmth spread through my body. *Traitor.* That particular combo was my undoing, and she knew it, with or without hypnosis.

"Why didn't you show me this photo last night?"

"You were drinking, depressed, and wouldn't have taken me seriously."

I handed her back the phone and gave her a clean spoon. "I don't do nice guys. I'm not ready. Stir, with a fresh spoon, please."

I hunted in a drawer for my favorite fruit knife. Someone had moved it. *Bastards.* Could nothing be easy? Susan stirred the chocolate with one hand and tapped on the metal countertop with the other. Her French-tipped nails were not helping my headache one bit. Her stern lawyer's face was replaced with plausible concern for my failure to see the prize within reach.

"Leanne, David's a Godiva chocolate bunny. The gold foil one in the special box with a fancy ribbon."

I didn't need a faux therapist to explain that my fear of chocolate bunny men was real. I put the knife hunt on hold, pulled a bottle of Grand Marnier from the spice cabinet, and considered my reluctance to meet the fabulous David. All that perfect made my stomach hurt. I moved toward my torturer. She smiled. Her intentions were honorable—moral even, but I knew I'd never be ready for a guy like David.

"I don't deserve chocolate," I said.

Susan set her spoon down, wrapped both arms around me, and became the mama bear that she hid from the rest of the world for a brief minute.

"Everyone deserves chocolate."

Back to business, I inhaled the aroma of liquid heaven, dribbled Grand Marnier into the pot in a steady stream, and gave Susan a half-assed smile. Happy felt years away, if not impossible. When she wasn't looking, I added a hefty pour of the liquor into my coffee mug and blinked until my eyes calmed. Steam wafting from a water bath will fuck with a woman's eyes.

"What am I making?" she asked.

"You are *melting* chocolate. I'm making mousse, and decorating four hundred flutes by myself unless you found another online school that you haven't mentioned," I said, rooting around in a drawer for my favorite knife.

"You call this work?"

I laughed as much as my tender head would allow. "Did you not hear me? Four hundred, in four flavors, delivered by five p.m., and the hostess is a testy bitch with deep pockets who entertains weekly."

"I hope Candy falls off a gondola and drowns."

Susan pursed her lips and stirred with more care and interest than I'd expected. Her usual approach to cooking was arranging takeout on a plate by color and nutritional value.

Goddamn. My knife was behind the bamboo steamers.

Maybe Susan had slipped a little hypnosis in last night. I wanted to meet this guy, and break my bad boy habit, but my getting information out of her was like a fox trying to sneak fried chicken out of a trap without getting caught. I gulped boozy coffee and tried to sound vague.

"Tell me more about the guy." I cut the juicy green limes into halves. The sweet tang cleared my head.

"I thought you weren't interested."

"If you smirk, your lip lines will get worse. Are you finished with the chocolate?"

With one hand on her hip, she lifted the chocolate-coated spoon and let the glossy brown satin flow like a waterfall into the pot. "David is this good."

Susan's joy about my potential happiness was palpable, and I loved her for it, but I wasn't ready for a chocolate bunny. A moldy marshmallow peep hidden under a bush from a decade old Easter egg hunt was more my style. I stared at the cutting board until the limes were a blurry green mass, then wiped my eyes on my apron.

"David sounds too good to be true. He's hiding something. Do you want to crack, squeeze, or whip?" I asked her.

"Who converted my kitchen into a S&M dungeon?" Neil asked as he shucked his backpack and offered his hand to Susan with a grin reserved for substantial lotto wins. "Not that I'm complaining."

She took in his ponytail, tattoos, and a single gold hoop earring the way the Sheriff of Nottingham regarded Robin Hood. The buzzer rang, and Neil headed to the back door to sign for the delivery of organic produce, eggs, and dairy that came in daily from Full Belly Farm, a dream of a farm north of the city. Neil carried back a box of fruit, herbs, and vegetables so gorgeous it could have been a Dutch still-life.

Neil leaned toward Susan. "I'd go for the whipping if I were you. No telling where squeezing will lead."

"I'm a divorce attorney. I know all about squeezing," she whispered back.

"Susan, this is Neil, the culinary genius behind Zen Soup. Susan's saving my ass today, so be kind. She only does take-out."

"It's Leanne's fault I'm here," Susan gave me a pointed look. "I also blame rising sea levels, melting ice caps, and junior chefs without impulse control."

"Candy is only an intern." Couldn't Susan keep her opinions to herself? Just for one day? Next time, I'd ask Comb-Over Norman to stir the chocolate.

Neil shrugged. "It's always someone's fault. Spend a few years on the *inside,* and you'll see." He peered into the chocolate and lifted the heavy pan out of the steamy water bath without potholders. "Let it cool."

Susan filled her cup with coffee and stirred in a whole five-calorie wisp of cream. She was way out of her comfort zone today. "What'd you do?"

"Let's say there's more to catch in a Mexican fishing village than fish."

Susan mouthed a silent and drawn-out *okay,* sucked in her cheeks, and forced her flawless face to relax for a minute. She couldn't resist any longer than that.

"I detest the no-fault thing. Someone is always responsible," Susan smacked the spoon onto the countertop. Chocolate rained on the stainless-steel counter, which she cleaned off without moving a single facial muscle. *Delightfully shocking. Is Susan losing her cultivated cool? What was that about?*

Neil went to the cold walk-in and emerged with two plucked chickens, heads and feet intact, and lay them on a thick, wooden board. A fleeting vision of Mom scooping up roadkill came to mind, and I looked away.

"Fault is an illusion by choice." He locked eyes with Susan, who stood her visual ground as he decapitated the birds then chopped off their feet with a steel cleaver.

"That guy didn't go to cooking school," Susan said, as Neil headed back to the walk-in. She handed me a fresh cup of coffee, creamed and sugared; her skin paler than normal.

"I'm the one that didn't go to school. Neil is Cordon Bleu, and you love his soup. You moaned and said the purple carrot cumin with coconut crème was better than sex."

"Oh my God, that soup? Excuse me; I need air," Susan said, fanning herself.

I cracked up. "Take a tray of cookies to the guys in the alley. They'll love you forever."

"The homeless ones?"

"They're my official tasters, and no one is gluten intolerant. Don't be judgy."

Susan bit her lip and loaded up a tray with miniature fruit tarts, éclairs, a stack of paper napkins, and a paper bag for trash tucked under her arm. She huffed her way out, the screen door slamming behind her. Neil returned while I was cutting the limes.

"What happened to Candy?"

"Venice is sinking. Can I ask you a question?"

"About Susan? She needs a long vacation in Columbia with daily massages."

"She relaxes three weeks a year and is married to a history professor with tenure, so calm down." I settled on the beaten, brown-leather couch, conveniently located smack dab in the middle of the kitchen, and put my feet up. "Have you been set up on a blind date?"

"Never got that lucky, but it's the best way to meet someone."

I sipped my coffee. "Why?"

"Real friends know us better than we know ourselves. They like us better, too."

He plunged chicken pieces into simmering water, and tossed in a handful of herbs and slices of fresh ginger. Susan came inside with an empty tray and a beatific smile on her face. I knew the regulars would love her—Norman in particular—almost as much as he adores my nectarine and ricotta tartlets with the lilikoi glaze.

Susan brushed a crumb from her apron, rinsed the tray, and dried it. She slid it back into a rack with one hand and winked. Excellent. She could help me out in between hypnotizing deadbeat dads for alimony and finding the scars I didn't know I had.

"I'm ready for squeezing," Susan clapped her hands together. "Who knew cooking could be entertaining?"

"Did you set David up with anyone else?" The fried chicken in the trap lured me closer.

"He's waiting for *you*."

I began to cave. Who says no to a fake therapist in a perky apron?

"I can't hear you over the mixer," I said.

"Why don't you want to meet him?" Neil asked, cracking eggs into a mountain of flour.

I turned the speed down by two settings. What the hell was going on today? Mom AWOL. Susan spoon-slapping? Neil interested in something other than a pot of aromatic broth?

"Don't you start," I said.

Susan focused her attention on my supposed failings. "Leanne dates terrible men. A not-so-subtle self-punishment, like a hair shirt made from beard stubble."

Neil cracked up, then got serious. Was he teasing her? "Sounds like deep self-esteem issues."

Susan gave an Oscar-worthy sigh. "Sad, isn't it? She refuses to accept the truth, even with my professional help."

"Give David her number. I'd like to see where this romance goes," Neil said.

"Do not give David my number. For the edification of those present who don't need to know about my personal life, Susan's *professional* help is sketchy at best."

"You know you're curious," Susan said.

"I'm amazed that you can recognize an inquisitive nature through a stubble shirt." I gulped down a third cup of coffee and turned the mixer on high.

"Leanne has boundary issues!" She yelled over the noise. "Meaning, she has none."

"I had boundaries with Scott."

Susan walked over to me and waggled two plump, juicy lime halves in my face.

"Ones he didn't choose to respect."

She returned the fruit to her station and squeezed with a vengeance not often used for small citrus.

Chapter Three

I pulled a mason jar from the cupboard, stuffed it with ice, and poured in equal amounts of vodka and grapefruit juice. I deserved a hefty cocktail after I got a lackluster thank-you from my client. So much for busting my ass to get her ten billion mousses with spun sugar Eiffel Towers delivered on time. I should've made sugar pigeons to crap on the towers.

I took my drink and perched on the edge of the couch, considering Mom's box with nothing and no one to stop me from opening it. With one more sip of holy water, I knelt before her treasure like it was a shrine, and I was the anointed keeper.

With my eyes closed, I pressed the emerald dress to my chest. I imagined Mom stepping into the crisp taffeta for an anniversary dinner with Dad, her nylons making a scratchy sound as she walked. She'd dance, her fingers, spreading like fans, drying her wet nail polish. She'd hold her breath, misting hair spray over her shoulder-length waves. She'd bend, dab a drop of her Miss Dior behind my ears, and tell me to be good for the sitter. Jeffrey and I watched *Happy Days* with TV dinners on our laps for a special treat, tinfoil over the cherry cobbler too hot to touch.

Surprisingly wistful for what never was, I sifted through a handful of dried, colorless flowers and found an old 45 in a plain white sleeve—*Black Coffee* written on the label—ready for a spin. I drained my drink, stuck the ugly ring on my finger, and went to the kitchen for a refill, taking *Verin and Vivi* with me. After popping a slice of rye bread into the toaster, the appropriate pairing for grapefruit and vodka, I sat on the counter and studied the photo in detail.

Mom looked glamorous and confident, her hair the magical shade between red and brown, like mine, except that mine was never as lush. Maybe this Verin, aka Dad, wasn't so creepy or old after all. He looked suave and dashing—a well-dressed James Dean. Why would she write Dad's name on the back if it wasn't him? *It has to be him.* People look different before they have kids, before they've aged in dog years.

All I'd known was an empty feeling where Dad should have been, never sure what was a memory and what was imagined—Mom's stories and the pretty photographs were almost too good to be true. I didn't know about the age difference. How could I? I'd never seen a photo of the happy couple before. Clutching the only known picture of them, I swallowed the lump growing in my throat.

I claimed that I didn't need a dad. The kind that showed up for baseball games and Christmas pageants and dreaded teacher parent conferences. A dad who wore drugstore aftershave and drank beer from a frosty glass as he lifted hamburgers off a smoky grill. A dad like all the dads in the neighborhood. Dads married to moms who wore pink Avon lipstick and who smelled like raw flour right out of the Gold Medal paper bag.

At my best friend Annie's birthday party, her mom told the other moms what a shame it was that Patricia couldn't make cupcakes for the spring bake sale. There was squawking, and I watched them clink glasses.

Later, when Mom tucked me in, I told her what Annie's mom had said, except for the laughing part.

"No one gets an award for making cupcakes from a box," she said, kissing me goodnight on top of my head. A few minutes later, something shattered in the kitchen, and I hid under my blanket.

I took my toast and a fresh drink back to the couch, flopped down, and yanked out the elastic band holding back my hair. Maybe Susan was right about the dead dad thing, how not having a dad impacted my ability to have a decent relationship. In a Dear Miss Kitty self-help book, I'd read that expectations are premeditated disappointments. Taking that wisdom to heart, I had no hopes and, therefore, no regrets. I put B.B. King on my turntable for a spin and willed my eyes shut to stop the leaking.

My phone rang with a restricted number right before the third verse. I loved the part where B.B. told his lover she'd be sorry someday, but I was the ultimate sucker when it came to mysterious restricted numbers. I needed a distraction from Mom's etch-a-sketchy box, and her inexplicable migration like a martini demands a queen-sized olive.

"Hello?"

"Leanne?"

"Who is this, please?" I asked.

"David. I'm a friend of Brett's." A moment of hesitation. "Susan said it was okay to call you."

That woman had no respect for me or anyone. I took a tiny bite of toast, not sure of my approach. Let him work a little? Sweat, perhaps? I bet he didn't sweat.

"Wow, this feels odd," he said. I detected a hint of nervousness, which I never saw in the men who offered themselves to me like holiday tinsel before a greedy magpie. "Could I start over?"

I knew he was the ultra-fabulous destiny David, but why make it easy? I didn't ask him to call. "David? Which, David?"

"How many Davids do you know?"

"Several, not including the one in Florence."

"Nothing like a plate of risotto, a bottle of red, and a view of the Arno."

"Are you selling vacations in Italy?" I asked.

"Sold my last one, but speaking of Italian, I'd love to take you to dinner. We can discuss all those other Davids."

This David was beyond my league. After losing his wife, he'd have *real* down to an art form, and I'd faked my way through romance since Eric Anderson in junior high asked me to go steady. Fake felt comfortable, like pizza, sweats, and leaving a new lover's bed before the obligatory breakfast became a command performance. Fake kept me reasonably safe, but he'd recently seen death up close and personal. He'd recognize the look and smell of fear.

"Susan says you're wonderful, perhaps even perfect, but I must pass."

"I'm far from perfect."

Earnest and humble? They say a guy like this is a myth. It was like something out of a romance novel. Maybe he was.

"Really? Not perfect? I'm working on being plug-and-play, but there's a lot of packaging to work through." I sipped my drink. "I'm going to be awhile. I'm sure you can find someone else to enjoy a bottle of Chianti."

"How about French?" His voice was smiling.

28

Did he still want a date? Turning a guy down was new territory. Was I doing it wrong? I'd let him talk for a bit and try again when I got the chance. I spied the hair tie on the carpet and pulled my hair into a ponytail so I could focus.

"I love Italian. I own at least thirty Italian cookbooks and worship Marcella Hazan."

"The first thing I mastered was her basic tomato sauce, but I added extra pepper. You can't take pepper out," David said.

"Pepper's a firm commitment."

I shut up before anything stupid slipped past the vodka. There was silence on the other end of the phone. I picked rye seeds out of the toast and listened to David swallow.

"About this packing material thing, are we talking bubble wrap? I love that stuff. My brother and I hoarded it," David said.

I had a passing thought about getting off the phone, but he had me at bubble wrap. Jeffrey and I'd had a huge stash. I snuggled into a mountain of recently gifted silk pillows courtesy of *the model*. We could be a while.

"Protection for your rock collection?" I asked.

"Nothing so tame. We'd tape it on the sidewalk and ride our bikes over it. Sounds like a Tommy gun." David added sound effects. "My granddad liked old gangster movies."

"That explains the Italian fixation," I said in my best Marlon Brando.

"You're quick for someone who hides in a box," David laughed.

Hot damn, he had my attention now. I begged any nearby deity that he wasn't a player. I'd had more than my share, and his voice was getting to me like freshly grated nutmeg in a silky béchamel sauce—unexpected yet enticing. Susan knew I was a sucker for a Barry White baritone, and it was double-swoon-worthy if crossed with an accent. I'd seen David's six-two well-defined frame, blue eyes, and runner's legs, but she hadn't mentioned the voice. I knew why. She knew that once I heard him, I would be a goner.

"Is the plug-and-play reference about dating or life in general?" he asked.

I wasn't going to meet him. I didn't need David reporting back to Brett, who would tell Susan, validating her need to sign up for the twenty-four-week therapy package. I steered the conversation away from my issues.

"You're sure you're new to dating?" I asked..

"I haven't dated for over twenty years."

"Your voice is killing me."

It's a great time to drop death into the otherwise lovely conversation. No wonder I preferred men without emotional intelligence. They couldn't be hurt. David loses his beloved wife to cancer, and asshole that I am, I don't just stab him—I poison the blade *and* twist the knife. Good thing I'd screwed up early on—a prudent reminder that I didn't deserve a decent man and shouldn't go out with him.

"Leanne? Hello? Are you still there?" Barry White sounded concerned.

"I shouldn't have said that. Look, I don't think ..."

"Divorced would be easier, right?" David asked.

I drained my drink and licked my lips. "Would you hate me if I said yes?"

"Go for it."

I'd had my chance to get out of Dodge and missed it. I inhaled deeply to clear my head and take a little boundary practice. Maybe Susan would give me a prize.

"It feels wrong dating a guy in your position. I feel guilty, like cheating, maybe worse. So, it's better if—"

"Jessica, my wife, wanted me to fall in love again. She insisted on it."

If I hadn't finished my drink, I'd have spit it out. I hoped that Jessica had been reincarnated as a tortoise, something slow and unobservant, so she couldn't hear me be a supreme asshole to her glorious husband. I gave myself fifteen compassion points for choosing a long-lived creature and padded to the kitchen for another drink.

"Leanne, I'm ready to meet someone. That's why I called you."

"Define ready," I asked.

"Plug-and-play?"

Out of vodka, I sat on the kitchen floor next to my wine rack and opened a bottle of cheap Merlot. My resolve to say no to this lovely, perhaps extraordinary, man slipped, but I owed it to Jessica-the-tortoise to not hurt him. I poured myself a glass, toasted my compassionate resolve, and tried not to slur.

"The truth is, I'd love to go out with you, but it's not a good time."

"I'll take the chance. I'll also throw in a gold-star sticker and a bottle of Chianti whenever you're ready as a reward for your honesty."

"I've got a lot of stuff on my plate."

"What stuff?" David asked.

"Do you work for Dr. Phil?"

"You got me. I call women, they tell me why they won't go out with me, and I sell the info. Go ahead; I've got my notebook."

"Since it's for profit, I'll spill. My mom's selling my childhood home, and I don't like it." I made for my marshmallow of a couch, my legs stiff, my back aching from the sugar towers.

"Nature only moves forward," David said.

A sexy voice and introspective? I took a long, slow sip and pulled a fluffy blanket over me. Happiness that I was unaccustomed to settled into my bones, and a smile found my lips.

"I never talk about emotional baggage with strangers."

"You can tell me all about the Samsonite. How about it? Dinner tomorrow?"

"I can't."

I put my feet up and over the back of the couch, stretching my legs in the air and wiggling my toes. Did I own a pair of running shoes? Did I want to?

"Day after?" David asked.

"You don't give up, do you."

"I let go of what I can't change; it leaves room for what I can. Something I learned the hard way."

He still wanted a *date* with me. It was an actual date instead of a quick and sleazy last-minute drink and a tumble I'd regret for months. I pulled myself up to a sitting position, blinking away the free head rush.

"Why me?"

"Do you like olives?" David asked.

"Did I miss something? When did we reach the stage of the favorite food?"

"What's your address?"

"No," I said.

Like I'd open the door for a hot stranger with food. Well, not since fake therapist session number four. My stomach growled, and I foraged in the fridge for a yogurt no more than two weeks past the best-before date.

"I'm sending you a pizza for dinner."

"I love pizza." I pitched the yogurt in the trash. "Did Susan put you up to this as part of my *therapy*?"

"Would she do that?"

"Without hesitation."

"Brett showed me a photo of you and Susan on the Ponte Vecchio. I couldn't stop thinking about you." David cleared his throat. "This is embarrassing—you haunted my dreams."

"You don't read Stephen King, do you? Haunted isn't generally a good thing."

"Captivated. Better?"

"Much better."

"I asked Susan about you. *Perfect timing*, she says. *Leanne's desperate for a serious relationship.*"

Desperate? Seriously? She deserved a seven-year bad sex hex, maybe twenty. After we hung up, one date agreed upon, and both yawning despite the scintillating conversation, I forgave Susan her meddling ways and cut the curse down to six months with good behavior.

Twenty minutes later the doorbell rang, and after consuming half of an excellent margarita pizza with olives, and tucking the rest in the fridge, I wondered if he preferred cherry clafoutis with or without creme anglaise? *Oh, shut up.* He doesn't deserve to be the caboose on the train wreck known as my love life. There would be no relationship with David or anyone else until I got my shit together.

I hunted for my stained and well-loved Marcella Hazan, The Classic Italian Cookbook. I snuggled into bed, and the book opened like magic to her basic tomato sauce recipe. I reached out to put it on my nightstand, but there wasn't room with all the self-help books. I slipped the book under my pillow. The right thing, for both of us, was to take a pass right after our first and only date.

Chapter Four

M om's new apartment was in a repurposed Art Deco bank building in the chic part of the city, and as I handed over thirty bucks for parking, I hated the place already. I missed the way our lives used to be. At least once a week, with a bottle of wine and takeout from the city, I would regale my most recent man-mess to an attentive and compassionate audience in our house.

A hot guy in a gray flannel suit joined me in the elevator. I ignored his tempting aftershave, the way his tawny brown eyes caressed my ego along with my ass. My gaze focused on the vintage panel, which illuminated the arrival at each floor with a golden star, reminding me of David.

On the sixth floor, I walked out to an audible sigh from Mr. Flannel, found Mom's black lacquered door, and listened to a sonorous gong announce my arrival. She was as giddy as a schoolgirl as she swung the door open, like a young woman in her first apartment. The familiar fragrance of Miss Dior tricked me into questionable comfort in this strange new world. Unusually tongue-tied, I handed over a bouquet of white tea roses and orange blossoms, her favorites.

She buried her nose in the flowers. "Come in. These smell amazing."

Mom wore a sleek violet tunic with skinny jeans and her hair styled to her shoulders, shiny like a new penny. A framed print of Billie Holiday had pride of place over the modern, glass-covered fireplace that burned fake logs with little heat and even less fragrance. A white faux fur rug, perfect for a fifties pin-up photo shoot, lay on the polished mahogany floor, making me wonder who besides Sandy-Shit-Selridge had influenced Mom.

"Looks like the place could use some color," I said.

"Black and white are colors. They're the only ones that don't require thought."

She might have moved, but she hadn't changed. I followed her into the kitchen and sat at the breakfast bar. The kitchen looked like pirates had raided a Williams-Sonoma and filled the galley with ill-gotten plunder. Martha Stewart would award Mom a medal for such a magnificent selection of cooking implements. The irony wasn't lost on me. Mom didn't like to cook. What was she up to?

"Which vase do you prefer?" She held up two clear square containers that come with upscale florist flowers. I pointed to the one on the left. Who was sending her flowers? I wasn't about to ask. Questioning Mom was worse than getting information out of Susan, like being a contestant on a game show with suspect rules and crappy prizes. My wise mind poked me in the gut and reminded me to stay focused. I love my wise mind, but she's a lot like Susan, always right, which explains why I don't listen to either of them as often as I should.

"Why'd you leave everything at our house?" I asked.

She filled the vase with tap water and added a shot of vodka and an aspirin. I put my hand out for the booze. She dropped two pills into my palm, passed me a glass of water, and tucked the vodka away in a plunder-filled cabinet. Water? Did she not know me anymore?

"*My* house, and Goodwill's picking up the rest this week." She stirred the boozy aspirin water with a long spoon, a swan carved along the handle.

"You realize this is unusual, don't you? Some might even say crazy."

"Not that it's any of your business, but what's wrong with new things?"

"I'm happy for you and your fancy cauldrons, but what about our stuff? You're giving away my childhood. Who does that?"

I had *Verin and Vivi* in my purse. Torn between showing and telling, I opted for telling since showing would mean the loss of the picture. If Mom would ditch over forty years' worth of our belongings at a thrift store, I hated to think what she'd do with my most recent and treasured possession. Mom gave me her famous zombie stare. She added hands on her hips in case I'd forgotten how terrifying she could be.

"This is ridiculous, Leanne. You've had years to take your stuff if it was important to you. I took a delightful butterfly ashtray you made in kindergarten, a ceramic worm Jeffrey labored over, and the family pictures that I wanted. That's all I need. Not everyone enjoys or needs memories."

"Explain why the house is a shrine to a man who died almost forty years ago. You kept his clothes, Mom. You have precious memories in your off-limits dresser."

She stopped fussing with the swan spoon and whirled around to face me, her mouth and eyes like a plastic baby doll—wide open with surprise. Interesting. She'd forgotten about the box and never meant for anyone to find it. Her eyes narrowed, and she gave me another zombie stare. I started to lose my nerve.

"You realize this is your fault? If you hadn't moved secretly, I wouldn't have found it, and I wouldn't need to know anything."

Once she mastered her trembling hands, she returned to the flowers. She arranged the orange blossom to impress Martha Stewart into giving her an award and a job.

"I forgot about the box." She picked up the arrangement and carried it to a thick glass coffee table in the living room. She set the flowers down next to a stack of vintage sheet music and a crystal elephant filled with peanuts, the tail a detachable rake.

"Is there something you're not telling me?" I wanted to show her the photo and ask why Dad seemed different in it than in all the other photos, but my wise mind poked me a second time, warning me to keep it out of sight and, for God's sake, to shut up.

"Leanne, pretend the past has a switch attached. You can turn it on or off at will. Some people thrive, they wallow, they live for the past. They keep that switch on to the point that it cancels out the present." She returned to the kitchen, flipped on the kettle, and waited to pour boiling water over tiny yellow flowers into a clear glass teapot shaped like a pagoda. "My switch is now off for a reason."

"I thought we were happy. You, me, Jeffrey. Did you hate it?"

"I said *now*."

The florist vases, the sexy white rug, and even the decked-out kitchen began to make sense. No wonder she didn't want anything from the old house, especially Daddy photos. Mom, for all her crazy, would never lie to me.

"Is this about getting over Dad? I can understand that. It's been a lifetime. You should move on. Maybe you're ready to date."

My wise mind told me to stop pushing, but the part of me that believed long-dead French chefs could be channeled for long-forgotten recipes was on a mission. My wise mind whispered that Mom knew more than she let on, but to proceed with caution to avoid upsetting her. My not-so-wise mind said Mom owed me answers after the house scare and to grill her hard, Susan-style.

"Imagine you died, and I cleaned out the house; I'd waste my entire retirement savings on psychics to contact you," I said.

"Thank you for the visual, but I'm not dead yet." She moved toward the refrigerator and peered in. "Some things, many things, are better left buried."

"Burying something doesn't always mean it's dead."

Dammit. The zombie stare for a third time. On steroids. One last stab before I slunk back to the uncomfortable land of I-know-nothing.

"Why'd you keep the dress? Just answer that."

"Are you staying for dinner?" Mom unwrapped a white-wrapped paper package from the fridge and dumped raw shrimp into a colander. "Paella and salad."

"Stouffer's doesn't make paella."

Boundary lessons with Susan were paying off. It was possible that the Sphinx would speak for the first time in my life.

"I bought real Spanish saffron." Mom held up a narrow glass vial and shook it over her head.

"As opposed to fake saffron?"

"Don't be so sarcastic; it doesn't suit you. I'm allowed to change."

She handed me a sleek, cobalt-blue mug and passed me a sugar bowl decorated with mystical symbols.

"Why'd you move? You left so fast. Did someone scare you away?" I laughed at my joke. No one and nothing scared Mom.

She stiffened her shoulders, rolled her lips inward, and swallowed her silly secrets.

"Set the dining room table, please."

She drew out the please to shut me up, which I did, and to remind me that good manners were more important than good grades. She said you could fake intelligence, as many people did, but you couldn't pretend not to look like a pig while eating dinner at Buckingham Palace.

Friday was the night we'd practice our manners at the fancy restaurant in town. Antonio's wasn't unique, but we thought it was when the maître d', a.k.a. Tony, gave Mom a silent and not-grabby hand kiss, which was appropriate, according to her. Was an inappropriate kiss like Pepé Le Pew kissing the confused black and white cat aka Penelope Pussycat? Oh, how I wondered.

She'd make me wear a dress that scooched up in the back while I tried my best to slink ladylike into the red leather booth, cold and smooth on the back of my bare thighs. I studied the dark green menu with Spaghetti spelled out in Italian and English, with a white cloth napkin on my lap. My heart softened with the memory; she was the best mom anyone could have, and I should leave her be.

"The shrimp shrank," Mom said, holding up the shellfish for better inspection. "And the clams didn't open."

My life has been spared. "Why are you learning to cook?" I opened a bottle of Pinot Grigio that was chilling in the refrigerator and poured a glass while she poked around her paella pan, scowling at the shellfish.

"I find cooking calming." She passed me a shriveled specimen.

I tossed the shrimp in the sink. "You put the shrimp in too soon, didn't you?"

Mom gave me a dirty look and dumped the paella, real Spanish saffron and all, into the trash. With her back to me, she scrambled eggs and put sourdough bread into a high-tech toaster.

"Why didn't you date after Dad died?"

"Why do you need to know?"

"I'm having a midlife crisis."

Mom adjusted the toaster dial like she was NASA mission control. "You're too young."

"I've run out of self-help books that help."

"What's your problem?" she asked, adding a thin thread of golden saffron to the eggs and sprinkling a questionable seasoning mix from a glass chicken into the pan.

"I'm comfortable with losers; a normal guy seems risky." I grabbed a coke from the fridge and finally swallowed the aspirin.

"Why don't you go out with normal and see what happens?"

"I'm not sure if I do something to bring out the asshole in men or if I go out of my way to find said assholes. Why didn't you date before you met Dad?"

Mom passed me an ice-filled glass for the Coke. How could I forget? Only heathens drink from cans. "I found the love of my life early, and don't swear."

"Yeah, a prince. You must have been lonely after he died. Didn't you want romance?"

"I had you and Jeffrey to take care of." She sprayed garlic butter on the toast from an aluminum mister and held out my plate.

"Answer the question," I said as I took the plate to the glass dining table.

"Your father made it impossible for me to love another man. Please, pour me some wine."

"According to the books, I shouldn't have relationship issues. Great dad equals ease with men."

"Books aren't always right."

"Did he do anything wrong?" I passed her a full glass of wine.

"I've told you a million times: he spoiled me for all other men. Eat your eggs."

"David's a widower. Sounds like he loved his wife."

"The normal guy? Why wouldn't he love her?"

I nodded and crunched the ice in my drink. "That's exactly my point. He's ruined for anyone else."

Mom took several small sips and dabbed at her lips with a cloth napkin. "People who have known great love want to experience it again."

"Aha. Then why didn't you date? I know you're not telling me something."

"Don't crunch the ice. It will ruin your teeth, and it has no nutritional value. Eat your dinner."

Defeated by her evasive maneuvers and my pathetic fear of her zombie stare, I headed for Kook, my happy place. The first order of business was a glass of pinot and organic eggs from the walk-in; each crate had the name of the hen that laid the eggs. The bride had insisted, and who was

I to argue with a detail-crazed woman about to ruin her life? The yolks filled one basin, and the whites rose in another. With dozens of eggs to go, I cracked them with my eyes closed, fueled by visions of Verin and Vivi at Taffy's a million years ago. I'd never looked at a man the way Mom looked at Dad. No wonder she'd carried a torch.

Snuggled under my yellow daisy comforter with a flashlight, a whole pack of iced pink and white circus cookies, and *The Secret of Shadow Ranch*, I was oblivious to everything outside my private world. Engrossed in ghostly horses, I didn't know that Mom had snuck past Jeffrey's bed until she peeled down my covers.

"Leanne, it's after midnight."

"Why are you still awake?"

"I can't sleep with the stupid wind noise." I didn't tell her my tummy hurt, and sometimes I'd cry imagining she died and left me alone with a strange man. I put the flashlight under my stomach so she wouldn't hear the click it made as I turned it off.

"Me too. Makes melancholy crawl like bugs up my neck."

"What's melancholy?"

"One part sad, one part lonely, and one part that makes it hard to sleep."

"I read to make it go away." I shoved the bag of cookies down the side of the bed.

She leaned down close enough to smell the icing on my breath. "What do you say to a moon party?"

We crept out into the garden like we did on many nights. Mom made hot chocolate with marshmallows and bundled me up like a human burrito in a wool blanket. We sat together in aluminum chairs with orange-and-lime-striped mesh seats; mine pushed down deep in the uneven grass to keep it from toppling. Jeffrey wasn't invited because he slept through the night and didn't like Mom's stories.

"Tell me the singing goat one again. I'll be quiet. Promise." I peered out from my blanket and wiggled my sock-covered toes with joy.

Mom laced her hands around her mug and cleared her throat. "Once upon a time, there lived a beautiful maiden named Ava. She had green eyes like an Egyptian cat and chocolate-brown hair that hung in long curls down her back. Ava had the voice of an angel, the most beautiful that the villagers had heard in five centuries.

"It's a terrible waste to keep a beautiful voice hidden between two mountains, two valleys, and two lakes, " they would say, passing her coins and flowers in the hope that she would never leave.

"The villagers didn't need to worry because an evil witch had enchanted Ava's six sisters into singing goats, and without Ava to protect them, they would be considered dangerous magic and killed for meat."

"Where did the evil witch live?" I asked. "Behind the first or the second mountain?"

"The first mountain, the first valley, and the first lake."

"They stayed sisters, right? Even though the witch turned them into goats, they stayed family?"

"Family is always family, even if they act like animals."

I popped a gooey marshmallow into my mouth and sipped hot chocolate in bliss.

"One day, Ava was singing 'I'm So Pretty' with the goats when a handsome stranger fell into the courtyard. The goats circled him, pawed the ground, and made angry clicking noises."

"Why didn't the goats like him?"

"He said that he had heard Ava singing as he floated above in a giant purple hot-air balloon covered with gold and silver sparkles. He'd leaped down to take her to a nearby kingdom where singers were treated like queens."

"Mom, why didn't the goats like him?"

"You have school tomorrow. We should call it a night."

What else hid behind two mountains, two valleys, and two lakes? I called Mom and cracked open the last egg.

"The singing goats story popped into my head. Do you remember that one? Did Ava have a green cocktail dress?"

"You're becoming obsessive," Mom snapped at me.

"Did she leave with the stranger?" I asked.

"No, she stayed with the goats and became the village manicurist."

Sarcastic equals annoyance, but I couldn't stop now. "I hear music. Where are you? It's late for live music."

"I'm hanging up."

"I'll bring you a Pavlova after I drop off the order with Levi and Paulka."

"A big one?"

"Yes."

"No more questions?"

"I respect your decision to leave me in perpetual darkness."

Thrilled with another opportunity for interrogation, I hung up and whipped the egg whites into a stiff mountain without the aid of witches or magic goats. She would talk. No one could resist the truth-telling properties of an almond vanilla meringue, a mélange of exotic fruit, and whipped cream courtesy of the organic cows, Stargazer and Moonchild.

Chapter Five

The following day, I parked my lavender delivery van by the trade entrance of The Flood Mansion, San Franciso's premier dream event site. I carried a single pastry box and found Levi and Paulka in the grand foyer directing minions. Paulka flipped open one of the lavender boxes, his cocoa-brown eyes wide with delight.

"Leanne, darling, the pavlovas are gorgeous, and I love the new box color; it matches the van," Paulka said, giving me a theatrical wink. "I wonder whose brilliant idea that was?"

Levi kissed me hello and took a quick peek. "I love how you make us look good."

"Paulka, call one of your efficient minions, please. I'm too tired to unload the van," I said, and stifled a yawn.

"Darling, don't you dare leave without saying goodbye."

Paulka tossed his hair and went through massive double French doors out to a marble terrace, where his well-dressed minion army arranged cascades of white blossoms over gilt-edged mirrors on round tables set for eight. The silver place settings dazzled in the morning sunlight, and with an array of stemware worthy of Louis XIV, shell-shaped pavlovas with edible pearls were the cherry on top of the sundae.

"What's this one? The Little Mermaid goes to Versailles?" I pushed my sunglasses up on my head.

Levi sighed. "This is only the shower. What happened to simple weddings with a handful of scattered rose petals?"

"You did."

I tailed Levi into a small library off the elegant foyer, and while he sat at an antique desk Susan would kill for, I waved the silky white feathers of a plumed pen like a magic wand. Should I tell him about the classified box of memories or get advice on the David's situation? I wasn't ready to tell him about Mom's curious keepsakes, so I went for Levi's favorite subject, my love life, or as Paulka liked to call it, The Tawdry Days and Nights of Leanne Spencer.

"Susan gave my number to a guy named David even though I told her I wasn't interested. We should boycott her birthday brunch."

"Which David? Hair or doctor?" Levi asked.

"Doctor. Oh, my God. Not you, too? Stop fanning yourself and fill me in."

Once he had the theatrics out of the way, Levi handed me back the plumed pen he had stolen.

"Dinner party a few weeks ago at Susan's. Paulka hyperventilated just this side of drooling. Susan insisted Dr. David check his pulse."

"Breathtaking, is he?" I said, batting my eyes at him over the feathers. "Hey, why wasn't I invited?"

"Susan wanted us to meet him *first*. In your best interest, of course."

"Aren't you two the thoughtful ones," I said.

"Don't be snippy. Everyone is trying to help you. Anyway, I said Paulka had a reaction to the spiced cashews, and Dr. David, bless him, pretended to believe me. He told Paulka to lay off the nuts, finish his

Hendrick's and tonic, and call him in the morning if he felt iffy. David is stunning and snuggly, if you know what I mean. It's an unusual combination. I wonder why Susan hid him for so long."

I was about to say something snarky, but Paulka returned with a minion holding a tray with demitasse cups and a silver pot of fragrant coffee. With a practiced flourish, the minion poured and vanished. Paulka kissed Levi on the lips like he had been gone for months instead of minutes.

"What'd I miss?" Paulka asked and perched on the arm of Levi's chair.

"Susan set Leanne up with Dr. David," Levi said.

"Wear something with lots of buttons down the front. When that darling man listens to your heart, you won't mess up your hair," Paulka said.

"Noted." I drained the tiny cup of excellent coffee. "See you two later. I'm off to interrogate Mom in her swanky mausoleum. You two will love it."

"Why did she move so fast?" Paulka asked. "Are bad guys after her?"

"You'll have to get in line for the answer."

"I've had enough of secrets," Paulka said. He raised both hands to the ceiling and was about to commence a lengthy sermon about secrets being the devil's flying monkeys or whatever when a flustered minion fluttered in with a bottle of pink champagne. He whispered in Levi's ear, leaving the bottle with a dramatic huff.

"They sent the wrong champagne. Paulka, call the winery and ask for Thorton; we need three cases exchanged ASAP."

"There's no such thing as the wrong champagne," I said, eying the bottle.

"Trust me, the vintage is glorious, but the bride's mother thinks pink is tacky," Levi said.

"Can I have a bottle to take to Mom?"

"Fabulous idea. You can deliver it chilled and find out why she moved and didn't send out a formal notice," Paulka said and scampered off to hunt down an ice bucket.

Levi filled his cup again. "Patricia's going through something intense. I've always thought of her as a fragile flower."

"Yeah, the poisonous kind with thorns. Trust me, Levi, she can care for herself and owes me answers."

"No one owes anyone anything." Levi crossed his arms. "If she needs nondisclosure, you should respect her space."

"Excuse me? You were my friend first, and I don't have many. Do you have to take her side?"

Paulka strolled back in, cleared his throat and tapped a coffee spoon on the ice bucket to get my attention.

"Leanne, darling. Forced confessions are like a quickie before a party. It's all fun and games until the two-hundred-dollar blowout resembles a tumbleweed."

"Another sex myth busted." I stood, kissed them goodbye, and settled my sunglasses over my tired eyes.

"I'm telling you, Leanne, be gentle—there's more to your mother than you think," Levi waggled a finger.

I walked out of the library, the icy bucket in my arms. Fragile flower? My ass.

Chapter Six

With the pastry box balanced on one hip and the ice bucket on the other, and with frost-bitten fingers a distinct possibility, I jabbed the buzzer with my elbow for the hundredth time. Answer the damn door. I couldn't waltz in like I used to, and I wasn't holding my breath for a key. Mom opened the door a crack, then pulled me in, reaching for the box.

"I brought champagne," I said.

"Did Jeffrey call you?"

"Why would Jeffrey call me?"

Like a game show hostess, I displayed the ice bucket and hoped she wouldn't guess why I'd brought over a two-hundred-dollar bottle of ready-to-drink truth serum. She gave the champagne a dirty look.

I followed her and reached into a cupboard for glasses. Her pristine kitchen was a disaster. The sink was full of dirty dishes, pots, and pans. She'd used everything possible to cook, God knows what. Levi guessed right: she was going through something. And no lipstick? Mom skipping lipstick was like the Pope blowing off Easter for a round of golf.

"Did Mr. Florist Flowers come by for lunch?" I asked.

"Your brother was here."

"On a weekday? Did you warn him that you were cooking?"

I popped the cork. The foam cascaded up onto the bar top, where it pooled and hissed; there was too much to contain within reasonable boundaries, just like Mom. I filled two glasses and handed one to her. She stared at it for a long time before taking a microscopic sip and putting it down.

"That's it? One taste?"

"I've never cared for champagne."

Mom filled a kettle at the sink and read the directions from a Fortnum & Mason tea tin out loud. I settled on a barstool and inhaled champagne fumes. I was dying to ask about Vivi, but she seemed closed up and unsettled, most unlike her usual bold and brassy self. The bubbles slipped down my throat, smoothing a path for the inquisition to commence.

"Levi and Paulka sent it as a housewarming gift, and this isn't just any champagne. They'll be crushed if you don't drink at least one glass. Two glasses, and they'd be thrilled."

"Champagne reminds me of your father."

"Oh. I'm sorry. Did you go for a painful walk down memory lane with Jeffrey?" My chest began to squeeze, and not in a good way.

"Something like that." Mom sat at the breakfast bar with the tea pot and poured a cup. We watched the leaves swirl and settle like a tiny storm. Was she reading the leaves? Ready to tell me my future? Taking an online class? How to be an accurate psychic in thirteen easy lessons? She reached for my hand. My chest did a double squeeze.

"Penny for your thoughts?" I asked.

"I have something to tell you before you learn from your brother." Madame crystal ball on-a-stick stopped fiddling with a new gold bracelet and exhaled a substantial breath. Our entwined hands unnerved me; we weren't a touchy family.

"Your father's risen from the grave."

"Risen, as in he never died, or more like a figure of speech?" My heart squeezed shut.

She let my hands go and sipped her tea while my heart released and pounded like a sledgehammer against my ribs. Trickles of cold sweat snaked down my back. The chill spread and sunk into my bones.

"I'd like to say risen à la Jesus, but the truth is, your father is more of a bastard than a holy man. Come; I know this is a shock to you."

She took my hand and led me to the living room. My legs wouldn't hold me up. I sank into her couch like a little ball. She covered my icy body with a thick throw and sat, hands in her lap, alert eyes fixed on me.

"He's alive? Is this why Jeffrey came over? Is this why you moved?"

"Yes, no, and kind of."

"I'm going to puke." I scrambled to my feet and ran to the bathroom, skin clammy, my stomach an active volcano. I dry-heaved until my ribs hurt and there was nothing left inside but questions.

"He was supposed to have stayed dead," Mom said, settling herself next to me on the cold marble floor. She brushed sticky strands of hair off my damp face and held out a glass of water, which I ignored.

"Stayed dead? You knew he was alive?" Tears broke through the shock, and my nose ran like a fire hose. I wiped my face with a towel covered with embroidered bees and tried to stop crying. I didn't want to scream in front of her, but my overwhelmed body had other ideas. "You lied to me? How could you?" The words spilled out in a child's voice from long ago.

"I didn't want to hurt you."

Mom swiped a box of tissues from under the sink and passed them to me as a peace offering.

I threw the box at her. "I don't want your fucking tissues." I stumbled to the kitchen to grab my purse and leave.

"Leanne, please don't go. Let me explain."

I stood next to the stool, poured another glass of champagne, chugged it, and filled the glass again. I was hoping for oblivion, but I'd settle for being slightly insensible.

"Please stop drinking."

"This is what people do when their dead father shows up and they discover their allegedly trustworthy mother lied to them for a lifetime." I grabbed a roll of paper towels and mopped my face. "You held a funeral for him, for fuck's sake."

Mouse-quiet, Mom sipped her tea. "It was a memorial for the three of us."

"Liar! What about the casket, flowers, and pallbearers? What about the photo album with Verin E. Spencer embossed on the leather cover?"

The horror on her face was the candle in the dark. No wonder she had hidden that photo. It wasn't the smoking and drinking. It wasn't the sexy pose you'd rather the kids didn't see. It wasn't a six-four-by-six memory to savor in the privacy of the heart heart's privacy either. It was the only picture of Dad in the whole goddamn house that was real.

"You duplicitous creature. That album is some poor bastard's funeral with Dad's name on it, isn't it? Are all the Daddy-n-me pictures someone else's? For fucks sake, answer me!"

"I can't think or talk when you yell and swear!"

"The Ferris Wheel picture, way up in the sky, tiny hands waving, the giant cotton candy in front of my face. The blurry Christmas mornings, Dad making sandcastles, the sun obliterating his face. Holy fuck. What an idiot I am. I thought you were just a shitty photographer!"

"I'm sorry." Mom dunked her hands in the sink full of dirty everything and grabbed a sponge.

"You're sorry? You faked memories. You faked my life. Did you watch the Hallmark channel for story ideas? I thought I could go to my grave, a real one, believing that you never lied."

"Leanne, I had no choice. You have to trust me on this."

Mom's hands were deep in the soapy water, pans slammed against the stainless sink. I kept an eye on the dirty knives lying on a cutting board.

"Why don't I believe you? I know. It's because you fucking lie. When can I meet him?"

"Oh, God. Anything but that. He's a terrible man."

"Un-fucking-believable. You were so devastated by the death of the best man anyone could ever know. You made his shit into a shrine. You made us celebrate his birthday and eat German Chocolate cake every year until I left home. Did he even like German Chocolate Cake, or did you make that up too? No wonder I can't tell the difference between a memory and a lie. Fuck!"

I put my head between my knees and sucked in air. There are no answers for those who yell, who swear. What a joke. There are no answers for anyone.

"The truth, Mom? I can't remember him, and now everything I believed is actually a lie. I have nothing. I have no Daddy, good or otherwise. You engineered an elaborate fantasy. No wonder I fell for it. Then again, how difficult is it to deceive a child?"

"Please stop. He wasn't a good dad, Leanne. He wasn't a good husband."

"Lots of dads and husbands aren't good. That's why Susan has a vacation home in Maui and several income properties."

Mom tossed more dishes into the sink, cracking a glass. She pulled out the fragments and disposed of them in the trash as if they were pieces of a dead rat. She rinsed a ribbon of blood off a finger. The monster could bleed.

I ripped off more paper towels and mopped the unstoppable tears. "You placed him on an unbreakable pedestal, like some Superman, and now, when it's inconvenient, he's the devil? Do you have any idea how fucked up that is, not to mention unbelievable?"

She continued to run water over her insignificant wound, or she was drowning me out.

"Why can't I meet him? Tell me."

"Call me later when you've had time to think this through." She snatched the champagne bottle off the counter and poured the remains down the sink, keeping her back to me.

"He wants to see me, right? Jeffrey's going to want to meet him. Oh, my God ... Dad's a grandfather. Does he know?"

"Jeffrey's met him, but you mustn't ever see him."

I hauled out the photograph lurking in my bag and slammed it on the counter, face up. She leveled a look of sheer venom at the photo, so intense that I was surprised the edges didn't smolder and burst into flame. My mind raced with all the possibilities she'd withheld without good reason. I was ripped in half between faith and confusion, something my wise mind said had always been true but never made sense.

"Tell me why I fucking shouldn't?"

"It's a complicated story; you shouldn't hear it now."

"Do you need more time to get your facts straight?"

When she didn't answer, I grabbed the photo, shoved it into my bag, downed the champagne, my eyes level with hers, then hurled the glass into the sink. I knew I was childish and cruel, but I couldn't stop, and I didn't want to. I remembered the Salisbury steak knife— terror clung to me even now. I grabbed my bag and my keys and headed for the front door.

"Fuck off, Mother."

Chapter Seven

Susan and Levi are my best friends, but Mom is my rock and pillow. She also stole my childhood, and Jeffrey knew. I had more than a few choice words for him, but I wasn't talking to anyone yet.

In third grade, I chose Sacagawea when we had picked a famous person for our big reports. I loved her then and I loved her now. She knew her way around unmapped territories under hostile conditions. Nothing could have been more apropos—I wanted her to comfort me like the baby on her back, without the need for words. Words cannot be trusted.

I tossed a few bucks at a bewildered valet as I retrieved my car. As the city faded behind me, I crossed the bridge onto simpler roads where I could unwind some thoughts, if not my body, which was still wracked by shock and loss. Tears flowed unchecked, while my chest ached with almost forty years of suppressed longing, and a dreadful melancholy settled into my bones, along with a gnawing fear. Alive? Why not reach out? What had Mom done to keep him away?

I fingered the blue beads around my wrist. My constricted chest had no room for mindful breaths to quiet the infinite questions. If he'd been a shitty husband, she would have divorced him. She'd told us that he was extraordinary, the best a man could be. I should have guessed it was a farce when she was quoting a razor commercial. Fuck. *Was* he a shitty dad? She obviously loved him; why else keep the photo?

I drove the back streets toward the house, the route Mom had taken on the Sundays when she looked for dead pets by the side of the road. Gathering roadkill should've tipped me off that something wasn't right. Hiding behind all that made her better than the other moms. She had been a pathological liar, and I hadn't noticed. Crushed within the brutal snare of truth, I'd found the reason I that was a shining beacon for assholes like Scott. I was a gullible fool, trained by my mother to accept anything dished out under the guise of love.

"It's a Small World," interrupted my torment; I jabbed at my phone to reject the call. It was time to get a new ringtone. Something imperfect. Something for a big, bad world.

"Hello?"

"I made reservations for seven. Okay with you?"

Dammit, I'd hit the wrong button, and I'd forgotten our date. My level of relationship stupid hit a new low. I'd dated so many jerks that I'd become one. I knew I was flawed baggage, but at least now I understood why. Being raised by a liar couldn't be good for a kid. My eyes filled with tears at the sound of his lovely voice, and I couldn't respond. I'd spilled several feet of my small intestines talking with him last time.

"Leanne? Are you okay?" David asked.

Silence would keep me safe from further intimacy. The pretense was well within my comfort zone, and, not wanting this gracious man to think I was unstable, I did what I always do and shoved my pain down deep where it couldn't find me.

"Leanne?"

"I can't go out tonight, or ever."

"This is a lot like Groundhog Day. Have you ever seen it? It's one of my favorite movies," David said.

"I warned you: I'm far from plug-and-play." The words caught in my throat, and I sounded like a sick baby frog.

"What's going on?" David asked.

"I can't talk right now."

"To me, or to anyone?"

This man and his béchamel voice; soothing, calming, luring me to spill my guts yet again. He made it hard to deny the reality that I wanted. Could his calm drive away demons? My wise mind whispered, *Go ahead, let this someone in.* Not possible, I will fuck it up and hurt him more than I can stand.

"This is a terrible way to get to know someone, listening to my endless crap. Let's talk about something pleasant, like the Bermuda Triangle."

"You're sniffling."

"Thank you, Doctor. I have seasonal allergies."

"Is this part of the plug-and-play thing, or did something happen?"

The road opened up without a car in sight. I slowed, rolled down the windows a smidge, breathed in the scent of oak trees, and turned toward the late afternoon sunlight. David's intuitive sense of giving me what I needed had found a way, despite my resistance. His voice flowed like warm syrup and placed a clean, soft bandage on my most recent wound. My wise mind took the wheel and slowed me down. I wasn't in a hurry to get anywhere.

"My dad died when I was four, except, my mom just told me that he's not dead, he's a horrible person, and I should never see him."

"Whoa." David exhaled. "Where are you now?"

"Heading to my childhood home, and if you're taking notes for Dr. Phil, it's my security blanket." I choked back a sob. "Do you want the address? Are you sending another pizza?"

"I'm thinking of wine and sympathy, in person."

"It's tea and sympathy, but your idea is better."

I cruised down my old street, shocked that I'd told David what I couldn't tell Susan or Levi. The street was a mix of beautiful Craftsmen and a few old homes that had seen better days, like a bag of fancy, chocolate-covered almonds with a few blistered peanuts at the bottom. I preferred the peanuts, with their saggy porches, weathered paint, and old bicycles on gravel driveways. Ours was a peanut.

"What the hell? Why's Jeffrey here?"

"Who's Jeffrey?"

"My brother. I don't want to see him right now. I might kill him."

"Leanne, we don't need to go out tonight," David said.

"Goddamn, I need a drink."

"Maybe he brought something."

"Jeffrey doesn't drink much. I'll tell you about it sometime."

"Promise?"

"I'm writing a memo on my soul."

"I don't sleep much; if you want to call later," David said.

"I thought that you were perfect?"

"Not a chance."

Chapter Eight

M om's house looked sad and lonely, like an old black lab abandoned a few days before a new puppy Christmas, losing hope
that their owner would return --a lying, soul-destroying monster of an
owner.

I parked behind Jeffrey's soccer-daddy minivan, fingers tapping on the
steering wheel. Do I reveal what I know about Dad, or hope he'll confess?
With Mom gone, I felt like a thief as I turned my key and opened the
door. Jeffrey lay plastered to the couch, an old basketball on his stomach,
a half-empty bottle of Captain Morgan's spiced rum by his side. Crap.
This was the mother of all days. Jeffrey didn't like booze. I cornered the
market on that particular vice.

"You're drinking?"

"Seems like a damn good day to get drunk."

Another myth shattered. I couldn't wait to see what would happen
next. I knew Jeffrey had a glass of wine now and again, but was he drunk?
I crouched in front of him, put my palms on either side of his face like
when we were kids, and forced him to look at me.

"How could you not tell me about Dad?"

"Good. Mom told you."

"You could have told me."

"She swore me to secrecy. She wasn't fucking around either; she made me do the weird handshake thing."

"Give me some of that rum."

The rage inside needed drowning. I slurped the rum down like a chocolate Frosty in July until the fumes stung my tender, swollen eyes, and the anger smoldered.

"Do you have anything to mix this with?" I asked.

"Cereal and milk. You're the chef; make something."

"Don't fuck with me, Jeffrey. I'm not in the mood."

He bent his head and howled into the basketball. He cried so hard that drool ran from his mouth and made a wet patch on the upholstery, the ball like a dying dream in his arms. Besides Mom's evil conspiracy to silence him, he knew something I didn't, which was not complicated since I knew nothing. Jeffrey must have had his reasons to protect me. We'd always had each other's backs.

"I'm sorry. It's been a shitty day." I took another swig. "There's something else, right? Is he in jail? I promise I won't go off the deep end."

"Marie kicked me out."

"Oh my God, Jeffrey. What in the hell did you do?" I lifted an eyebrow in the style of Paulka.

"Nothing."

"Jeffrey?"

"I cheated with an internet option. Brunette within five miles."

I thought about patting his back through his white orthodontist coat, out of habit more than concern, while he choked on his sobs. A charter member of the gut-wrenching world of betrayal, I wondered how Marie was doing, closed my eyes, and tipped back to oblivion.

While I kept natural emotional desires in check and stayed safe, pretending each horrendous relationship was good enough, Jeffrey cheated, all the while carving pumpkins with his kids, hanging lights on the Christmas tree, and never forgetting a wedding anniversary. Both of us were liars, destroyed on the inside because Mom believed lies to be the kindest of truths. What a bunch of crap.

"Did you bring any tranquilizers from work?" I asked.

"Don't be stupid."

"Losers who cheat with internet whores shouldn't judge."

Jeffery renewed his howls.

"I'm sorry. I shouldn't have said that." I drank until shame felt more like a memory.

He hung his head, forehead smashed against the ball, rolling it back and forth.

"I deserved it." He looked up from the ball. "Somewhere between the kids' soccer games and waiting in line for 'It's a Small World,' I got lost."

"I'm surprised it's not your favorite ride. All those pretty girls in scanty costumes. Do you like the belly dancers best? My money is on the can-can girls. Hard to resist a three-foot woman in black feathers."

"Shut up, Leanne."

"What? Like small, sexy crows? Hey, I'm trying to cheer you up. He wiped his face with the basketball. "She doesn't want me anymore."

"There's a pile of firewood outback," I said. "No reason to wait until dark, and I'm in the mood to burn something."

"A moon party, huh?"

"You knew about those?"

The tears I'd managed to keep in check threatened to spill. The image of a little Jeffrey pretending to be asleep hurt my heart. The knowledge that he'd been wide awake and alone killed me.

"No one sleeps that much." He gave me the saddest smile I'd ever seen and looked down at the floor, his eyelashes flat, wet crescents on his face. The primal desire to burn away my pain, purify my soul, pulled me to the firepit. The screen door slammed behind me. *If only it were that easy to walk away from the past.*

The fire sizzled, sparks flew, and Jeffrey refused to move—the basketball glued to his lap.

I yelled through the screen door, "Come outside. You're missing the party. Hurry and bring the rum and the Lucky Charms. The valley of despair is threatening, and I'm hungry."

Jeffrey poked his head out the door and shuffled to the stone firepit, a fresh bottle of rum in his grip. He collapsed on an Adirondack chair, banana yellow showing through the new white paint.

"Do you remember when we looked for the eyes in the back of Mom's head?" Jeffrey said. "Too bad she woke up." His words slurred into near gibberish. "I shouldn't have parted her hair."

"It was the only way to look for the extra eyes. Do you remember screaming? It's true!" I laughed into the bottle.

"She was face down in her pillow and saw me! I was a trusting child who took everything literally, and I didn't scream."

"I've never trusted anyone completely, except for her and you, I guess," I said and poked the fire with a stick to keep it going. "She set us up."

Jeffrey reached for the rum, took a long drink, and stared at the stars threaded between the clouds. The fire crackled and blazed, sparks ascending like little devils. I poked the heart of the heat. The embers burned brighter, more demons free to escape into the night and leave us alone.

"I'm a fucking idiot. Why did I think Marie wouldn't find out?"

"You inherited Mom's uncanny ability to bullshit those who you love?"

I put my hand out for the rum, closed my eyes, and took a long swig. The booze slid down without burning. My throat was numb, feeling no pain. That didn't make laying into Jeffrey any easier, yet the moment had arrived.

"Why did Mom lie?"

"He was a fuck-up, and she wanted to protect us. Marie's right. I shouldn't be around my kids. I'm a fuck-up too."

"Marie is a whole new level of pissed that you've never experienced. Did you think she'd book a swingers cruise to Bikini Babe Island to celebrate your newfound ability to cheat?"

"Shut up, Leanne."

The countless times I'd been cheated on got the best of me. I poked Jeffrey in the chest. "You messed up once?"

"Yeah, one time," Jeffrey said and swatted my finger away.

I wanted to believe him, but I didn't. I'd known too many men who lied as they breathed.

The Captain and his golden truth serum allowed me to see Jeffrey, the man, instead of Jeffrey, my baby brother. All my empathy for him evaporated. The rum hadn't saved me from the valley of despair, and my heart ached. The sad reality that Jeffrey was just another asshole didn't destroy me as much as mom's betrayal had. Nothing could hurt me like that anymore. There was nothing to lose by calling my so-called rat bastard dad and getting his side of the story.

"Mom told me you have Dad's number."

"No, she didn't."

"Give me the number, or I'll tell Marie about the stolen Playboys, the gateway drug you kept under your bed as a child."

"I was twelve, and I didn't steal them; I found them in Kevin Schneider's dad's trash." Jeffrey snatched the bottle as it slipped from my grasp and took a swig. "I have to tell you something, and you won't like it. There's a reason Mom left the pictures."

Jeffrey threw sticks onto the fire. I tried to count the sparks swirling up into the night sky.

"Yeah, she said she doesn't want the memories. I'll pack them up tomorrow." I nabbed the bottle back, waiting for Jeffrey to confess what I already knew. Redemption is a beautiful thing.

Jeffrey shook his head and put his face between his knees.

"Don't take them. Not Dad. Not us. The pictures are of another family."

I knew in my bones that something was off with the photos. Too many years of an intentionally cruel fallacy crumbled what little hope I had of trusting Mom ever again. The shaky feeling hit me in the gut, slithered up my chest, and consumed me. Hearing Jeffrey say it out loud made it true. I felt like someone I loved had died.

"You're absolutely sure?"

Jeffrey looked me straight in the eyes and nodded. I wanted to run inside, confirm, and see the wretched tangible truth, but what was the point?

"How long have you known?"

"Three years. Marie figured it out."

"You're a chickenshit, Jeffrey. You had no right to keep secrets from me."

"I know." Jeffrey shook his head. I shut my eyes. I didn't want to cry in front of him. I wished he was wrong. Mom hadn't confessed to the faux family pics.

"There has to be a mistake. I can't believe she'd fake family photos..." Years of believing the liar made it hard to wrap my brain around her latest betrayal, not to mention that I wore the gullible crown rain or shine. "You're one hundred percent sure? Of course, you are. Marie is pretty good at seeing what's in front of her face."

Jeffrey looked like I'd kicked him. I didn't care. "I forced Mom to confess, then I hired a detective to find him. She bought the pictures at a garage sale. The suits, his robe and slippers, the jackets she couldn't bear to give away? Thrift stores. Never his. The daddy smell? She sprayed Old Spice on the clothes. Oh, and the bowling trophies..."

My eyes flooded with tears, with unfathomable hurt. I put my hands over my ears.

"Shut up, Jeffrey. I don't want to hear any more."

My stomach hurt from booze without food and the irrefutable evidence that Mom was heartless and crazy. I should have slowed down to sober up, go home, but getting numb enough to ease the increasing agony became the more pressing need, and I couldn't leave Jeffrey now.

"I couldn't believe it, either. I studied those photos with a magnifying glass. I mean, who does such a terrible thing, right?" Jeffrey slurred so badly that terrible came out as terrorville, so I took the bottle. He wasn't half wrong.

"When did you start getting up close and personal with the internet?" I asked, pretty sure that I could guess the time frame.

"About three years ago." He put his hands on his thighs and stood over me, geared up for something unpleasant. "I'm going to call Marie. Slow down on the booze, would you?"

I nodded and put the bottle on the grass within easy reach.

"Jeffrey, rule number one when drinking: never have a serious discussion with a pissed-off wife. Rule two: see rule number six." I realized what I'd said, but I didn't care. Numbers were never my thing.

Jeffrey gave me a dirty look. I stretched for the bottle and drained it out of spite. If it had been Mezcal, I would've choked on the worm.

"Maybe she's calmed down," he said and left me by the fire.

I stretched out on the new lawn, staring up into the stars until they became a hazy oneness in the night sky. A dog barked somewhere in the neighborhood. Tears slid from my eyes, and the not-so-gentle torrent watered the dead beneath me.

Chapter Nine

I woke up curled into a sad and stiff little ball on top of spilled and scattered Lucky Charms.

Jeffrey walked over, pale as a ghost. "She's interviewing lawyers tomorrow. She's gonna get a shark."

He slumped into his chair and cracked open the top on another fifth of rum. What was left of his dirty-blond hair tried to shimmer in the moonlight but couldn't, worn out by working so hard to be more than it was, like the rest of him. I rolled over, rested my face in the cool grass, and poked at the cereal.

"I'm looking for a green clover, but all I can find are pink hearts, yellow moons, and orange stars."

"Your leprechaun voice hasn't improved over the years."

I held up a multicolored, squished, moon marshmallow and popped it in my mouth.

"I found our old sleeping bags in the garage," he said and tossed one to me.

"Let's sleep under the stars," I said and patted the glossy grass.

"No way. Creeps me out," Jeffrey said.

"Chicken."

I was well and truly sloshed inside my musty Scooby-Doo sleeping bag, my head like a helium balloon without a string. The doorbell rang, and Jeffrey slithered out of his Flintstones bag, fished his wallet from his jeans, and headed inside.

"No hookers in Mom's house!" I yelled and snuggled deeper into my cozy nest. It was difficult. I'd grown at least a foot since the last time I'd used it.

"I wish I hadn't told you!" he yelled back. It could have been a minute or an hour when Jeffrey reappeared and held out a steaming cardboard box and cracked the lid open. I inhaled the delicious scent of hot pizza but reached for the bottle of diet coke and a paper cup he was holding in his other hand.

Good old dependable, teeth-wrestling Jeffrey. He got something to mix with the rum.

"You sure you want to know what Mom told me?"

"Why wouldn't I?" I asked, making an actual drink, instead of downing the booze, pirate-style.

"You could stay with the picture you have of him."

"The pictures are fake."

"There is that."

"I can handle the truth."

He set the pizza on the grass between us and passed me a huge slice, dripping with greasy cheese.

"Doesn't it depend on what the truth is? Once you hear it, you might change into someone who can't handle it."

I folded the slice in half and took a big bite. The pizza was glorious, and we ate in silence. Jeffrey wiped his hands on the grass. I threw him a brown paper napkin and watched him wipe tomato sauce off his five o'clock shadow. Could I handle the truth? Probably not, but the almost compulsive need to know shoved all reason to the back of the logic bus.

"Truth or dare?" I asked.

"Truth."

"How did you find Dad?"

"Dare."

"You know the rules, Jeffrey. You can't change your choice."

Jeffrey traded the pizza for his basketball and dribbled it around the brick patio. The basketball didn't have much air; it squished more than bounced. I could hear Jeffrey thinking over the squishing. I ate another slice and waited until he stopped playing basketball, returned to the fire, threw on an armful of wood, and got into his sleeping bag.

"I'll tell you about Dad later, but first I'm going to tell you a story."

The night air had turned misty and cold. I snuggled down into my bag, the Captain nearby in case I needed to escape another shock.

"A long time ago, a girl married this guy who made a lot of promises but didn't come home all that much."

"Is this about you?"

"Are you going to ask a bunch of questions?"

"You're grumpy when you drink."

"You're annoying. Shut up, or I won't tell you."

"Fine."

"They had two kids. One night, the little guys were horsing around, and the girl fell on her little brother and broke his arm."

"Is this about Mom?"

Jeffrey poured Diet Coke into what was left of the rum, spilled most of it, and ignored me.

"Her husband, as usual, wasn't home, and had the only car. There was one hospital in the town, and they took insurance or cash. She didn't have insurance, and her husband only gave her money when he remembered to, so she asked the neighbor to borrow their car."

"Why didn't Mom ask the neighbor for money?"

"I don't know, but she didn't. She put both kids in the car and drove to the Bottomless Cup, a dive bar a few miles up the road. She left the crying babies in the car and found her husband."

"Mom left us in the car?"

"Leanne, shut up." Jeffrey stuffed half a slice in his mouth and chased it with his rum and Diet Coke, the foam running down his chin. I threw more napkins at the irritable, rabid squirrel boy.

"The guy's lap was covered with a trashy brunette, and his glass was empty. He told her he'd withdrawn six hundred dollars, all their savings, and wasn't coming home. She drove the kids to the hospital, hoping someone would take pity on them. The hospital didn't have pity, but they did have a phone."

"Oh, boo-hoo, Jeffrey. She's probably lying about that too."

"Talk to her."

"No."

"You're a woman. Don't you feel sorry for her?"

"Most guys are assholes. It doesn't mean you keep kids away from their dad. Why do you

believe anything she says? She lied to you, too." I fished around on the grass for my car keys.

"I told you I met him. He's a fucked-up guy."

"Oh my God, Jeffrey." I tried to stand and slipped down into a chair, the seat too deep and slippery to bother fighting. "He's our dad, and she could be crazy."

"Goddammit, Leanne. Do yourself a favor: believe Mom and me, and let it go."

"Our childhood was one big, fat lie. I can't believe you're taking her side."

"Do the smart thing. Keep pretending he's dead."

"Pretending works so well for you. I'm going home."

"Get back in the bag."

"You can't make me."

Jeffrey grabbed my keys and hurled them to the back of the dark garden where he knew I wouldn't go.

My brain had melted, the way that praline does before it's stretched and set. Jeffrey slept in peaceful post-rum-and-pepperoni bliss, his pain on hold. Except for the worst hangover of my life, it was an exceptional night. A seriously flawed Jeffrey had made me feel so much better about myself. Bitch.

"Cheater. Wake up. I need coffee."

Jeffrey emerged from the bag with his eyes closed tight, his hands clutching his head. "Did I call you last night?"

"No, I needed to come here. I didn't know you'd moved in."

"It's temporary. Why'd you come?"

"I thought I'd feel better here."

"Do you?" Jeffrey asked.

"A little, but nature doesn't go backwards."

Jeffrey burrowed down deep into his sleeping bag, only his hair sticking out. It could've been the praline brain or his messy bed head, but I desperately wanted to be ten again. I yearned for the smell of frozen French toast warming in the oven, fighting Jeffrey for the last glass of orange juice, and choosing dare because it was always the safer option.

That realization sobered the last drunken tendrils of the Captain's recent occupation while I hunted down my keys in the garden. Could I accept why Mom lied? Did I have the necessary compassion to forgive her the way that Jeffrey had? I went to the bathroom, found an old brush, and made my hair decent. I rinsed my mouth, looked at my drained self in the mirror, and prepared to rob my baby brother.

If Jeffrey had hired a detective, he'd kept Dad's number. While he snored, I scrolled through his phone until I found Verin Spencer. Oh, my God. Him. Hands shaking, I dropped the phone and got the numbers wrong several times before I copied them correctly into my phone. I blew Jeffrey a goodbye kiss and snuck out. What would I say to a man who was my father but never my dad, who may or may not be a rat bastard?

Chapter Ten

D esperate to soothe my aching limbs, I peeled off yesterday's clothes and submerged my weary body in my tub for a soul-searching soak. I thought about calling David, but any more of my crap this early in the game would scare him off for good. Seventy gallons of jasmine-scented bubbly water convinced me to get up the nerve to call Dad. Mom didn't have my back, not the way that I'd believed. Conflicting thoughts pinged away in my soggy brain, the inside of my skull a rusty old pinball machine in the back of a dive bar.

Was this the first time that Dad had been in touch? How would I know? The unfairness of it was overwhelming. I continued to play with the possibilities until my phone rang and snapped me out of a reality that I barely believed, let alone accepted. Levi. No wonder I was compelled to answer the phone.

"What's wrong?" Levi said. "You always call back. What happened with Patricia?"

"How'd you guess?"

"Did you just meet me?"

Levi knew the most intimate details of my life and never judged. He'd stopped me from calling women I hadn't known were wives. His was the shoulder I'd cried on, vowing countless times to hire a real therapist.

As much as I needed his words of wisdom, I couldn't confess Mom's treason. It would be all the more real if Levi knew, and painful for both of us. Levi worshipped Mom. He'd adopted her since his own mother refused to acknowledge his marriage to Paulka. Shame pricked my heart, and at that moment, I became like her. I covered her ass at the expense of trust.

"She's picking her stuff up next week," I said. "And it turns out that she did tell me about the move, but I forgot."

"See, you were worried for nothing. Did she like the champagne?"

"She loved it."

New tears fell into bubbles no longer brilliant with rainbow iridescence. I pulled the plug and watched them circle the drain. This time, the bath didn't help with the slimy feeling that lived under my skin. Goddamn it. I hated how the past continued to poison the present.

"Leanne? What's going on? My Spidey-sense is tingling."

I wasn't ready to confide everything I knew to Levi just yet, but there was something I could share.

"Levi, I found a photo at the house. It was of my dad before I was born. He looks like the kind of guys I've been dating all my life."

"No wonder you count ex-lovers instead of sheep. I told Levi that you weren't a slut by nature," Paulka said.

"Paulka, I'm not in the mood, but you are correct. Sluts are made, not born. Levi, take me off speaker, please."

I reached for a towel, hauled my limp carcass from the tub, wandered into my bedroom, and dropped it on the floor. Exhausted, I climbed naked into bed. Even putting on a t-shirt seemed like more work than I could handle.

"We are both concerned for your wellbeing." I heard kissing noises. "Are you sure you're okay?" Levi asked. "Something is wrong, and you're not telling, or you're sick."

"All the running around has made you sick, and Susan's birthday brunch is Sunday. I'll be right over with Eau Minérale on the tiny ice and some fabulous pills I picked up in France." Paulka said.

"I'm good, Paulka, just tired," I said. "Sorry I was snippy. See you guys on Sunday."

I couldn't be bothered to turn on the heat and huddled under the covers until hunger drove me to the kitchen. Mashed potatoes were my usual offering to the goddess of misery, and it seemed fitting to make the customary gesture. Skin on organic russets, butter, heavy cream, and lots of freshly ground pepper whipped into creamy clouds of Idahoan joy. The last twenty-four hours deserved a meaningful sacrifice. I'd commit to a ten-pound weight gain and put a trust but verify tattoo on my plumped-up ass. Susan would be thrilled. I headed back to bed with carbohydrate sedation in my favorite vintage Pyrex bowl.

As the glorious offering bolstered the confidence necessary to call Dad, the doorbell rang. Levi and Paulka, no doubt, with fancy water, tiny ice, and suppositories from Paris. I pulled an apple-green nightie, a recent gift from the dynamic duo, off the floor and over my head, and swung the door open.

"Are you going to invite me in?" Scott asked.

Idahoan joy turned to lead in my gut, and I chastised myself for opening the door without checking the peephole.

"My mother told me never to let a stranger in the house," I said, the total weight of my mother's ancient advice dawning on me. She didn't want dear old Dad waltzing back into our home uninvited, ruining the status quo.

"Since when am I a stranger?"

"Did I say, stranger? I meant strange. Go away, Scott. I broke up with you."

"I came to talk. Please? Let me in."

There was a significant pause, and in that moment, that opportunity, the one that gauges without compassion if you've learned your lesson, presented itself. What that moment never takes into consideration is the cobra-like ability of the asshole in question to use your goodness against you. I ushered Scott inside while my wise mind railed with frustration. The potatoes lay like rocks in my gut.

"It's been a while. You look beautiful, as always."

"I suppose you want a drink?"

"Whatever you're having," Scott said.

I put my bowl on the coffee table. "What I'm having doesn't translate into a glass. Pinot okay?"

"Sure, and could you put some clothes on? That thing you're wearing is short and distracting." He took a seat on my couch, and I gave him a dirty look while I poured him a glass of wine from the open bottle on the coffee table.

"I thought you were a chartered member of the less-is-more club?" I said and passed him the wine.

"Believe it or not, I've changed."

"Be right back."

Jeans, T-shirt, lip gloss, and a quick flick of mascara—my wise mind shook her head in dismay. It was a bad habit, but makeup meant nothing. I reached for a spritz of perfume and sprayed my T-shirt, a little on my neck. I did this for the pizza guy, the meter reader, and the occasional Jehovah's Witness. Why not for Scott?

"You didn't have to put on makeup for me. You're always beautiful." Scott said, and stood up as I walked into the room. I tried not to gag. "Does this mean I have a chance?"

"What are you, the weather? Cloudy with a chance of asshole? I don't think so. Sit."

"I've had two weeks to realize how much you mean to me."

"It took you two weeks?" I asked, and sat on the opposite end of the couch. I poured wine into an empty mug and swallowed half of it.

"You didn't respond to my calls or texts. It took two weeks to be able to tell you."

"You cheated again, Scott. There's nothing to talk about."

He reached across the upholstered divide, pulled me in close, and pressed my head down on his chest. I listened to his heart beat to the rhythm of Donna Summer's "Bad Girls" and scooted out of reach. Susan would've been so proud of me, until shame showed up, lit a cigarette, and settled in for the usual show. Scott looked sincere, earnest in a sexy Boy Scout way. His fragrance, manufactured for the sleazy masses, dragged my appalling need for affection out into the open. It called to me the way cartoon fingers appeared out of an apple pie cooling on a farmhouse window sill, beckoning hungry baby bears in for a tasty morsel.

"I'm seeing a therapist and I've realized that you're all I've ever needed." Scott stroked my hair. Hard, like I was a feral cat and if he let up, I'd scratch and run.

"I don't have fake boobs."

He tweaked my nipple, just in case I didn't know what boobs were. "I love your boobs. You're the whole package."

"Every girl you cheated with had fake boobs. Did you reach your quota?"

"Sweetheart, please don't do this."

"Nothing's changed, Scott," I said.

"I've changed, and I miss you."

"Missing isn't loving."

I sipped the wine to cool my jets. I wanted to believe he'd changed, not because I loved Scott, but because I was extra lonely and vulnerable, and David, as wonderful as he seemed to be, was an unknown variable. Like a failed Weight Watchers disciple with a blueberry cheesecake and a free Saturday night, I reached for a fork.

"One more chance, Leanne. I promise it will be the last time I have to ask."

With sweet softness, he pushed me against the couch pillows and kissed me into starch-fueled stupidity. Before I knew it, my shirt was over my head, he'd unclasped my bra with one practiced hand flick, and had me close to the point of no return. His hands soothed away doubt along with my jeans.

He nestled his lips into my neck and murmured into my ear, "I never meant to hurt you, baby."

Those words triggered a clarity I didn't know I had, almost a memory, disturbing and odd. My stomach lurched, and Idaho's finest rose in my throat as I pulled away from him. "I'm not doing this."

"We were good together. You know that." Scott reached for me, caressing my neck.

I swallowed down acute nausea. "Scott, I need you to leave."

"Your breasts are heaving. They want me to stay." He winked, licked his lips, and bent his head.

"It's called a panic attack." I pushed his head away. "For fucks sake, leave my nipples alone."

"I love you, Leanne."

"You don't, Scott. You don't have a clue what love is."

"Love means never having to say you're sorry."

Scott looked so sincere in his stupidity that I laughed in his face. Such idiocy fed my growing resolve to take better care of myself. I tossed the imaginary cheesecake in the imaginary trash and sat up straight and naked, my jets meat-locker cold.

"You met someone, didn't you?" Scott said.

"I'm surprised that you have any perception of someone other than yourself. Give me back my pants."

"Bitch."

"Finish your wine, Scott. It's excellent, and I'm not going to drink it. Your lips touched it, and I know where they've been."

"Too bad you're not as sexy as you are funny."

Once in a lifetime, you know the perfect thing to say and have the courage to bring it forth with no fear of repercussion. I thought about covering my nakedness with a throw pillow, to keep the distractions to a minimum, but my wise mind enjoyed Scott being lectured by a mostly naked woman with perky nipples.

"I'll use small words so that you can keep up."

"You're making a mistake, Leanne. I won't give you another chance."

Doubt elbowed me in the gut. What if I had made a mistake? He had a therapist; hopefully not from Susan's sketchy online school, but I'd take what I could get. My mouth dried out and my heart thudded and skipped a beat. David flickered across my mind, a bright flash of promise. Scott reached for me, put a finger to my lips to subdue me, make me his naïve fool once again. I shoved doubt out the second-story window and put my shaky hands on capable hips to still them.

"I understand that men are slow creatures. Introspection doesn't happen until they've fucked up decades of relationship potential with a criminal amount of collateral damage. Count yourself lucky, Scott. I'm your wake-up call."

I stood up slowly, so he could see what he'd be missing, licked a drop of wine from my fingers, grabbed the potatoes, and sauntered to my bedroom.

"Let yourself out. I'm going to bed. Alone."

Chapter Eleven

My heart pounded with exhilaration as I lay on my bed, toes in the air. The front door slammed, and I reached for the spoon to celebrate. The potatoes were cold, but their potent magic was no longer needed. Scott had been the sacrifice. I took my bowl into the kitchen, tucked the spuds into the refrigerator, and poured a vodka and ginger ale.

Fat raindrops splattered against the window as I perched on my couch and called Dad. My mouth became desert dry, and panic rose like a new moon, making it impossible to talk, let alone think. I hung up on the third ring. The thought of David's voice soothed me from afar. I pushed panic back into the dark places where it rested but never slept. Should I invite him to Mobs' soft opening? My ultimate debut in the heady world of the San Francisco restaurant elite? Would it be too much too soon? Was I ready to share amaretto apricot panna cotta with a dark chocolate drizzle? I kept men far away from the best part of my world, and from the best part of me.

A Magic 8-Ball had earned a place of respect on my coffee table for often-needed woo-woo. I flipped over the twentieth-century oracle, and "you may rely on it" flowed up through the mysterious liquid. Unlike my mother, the ball never lied. I called David, vodka drowning the butterflies in my stomach.

"Hi," I said when he answered.

"She calls."

"You said you're up late."

"She listens."

"I can leap over buildings in a single bound, too."

"With or without a cape?" David asked.

"Depends on the rest of the outfit. Is it too late to call?"

"About twenty years, but I'll forgive you."

"I don't usually find doctors amusing."

"See what happens when forced to choose between medical or clown school? Did you know they have therapy for kids now? Ruined my dream of a life in the circus."

The butterflies settled, and his loveliness softened my edges. "Speaking of therapy, do you think a real therapist can help someone if the person doesn't admit they have a problem?"

"As opposed to a fake therapist? You don't do the idle chit chat thing, do you?"

"I thought you might know."

"Do you need a referral?"

"I'm fine."

They say only two things have the power to motivate people: the proverbial carrot or the sharp stick. I was tired of painful sticks. My first carrot would be David, glazed alongside a creamy pesto lasagna and a chilled bottle of Pinot Grigio.

"I'm surprised that you didn't call sooner. I was worried about you."

Sweet concern and a definite you-are-an-asshole-Leanne came through loud and clear, but instead of pissing me off, I found his annoyance reasonable. I should have called him. I wanted him even more now. How often did you meet a grounded, handsome man?

"I'm sorry. I should have called, but I wanted to get myself together first."

"Right, plug-and-play. I forgot."

I'd wondered what could be responsible for my underwhelming relationship skills for years. A couple of glorious phone calls and I'd fucked it up already. What was wrong with me?

"Wow, I sound like a jerk. My day followed me home, and my bedside manner is a little off," David said.

"What happened?"

"I lost a favorite patient. Alice McKinney. Ninety-two years old. Gorgeous white hair and lavender eyes. According to her, she was a dead ringer for Elizabeth Taylor."

"I didn't know doctors were allowed to have favorites."

"My specialty is geriatric medicine. I've learned to make my peace with limited time, but the reality is painful." David cleared his throat. "Anyway, yes, I have favorites, and Alice was one of them."

"I'm sorry. I should've been more sensitive. That's a skill I haven't mastered, according to my honest friends and family."

"There are schools."

"I'm in an accelerated program under duress. What's that noise?"

"My dog is sniffing the phone. Eddie's a good judge of character."

"I've never had a dog."

"Did the wolf get you on the way to Grandma's?"

"I have attachment issues."

"Distance, so you don't get hurt? Or a deep phobia of duct tape?"

I cracked up. Susan was right, not that I'd tell her that: hanging out with this guy would be good for me.

"Would you like to come with me to a restaurant opening? Italian. Tuesday at seven?"

"I'd love to." I paused. "Would you mind picking me up?" The butterflies came back, plastered and swooping around my gut. "I'd like this to be a real date."

"I'll bring you flowers and candy in a heart-shaped box."

"Will you wear your best bubble wrap?" I asked.

"Yes, and a matching tie."

Chapter Twelve

I let myself in through Susan's kitchen door carrying two pastry boxes. Paulka took the star-shaped quiches and set them on the white
marble counter after he peeked inside the box.

"Why are you two playing host? Where's the birthday girl?" I said,
setting down the box of warm scones.

"Baby stars of cheesy delight! Can I have a nibble?" Paulka asked.

I nodded and he popped a miniature quiche in his mouth, an obvious
foodgasm the only reward I needed.

"The birthday diva dusted organic merde all over her fabulous dress,"
Paulka said through a mouthful of flakey deliciousness. "OMG. Lobster
and chive? This is Meg Ryan good. Levi, taste the glory."

"Susan had a slight wardrobe malfunction," Levi said and wiped
crumbs off his lips with his fingertip after taking a bite.

"Au contraire my darling, the need to change was desperate." Paulka
reached for another star.

Levi snared the savory star from his beloved and turned to me. "She
was cutting flowers for the table, a tiny smudge got on her dress, and
Paulka *had* to say something. How are you doing? Still sick?" Levi raised
his eyebrows and popped the quiche into his mouth. "Oh, this is Meg
Ryan good."

"I wasn't sick. I'm hiding from the police. I smothered Scott in breast implants, and I was the last person to see him alive. Oh, and you'll be thrilled to know that I have a date with Dr. David."

"I treasure the way you embrace next. Almost an art form," Levi said and high-fived me.

Brett, the wonder husband, strolled into the kitchen. Next to the pale blue subway tile, rich mahogany cabinets, and a gorgeous eight-burner licorice-black and chrome refurbished stove, he looked like a model in House Beautiful—the June issue, for Father's Day.

How did Dad feel about Father's Day? He was ripped off. So was I. The smoldering fire beneath the fragile surface of the mundane flared and sent up sparks. Another thing that Mom stole from us.

"Hi, Brett."

"Hey, Leanne. Mimosa or coffee?" Brett asked and gave me a peck on the cheek.

"Mimosa, please."

Brett poured fresh squeezed Ojai Pixie tangerine juice topped with prosecco from a chilled vintage coupe, passed me my drink with his usual sweet demeanor, and began to grind beans in small, mindful batches. I was dying to ask him about David, but that would be for later, when the Levi and Paulka circus wasn't in town.

Paulka floated a white blossom in my glass. "Susan says the flower's organic and edible. She grew it from a seedling. She thinks you'll be impressed."

"Susan's idea of farm to table," Brett said. He had a dry sense of humor that matched my own. No wonder he and David got along.

Paulka dropped a few more flowers in my glass. "The birthday diva is taking forever, and I'm hungry."

"Stop with the flowers, Paulka. It's a drink, not a funeral arrangement." Levi took all but one blossom out of my glass. "When can I see the photo?"

Levi knew something was up, and I needed a day to forget. Maybe more than a day. Perhaps the rest of my life. Pretending to not hear Levi, I grabbed Paulka's hand. "Let's go get her."

The staircase was beautiful. You couldn't help but glide like a glamorous old-school movie star. Its glossy, aged wood was complimented by a dark blue and ivory floral runner held down with the original brass fittings. Brett and Susan had endured the last four years in an extensive restoration, paying experts obscene sums of money to resurrect the derelict home to its former magnificence. I loved the way that the house held space for the past, though the last time I checked, Victorians didn't have heated floors and Jacuzzi tubs.

Paulka used the last few feet of the spacious landing to show me modeling poses. We rounded the corner and swept into the master bedroom, which featured a mahogany four-poster bed hung with sheer white silk; a bed for angels or overpriced lawyers. Her royal highness had her phone glued to one ear while she lined her lips with a nude pencil.

"You're in the neighborhood, and there's plenty," Susan said to the phone.

"Plenty of what? Who are you talking to?" I said and flopped next to Paulka. We reclined on a spectacular assortment of pillows, and Paulka snapped pictures of the tiny tags, for reference purposes.

Susan settled her phone on the vanity between anti-aging potions. "My mother's so thoughtful. Did you know my best years are behind me?"

"I'm sorry," I said.

"What happened to your hair? Did you fly over on a broom?" Susan said, and scowled into her mirror, tapping around her eyes.

"Yes, my car was in the shop," I answered.

"Let me fix it," Paulka said, fingers twitching as he reached for my hair.

I gently slapped his hands away. "Go downstairs. I've got this."

"Come on, Paulka, the mimosas are calling," Susan said. "Leanne, would you mind fixing the pillows?"

"I got you a big box of OCD for your birthday!" I yelled after her.

"Good," Susan said. "I'm almost out."

I fixed my hair and headed downstairs, ignoring the cell phone buzzing in my jeans pocket. David's béchamel voice drifted from the kitchen, and I divined just who and what Susan was up to. Fix the pillows? Unbelievable, even for her. I peeked around the door to get a preview. He had a sugar-dusted cardamom scone in one hand, and a mug of coffee in the other, chatting away with Brett. I'd make Susan pay, but in the meantime, the sight of him made me breathless, almost dizzy. This was the guy I'd wanted to pass on? The ultimate chocolate bunny? Necessary radiated from him like a fig leaf on a bronze statue.

Paulka mimed a phone behind David, so I took a few steps back and pulled the phone from my pocket.

Paulka: *Let down your hair and fluff it like JFK.*

JFK?

I pulled out my ponytail, shook my hair loose to Paulka's silent approval, and walked through the threshold. The tiny hairs on my arms stood at attention, and I felt like life as I knew it was about to change forever.

Brett nudged David and handed me a fresh drink. "David, meet Leanne."

"Is it Tuesday?" David smiled broadly at me, a grin that made star-bursts of the lines around his eyes.

"Sunday, last time I checked," I remembered to breathe, and took a deep inhale.

Susan sipped her mimosa. She looked like a cat that had swallowed an entire organic turkey.

"You two sound like old friends. Come along—we shall dine al fresco in the rose garden," Susan said, and we all tailed her to where brunch waited in pastel perfection.

I knocked my knee on the cast-iron table leg as I sat down and swore under my breath. David sat next to me, looking sympathetic, and I forgot all about the pain. The last time I'd reveled in such excitement, I'd won a dessert contest at fifteen with classic Baked Alaska. David grinned, and I smiled back, as Susan noted, like long-lost friends, or more like long-lost lovers. My body tingled, on high alert due to his masculine mojo.

"Strawberries?" He asked.

"Always."

Something rare and magical was happening, as he spooned strawberries onto my plate. I ignored my phone buzzing in my pocket.

"Leanne, your phone's the awkward guest," Paulka said with an engaging pout toward David.

I fished it out and looked down at the screen. "Marie, my sister-in-law. I'll call her back later."

"You better see what she wants," Levi said. "Could be something with your mother."

I had a damn good idea what Marie needed. She was either looking for Jeffrey or wanted to know where the body should be delivered.

I wasn't thrilled with Levi's interference, and whatever Jeffrey had done could wait, but since I didn't want to look like an unfeeling ass, I stood and waved the phone at everyone.

"I'm so sorry. Don't wait for me."

David looked concerned. Occupational hazard? He must be overly familiar with bad news. I stepped away from the table and called Marie.

"Hi, Marie. Everything okay?"

"Jeffrey's been in an accident. Can you come to the hospital?"

An accident? The hospital? My entire body shook, and I couldn't stop shaking any more than I could speak. My brain knew the words, but I couldn't get them past my mouth.

"Leanne?" Marie was crying.

"Oh, my God. I'll be right there. Did you call Mom?" I managed to squeak out.

"She's here."

"What happened?" I whispered, my mouth dry, my chest squeezing viselike tight. Part of me didn't want to know.

"He hit a tree."

Chapter Thirteen

C ars whizzed by, bringing visions of Jeffrey and the unknown closer. I remember him getting busted for sneaking ice cream money
from Mom's purse, the science experiments we made when she wasn't
home, the burned brownies he baked when I flunked my first driving
test. Jeffrey's life flashing before my eyes couldn't be a good sign. The
gnawing in my stomach and the squeeze in my chest got worse with every
mile.

David had offered to drive me and now he gave me some tissues. I
plucked a handful and held them tight in my palm. My eyes began to
leak.

"Hey, we don't know anything yet," David said.

His voice held the promise that everything would be okay. It wrapped
me in a comfort I'd only dreamt about. I took a long slow breath. He was
right. We didn't know anything.

"I'm sorry. This isn't the way I imagined our first date would go," I
said.

"Our first date is Tuesday," David said, his eyes not leaving the road
as he laid his hand briefly on my arm.

"What about today?"

"I didn't ask you, you didn't ask me, so this isn't a date."

"Susan didn't tell you I'd be there?" A discussion of Susan's plan gone wrong was an excellent distraction from the frantic beating of my heart, which had started up again. *We know nothing. He'll be fine.*

"No," he answered.

Up until now, David had been anything but a man of few words, even a bit on the chatty side. Was he in on the plan? Was he lying? He was lying. My wise mind checked in and waggled a finger in my direction. *He's fine. David's fine. Everyone is fine.*

"Did she tell you I'd be there?" David asked, so nonchalant. Testing? He wasn't a bit bothered by Susan's masterful manipulation.

"Are you kidding? She's all about the surprise attack."

"I wonder if Brett knew." David ran a hand through his hair, then gave me another reassuring pat, this time on my leg.

"Brett, the Wonder Husband? Never. She runs the show."

The warmth of his touch lingered. Like a tiny pebble tossed in a lake, his touch widened its reach and slowed my heart to almost normal. I wished David hadn't come along. I didn't want my first promising partner to witness whatever drama waited in the ER. He could have stayed at Susan's, or taken a brisk run in the park, or called in a prescription for industrial-strength Preparation H. Anything but being here with my family and me.

"Thank you for driving."

"It's not discussing all those other Davids over dinner, but I'll take it." He added a smile.

I couldn't believe him. I wanted to, but no one was that perfect.

"Love in the ER your thing?" I asked.

"Better than moonlight on a tropical beach." Kindness I could handle, but a romance with kindness set off my hard-wired distrust device. I floundered in water so deep I had no choice but to reach for a lifeline to distract us both. His car. Car topics are safe, friendly, and this classic beauty was obviously loved.

"I wouldn't have guessed you for a vintage car guy."

"It's a 1965 Chevelle Malibu convertible. My pride and joy. It was Dad's, and Eddie likes the breeze in what little fur he has."

"My mom drove something like this when we were kids. She had a different car almost every week. Once Jeffrey and ..." My eyes filled with tears. I choked up and turned my head to the window again. I wondered if I should call my supposed rat bastard of a dad in case Jeffrey didn't make it. Don't think. He'd be fine.

When we arrived at the hospital, David parked under the Doctors Only sign and cut the engine.

"You sure you want me to come in? Things could be uncomfortable with your mother. Patricia, right?"

Concern was etched in his soulful eyes, along with something I didn't recognize and would have to analyze later when I could think straight. I put my windblown mess of hair into a ponytail, grabbed my purse, and steeled my heart for anything.

"Let's go," I said. Might as well throw him into the deep end and see if he could swim.

David took my hand as we went through the automatic doors, not as typical visitors, agonizing in waiting rooms, desperate for news of any kind, but as VIPs. His hospital privileges acted like backstage passes at a concert. His magical hand in mine slowed down my chaotic thoughts and my stomach pains became manageable. My heart was back in my throat, but I wasn't alone. Within minutes, we knew that Jeffrey had been admitted with a head injury and a broken leg. An escort ushered us to the formidable ICU.

We found Mom and Marie on either side of Jeffrey's bed, the chilly room cordoned off with stripy beige and green curtains. Motionless and pale, Jeffrey lay with his head bandaged, fresh blood seeping through. He had an IV in his arm, and colored wires hooked up to monitors that made ominous noises that scared the crap out of me.

Marie threw herself into my arms and held me tight. I squeezed her back, but couldn't look her in the eye. I understood her pain, the anger over Jeffrey's cheating, and the terror that she'd lose him over something so stupid. David read the monitors and studied the whiteboard with its medical hieroglyphics in purple, red, and blue. Mom sat finishing-school straight and held Jeffrey's limp hand, her face a pale, blank mask.

"Marie, this is my friend David. David's a doctor. He knows the ropes around here." This was the first I'd seen of Mom since I'd told her to fuck off, and as David had guessed, I hadn't had time to thaw out. Neither had she—difficult to come back from such an exit with hugs and kisses.

"You must be Patricia," David said. "Nice to meet you."

"Good to meet you, David," Mom replied.

I gave him bonus points for taking the lead and hoped he didn't think I was childish for freezing when I saw her. He gave Mom a measured smile, his bedside best in an uncomfortable situation. I pulled a chair closer to Jeffrey, sat, and took his other hand.

"Leanne, I'm going to call an ortho buddy of mine to look at the x-rays and find out who's on call for neurology. Anyone want coffee?"

I nodded and put three fingers up. I didn't trust my voice.

David put his reassuring hand on my shoulder. "I know it sounds crazy, but after doing this for years, you develop an instinct. He'll be okay, I promise."

David didn't know this went way beyond busted-up body parts. Jeffrey's head might heal and his leg would mend, but he wouldn't be okay. He'd have to work on all the parts doctors couldn't see, and those parts took a lifetime to heal, if they ever did.

Marie touched my arm. "I'll be in the ladies' room for a minute. Don't leave him alone."

"We won't go anywhere," Mom said.

The second Marie left, tears welled up and ran down Mom's face in a torrent. I'd never seen her lose her shit and I didn't want to ever again. Susan would analyze each sob. Levi would hold her close. Paulka would cry in sympathy and offer gifts of home décor. Me? Like a mighty river destroying everything in its path, profound guilt gurgled up from its source. Jeffrey's accident was my fault. It was my job to watch out for my baby brother. I'd known the guilty feeling forever, but I didn't know why.

"This is my fault." She sobbed harder.

"Jeffrey's an adult. This is on him, not you."

The lie rolled right off my tongue. Not surprising—I learned from the best. She fished a tissue out of her purse and dabbed at the blood on Jeffrey's face. I saw his mouth twitch, and someone walked over my grave. My lungs were running on empty, and I took tiny sips of the Lysol-scented air, willing myself to keep my shit together.

"What if he has brain damage? What if he'd killed someone? What if he dies?" she whispered.

"Jeffrey doesn't have a brain to be damaged."

She didn't laugh. I didn't think she would.

"Mom, he didn't kill anyone, and David said he's going to be fine."

"He's not fine, Leanne. He was drunk."

I thought about telling her that the sleazy internet option made him drink. His outrageous lack of judgment. She'd be livid instead of heartbroken, but I wouldn't tattle on Jeffrey, even if he deserved it.

She shut her eyes as if she couldn't bear to see the destruction of the fragile world she'd created. I moved to the whiteboard, my back to her, and pretended to read what I couldn't understand. A nurse came in, checked the beeping machines, and changed the numbers on the whiteboard.

"Is he improving?" I asked the nurse, my voice shaky and small.

She smiled and patted my arm. "The doctor should be in soon."

I stared at Jeffrey's latest vitals until they were burned into my brain.

I moved a chair next to Mom and reached out my hand. The immeasurable hurt in her eyes took me to an edge I avoided at any cost. Mom took my hand, and squeezed it hard, her eyes staring straight ahead. Raw, unfiltered pain slithered inside my body, suffocating me. I imagined cold, wet cement filling my veins, stilling the agony.

"I didn't know how you take your coffee." David came in like a food truck, loaded up with pastel-colored packets of everything possible to dump into coffee, plus bagels, muffins, and a fruit plate. I gave him extra points for the dazzling smile with the thoughtful catering service, and Mom let go of my hand.

"People forget to eat." He shrugged and passed me a steaming cup and Mom a raspberry muffin.

"These are my favorite. Thank you." Mom set the muffin down and took a coffee.

"Did you find anything out?" I nervously peeled the tops off way too many tiny creamer containers and dumped them in my cup until the coffee was as pale as Jeffrey.

"Good news. I talked with Jeffrey's neurologist, Dr. Gregorian—he's a buddy of mine and the best in the business. He was on call when Jeffrey came in."

"Is that the good news?" Mom asked.

"Dr. Gregorian said the MRI is precautionary. He'll talk to you after the tests, but he's not worried," David said. He opened as many tiny creamer containers as I had and tasted his coffee. "Not bad for hospital coffee," he said, looking at me, his gaze then taking in Mom. "You two look like sisters. How—"

Marie stepped back into the room before he could say any more. The morning's terror was camouflaged with pressed powder and fresh lipstick, and her wispy blond hair framed her angelic face.

David stood to give her the chair. "How're you doing, Marie?"

Marie leaned into David, and he put his arms around her. Face powder imprinted her petite nose on his navy shirt. I wished he'd met the family under better circumstances, like at a picnic in a park, but he didn't seem to mind, and we hadn't had a picnic in years.

A nurse wheeled in a gurney, and David helped get Jeffrey aboard.

"Please be careful with him. He doesn't like tests," Marie whispered through fresh tears.

She kissed Jeffrey gently on the lips before the nurse wheeled him out of the room. She slumped next to me. Tears streaked through her fresh makeup.

"This is my fault, Leanne. I shouldn't have kicked him out."

I was acutely aware that David was about to get an earful, but I was tired of secrets. It was much better when everything was out in the open. I was tempted to tell David that Mom lied about raspberry muffins being her favorite, but I decided to cover her worthless ass.

"You did the right thing. Maybe he'll straighten up now," I said.

Mom gave me an inquisitive stare, which I countered with one of my own. Jeffrey's story wasn't mine to tell.

"Jeffrey's going to be a while." David said.

"Marie, why don't you go home and check on the kids. I'll stay here."

"How long do you think he'll be?" Marie asked.

David glanced at Jeffrey's vital signs and turned back to her. "I'd guess about four hours. There won't be any news until then."

"I'll be good in the cafeteria. The kids are with a friend." She smiled at David, then leaned over and whispered in my ear, "If David's lost, don't give him back."

"What if someone posts a sign?" I teased and squeezed her hand.

"Keep him, no matter what." She squeezed back. "You guys don't need to wait with me. I've got phone calls to make. I'll be busy till Jeffrey's done."

"David, if you wouldn't mind, I'd like to steal Leanne away for a few hours," Mom said, eyes on me. "We have some things to discuss."

David nodded.

"Let's talk here," I said.

Mom obviously intended to pump me for information on Jeffrey, and that was on a need-to-know basis. Payback is a bitch.

"We aren't going to intrude on Marie," Mom said.

I glanced over at David to see how much of the unsaid he picked up on. He shrugged ever so slightly.

"Marie, how about we head down to the cafeteria, and I'll fill you in on Jeffrey until Dr. Gregorian is available," David said. He seemed to be an expert at reading the signs of an uncomfortable family drama. I bet he'd had a lot of practice. "Gift shop, too. I need colored Sharpies."

"What do you want with Sharpies?" I asked.

"For the kids, so they can draw on his cast when they visit. I bet they can come by tonight," he said and gave Marie a reassuring nod.

"Save a thigh for me," I said. "I've got a lot to say."

Chapter Fourteen

M om sat on my couch and flipped through the vintage cookbooks piled on my coffee table. "Pink drapes in a living room? Unusual," Mom said.

"Paulka gave them to me. *Rose Glacé*, not pink. Coffee or wine?"

"Tea, please. Why didn't David know how you take your coffee? He seems like the kind of man who'd pay attention to the little things."

"Fishing for details?" I asked as I put the kettle on and opened a bottle of wine for myself.

"I have keen powers of observation, and you two seemed cozy," Mom said.

"Enough about me. Since you wanted to talk, let's talk about you."

She pointed at a page in the magazine. "This almond chocolate thing looks divine. You should make this." She flipped through a few more pages. "Is David a real doctor?"

I poured hot water into the teapot and threw in a teabag. "No, he's a plumber. That's why he has hospital privileges. He fixed the toilet last week in the ER." I carried in a tray with tea for her and wine for me. "What discussion topic was burning in your mind? Dad, Jeffrey, the unseasonably balmy weather?"

"Give me a moment to warm up. The past isn't the easiest thing to discuss. I'm not like most people who can't wait to dredge it up and roll around in it like a pig in a mud bath. That's what most people do, Leanne. They relive the past, thinking they'll feel a bit better with each soak in the dirt."

"You might feel better if you got it all out, cleared the air?"

"My air is fabulous. I don't need to stink it up with what is long dead as far as I'm concerned."

She wasn't going to make this easy. To let me in on her supposed torment was more painful than lying about it. I poured myself a big glass of wine.

Mom sipped her tea and stared out the window, her lips a line in the sand, reluctant to divulge anything. Hesitation filled the air along with her perfume. I had a soft spot for her fragrance—it reminded me of goodness, laughter, and Mom always being there. I started to thaw, becoming more of a curious cat than a hostile honey badger.

She fussed with a luxurious mohair and sequin throw, another hand-me-down from Paulka, and arranged herself on my sofa the way an opera singer poses before an opening aria. It's an unconscious move to shield herself from who knew what. A few sessions ago, Susan pointed out that I did the same thing. Ridiculous.

"At Christmas, we wrote letters to Jesus and Mary instead of Santa Claus," she said. "My mother believed murderers should get two consecutive life sentences. One for killing and one for lying."

"Why are you telling me this?"

"I need to start somewhere."

"Carry on."

"My father was a saltine cracker of a man. Bland but useful. He was in the insurance business." She reached for the wine and filled her empty teacup. "He ate three scrambled eggs every morning of his life, wore the same two ties, both dark blue, and worked six days a week. Later in life, I realized my mother was in the insurance business, too. Religion's a kind of insurance. Speaking of saltines, do you have any crackers? Cheese?"

A stroll in the past was hungry work. I grunted, rolled my eyes at the delay, and got up to make us a snack. Being in the high-end food business with the Napa Valley at my beck and call as a purveyor had its perks: Comice pears, hand-crafted cheese, and a bowl of fresh walnuts. It was the basket I'd forgotten to take for Susan's brunch. Maybe the high fat content of the decadent brie would smooth the way for Mom. I set the bamboo tray down and eased up on the reins.

"I won't be mad, but is it possible your parents aren't dead?" I said and handed her a slice of pear liberally slathered with cheese.

"They died in a house fire. Strangest thing, Leanne. After the firemen put the flames out, they found them in bed together. Astounding, since they'd had separate bedrooms for years and it was in the middle of the afternoon and on a Wednesday. Her St. Tarcisius candle started the fire."

"That's so sad."

"I thought it sweet that they died together."

"No, Mom. It's tragic that they died in a fire."

"Well, that's what happens when you leave candles burning unattended. St. Tarcisius burned day and night. Ironic, she picked a saint beaten to death for hiding things."

Considering her parents had burned to death, she seemed almost blasé. Very odd.

"Why didn't you tell me about the fire?"

She finished the pear, spread a cracker with the brie, and took her time. "I told you that they died in their sleep, which is mostly true. Besides, you didn't know them, and what's the point of traumatizing children?"

I palmed my face in my mind. *I don't know, Mom. What is the point of traumatizing children?* I knew better than to say what I thought or raise my voice. I had a sneaking suspicion that the grandparent pictures were also fake. Patience, young Grasshopper, I told myself, as I topped up my glass and filled her teacup with the wine. It was shameless, but I had to hedge my bets, and cheese as a weapon had yet to be tested.

"The grandparent pictures are fake, aren't they?"

"I'm sorry, but she refused to meet you, and he wouldn't consider it if she didn't. I wanted you to think you were loved."

"Why didn't they want to meet me?"

"You were born out of wedlock with the devil in attendance, according to her, although he was late for your birth by a case of scotch and several, no doubt sleazy, women."

"The devil? Who's the devil?"

"Your father. The only thing your grandmother was right about."

Chapter Fifteen

San Francisco, California. May 1962.

"Looks like you're waiting for someone special," the man said, and slid onto the metal-topped barstool next to Patricia, giving her a well-practiced once-over.

"I didn't know Dick Tracy liked chocolate milkshakes," Patricia said, like she wasn't flattered by his attention.

"I'm not a detective; I'm a radio guy." He licked ice cream off the straw and pointed it at Patricia. "Girls don't usually dress up for a soda in a diner."

"I'm meeting a friend, and you act like a detective."

"Why would you think I'm a detective? Got something to hide?" he asked.

"Only from you."

"You're sassy for a young thing."

"Are you using your radio voice or your real voice?"

He stuck the straw in his shake and stood; six feet of defined muscle loomed over her. Patricia took in the pressed navy suit, shined shoes, and fancy gold watch, and took a sip of Coke to wet her mouth. She wondered if she'd gone too far since he didn't smile or laugh at her joke, and she felt a jolt in her gut like she'd done something wrong.

"Tell you what, I'm going to wait at the lunch counter. If your friend doesn't show up in ten minutes, we'll blow this place, and I'll buy you a real drink."

He took his milkshake and a newspaper from the rack and eased himself onto the last barstool at the counter. He dipped the straw in the glass and sucked up the shake, his thumb over the top of the straw. He released it, and a drop of creamy ice cream fell into his mouth. She saw a shadow of a dark beard on his chiseled jaw as his blue eyes stole glances at her. His voice was like the hot caramel simmering behind the counter. No wonder he did radio. Connie Frances sang "Lipstick on Your Collar" while Patricia smiled at him and sipped on her Coke.

It would have saved her a whole lot of trouble if she'd taken the time to listen to Connie's words instead of his. He waited six minutes before he slipped off the barstool and slid in next to Patricia.

"Doesn't look like anyone's showing up. So, princess, about that drink?"

"I'm twenty."

"Got a fake ID?"

"Sure, I do."

"With your figure, I doubt you'll need it." No one had ever said something so fresh. She loved it. "I'll grab us a cab," he said.

He put his hand out while a smile played on his lips; a dimple appeared in his left cheek. She glanced up at him and felt taken care of and important. She looked down at his hands; no gold ring would steal him away. He looked like the young lawyer in a motion picture she'd seen last week. Too bad he wasn't a lawyer or an actor—what a waste, all that handsome hidden inside a soundproof glass booth. A captivating thought took hold; being a radio guy, he'd know all about the music business.

After a quick cab ride, he whisked her into his favorite bar, Bluebeards. They settled into an old, black, button-backed leather booth, his thigh against hers, making her green dress rustle under the table. Rusty anchors, fishing nets, and dusty starfish graced the walls. A cheese ball covered in crushed walnuts sat alongside a plate of crackers on the long bar. It was a pirate den with serving wenches, a swarthy bartender with an eye patch, and Christmas snacks in May.

She played with her fake pearl bracelet and hoped he thought the matching necklace made her glamorous. "I love this place. Is that a real fish?"

"That's a swordfish from Mexico, stuffed and mounted. Grasshopper or a Tom Collins?" he asked and lit a cigarette.

She wanted to seem mature, so she made her voice breathy and licked her pink lips. "I'll have what you're having." She knew that was the thing to say when you didn't know what to order.

"Bourbon on the rocks. Throw a couple of cherries in one of them. You smoke?"

She shook her head while noticing that he gave their order to the cocktail server's ample cleavage. Patricia couldn't blame him; the purple bodice spilled forth its contents like the Mississippi flooding its banks.

"I suppose I get the one with the cherry."

"A beautiful woman needs something pretty in her drink."

"You think I'm pretty, huh?"

"You're exquisite."

She didn't know what to say, and her cheeks flushed. The only time she'd heard anything referred to as exquisite was a rare purple orchid at the church flower festival. She sipped on the drink until a cherry rolled back into her throat. He rubbed her shoulders while she hacked like a seal pup. Once she'd caught her breath, she noted her body was warm and aroused from his touch. She knew it was wrong to want his hand on her. Her mother had ground into her head that a man's hand could ruin a girl's life. She tossed back the drink to quench the fire in her practical parts, as her mother christened them when Patricia became a woman.

"Hey, go easy on that thing," he said.

"You ordered the dangerous drink."

"A baby could drink bourbon. The cherry? That's the dangerous part."

"I'm okay with a little danger."

"What about a lot?" he asked.

"You mean like dangerous rocks ahead?" Patricia said and smoothed his cheek with her hand. She scooted closer to him, heady with her sophisticated repartee, the booze making her brave.

"Yeah." He put his hand on her lower back. "We better cover up the ice, so you're safe."

He took his hand off her back and waved the wench over. "No cherries this time. She can handle it straight." The cocktail server flashed him a dimpled smile. No surprise there. He was James Dean sexy. Dreamy or not, Patricia realized that she sat with a stranger.

"I forgot to ask your name," Patricia said, surprised at herself. She'd had manners drummed into her head from childhood.

"I'll take it as a compliment." He winked and took a sip of his cocktail. "You were distracted by my obvious charms. Happens to the best of them."

"I'd still like to know your name."

"I'm Verin. Nice to meet you." He put out a hand and shook hers.

She giggled. "Never heard that name before. Is it a family name?"

"My dad named me after the demon of impatience."

"Names are stupid. I hate mine. It's Patricia, but I go by Vivienne."

"Vivienne it is."

"Call me Vivi. That's my stage name."

"Enchanté, Vivi." He took her hand and kissed it. Twice. His kiss was delicious, like vanilla ice cream on hot apple pie. "How about we order some food? Talk about your stardom?"

"A star? I wish. I sing jazz around town, that's all."

The pirate wench came by to take their order. Verin spoke to the valley in her bodice. Patricia adjusted her neckline a little lower.

"Chateaubriand for two and all the trimmings."

"Would you like a bottle of wine with that, sir?" The waitress was flustered around him, giving him the eyelash treatment. He gave her a grin. It was a bit too friendly, considering that she wasn't his date.

"French champagne, your best."

"I better call my roommate. We had plans tonight," Patricia said and picked up her handbag to look for some loose change.

Verin trickled a handful of coins into the open bag. "Hurry back, beautiful. I'm missing you already."

She had nothing to compare with, but this heady feeling couldn't be alcohol alone. She was beautiful and sophisticated, elevated by his knowing ways. This was much better than Friday fish sticks with St.

Tarcisius and a fresh batch of oatmeal cookies. She fixed her lipstick in the ladies' room and studied her reflection in the mirror. She looked different, radiant, and a little drunk. Patricia fumbled in her purse for one of Verin's nickels and shut herself in the phone booth. The hinge was broken, so she held it closed. He'd never give her a second look if he knew there wasn't a roommate and that she lived at home with a crazy mother.

"Hi, Mom. I'm going to be home a little late. Ginger got free tickets to *Ben Hur*."

"What about your studies? Don't you have homework?"

"Mom, please."

"There's nudity in that picture."

"It's Moses, Mom. God wants me to see it."

"Don't be fresh with me, Patricia. Are you all right? You sound odd. Are you getting sick?"

"Couldn't be better. Ginger said I could stay at her house."

"You come home right after the picture."

"I'm seventeen, not a baby. I'll study after the movie; I promise."

"I don't know what the devil has got into you, but I want you home by eight a.m. tomorrow to do your chores. I'll save you some fish sticks."

Chapter Sixteen

P atricia's dress slithered underneath her as she scooted into the booth. Verin watched, a sweetheart of a protector. She adjusted the dress to cover her thighs and reached for her drink. She wiggled her nose at the bubbles she didn't expect.

"I've never had champagne before."

"You look like you'd drink it for breakfast."

Patricia caught her slip and shrugged. "I mean, I haven't had this kind."

"What kind did you have?" Verin said, placing another smoke in his mouth.

"German champagne, maybe Swedish. Did you notice our names both start with a V?"

"It's fate, baby." He lit the cigarette and blew a ring over her head.

She tipped the champagne to her lips, looked over the rim, and lowered her eyelashes. He lifted his glass at the same time.

"So. Tell me, baby. Why are you dressed up for a cocktail party in the middle of the afternoon?"

"I had a meeting with this guy, Jack. I wanted to look good, like a professional singer. I guess he didn't remember our appointment."

"I don't think he'd forget a date with you."

"It wasn't a date. I sang with his band the other night at the Cupid and Crow. He has another gig lined up for me."

"I bet he does."

"Sounds like someone's jealous," Patricia said and walked her fingers up his arm.

"You can sing, huh?" Verin finished his cigarette and reached for a celery stick from the relish tray.

"Decide for yourself."

Patricia drained her champagne, kissed Verin on the cheek, and made her way to an older Black man wearing a porkpie hat playing background tunes at an upright piano next to the bar. She was close enough to smell the cheese ball. She leaned down and whispered in his ear.

"'Black Coffee'? Sure thing," he said, giving Patricia a huge grin. "What key, gorgeous?"

"C major, please. What's your name?"

"William, but for you? I'm plain old Billy."

"Thanks, Billy."

She patted her updo, making sure her hair was in place, smoothed her tight dress down, and pressed her lips together, careful not to lick her lipstick off. A little woozy, she wished she hadn't had that last glass of champagne, but it was too late now. She closed her eyes and breathed in confidence along with the smoky air. Patricia put her hands on either side of the microphone and held it like a lover's face. Her eyes found Verin's. She pretended she understood the lyrics as she sang to him.

Wild applause and a few catcalls followed as she floated back to her table. Billy wanted her to sing another song, but she couldn't wait to get back to Verin. He held his glass for a toast, eyes full of surprise and heat.

"Baby! Incredible! You're something else. Like Ella Fitzgerald, but prettier." He got up and helped her slide into the booth.

"She's a much better singer. I can't believe I did that. I'm not usually so daring."

"Why the hell not? Daring suits you."

The wench set down their dinners, making the table sway and the glasses rattle. Patricia noted that this time, Verin ignored the banks of the Mississippi.

"Tell you what, baby, how do you feel about a little more singing tonight? I've got a friend with a combo over at Taffy's. We'll swing by, show off that sultry voice of yours."

"You'd do that for me?"

"Why not? I bet you could be a star."

"Oh, Verin."

"I'd like to see the sun come up with you, baby." Verin took her hand in his, kissed her open palm. Dampness pulled her dress tight against her skin, fire in her face. He pulled away and cut into his steak. He must be over thirty; men over thirty expected to see the sun come up. She would figure it out after she sang at Taffy's.

The cab pulled up in front of the nightclub. Verin tossed a five-dollar bill to the taxi driver, grabbed Patricia's hand, and escorted her to the red velvet rope. He pushed a five into the hard palm of a muscled-up guy poured into a midnight-blue tuxedo.

"Hey, Bruce, get that gig in Hollywood yet?"

"Soon, Verin. Thanks for asking. I'll get you and the lady a table. Mikey, watch the door."

Bruce ushered them toward the most gorgeous woman Patricia had ever seen. She wore a long, silver, sequined dress with a slit up the thigh, and her shiny black hair was piled high on her head and held with diamond clips. She dismissed Patricia with a sweep of inky lashes, her smile hard and without warmth.

"I'm Lillian." She put out a hand with crimson nails filed to sharp points, and let it circle down until she clasped her own tiny waist. Patricia had expected a handshake, and let her hand drop against her side, feeling foolish.

"Champagne or bourbon, Verin?" Lillian lit his cigarette with a fancy jeweled lighter as she moved closer, her perfume filling the space between them. Patricia recognized the expensive scent from the makeup counter at I. Magnin; Shalimar. Lillian raised herself up, presenting a cheek for Verin to kiss. Was she looking for a thank you for lighting his smoke? Bile filled Patricia's stomach as she watched his lips linger longer than necessary on the smooth, porcelain cheek.

"Surprise me, baby. You know what I like," Verin said. Patricia guessed that Verin and this sparkly column knew all about each other's practical parts.

Lillian sat them at the best table, on the edge of the dance floor, and swayed over to the bar. After taking a mental note to master Lillian's sultry walk, Patricia gazed around the most gorgeous room she'd ever seen. Real palm trees reached toward twinkling lights set into a midnight-blue ceiling. White silk flowed from golden hooks, draping blue velvet booths that lined the walls around a silver-glittered dance floor. Midnight-blue velvet draped the stage, hundreds of sparkly silver stars hung above the band. It was heaven with endless booze and thick with cigarette smoke.

A young, blond cocktail waitress in a short sequined dress brought a bottle of champagne in a fancy ice bucket along with an expensive-looking bottle of bourbon. A bald man, skinny like a pencil in a gray sharkskin suit, sauntered over, pulled up a chair, and sat down backward.

"Hey, Verin. Who's the girl?"

"Sam, this is Vivi. Vivi, meet Sam. Let her sing a little. Trust me, she's something special." Verin put his hand on the waitress's rear. "Bring us another glass, sweetheart." He gazed at the blonde's back as she hurried off.

"What are you doing with a kid, Verin? Hey, Vivi, you got an ID? Don't want to get busted for enticing a minor." Sam gave Verin a dirty look, tossed back his drink, and stood.

"It's okay," Patricia said. "I don't have to sing."

"No, baby, he's gotta hear you," Verin said. "Jesus Christ, Sam, lighten up. She's not taking her clothes off; she's got a voice. Do 'Black Coffee,' baby. She slays it, Sam."

Sam finished his cigarette, stubbed it out in the silver-star ashtray, and tucked another between his lips. He blew out a big cloud of smoke, shook his head, and studied Patricia. "All right, kid. One song. Verin, you better be right."

She followed him to the stage, her mouth bone dry, her heart thudding. She'd make Verin proud. She had to.

Patricia lost herself in "Black Coffee" and surrendered to "Mood Indigo." She became a wounded lover, a temptress with a conscience, and a heartless siren. Heartache and relentless passion showed in her face and the pitch-perfect notes that flowed out of her without hesitation. Sam chain-smoked, and the band never took a break.

She sang while the bartenders washed last-round glasses, and her voice stilled the rowdy, well-dressed crowd. She stripped down to her soul for the finale and sang "Come Rain or Come Shine" straight to Verin. He hadn't taken his blue eyes off her all night, but the bourbon was down to half a bottle and a fresh pack of Lucky Strikes waited on the cocktail table.

Sam escorted Patricia back to Verin. He pulled her down on his lap, arms tight around her body. The photo girl came by and snapped a polaroid.

"Verin, you gotta get this girl in a studio. I'm serious. Vivi, you come back anytime. Do you hear me?" Sam said.

"Thank you so much, Sam. You don't know what this means to me." She detached Verin's arms from around her waist and stood to kiss Sam on the cheek.

"Hey, those are only for me." Verin laughed and pulled her back down hard.

Butterflies in her stomach, false poise on her face, Patricia came in closer and smiled. "Oh, Verin. I have lots of those for you."

As soon as she moved in for a kiss, Verin gently lifted her off his lap, checked his watch, and put his hands in his pockets.

"Come on, baby, it's late. Let's get you home."

"What about the sunrise?"

"There are three hundred and sixty-five mornings a year, baby. We've got plenty of time."

His palm on the small of her back, Verin guided her outside. Bruce whistled for a cab, handed Verin the photo, and held the car door open. Verin slipped him another five and slithered in next to Patricia.

"Penny, for your thoughts," she said, reaching for the photo as the cab took off.

"Sam's right. You're a beautiful, talented kid. I shouldn't be falling for a kid."

"Don't be like that, Verin. I'm advanced for my age. I know what I'm doing."

"You've had a boyfriend?"

"Yes, lots of them."

Her heart skipped a beat. She'd lied to him again but didn't want to be the kid. She didn't want the best night of her life to be over. She scooted close enough to see his once clean-shaven face had dark shadows; he'd become swarthy and sexy. He looked like a pirate captain in a banker's suit. She swallowed a giggle. No wonder he liked Bluebeards. She'd read in a movie magazine that pupils dilated when aroused. His pupils were dilated to infinity.

"I know what I'm doing," she said again. Whispers of bourbon closed the gap between them. "Kiss me, Verin." She shut her eyes and raised her face. He touched her long, dark lashes and the hint of delicate bones behind flushed cheeks as she puckered her lips. He stroked her face with two fingers and closed the gap between them.

"What kind of a kiss is that? My uncle gives me more romantic kisses."

"Some uncle you got." He smiled at her.

"I thought you liked me?"

"I do."

"What did I do wrong?"

"Nothing, baby. Trust me, let's take it slow."

"I don't want to take it slow. I've never felt like this about anyone."

He laughed. Patricia clenched her hand into a fist. He pulled it apart, finger by finger, and kissed her open palm, never taking his eyes off her. He placed her hand by her side.

"I'm taking you home. We'll talk later. Give me your number."

"The phone's out of order."

There was no way she could risk Verin calling. She'd never be allowed out ever again.

"I'll find you."

Patricia gave the driver Ginger's address, and they drove in silence. Patricia wouldn't look at Verin. She got out before he could help her and hustled to Ginger's porch. She could feel his eyes on her back as she pretended to find a hidden key by the front porch, slipped off her heels, and gave him a little wave as he rolled up the window and the cab pulled away. She waited until the cab had turned the corner and walked down the street to her house, confused and rejected, while tears ran down her face in the early morning light.

Chapter Seventeen

Patricia's mother, Rosalind, stood on a stepladder, a bucket of foamy water on the counter, and a dishrag in her hand to wipe down the kitchen cabinets. Patricia looked up at her, a willowy brunette with natural auburn highlights and cheekbones to die for. She could have been a model, but instead, she wore a plain, mud-brown dress from her neck to her ankles, a faded floral apron, and no makeup. St. Tarcisius disapproved of makeup.

"Get your homework done?"

"Don't I always?" Patricia opened the fridge, took out a milk bottle, and tipped it to her mouth.

"The sun is barely up, and she's in first place for Miss Manners 1962."

"At least I'm in first place for something."

"You look terrible. Are you getting sick?" Rosalind said and passed her a glass.

"It's my new look. Do you like it?"

"Do you want eggs to go with that attitude?" Rosalind climbed down, meticulously uncovered the butter dish, and dabbed a pat on the cast-iron skillet. "Why don't you take your milk and sit at the table like a lady?"

"I'm almost done."

"Sit. I'll make you eggs."

"Can I have coffee if I eat eggs?"

"You stayed up too late seeing that picture, didn't you? And no, coffee will stunt your growth."

"I'll take the chance."

Patricia sat at the kitchen table and traced the initial V on the blue checkered tablecloth. Scrambled eggs sizzled in the pan, making her hungry. She thought about Verin, wondering where he lived and how she could see him again.

"You think you're something special, don't you?" Rosalind said as she set a plate before Patricia, added a fork and knife, and tossed a cloth napkin at her. "Always have something to say. Why can't you set a decent example for your baby sisters? Such blessed girls, and there's you, Miss Mouth, from the day you learned to talk. I wish you'd been mute."

"Jesus, Mother."

"Don't take the Lord's name in vain, Patricia. No toast for you," Rosalind said.

"Everyone's perfect at five. Give them time."

"Rose and Lily will always be perfect. Mother Mary came to me during their birth. 'Rosalind,' she said, 'these babies are special angels. Keep them pink and with a purpose."

"Mary didn't have a comment when I popped out?" Patricia shoved eggs into her mouth and drank her milk to wash them down. "Was she busy setting the table for the Last Supper?"

"I mean it, Patricia. Watch your mouth, and no, she didn't."

"Bob's not so perfect."

"Your brother's serving his country and God, although not in that order. Small mistakes are forgotten for a man in uniform. Use your napkin."

Patricia wiped her lips. "Sue isn't small."

"There's no one named Sue for you to concern yourself with, and Bob's a good boy. Bacon?" Rosalind seized a burnt piece of bacon and held it out with tongs.

"I'm done."

"Start with the baseboards, and don't soak them. If I wanted to flood the hall, I'd call the fire department. Last week you got the runners damp. Mildew hangs around like flies on a drunken sailor." Rosalind started on the breakfast dishes.

"What do you know about drunken sailors?" Patricia said, playing with an apple from the fruit bowl.

"Don't be fresh with me, and put your pity-party face away. I won't have it. You have six hours of housework, that's all. At seventeen, I cleaned the house ten hours a day, whether it needed it or not. Later, take the twins to the park, and no sandbox. Last time, they turned my rugs into the Sahara. I need a little peace today. Don't play with the fruit."

"You need peace from the little angels?"

"I'll enter you for Miss Manners 1963. No doubt you'll win that one as well."

Patricia put her dishes in the sink and retrieved a bucket, sponge, and Spic and Span from the pantry. The other Holy Trinity, according to her mother. On hands and knees, Patricia started to the left of the front door and worked her way around the house. She scrubbed the ornate baseboard she'd grown to detest.

Pink polish flaked off her nails as resentment churned, the baseboards pristine from last week's needless pilgrimage. Damn this stupid old house. She imagined Verin at her front door, a glass slipper in his hand, a cigarette hanging from his lips, and a sexy "Hey, baby, drop something?" She said a heartfelt prayer that he wouldn't ever come over. Her mother would scare him off for good.

A few hours later, breathing in fumes from the Spic and Span, Patricia pushed sticky hair off her face, exhausted from lack of sleep. She'd tried to catch a few hours in the back seat of her dad's station wagon before coming into the house, but she couldn't get Verin off her mind. Why hadn't he wanted her? Patricia watched Verin eyeball the Mississippi's bosom, inhale the club hostess's neck, and appraise the blonde with the drinks like she was a prize show dog. She decided those women threw themselves at him, and, with such good manners, he had no choice but to be polite. Why didn't he want her like that?

In the car, she could feel his hand on her face, the small of her back, and her thigh. He had said that he needed to smooth down her dress; he couldn't have it riding up for the cabbie to get a look. His fingers lingered on her stocking tops; he apologized when he touched her garter belt. Patricia had never been on a real date and had only kissed a few guys on the rare occasions when she managed to convince her mother that she had a sewing evening with Ginger.

"Knitting class" had bought her six weeks of parties and her first taste of gin. She'd kissed hormonal, sweaty boys, but never a man. She concluded that this was how it went when they liked you, and crawled into the bathroom. Working her way around the tub and behind the toilet, she decided that Verin was falling in love, which was why he'd acted like a gentleman.

She stood up, stiff, tired, and elated with her pinpoint perception. She peered into the mirror. Jesus, she did look sick. She needed a nap. She made a kiss face at herself and decided she'd have to make the first move with Verin.

Her mother yelled, "Patricia, come downstairs. There's a man at the door for you."

She was wide awake now, frothy visions of romance replaced by abject terror. Verin was downstairs with her mother. He must have circled back and seen her go into the garage. He had waited until an appropriate time to say good morning and whisk her away for a romantic lunch. She could hear muffled voices coming up the stairs, and from the sound of it, they were in the parlor with St. Tarcisius, fresh cookies on his plaster feet.

Wearing stained capris, an old striped shirt of her father's, and yesterday's makeup smeared under her eyes, she looked like the sailors her mother feared. Frantic, she zipped into her bedroom and pulled out a white lace dress. Nothing seduction-worthy but a ticket out of the house for the afternoon if she was lucky. She'd tell her mother he had tickets to a church lunch—his church. She'd love that.

Her hair was a sticky mess from yesterday's hairspray. She moved it into a ponytail and tied it with a white ribbon. She checked herself in the full-length mirror and took the stairs two at a time, slowing down for her grand entrance, head up like the queen of the holiday parade.

"Jack? What are you doing here?"

"Hey, Vivi, I felt bad standing you up yesterday. I asked around, and Ginger gave me your address. Peace offering?"

Jack handed Patricia a small bouquet of carnations tied with a pink ribbon. She couldn't believe it. Maybe this prayer stuff worked. Verin coming to the house would have been a nightmare. Jack, the band leader? Only a horrible dream.

"Should I call you Vivi now?" Rosalind said in her scary-quiet voice, an octave lower than usual.

"Jack's confusing me with someone else."

"I swear the other night you said your name was Vivi?" Jack said.

"Patricia, where were you the other night?"

"The library with Ginger. Remember, Mother? My report on Andrew Jackson?"

"I got the gig. You sing on Monday, Wednesday, and Friday. I can pay you ten bucks a night. You in?"

Rosalind put both hands on her bony hips. "Patricia Jane, what is this boy talking about?"

"I got a paying gig, ma'am. Your daughter sings like that bird that sings good," Jack explained.

The scrambled eggs twisted in Patricia's gut, threatening to join the cookies on St. T's feet.

"Are you referring to a nightingale?" Rosalind asked.

"That bird is so good they named a nurse after it." Jack slapped his knee.

Patricia took a deep breath, hands over her stomach. Her mother grabbed a cookie from St. Tarcisius' feet and took a small bite, crumbling the rest in her fist.

"I'm sorry, Jack, but I couldn't possibly sing on school nights," Patricia said. "I told you I could sing for your church as a soloist. Remember? Jack?"

"Tell us, Jack, where is this gig?" Rosalind said. "Our Lady of Blessed Liars? St. Grounded for Life? I love music. I'll get a ticket."

Jack knew music but was dense as a swamp when reading signs. While Jack had her mother's undivided attention, Patricia mimed singing, pointed at her mother, and put an imaginary gun to her head. He finally got it.

"Ma'am? Oh, I'm sorry. I get confused. I got dropped on my head as a baby. I saw Vivi, I mean Patricia, in the library the other night, and we talked about the Civil War. Did you know they ate hot squirrels Monday, Wednesday, and Friday? Even the Catholics. They sang on the battlefield, hymns mostly, so I thought—"

"That is the biggest malarkey I've ever heard," Rosalind said. "Please go. My daughter will not perform like a trained poodle for anyone."

Jack frowned at Patricia, made the sign for crazy when Rosalind turned away, and slunk out the front door, closing it quietly.

"A dog, Mother?" Patricia said. "How could you embarrass me in front of Jack?"

"Embarrass you? You embarrass yourself, Patricia—or should I say, Vivi?"

"That's my stage name. I will be a singer, whether you like it or not."

"Do you know what happens to nightclub singers? You'll be passed around like a collection basket. Men lined up with filth in their minds to watch you. They don't care about your voice."

"You don't know anything."

"I know you'll be nothing but a side of beef to be portioned into choice bits until you are leftovers for street dogs." She crossed herself and ate another cookie. "If you must have a career, become a nurse or a schoolteacher, something respectful. You will not, I repeat, you will not set foot on stage, or you will be out of this house for good. Do I make myself clear?"

"I hate this house, and I hate you." Still holding the small bouquet, Patricia ran up the stairs to her bedroom.

"The devil has many weapons, Patricia Jane!" Rosalind yelled up the stairs.

Patricia threw the flowers across the room, and a small note rolled out. *Sorry, I forgot about our meeting. Hot Squirrel on Monday if you want to sing. Jack.*

Patricia opened her door and yelled down the stairs, "It's my life, Mother!" She slammed her door, the note in her fist.

Chapter Eighteen

T he Hot Squirrel was a far cry from the glamour of Taffy's, but it jumped with a hopped-up, booze-filled crowd who loved the new girl. Guys pushed drinks at the band all night and threw phone numbers to Patricia, who ate it up with a soup spoon.

"What's my beautiful baby doing in a joint like this?"

Patricia threw herself into Verin's outstretched arms, pressing herself against his navy suit and inhaling the scent of a fresh shave.

"My gig, Verin, and they pay me."

"They should pay you, baby. You think the crowd's here for the beer?" Verin called for a server to clean off a barstool before he sat down. She laughed and threw him a dishrag. Verin scowled, wiped down the sticky barstool, and sat, crushing peanut shells beneath his shiny shoes.

"How long have you been listening?"

"From the first moment I laid eyes on you." He touched her cheek and motioned to the swamped bartender, "Hey, a scotch over here, and keep the tab running. You want a drink, baby?"

Patricia shook her head. "I didn't have your number. I couldn't reach you."

"You reach me, baby."

"Are you making fun of me?"

Patricia wondered why he sounded like a movie script. Did he ever have an original comment? He lit a smoke, inhaled deeply, and ran one hand over his cheeks and chin. He looked like that statue of The Thinker from ancient history class.

"Those are compliments. If you don't like them, say so, and I'll stop." Verin slapped the bar. "Hey, what are you doing back there? Growing the barley?"

"I'm sorry," Patricia said. She put her head down, the magic of the night evaporating along with his cigarette. When he finished the smoke, he put a manicured fingertip under her chin, lifted her head, and kissed both cheeks.

"Word around town is the Hot Squirrel's got a new girl. A smoking brunette with some serious pipes. I figured she had to be you."

The bartender put a healthy pour in Verin's glass. "Sorry about that, mister—it's packed in here because of her." The bartender gestured to Patricia and put down bourbon and a Coke. "Here you go, doll, on the house."

"I have one more set. Can you stick around for a while?" Patricia moved closer to Verin.

He reached out and ran a finger across her bottom lip. "If your new friends can spare you, I'll steal you away for a late supper."

"Can we go to the pirate den?"

"Anywhere you want."

Patricia squealed, gave him a quick kiss, and hurried over to the stage with her drink. Jack put out a hand and helped her up.

"Who are you glaring at?" Patricia said and took a sip.

"What's with the old guy in the suit?" Jack said. "He's at least thirty."

"That's Verin. He might manage me."

"I bet, and as often as possible."

"I don't know where you get your garbage, but you're wrong about him."

"He's a player, Vivi. I've seen him with lots of girls."

Patricia hated the sick feeling that stole over her. It took her confidence away and made it hard to focus. She didn't want to think about Verin with anyone but her.

"Damn it, Jack. Are you my mother? Play my song. People are looking."

Patricia found Verin in the crowd. He nodded and sipped on his drink, his eyes only on her. Jack was jealous. That had to be it. She grabbed the microphone and ensured Verin had no reason to look at anyone but her. She hissed at Jack to play "Fever" and worked the crowd into a frenzy. She sent the Romeo and Juliet verse straight to Verin. He reminded her of a Greek god, one with a cigarette in one hand and a drink in the other. Jack was crazy; she didn't have to worry about other girls. The curve of Verin's lips told her how much he adored her, and so did the kiss he blew. Jack was an idiot.

"Hey, Vivi. We're going to get a bite. Late-night noodle place in Chinatown." Jack set his bass into its case, snapped it shut, and waited for an answer.

"No, thanks. I have dinner plans with Verin."

"Here's your split." Jack handed her two five-dollar bills and a fat handful from the tip jar.

"Looks like they like us."

"They like you plenty. Hey, Vivi?"

"Yeah, Jack?"

"Be careful, okay?"

"You're an old mother hen. He's not what you think." Patricia peered into her compact and fixed her lipstick.

"He's not what you think, either," Jack said under his breath as Verin sauntered to claim Patricia.

"Ready, baby? Here's your coat. Better put it on; I don't want any of these low-lifes staring at my girl. See you Monday night, Jack," Verin said, slipping the coat over Patricia's low-cut cocktail dress. He buttoned it up to her neck and tied her scarf around her hair. She was his precious doll. No one at home took care of her like Verin. No one's fingers could send sparks down her body, either. It's too bad her dress didn't have a flameproof lining.

The delicious aroma of roast beef, fried chicken, and lamb chops wafted out of the restaurant as Verin held the heavy oak door open for Patricia. She thought she might order one of everything tonight. She was crazy hungry; she hadn't eaten a thing before she sang, and it was past midnight.

"The usual table, Verin?" The maître d', dressed like a pirate, adjusted the fake parrot on his shoulder.

Verin palmed the guy a couple of bucks. "Better buy your bird something to eat. It's looking a little skinny."

Patricia giggled, took Verin's outstretched hand, and led him past the piano.

Billy tinkered with a smoky melody and gave Patricia a big grin. "Well, lookie here. How about a sweet song for the crowd? They're mighty tired of my ugly mug."

"She's done for the night, Billy. She's got to rest her pipes."

"That's a damn shame. I suspect you want the princess all to yourself, Mr. V."

"I certainly do, Billy." Verin popped a twenty-dollar bill in the tip jar, gave Billy a hearty pat on the back, and settled Vivi into a cozy, candlelit booth.

"Do you like lobster, baby?"

"I've wanted to try it, but my mother thinks they carry the plague."

"Is that a fact?"

"She doesn't know anything. I'd love the lobster. An extra-big one?"

"Whatever my baby wants, she gets." Verin lit up another smoke. Patricia squirmed in her seat, high from performing.

"Jack gave you a hard time. Does he have beef about something?" Verin said and stroked his chin.

Her stomach started to churn. Patricia took a roll from the bread-basket, buttered it, and popped a piece in her mouth. She figured Verin could be the jealous type, and Jack had given her a gig.

She blinked and ran her hand down Verin's arm. "There's nothing to worry about."

"Why don't you want to tell me?"

"There's nothing to tell. Where do you suppose the waitress is?"

"Come on, Vivi. There are no secrets between us. What did Jack say?"

Vivi buttered more of the roll, popped a big piece into her mouth. He tapped a finger on the table while she chewed, and swallowed. "People don't understand you."

"Am I difficult to understand, baby?" Verin twirled a strand of hair that had escaped Patricia's updo. "Well, am I?"

"Jack said I should be careful of you." Patricia's stomach fluttered again. She finished the bread. "Boy, I sure would like a drink."

"Now, why would he say that? What did you tell him, Vivi?"

"I didn't say anything." Patricia fiddled with the saltshaker until Verin took it away and held her face in his hands.

"Vivi, talk."

"He told me that you have lots of girls."

Verin laughed, and Patricia started to feel better. Good thing she'd eaten the roll.

"I suppose if you're a guy like Jack, anything over one would seem like a lot."

The waitress strolled over, pen and pad in hand. Patricia recognized her from the first night: dark hair piled up on her head, blood-red lipstick, and the same low-cut purple bodice. Cheap jasmine perfume clung to her like barbecue sauce on baby-back ribs.

The wench shot Verin a dirty look. "I suppose you want your usual."

"I'd like a daiquiri, please," Patricia said.

"You got ID?"

Patricia wondered why the waitress was so difficult.

"I'm her ID, and you served her the other night," Verin said. "Make that two daiquiris. Might as well try something new, right, Vanessa?"

Vanessa flushed red and scribbled on the pad.

"And if it's not too much trouble, the biggest lobster you've got for the lady. I'll take the filet mignon, barely breathing."

Vanessa jotted down the order and made straight for the swinging kitchen door, ignoring a nearby table waving an empty wine bottle.

"Something seems off with the waitress."

"It's late, Vivi. She wants to finish her shift, get a drink, and go home. Be grateful you'll never have to wait tables."

Patricia unfolded a napkin and smoothed it on her lap. "Why do you know her name?"

"Because I eat here a lot. Enough about the waitress."

"Did you miss me, Verin?"

He sucked on his cigarette and ignored her. He looked like his mind was on other things. Maybe the waitress.

"Verin?"

"I think about you all the time, baby."

The wench brought over their drinks and dropped off a white paper bib. "Better put it on. Things could get messy around here," she said.

"A bib? I don't need one of those," Patricia said.

"You want to get melted butter on your pretty dress? Some stains never come out." Vanessa looked preoccupied with more than butter stains and hurried off to another table.

"How often do you eat here, Verin?"

"Already keeping tabs on me?"

"Do you think the waitress—"

Verin stubbed out his cigarette with a vengeance. "Damn it, Vivi. Do you want her to sit with us? I'll go, so you two can enjoy dinner together."

"I'm sorry, Verin."

"No more talk about the waitress?"

"No."

"That's my girl. Drink up, then right after dinner, I'm taking you home. You need your rest. I've got a surprise for you tomorrow at ten a.m. sharp."

Patricia's stomach hurt. She must have finished that daiquiri too fast.

Chapter Nineteen

P atricia sat with her arms wrapped tight around her body, freezing on the couch, the scratchy fabric rough against her legs. Her heart was in her throat, and she had no breath in her lungs. How was she supposed to sing? The ashtray on the coffee table overflowed as Verin stubbed out his cigarette and lit another. Was he annoyed with her? Was it her fault? He'd taken her for breakfast, where they'd first met, and ordered her coffee, waffles, and bacon. He'd booked a recording session for right after breakfast.

She was terrified, insisted she wasn't ready, and didn't touch her food. He paid the check, placed a firm hand on her arm, and they walked to the studio. A bell rang as Verin opened the door. Patricia kept quiet and looked around. A metal can stuffed with empty beer bottles. Half a pot of hot coffee simmered on a rusted hot plate. She wanted a cup but was too nervous to ask, so she calmed herself by looking at pictures of singers hanging on the smoke-stained walls.

"Vivi, we're ready to record." The sound engineer's voice came over a speaker.

"What if I mess up?" Patricia asked Verin.

Verin cradled her head between his hands, his eyes locked on hers. "You're killing me. Baby, they can start over. Sing like the first time I heard you, and you'll be fine."

"I don't know this band, Verin."

"They're studio musicians. They can play anything. All you have to do is sing."

Tears slipped down her face; her voice caught in her throat. How could she sing now? "I'm used to Jack. He leads me in."

"Screw Jack. Do you want to do this or not? I went to a lot of trouble to set this up." He tapped out a cigarette from the pack, lit it, and blew the smoke over her head.

She wiped tears away with the hem of her rose-pink dress and wondered why he was insistent. Didn't he understand how vital a recording was? Wasn't it reasonable for her to decide her future?

"Stop with the nervousness, little girl, or we can leave. I thought you were ready for this."

"Verin, please stop pushing. I've never been in a studio before."

"Goddamn, Vivi. I thought you wanted this, or I wouldn't have wasted the money."

Allen, the sound engineer, left his booth and came over. "Hey, Vivi, let's test out the mic. Can I get you a glass of water?"

"Thank you. I'm a little nervous. I've never been in a studio, although some people don't seem to understand that."

Patricia swallowed back tears until Allen put both hands on her shoulders. He wore dark glasses, so she couldn't see his eyes.

"Hey, Vivi, all singers get nervous. Sink into the words and concentrate on the music."

"What if I mess up?"

"We'll start over."

"Didn't I tell you that?" Verin said, crossing his legs, his foot bouncing. His eyes were hooded, and he stroked his chin-a gesture he often made when things didn't go his way. Verin stared at her, his face stern and unforgiving. Foolish, she stood before him, a chastised child, ready to cry again.

"I'm sorry, Verin."

"That's my girl. Get in there. You'll be fine." Verin swatted her on the rear, and she felt the sting as she walked away. Patricia went into the recording booth feeling slightly dizzy and a little nauseated. Her throat all but closed from fear. Verin's face had scared her. How was she supposed to sing when she was a nervous wreck?

Allen adjusted her headphones, fixed the microphone, and gave her a thumbs-up. She waved at Verin, who sat outside the booth in a torn leather armchair, cigarette in one hand, coffee in the other. How many girls were this lucky? What would another girl give to be in here right now? Professional musicians in a real recording studio? Men liked sassy confidence. Especially guys like Verin. She swallowed a big ball of fear and gave him her best smile.

Patrica left the booth and settled into Verin's lap as her voice came over the speakers. "Do I sound like a real singer?"

"All you, baby. Damn impressive, if you ask me." Verin ran his finger along her cheek.

"I sound like a real singer on the radio. Allen? Could I listen one more time?"

Allen chuckled. "Sure thing, Vivi. You sound incredible. See, nothing to it." He winked at her, and she hoped Verin didn't notice. "I'm going to let the guys go now."

"I'll tell them. Be right back." Verin lifted Patricia off his lap and gave her a big, loud kiss. He had been right to push her. He knew what she needed. She watched him with the guys. They liked Verin. He set people at ease and made them feel special. She'd been stupid, and he'd been right. There was no reason to be nervous. She watched him count out cash, pressing crisp bills into each palm. The drummer put up a hand and shook his head. Verin insisted and tucked the money into the drummer's scruffy jacket pocket.

Verin gathered Patricia's Angora sweater from the couch while she lingered by the door, listening to herself sing. As he settled the sweater around her, he gave her shoulder a slow, deliberate, lingering kiss. Her knees became weak as his hands settled on her hips. She didn't know what had changed, but she liked it.

"Ready, baby?" Verin asked.

"Thank you again." She put her hand out for Allen to shake. She'd already learned not to be too friendly with other men when Verin was around, not that he had anything to worry about. She was his now and forever.

Allen smiled at her and shook her hand. "I'll have a copy ready tonight. Go easy on the kid, Verin. You got a real gem there." He patted Verin on the back.

"Don't I know it?" Verin herded Patricia toward the door, his arm around her.

Patricia's cheeks flamed. Someone believed in her. "Verin, how do I get the record to an agent?"

"I'll handle that, baby. I know people."

"Could we go somewhere and make a plan?"

"I'm feeling like champagne and oysters." He stepped onto the busy sidewalk and hailed a cab.

"You spoil me, Verin. Where are we going?"

"How does the Rosewood Hotel grab you? Get in, baby."

A hotel? Patricia stood next to the open car door like a deer in the headlights, blinded by possibilities she couldn't comprehend. People rushed by her on the sidewalk, laughing, talking, and grabbing food on a lunch break. She only saw Verin, his body framed in a hazy outline. Blood rushed in her ears; her stomach dropped the way it did when she was hanging high on the Ferris wheel.

"The Rosewood?"

"Best hotel in the city."

"They don't let you in unless you wear a ring."

Verin laughed. "I don't know where you heard that, but if it's true—we better get a ring."

"Now?"

"Say you don't want a ring, and we can be friends, Vivi. Nothing wrong with being friends."

"I don't know what to say, Verin."

"Are you getting in or what?" the cabbie yelled at them. Verin pulled a wad of cash from his pocket, peeled off a couple of bills, and tossed them in the window. "Cool your meter, and give us a minute."

"Vivi, am I going too fast? The way you sing and the signals you give me with that smoking body, I sometimes forget you're a kid.. Maybe you don't like me in that way. I never want you to feel uncomfortable. Do I make you uncomfortable, baby?"

Verin's firm hands were around her fingers. She hadn't taken a breath. She couldn't speak. His eyes searched hers. He looked so wounded and sad. Could he be afraid she didn't love him? It was all too fast, but she didn't want to hurt him or lose him to the gorgeous club hostess, the Mississippi girl, or all the other girls that gave her jealous stares whenever they were together. Verin was a catch, and she knew it.

"Well, baby? What's it gonna be?"

"I want it all, but especially you." She threw her arms around his neck and brought him close to her.

He gently pushed her away. "You're sure? I don't want to pressure you."

"A ring means forever, right?"

"Jeez, are you getting in or what?" the cabbie growled at them. Patricia slid across the back seat. Verin moved in next to her, slammed the car door, and planted kisses all over her face while she laughed.

"Rosewood Hotel."

"We're meant to be together," Patricia said, leaning into Verin's shoulder.

"Put your hand in my jacket pocket."

"There's a little box in here."

"Open it."

Patricia's fingers tingled as she pulled the box from Verin's pocket. The velvet box had patches of fabric missing, like a mangy dog, but she didn't care. She flipped the top, and inside was a ring. The band was scratched and dented, with a yellow stone in the center and two minuscule diamonds on either side. It didn't sparkle the way a diamond should, but she'd never seen a yellow diamond. Maybe they were different.

"Is it real?"

"It's real, baby. It was my grandmother's." Verin ran a hand over his chin, his eyes misty, and he cleared his throat. "I know it's not a big diamond, but I'll buy you a huge one someday."

Was he proposing? Shouldn't he ask her father? No, Verin was smart. Her parents would never agree, and no one could kneel in a cab. Still, something was off.

"Are we ... engaged?"

"That's a word, baby. For now, let's keep it between you and me. No one else needs to know."

"I understand. Not to mention, my mother will flip if she finds out." Patricia twirled the ring on her finger. He hadn't put it on for her. He must have been too overcome with the moment. "Verin, do we need a suitcase to check in?"

"Just flash the ring, baby."

Chapter Twenty

"**M**om! How can you stop there? What happened at the hotel?"

"We shared several bottles of champagne, Blue Point oysters nestled in ice, and lemon, lots of lemon."

"No, Mom, after the oysters."

"I have no intention of telling you."

I slapped the soles of my feet to wake them up.

"Not those kinds of details. I want to know about Dad and Rosalind. Did she go crazy when she found out? What happened to your singing?"

"My only record is the one you found."

"I knew it."

"Congratulations. Have you considered working for the FBI?"

I floated to my bedroom, returned with the forty-five, and held it to her, momentarily quenching my suspicion and anger.

"How about some Black Coffee?"

Her face blanched, and I congratulated myself on leaving the yellow stone ring on my nightstand. I tucked the record under a stack of old Bon Appétit magazines on the coffee table. Why didn't she want to see it? Who wouldn't be curious to relive what sounded like a dream of a day?

I poured the rest of the wine into my glass. I wish I'd met my grandmother, Rosalind. Dad sounded like a guy straight out of an old B movie, and come to think of it, so did Mom's story. The whole thing seemed too smooth, too easy, the way butter soaked into hot potatoes. This was some old fifties movie she'd watched when she couldn't sleep. Goddamn it. She'd tricked me again.

Mom leaned into the cushions and played with her bracelet. The mood between us changed. Did she think I'd be bought off with a movie script instead of the truth after all this time?

I picked up my wine, "Great story. Now tell me what happened."

The unwelcome sound of Pachelbel's Canon filled the air. My fancy doorbell was another one of Paulka's hand-me-down decorator items because he liked a grand entrance and left nothing to chance. Having learned my lesson with Scott, I walked over to the door and peered through the peephole. I loved visits from Levi and Paulka, but not right now. I thought about lying low, but it was unusual they'd stop by on a whim.

"You must be a wreck," Paulka said as he busted in. He touched my forehead and fussed with my hair like a bereaved spider monkey.

Levi slapped Paulka's fingers away from me. "Paulka, stop it. Dr. David said Jeffrey's not in danger." Levi handed me a glass container of leftovers. "From Susan. You didn't eat."

"Thanks. When did you talk to David?" I asked.

"He came back to the party. The entire time, he was on the phone with his doctor friends at the hospital," Levi said. "Answer your phone, and you'll learn many things. David said you didn't answer, so we decided to swing by and check on you."

Paulka shook a bottle in my face and patted my eyes. "Eye cream with organic witch-hazel extract. I know how puffy you get." I waved the bottle away and grabbed my phone. I'd missed several calls from David and one from Marie. Damn. David had said it would be four hours before they'd call us. Good. I preferred him flawed.

"Marie left a message. Dr. David was right—he's going to be fine," Mom said, blowing out her breath and slipping her phone back in her purse. She rose from the couch to greet Levi and Paulka.

"Patricia darling, you must be consumed with angst." Paulka kissed her and held her face to stare into her tired eyes.

"I'm much better now," she gently removed his palms and helped herself to the leftovers.

"Should we go? Quiche and run?" Levi asked, making himself comfortable in my overstuffed armchair.

"Leanne, make cocktails for these two. We should celebrate the good news," Mom said and nibbled on a quiche star.

I don't bother with fancy cocktails, but I'd been playing with boozy gelato ideas for an event. Fresh mint, smashed peaches, simple syrup, and rum. A splash of seltzer and Paulka's favorite glasses, the swirly ones he brought me back from Portugal last summer. Armed and dangerous with peach mojitos, I enlisted my unwitting accomplices in the divine search for truth.

I passed out the aromatic drinks in their frosty glasses. "Mom was a professional singer back in the day. Isn't that fabulous? Mom, I'm sure Paulka would love to hear your stories."

"You have the figure for it. As my tatala used to say, the ears follow the eyes," Paulka sipped his drink. "Mmmmm. This is glorious."

"Did you perform after you had me?" I asked. Lying to innocent children was one thing, but lying to my friends?

"Mothers shouldn't perform in public, according to your father."

"Such a beast. Afraid you would be swept up and away by Hollywood? Damn men," Paulka said.

"Paulka, don't project," Levi said.

"Didn't you model before you met Levi?" Mom asked.

Damn, she was good—a true professional at diverting the attention away from herself. Before Paulka geared up to recite page two thousand and thirty-five from The Life and Times of a Hot Soviet Model, I shushed him. Paulka hated being cut off, but desperate times—

"Mom, what happened after the hotel?"

Paulka cleared his throat. "Do tell, Patricia. I adore family history. My mama is a professional monkey-veterinarian, and my father is a respected bread scientist."

Levi, subtly like a spider has legs, set his drink down hard. "Leanne, we booked an October wedding at the Vatican. They know papal people. Can you make it?"

Seriously? The Vatican? I knew damn well he disapproved of my tactics, but he was supposed to be my friend.

"Will their papal people be calling our people?" I asked, letting him know I was on to his betrayal. How could he side with Mom over me?

"Why don't I know about this wedding?" Paulka pouted at Levi.

Levi shushed Paulka and continued to stuff the conversation with bullshit.

"They expressed a desire for seventeenth-century Venetian desserts."

"October, right? Something with pumpkin and wafers?" I said and gave Levi a dirty look. "So, Mom—"

"If you'll excuse me, I think I'll freshen up. It's been a long day." Mom slipped her purse over her arm, smiled at us, and strolled into my bathroom.

Game over. She'd kept secrets for over forty years. That took some talent. I'd have to step up my game—time for her to accept that lies and secrets were not interchangeable. I drained my drink and headed for the kitchen to make another.

Levi followed close behind and grabbed my wrist. "What the hell is wrong with you? Her son almost died, and you're behaving like the Inquisition on steroids."

"Don't listen to him, Leanne. We know nothing about steroids," Paulka said, trailing behind Levi.

"Damn it, Levi," I said. "The Vatican? I was so close. She told me how she met my dad, although there's something fishy about that, too."

"For God's sake, Leanne, lighten up," Levi said. "She's not going to confide anything if you hound her. She'll open up to you when she's ready."

Paulka put his hands in the air. "What is she? A sunflower? Leanne has the right to know about her father. He could be a spy."

"It's my birthright to know about my past," I said, keeping my voice down.

"It's her past, too," Levi said. "Did you forget that she has some skin in this game?"

"My dad's not dead."

Levi stared into my soul. I watched the wheels turning. Paulka gasped and slid to the floor. By George, I think they finally got it.

Levi, always a smidge faster than Paulka on the intel uptake, spoke first. Paulka, still in a daze of faux shock, stayed supine on the carpet.

"She *must* have a reason, Leanne. A damn good one. You want her to justify why she lied to you, to make it all better? That's not how it works, and you, my love, need to leave her alone; she'll tell you more when she's ready."

"All right, Levi. I'll back off, but stealing my dad from me is inexcusable. You have someone who loves you. Ever wonder why I don't?"

Tears dripped down my cheeks. Paulka plucked two fresh hankies from his bag, tossed me one, and dabbed his eyes with the other.

"Are you terrified someone will leave you?" Paulka asked and sniffed into a hankie. Damn. I'd never thought of that.

My mother gave a fake cough, walked into the kitchen, and put her glass in the sink. I wondered what she'd heard. Levi had called it, all right. I wanted the story, the whole story, and nothing but the story to justify her lying. Maybe it didn't matter, but nothing could sway me to trust her again, and I wasn't sure I would ever forgive her.

"I'm going to check on Jeffrey," Mom said.

"Do you want a ride to Susan's? Pick up your car?" Levi asked me.

"No, thanks. I'd like to spend more time with Mom. I'll grab an Uber or something."

"Bring the eye cream," Paulka fished in his bag and pressed the bottle into my hand. "You're going to need it."

Chapter Twenty-One

F urious with Levi, I drove with Mom to the hospital in silence. She looked pensive, no doubt planning what fanciful tale to tell next. All lies have a degree of reality; some of her stories could be true. I put fifty bucks on Rosalind. Something about her crazy mother made perfect sense, considering the poisoned apple hadn't fallen far from the diseased tree. Mom's gaze was straight ahead.

"You didn't forget about the box," I pointed out.

"You'd be amazed at what the mind can hide, Leanne. We bury what we can't cope with until we're ready to deal with it."

We reached the hospital, went to the ICU, and found Jeffrey in a regular room on the third floor.

Marie put a finger to her lips and shushed us when we walked in. Mom kissed Jeffrey and planted herself in the chair next to the bed. I poked his arm to confirm he was asleep. Highly possible he was faking it to avoid a spectacle with Marie. His little boy face didn't stir. I prayed he'd found his rock bottom and that he'd work it out with Marie so that my future drinking buddy wouldn't be my brother.

"If you two are okay, I'm going to head out," I said, sliding dark glasses on and grabbing my purse. The Sphinx was on lockdown for the night, so I might as well see what I could accomplish with The Meddler.

"Thanks for bringing David. He's wonderful," Marie said.

"I guess we'll have to wait and see how deep the wonderful goes, right, Mom?"

She didn't say a thing, just took Jeffrey's limp hand.

I left for Susan's, my mind on a drink and a come-to-Jesus reckoning well overdue.

I let myself in with the hidden key when she didn't answer and found her in the living room next to a cozy fire, her laptop almost smoking from her flying fingers. Her eyes scrunched in concentration while she worked on her homework—otherwise known as my life.

"Sit. I'm documenting your first meeting with David."

"Did you open your birthday presents?" I asked and flopped down on her couch.

"Yes, thank you for the homemade cookie coupons. Touching and fattening in equal measure."

"You're lucky I got you anything. You had no business inviting David without telling me and hosting a pre-meddling dinner party for that matter."

She laughed and waggled a finger at me. "Me? You had no business making a date without informing me of your progress. You shouldn't mess with my data."

"I'd love to believe you're kidding, but I know you're not. You should make me a drink to apologize."

"A decent friend would have filled me in, especially since you're my final project."

I laughed, leaned over, and kissed her on her head. "I give up. You win. Can the project have a drink now?"

"One drink. I'm glad Jeffrey's okay. Oh, I hear your first date is at Mobs. I can't believe you aren't taking me." Susan headed to the kitchen. Big ice cubes dropped into a glass, followed by the slushy sound of crushed ice. Wow. Susan was trying to cook.

"David told you?" I yelled. "Can't I have any secrets?"

"You're paranoid."

"I knew I shouldn't have come here."

Susan returned with a Diet Coke and bourbon decorated with purple and green grapes. It looked like something a six-year-old bartender would make. "Would you like to practice a breathing technique? You look edgy."

"I was edgy, and now I'm exhausted. You can torture me on Tuesday any way you want as per our arrangement, but for now, special breathing isn't necessary."

"You already look tired and stressed, and I need to tell you something iffy."

"Iffy? Is that a legal or psychological term?" I sucked down the drink and chewed the ice.

Susan raised her eyebrows and pursed her lips for a second. Did she wonder what chewing ice means? Would she add ice chewing to my questionable antics?

"Well?"

"Ask David about Crystal."

"It's a little early to register for a wedding, isn't it?"

"He's dating someone named Crystal. Brett told me tonight."

Fuck. I went straight to Kook and started on desserts for the Mobs opening. It had to be healthier to pound nuts with a mallet and whip cream by hand than beating up on myself for being an idiot. I cranked up The Allman Brothers "Whipping Post", slapped stainless molds down hard on the counter, and retrieved eggs, sugar, cream, and chocolate for gianduja semifreddo. The semifreddo and I both needed a day to chill before meeting David, assuming that I still wanted to. I didn't.

I grabbed my heavy rolling pin and a bag of imported Italian hazelnuts, shook the innocent brown orbs out onto a clean cloth, tucked them in, and whacked them into compliance. Damn liar. Was it too much to want an honest man? Did they exist? Anywhere? I should have known Mr. Pizza-Delivered-Tell-Me-Your-Troubles had to be too good to be true. I'd let my guard down, and for what, to be charmed by a conniving prick with an honorable profession?

The song was over and my angst was still burning. I fired up YouTube on the kitchen TV to watch the one guilty pleasure which never let me down, The Galloping Gourmet, my childhood crush. I faked many a tummy ache to stay home from school lusting after Graham Kerr with his decadent dishes and thinly veiled dirty talk. I fell in love, never knowing that my dream man, a likable, sexy lush with questionable recipes, would be the best I could do. I'd toast him with a cocktail glass filled with 7-Up and a pimento-stuffed olive whenever he called for a "short slurp," and dream about our future together.

I had planned for Graham to leave his wife, Treena, and run away with me. We would dine on sweetbreads in a cognac-laced sauce. I realized that my plan had serious flaws when Mom told me what sweetbreads were. David's omission was reminiscent of the sweetbreads. Until you knew the reality, sweetbreads sounded delicious, like spectacular French toast. David seemed all kinds of special, not like another asshole with an all-night buffet of women to juggle.

I heaped sugar into a huge copper pan, added vanilla and water, and put my muscle into a thick sugar syrup while I watched my first love lard a piece of meat. Graham impaled the rump roast with several thrusts. Someone knocked on the big steel exterior door. I figured Norman was peckish and wanted a snack. I put the copper cauldron on the stove and looked up at the security monitor to confirm, but there was Levi with a bunch of orange tulips. Why couldn't I find someone like Levi? He waved up at the monitor, and I swung the door open.

"I figured you'd be here."

"Lots to do." I turned down the volume, leaving Graham to braise his rump in silence and beer.

"Paulka said I made you cry. I'm sorry."

"You didn't do anything wrong. You never do." I handed him a glass canister from a rack. "I'm the one that should be sorry. For the record, I want to be a better person, but Mom's so frustrating."

"I wonder which side of the family your obsessive nature comes from?"

"I'm not obsessive. Her method of imparting information is how the Chinese got the idea for water torture. It's all such bullshit, Levi. If my dad was actually dead, I wouldn't have a problem."

My eyes filled with tears, and my wise mind gave me a hug. *You'd still have a problem.*

"Are you meeting him?" Levi filled the canister with water and threw me a dishcloth.

"She doesn't want me to, and neither does Jeffrey. Since she started with the stories, I don't know what I believe anymore." The sugar syrup thickened, and I took it off the heat.

"Don't see him."

"Tea?"

Levi nodded, and I pulled a metal teapot off the shelf and stared at fancy tins of Earl Grey, Mint Mischief, and Orange screw-the-bastard-doctor with Indonesian clove. How enamored of David was Levi? Would he take my side?

"I have to meet him. I need to make sure that my mom isn't some batshit-crazy lady who drove a good man away, and Levi, even if he's an asshole, he's my dad." I threw two Earl Grey bags into the pot.

"For what it's worth, I get the feeling you should trust her."

"She faked a funeral, Levi."

I poured hot water over the tea bags. The steam swirled and left ghost kisses on my face. I wiped my eyes with my apron and set mugs and the teapot on the butcher-block table. I noticed that Graham had pulled a Margaret Thatcher lookalike from the audience to taste the finished rump roast. As he poured hot, slimy oysters on the overcooked meat, I realized that our differences were vast and that we could never have been.

"I'm going to cancel my date with David."

"Your mom made one mistake and never took another chance. Do you want to be like her?"

"I've taken plenty of chances home, Levi. None of them have worked out."

"You stacked the deck with jerks because, for some reason, you think that's all you deserve. David's special."

Levi arranged the tulips; each stem, every possible angle lovingly considered. He never made mistakes. Must be nice to live in a perfect world.

"Because he's a doctor, and your mother would love him?" I asked.

"No, because he went to the hospital with you. How many guys would do that?"

I settled a lemon slice into both cups, poured in the steaming tea, and hoped against all odds that Levi was wrong. "Maybe he had to check on a patient."

"You'll regret it if you don't at least try." Levi finished with the tulips. The simple arrangement looked glorious in its simplicity.

"He's a liar. Drink your tea."

"Now you're being ridiculous." He gently blew on the tea to cool it down.

"I am not. He's dating someone named Crystal, and he didn't tell me. He said he was new to dating."

"Is he a bakery? Did you take a number, and he skipped you? Are you really that literal?"

"It feels sneaky, wrong. It's a bad way to start a relationship."

Face down on the table, I put my arms over my head as exhaustion settled in.

"Let's go back to this obsessive nature of yours." Levi stroked my hair with one hand while he stirred honey into his tea with the other.

"Swear you won't tell Paulka or Susan, but I thought David might be The One." I bent my head, soaking up the petting like a neglected feline.

"He could be, but you'll never know." Levi took his hand away, and I heard a cookie crunching. Macarons. Levi loves them.

I put my elbows on the table and my face between my hands. "The One doesn't start a relationship while dating someone else."

"What relationship? You talked on the phone. He bought you a cafeteria muffin." Levi waved a cookie in my face.

"It was more than a breakfast pastry."

"For God's sake, Leanne. Do us all a favor and go out with the man."

"What about the Crystal situation?"

"Paulka will take you shopping at ten." Levi looked down at his watch. "He says you need something spectacular for your date and he's worried about your mental state."

"Do I have to?"

"Yes, you do. He'll make you look fabulous, and David will drop Crystal like a cheap Tiffany knockoff. Can I take a few of these for the kids?"

"I thought I was ridiculous?" I couldn't help smiling at him, so I packed him up a dozen chocolate macarons.

Chapter Twenty-Two

I walked Levi to his car, cleaned up the kitchen, and headed home. I'd need my rest to shop with Paulka. The last time Paulka insisted his new look, dawn-to-dusk-chic-to-chic dressing, should be my new look, I mocked the mummy-like layers and threw all but one black sweater out of the dressing room. He didn't speak to me for a day, and we hadn't been shopping together since.

Once home, I headed straight for my tub. I unclasped my bra, and the light brown dust of finely crushed hazelnuts drifted to the bathroom floor. I filled the tub with steaming hot water and vanilla-scented bubbles and settled myself into luxurious tranquility. More dust floated to the surface, an embarrassing reminder of the impromptu nut-bashing session. I wanted David to call, let his magic voice lull me into a safe place, and chip away at my bad behavior and marrow-deep insecurities.

I could call him, but I'd say something stupid. I lay back and closed my eyes. What I needed was the saintly wisdom of someone who didn't know my entire catalog of self-sabotaging man mistakes. I imagined stirring butter and flour into a rich brown roux with Graham as I slipped lower into the sleep-lulling warmth of the water.

Graham cupped my chin in his palm and squeezed my cheeks into a kissy fish face. "You've got to see what's in front of your nose, lovey."

"David and I got complicated before it started."

"You're the one making it difficult. Doesn't have to be that way. Dice the green peppers. There's a good girl. Let's have a short slurp." Graham opened a bottle of red wine and filled two glasses.

"Should I cancel my date with David?"

We clinked the glasses together. "Why would you do a daft thing like that?"

"You're right. I'll think of David as strawberries. Simple, perfect, nothing more needed." I kissed Graham on the cheek and wondered why we were cooking naked.

"Not true, love. You need a bit of freshly ground pepper to bring out the depth of the berries." He patted my ass, which woke me with a start, and I spat out cold vanilla and nut-dust water. I hauled my spent body out of the tub before I drowned, made a double espresso, and threw on something that was bound to offend the delicate textile passions of Paulka. Phantom Graham was right. Love didn't need to be this hard.

I met Paulka near North Beach at his current favorite boutique, Toute la Journée Toute la Nuit, a glorious mix of high-end new and classic vintage clothing. Eight hundred square feet of gold-glittered floor, enormous dressing rooms draped in floor-to-ceiling white chiffon, the best skinny mirrors money could buy, and a complicated-looking espresso machine on a beautiful black lacquered Art Deco bar. Paulka expertly flipped through gold armoires filled with beautiful dresses. I followed behind, looking at the insane price tags.

Paulka held out his first find and did his famous Tim Gunn impression. "A gorgeous green. Fabulous but subtle cleavage. David will surrender in minutes. Try it on."

"It's dinner, not Gettysburg."

"She's such a brat today. What is wrong with you?"

"I'm exhausted. Can you please speed-style me?"

Paulka waved over the owner. "Relax, my darling little schnitzel. I've got this. Prescott, would you be an angel and make Leanne a silver lynx brew?"

"I've had coffee," I pointed out.

Prescott tapped my nose gently with a finger adorned with a heavy gold signet ring. "Not this coffee. A tribe of witches in Columbia grows it. You drink it black." He hurried off to the espresso machine.

I pulled out a simple blue dress and put it back. "Damn, Paulka. I can't afford this stuff."

"Prescott will give us an über-special, fabulous deal."

"If you say so, but you're trying on. I'm too tired."

"I thought you'd never ask."

Paulka proceeded to model his favorites. I lost count between a silver lamé skirt and top combo and a floor-length sequin number. I was positive Cher would call any minute and demand the return of her clothes. He walked the length of the boutique to the delight of the well-dressed staff and a studious Prescott, who'd brought me a thimble of coffee. When the style committee crossed their arms, it was a hell no. A raised eyebrow meant possible, but turn around three times and let us ponder. According to Paulka, I had to wear an über-sexy dress since the hot doctor had saved his life. Apparently, David suffered hospital staff in pantsuits, and no one really likes a pantsuit.

"I like the black one," I said, wide awake now and enjoying the attention.

The staff applauded with fingertip claps and went back to business.

"A shadow of vintage glamor yet doesn't scream Grandma's closet. You can borrow my pearls—twenty-four inches; they'll wrap around twice."

"No, Paulka, I don't do pearls. They feel serious. I don't do serious."

"These aren't just any pearls. These are antique baroque pearls stolen from a princess by my great-grand-mère. She gave lap dances to a czar."

"Your capacity for romance has no limits."

"At the risk of shocking you senseless, I used to be like you. Didn't believe in romance, didn't believe in love, thought soul mates was a fabulous name for a shoe brand. Then, I met Levi. My love magic says David could very well be your Levi, so get serious."

"Thank you for the pearls of wisdom. Those I am happy to take."

"Merci." Paulka kissed me on the cheek.

Prescott put my new dress in a black box and tied it with a velvet ribbon, which he handed to Paulka, who wiggled all ten fingers at my credit card until I put it back into my wallet.

"Because I adore you, and David is one in a zillion." Paulka passed the package to me with a bow worthy of royalty.

"You didn't have to do that, but thank you."

"Levi's making crab and asparagus ravioli with the kids. Come for dinner and pick up the pearls. They haven't seen Auntie Leanne for ages."

"Sounds delish, but I can't. I need to work."

"Why on earth did you invite David to this thing? Seriously, isn't there enough pressure without a first date?"

I was hungry to see David, but Paulka had a good point. The Mobs thing was career crucial. "Do you think I should reschedule?"

"And let him know you're a temperamental, flaky bitch? The damage is done. You'll have to make do."

"Flaky?"

"Always here to help." He gave me his best cheeks-sucked-in model pose. "Try not to stress, darling, and go straight home. The silk needs to nap."

Twitching from the witch's brew, I was thrilled that I had the kitchen to myself and could cook alone so spicy main dish scents wouldn't sneak into delicate dessert flavors and because I didn't feel like chit-chat. I put on Chris Isaak's "Heart Shaped World." I found my happy place swirling organic raspberries into the mascarpone, lacing Modica bittersweet chocolate with Sicilian orange zest, and poaching pears in red wine.

Jeffrey and I had an almost supernatural ability to think each other into calling, so I wasn't surprised when his signature "Meet the Flintstones" ringtone crashed my party.

"Marie should give up the lingerie business and get a job with the CIA." Jeffrey's voice was dull, like used sandpaper. "Can you pick me up from the hospital and take me to the old house, please?"

"Why? Don't you want to go home? Where's Marie?"

"Marie went through my phone and the computer while I was sedated. She took my stuff to Mom's old house this morning, but she doesn't want to see me."

"What'd she find?"

"Naked girls. I mean women—you can't call them girls anymore. They get offended. And she read my chats."

"I'm not helping you anymore." I poured myself a glass of red wine. I needed it more than the pears did.

"Okay, I'm sorry, and I'm kidding. I'm not that much of a jerk. Marie found my secret file. I'm impressed. I labeled it dog supplies."

"Obvious, don't you think? You don't have a dog."

"Not funny."

"How could you be so stupid? You have everything anyone could want!"

"I don't need a lecture. Come and get me, please? The hospital released me, I can't drive, and Mom's is the only place I can go."

"I can't, Jeffrey, I'm swamped." My phone beeped. "I have another call. Oh, it's David."

"The nice boyfriend that came to the hospital? See if he can help me."

"He's not my boyfriend, and I'm not asking him. Don't you have any friends you can call?"

"My friends are our friends."

"Give me five, and I'll figure something out."

Chapter Twenty-Three

T hrilled beyond reason that David called, regardless of the Crystal situation, I smiled into the phone. I had that under control,
thanks to Paulka. "Do I have lots of drama in my life, or do you have mad
timing skills?" I asked.

"It's my superpower," David said.

"Knowing when I'm stressed? Wouldn't you prefer to be invisible?"

"I gave up my invisibility superpower last year. People run into you all
the time, there are bruises you can't explain, lots of questions, and the
next thing you know, the cat's out of the bag."

I cracked up and saw a happy version of me in a mirrored serving
tray. I had enough powdered sugar on my face to look like the Pillsbury
Doughboy, courtesy of the cannoli shells filled with brandied nectarines
and ricotta crème. I wiped my face, plopped down at the butcher-block
table, rested my head on my arms, and surrendered to the human in
distress that David conjured in me. Good. It's normal to need help. I
finished my wine and poured what was left in the bottle into my glass.

"I hate asking for favors, but I'm in a serious bind."

"What do you need?"

"Just like that?"

"If you want me to hide a body, I'm going to say no. If you need chocolate chips or a weekend on a beach, I'm your guy."

"You're sure?"

"Is this a test? I met a woman a few months ago who wanted ten years of tax returns and a polygraph."

Was he talking about Crystal? Wasn't coffee considered dating? Could this be yet another woman, maybe a hot brain surgeon he'd forgotten to mention?

"Did you ask her why?"

"I went to the restroom and waited until she left. I tried online dating, but it's difficult. There's been more than a few odd dates. I'm grateful we met the old-fashioned way."

He wasn't an innocent babe in the dating woods, after all. I was justified in making him pick up Jeffrey. They had a lot in common and would have plenty to talk about. My wise mind stepped in and gave me the customary slap of perspective. David wasn't a liar; he was a decent guy, and Levi was right; I'd taken new to dating literally. I didn't know if he'd dated hundreds of women or three, but either way, it shouldn't matter. As Levi had pointed out, David wasn't a bakery, and I liked him enough not to jump to crazy conclusions.

"I swear it's not a test. I'm short an assistant and behind on orders, and Jeffrey needs a ride from the hospital to Mom's old house. I don't trust anyone else to move him with the broken leg."

"Would he be comfortable with me? I doubt he remembers much about the hospital."

"He remembers. He likes you. I suspect a lot of people like you. You have charisma. Even Mom liked you, and she's not overly fond of anything with a penis."

Stupid woman. Why would you utter the word penis? I finished the dregs of my wine and uncorked another bottle.

He laughed. Right. He's a doctor. It's a medical word, nothing sexual.

"Glad you think I'm popular, but Jeffrey was under the influence, so it doesn't count. Doesn't he want to be home with Marie and the kids? By the way, I met everyone last night. Great family."

"Yeah, really great. Look, I can't tell you the circumstances, but he can't go home."

"You really do have a lot going on. Okay, I'll pick up Jeffrey, and how about I take you on a pre-date drink after I get him settled?"

"No time, remember?"

"You drive a hard bargain, lady."

"Would you hate me if we met at Mobs instead of my place?"

"I'll cancel the horse-drawn carriage."

"Thank you."

"Anything else?"

"Ah, no."

"Why don't I believe that?"

How did he know? The Crystal question burned in my mind, charring scarce sanity into oblivion. I hated that I had to know.

"Not to sound like an ass, but are you dating someone?" I took my wine into the walk-in fridge, sat on a turned-over milk crate, and counted quarts of heavy cream. I'd have to share my latest calming technique with Susan.

"Is that a problem?"

Is that a problem? Well, David, it's a huge issue. I'm trying to trust you, but I'm not thrilled I'm sharing you with someone who belongs on a wedding registry. On the other hand, I'm not accustomed to a straightforward yes from anyone in my world, so maybe I should be grateful you're honest. Perhaps this is the defining moment for us to dodge the bullet that arrived ahead of schedule. I wish I weren't so damn insecure, but I'm trying harder than I ever have, so throw me a bone.

"Leanne? Are you there?"

"This is hard for me and embarrassing, but I've had a history—think Jurassic period to present day—of dating guys who I didn't know were taken."

"I've been dating someone for about four weeks. She's a brilliant heart surgeon, but I'm not in love with her, or likely to be, although I enjoy her company."

I bet. They could bond over aging and clogged artery studies. What now? Do I admit I didn't like the insecure baker versus probably attractive heart surgeon odds? It sounded so needy, so weak, so honest. She wouldn't have to buy a sexy doctor outfit for fantasy night, as she already had one.

"I appreciate radical honesty, so if even a coffee in the cafeteria with her makes you uncomfortable, let me know."

"I'm uncomfortable."

"Good to know," David said.

"What happens now?"

"I let her know I met a baker I'm intrigued by, and if I need a heart transplant, to not hold this against me."

"I'm a pastry chef."

"You get the idea. Feel better?"

"Thank you. For once, I feel like I have a choice in my life. Do you understand that? How it feels when you don't have a choice?"

"More than you could imagine." There was silence. David cleared his throat. I listened to water running, filling a glass, a gurgle as he swallowed. Jessica. The tortoise.

"I'm sorry. Of course, you would understand."

"It's tough when circumstances take away choice. Like I said, control what you can and don't worry about what you can't. So, do we have a date?"

My wise mind nudged me. David's voice was soft, asking, not assuming. I'd never met anyone like him, and I might never again. I took a deep breath and chose to believe in the good guys—at least this good guy.

"I have no issues with Crystal."

"You have an excellent reconnaissance network."

"And a hot dress."

I heard a sharp intake of breath. The silence was electric. He made a humming sound.

"Okay, where am I picking up Jeffrey, and what time should I meet you at Mobs?"

"Jeffrey, as soon as you can. Seven at Mobs would be great, and are you sleeping with her?"

David chuckled. "What happened to no issues?"

"It's a process."

There was a long silence on the other end of the phone. Radical honesty came with a high level of anxiety.

"If I had slept with her, would you change your mind about dating me?"

"Yes. I wouldn't want you to break up with someone over me."

"Because I might do the same thing to you?"

"Yes."

"I'll bear that in mind."

Mobs sent a minivan to pick up what I hoped would put us all on the map, and I raced home for a quick shower, the beautiful black dress, and Grand-Mère's stolen pearls. I drove to North Beach, gave my car to the valet, who dressed like a 1920's gangster, and walked through Mobs' brass and glass revolving door.

Hundreds of black-and-white photos in ornate gilt frames hung from the floor to the ceiling, Hollywood's movie mobsters rubbing shoulders with the real deal on crimson-papered walls. Starched white table linens and gleaming silverware graced deep booths while a stunning Murano chandelier lit up the twelve-foot family table in the middle of the floor.

It was easy to imagine Don Vito Corleone talking business in the red leather banquettes, big plates of steaming pasta in front of the associates in black suits, stubby necks draped in white linen napkins like dangerous penguins. I took a glass of red wine from a passing server.

Michael, in a classic black tux with a red carnation in his lapel, said, "Buona sera, Leanne! Can you believe this?"

"Michael! I'm so proud of you. This place is gorgeous, and I can't wait to taste the pesto gnocchi!" I had to yell since the Frank Sinatra impersonator crooned "New York, New York" more enthusiastically than the original.

Michael, a fifth-generation Italian, and his wife Charlotte, had several successful pizza joints, but Mobs was their dream restaurant in North Beach's heart.

"You're one bella signora, Leanne. Stunning, like the desserts. Holy moly! Sam Blakely wants a word with you."

"The restaurant critic? He's here?"

"In his three-hundred-pound birthday suit. Thank God, that man loves food. He's sampled plenty and taken a ton of pictures. I think we hit it big."

Charlotte made it through the crowd, radiant in a crisp navy dress with plenty of Italian gold around her neck. We kissed cheeks and beamed at each other. "Samuel Blakely is looking for you. Something about genius and desserts in the afterlife?"

"He's gotten into the angel and demon cannoli." I clinked glasses with Charlotte.

Michael crossed himself, laughed, and kissed my forehead loudly. "You're a saint." One more kiss for me, and he whisked Charlotte away to schmooze with the who's who of San Francisco's food and wine world. I made my way to the bar, a perfect replica of the Godfather's desk, only higher and without the cigar ash. David waited on one of the crimson barstools with a Campari and soda in hand. He wore a dark blue suit, tailored white shirt, and garnet tie to heart-stopping perfection. Samuel Blakely would have to wait. I wanted to share myself with David, every detail, including the bad stuff. Comfortable was strange new territory for me, except for the Crystal question that stuck like al dente pasta on a brick wall.

"You made it," I said. I leaned over and, insecurity be damned, kissed him on the mouth.

David kissed me back with gusto. "Congratulations. You didn't mention you're a celebrity chef. I'm speechless."

"This is Michael and Charlotte's bambino. I'm lucky they wanted me."

David's eyes sparkled as they gazed upon me with a head-to-toe sweep. "Your ego is the only understated thing about you tonight. You look superb."

"It's the dress."

He kissed my hand, silent and not too grabby.

"Can I steal you away to a quiet table?" he asked, offering me his arm. We made our way through the rambunctious crowd and settled into the booth furthest from the action. A tuxedo-clad server passed us Chianti-red menus, the velvet cover unexpected and deliciously soft. I opened the menu where traditional Italian courses were hand-lettered on a gold-edged mirror. My reflection looked back at me, wide-eyed, delighted, and slightly trembling with anticipation.

"No one's gonna get whacked in here. You can see the hitman sneaking up from behind," David said.

I laughed and set my menu on the table. I smoothed the heavily starched napkin on my lap.

"Do you have enemies?" I asked with an eyebrow raised.

"I will after I order a Banfi Brunello di Montalcino Poggio all'Oro off the violin case."

A server brought an outrageous plate of antipasto, focaccia, and labeled bottles of Virgin Mary olive oil and balsamic vinegar. Another server took David's order for the wine.

"Your accent is insanely good. I'm not going to tell you what that does to me."

David didn't need an accent to make me hot and bothered. I could blame the spicy anchovy antipasto for the flush on my face and the heavy breathing. He reached over the arrangement of fragrant red roses and kissed my hand again. The kiss sent shivers up my arm and down to the places I'd sworn I left home for safekeeping. Good thing I'd worn pantyhose, the modern-day equivalent of a chastity belt. I poured olive oil and a sprinkle of salt on my bread plate. David tore off a piece of bread, used my salted oil, and popped it in my mouth. Oh, my. I chewed slowly, didn't lick the oil I could feel on my lips, and tried to get my libido under control.

"When I was a kid, Mr. Antonio gave hand kisses to my mother. Must be the Italian vibe stirring up memories," I said.

"Who's Mr. Antonio?"

"He owned the Italian restaurant we went to as kids. Remember I had a story about Jeffrey? I think you've earned it." I dipped bread into the oil and handed it to David.

"Ah, yes. The Why Jeffrey Doesn't Drink novella. You remembered your promise."

I always do.

"When we were kids, Mom took us out every Friday to practice our manners. She'd sit between us, and teach us how to order, 'Three Shirley Temples, please. Two with extra cherries and one with extra scotch, please.' Jeffrey switched the drinks one night when Mom went to the ladies' room. She returned to the table quickly, since she didn't like to leave us alone, and watched him drain the drink like strawberry Kool-Aid."

"Didn't she notice the drinks looked different, and isn't a Shirley Temple made without booze?"

I served David sliced tomatoes, olives, and creamy burrata, delicacies flown in from Italy, and made a plate for myself.

"Mom has her way of doing *everything*. Her eyebrows lifted so high on her forehead that I thought they would fly off like butterflies and circle the other diners. Five minutes later, Jeffrey said he didn't feel good, so Mom told him to 'Please put the napkin down nicely, and not on the plate,' and escorted him to the ladies' room."

"What did you do?"

"I had to go with them—not safe for little girls to sit alone."

"Poor Jeffrey." David shook his head and dug into the antipasto.

"He threw up bright red cherries, fettuccine, and salad with authentic Italian dressing. When he was done, she put cold water on a paper hand towel and wiped his clammy forehead, humming along to 'That's Amore.'"

"That is amore. Did your mom say anything?"

"Not a single word."

"Does Jeffrey still have a drinking problem?"

"He's having a rough time right now. Thank you for helping him today. Is he doing better, from your professional point of view?"

The server brought the wine, poured a taste for David, and hovered. David didn't make a big production, but I could tell he knew his way around a good bottle. He nodded and took the wine from the server, filling both of our glasses.

"We had an enlightening conversation. By the way, your mom's house is terrific. I'm surprised it hasn't sold yet. The neighborhood reminds me of the place where I grew up."

I smiled, sipped, and smiled again. This guy felt like home.

"I dropped Jeffrey off and then went back with a recliner. You know, for his leg. Love the neighborhood, great place to be a kid."

"Jeffrey opened up to you?"

"It's a bedside thing."

"Did you put a spell on him?"

David laughed, a warm, sexy, authentic sound of delight. "The witch doctor class was past my budget. I put myself through school."

I ached inside at his sweet perfection and knew that I should hold back any word of insecurity, but thoughts formed and slithered past my lips because every lie by every man I'd ever known had burned my trust reflex into charred toast. The sooty black crumbs had led me to a lonely existence, but that didn't stop me from pushing into places that were none of my business.

"If you wanted to play naked Twister, do you have a friend handy?" I asked, cringing from within but needing to know if he'd slept with Crystal, but not wanting to ask again. It was crazy how much the possibility bothered me—utterly bizarre, unlike me, but my wise mind was thrilled. Boundary progress, indeed. Susan would give me gold stars for taking care of myself.

The server came for our order and, like all great servers, observed the intensity between us and smoothly backed away from the table. David had no pretense. He was calm like the summer sea off the Italian Riviera, his eyes true blue and trustworthy. He sipped the incredible wine, wiped his lips with the napkin, and reached across the table to hold my hands.

"Twister is in the closet, hidden behind my winter coat. But for you, I'll take it out and move the furniture."

Chapter Twenty-Four

We stayed until the last wild boar meatball was gone, and Michael's grappa-fueled toasts turned into tearful words of gratitude to both the living and the dead. David's arm stayed linked with mine, and for the first time in my life, I was part of a couple with a healthy history, however brief, and a possible future. Heady stuff, and not because I was drunk. I'd paced myself, not wanting to miss a minute of this remarkable man.

David set his glass down on the bar, leaned against me, and whispered in my ear, "I turn into a pumpkin at three a.m. Can I walk you to your car?"

I hoped a walk to the car meant a goodnight kiss and not a concern for my safety. I'd be the one turning into a pumpkin if the perfect night ended without one.

I nodded, grabbed my wrap and bag, and looked around to say goodnight to Michael and Charlotte. They were engrossed with family and another round of pasta, so I blew a kiss and, with David's arm around my waist, we went off into the night.

"You sure know how to show a guy a good time. You spoiled me for any future first dates."

Insecurity nipped at me like the cold mist rolling in from the bay until he put his other arm around me and drew me close, his back against my car.

He nibbled on my neck. "I'm kidding."

My wise mind gave me a gentle nudge to return the nibble, which I did.

"This was the best night of my life," I said.

"You're lucky. You found the world that works for you. Not many people can say that."

"I wasn't talking about work..."

"Oh."

We stood, arms wrapped around each other, the energy between us breathing with a life of its own.

"I hope this doesn't make you climb back in your bubble wrap, but I've never felt like this with anyone," David said.

The word anyone hung between us. Anyone meant his wife, Jessica, and momentary guilt, along with amazement, rattled my cage because I felt the same way.

"I won't get back in my box, but I'd love to sit in the car. I'm freezing."

He opened the doors, and we huddled inside in the back seat, the engine purring. My back seat was a collage of clothes, pastry boxes, and ancient cookbooks, but at least it smelled good, and he didn't seem to mind the disaster.

"Are you still on pumpkin time?" I asked and pushed the mess to one side.

"I'm happy to be round and orange with you."

I snuggled up against his body and inhaled his glorious scent, a sense of forever close enough to taste. "What about the carving part?"

"As long as I have a smile, I'm good."

He brushed my cheek with his hand and looked into my eyes until he found the real me I hid from the world. She was the one who was guilty without reason, who believed I'd always let down those that I loved. That I'd never been good enough. That given enough time, I would fuck this up, and he was making a huge mistake. I'd told him I wasn't ready, and if he were as smart as I thought, he'd believe me.

Was that why he didn't kiss me? Making the first move had never bothered me. I liked the power and control of seduction, proving I was desirable and wanted. This time, I wouldn't dare. I closed my eyes to hide my disappointment. He'd realized he should walk away while he could, believed the night's magic was the glamor of a splashy restaurant opening, and had nothing to do with me.

In the safety of silence, warm, soft lips touched mine. They lifted ever so slightly and touched again with a whisper of pressure, a promise of more. His arms pulled me closer. I couldn't tell where I stopped, and he began. His lips disappeared, and with a slight trembling, his mouth came down on mine and stayed. I reached to meet him with no hesitation; nothing held back.

I opened my eyes, hungry to see his beautiful face up close. His eyes were closed, lost in the moment. I felt his rough midnight beard and listened to his breathing deepen. The spaces between each breath grew. After dinner, he'd fallen hard for my amaretto apricot panna cotta with dark chocolate drizzle. Tasting it as his tongue teased mine was heady bliss. I closed my eyes to meet him in this beautiful new world and surrendered to something I'd only read about in fairy tales.

When his breath turned into a soft groan, he stopped and leaned back, his eyes raised to the car's ceiling, one arm still around me. With nothing less than sweet mischief, he drew a heart on the steamy window and an arrow right through the center. I looked through the heart into an empty parking lot.

"It's late," I said, tangling myself in his arms again, hiding from the future.

David kissed my forehead. "My dog's going to ground me. I'll have to sneak into my house."

"Better take your shoes off."

"Can I see you tomorrow?"

"Only if you're not grounded. I don't want to get on your dog's bad side."

"Edison doesn't have a bad side."

David helped me into the front seat. We had a short but equally incredible goodbye kiss, and I watched him head to his car, wave, and disappear. My heart had never known such lightness and my mind filled with a happiness I couldn't have imagined was possible.

Chapter Twenty-Five

I slipped out of my dress and the pearls with the questionable past, made a cup of tea, and sank up to my neck in happy bubbles of rose and sea salt—time to call The Meddler. Susan deserved to know that her plan was the best thing since prehistoric creatures crawled out of the slime. I couldn't wait another minute to tell her.

"Leanne, it's after 3:00 a.m.," Susan whispered. "Hold on a sec."

"I will no longer mock your fake therapist hobby again." I made loud, kissy sounds.

"It's not a hobby; who is this, and what have you done with my friend Leanne?"

I popped bubbles with my toes. "I'm in love with him."

"You're infatuated because he's good to you. Since you're confused, I'll explain. That's not love, it's appreciation. Slow down."

"Whoa. After your world-class manipulation, am I supposed to put on the brakes?"

"Yes, as soon as I get my robe on. Okay, I'm sneaking downstairs. I don't want to disturb Brett."

"I see you're considerate of some people."

"I'm the gold standard of considerate."

"You sure you don't need sleep? A trial or public hanging tomorrow? You don't want to be off your game."

"I'm never off my game, and we don't hang, we sue."

"Why didn't I call Levi and Paulka?" I slathered my face with cleanser. My makeup rinsed away along with my good mood.

"Because they have children and need their rest."

My impulsive nature needed a severe tweak. Did I think she'd give me an A and delete my file? I plastered the wet washcloth over my face.

"Lucky for you, I had a Be Your Best Relationship class tonight." Susan put me on speaker. The tea kettle whistled, and she rustled around opening drawers, so much for not disturbing Brett.

"Oh, joy."

"Love is the opportunity to deal with our shit."

"If you put that on the side of a bus, change shit to stuff." I poked bubbles into oblivion. Couldn't I have a little illusion?

"David's fabulous. He has no issues," Susan said over a mouthful of what sounded like a contraband cookie.

"Then what's the problem?"

"You. I gave you perfection, so you'd have a positive reward to work on yourself."

"Did I say world-class manipulation? I take that back. You're an Olympic sport."

"Leanne, we've known each other longer than I'd like to admit, and I love you. Use David as your messenger and be the good-catch girl I know you can be."

"Do you recognize how unbelievably manipulative you are? I'm going to review your supposed school. It should be shut down."

"David is plug-and-play. You won't get a second chance if you mess this up."

"I hate you right now."

I leaned back and picked up my mug. The tea was stone cold. I don't remember signing up to be the communal puppet—everyone pulling my strings to keep me safe from myself. *Bullshit.*

"This is exactly why I said I wasn't interested, but you, supreme meddler of the universe, didn't listen. I know I'm not ready."

"Get some more info from your mom, and we'll dig your way out of the past."

"We? What I need to do is see my dad as soon as possible."

Would he have answers? What if he confirmed everything Mom said? It couldn't be true. What if it was?

"I don't advise it."

"Excuse me? Did I accidentally put you on retainer?"

"He ditched you as a child. Trust your mom."

"Have you been talking to Levi again? Another secret meeting?"

"We have your best interests at heart. I'm going back to bed now. Goodnight."

I dropped my phone on a fluffy towel and sank under the tepid water until I couldn't breathe. Susan was right again. How could I be in love? The date had been remarkable, the kiss sublime, and Charlotte had whispered when we left that they'd be honored to host our rehearsal dinner. I wasn't fit to believe myself, let alone anyone else. No wonder my handlers had tightened up on the reins. I decided to go to Mom's. I'd be gentle, like Levi advised.

"Mom, answer the door."

I'd been knocking for five minutes. I knew she had to be awake. The wind rustled leaves and a distant train needled my soul, so she wasn't asleep either. High heels clicked toward the door, and after a series of theatrical sighs, and multiple locks clicked, the door opened.

"What took you so long? Why are you dressed up?"

"Damn it, Leanne. Even The Grand Inquisitor slept once in a while." She turned her back to me and headed to her bedroom. "Leave your torture devices on the counter, please." Mom sat on her bed and slipped off silver high heels.

"Why are you wearing an evening gown? Are you picking up an Academy Award for best actress-slash-liar?"

"Do I come to your home and interrogate you?"

"No, because I've got nothing to hide. You, on the other hand, are interesting. Did you have a date with Rudolph Valentino?" I made myself comfortable at her vanity, inhaled her perfume, and wished I could be more like Levi.

"I should have burned your Nancy Drew books. I didn't have a date. I had a job interview."

I had visions of her in a long gown, like the gorgeous woman in her story, with the diamond clips in her hair. Drinking top-shelf scotch with cigar-smoking men in swanky clubs. Walking up the stairs to a tiny apartment in the morning, her purse filled with fifties, money for the powder room. I shook my head to remove the unwelcome thought, my brain an Etch-A-Sketch that I couldn't shake clear.

"Job interview? I didn't know Denny's requires formal wear for the late shift."

"Enough, Leanne. What do you want?"

"I want your approval to see my dad."

"Since when have you asked permission for anything?"

"I don't want to upset you."

Mom walked into her bathroom. I followed her and watched her remove false eyelashes and slather cold cream on her face.

"Well, isn't that special."

"I'm half him, you know."

"Half of nothing is still nothing."

"I think we went to a jewelry store together when I was four? He picked out a bracelet with a gold heart. It was a charm bracelet. He said he'd buy a new charm for every birthday."

"Do what you need to do." She pointed to her bathrobe on a hook behind the door. I passed her the robe and sat on the edge of the bathtub. "But be careful. He's like letting a hungry snake sleep in a basket of newborn kittens."

"Why'd you marry him?"

"I plead young and naïve, grand inquisitor. Leanne, your life is your business. If you insist on seeing him, I won't interfere. He can be quite engaging when he wants something, and if he wants to see you, he wants something." She wrapped herself in her pink bathrobe and wiped the cold cream off with cotton balls.

"Last chance to talk me out of snake charming, Mom. If there's something that I need to know, tell me."

Mom picked up a brush and ran it through her shoulder-length hair, eyes on the bathroom mirror. My heart sped up in my chest; it was never good when she wouldn't look at me.

"The worst part wasn't the cheating. I didn't leave because of that."

"What did he do?" I swallowed the lump in my throat, along with my fear of the unknown and thrill of learning more. She seemed genuinely ready to be truthful. Jeffrey's words came to haunt me. Would knowing the truth change me into someone who couldn't handle it?

"The first thing each morning, the sting of stupid, like a sharp, painful slap to the face, the minute I woke up. I knew I'd ruined my life. I couldn't let him ruin yours, too."

"How did he ruin your life?"

"He hit me, and other things." She put down the brush and rubbed night cream into her face. "The first time, he said I had a bee in my hair, he had to swat it. My head was in the way of his hand. Imagine that. He'd hit me and make up some garbage. He'd say he didn't mean to trip me or push me down, or he'd flat-out lie and tell me I dreamt it. The next day, he'd bring me flowers or a bottle of perfume that we couldn't afford. I didn't know what to believe, so I lost more of myself daily. I didn't want you to grow up seeing a bad example of a marriage."

"It was still extreme to pretend that he died."

"Times were different, and so was I."

"Are you done protecting me?"

"You never stop protecting your kids, Leanne. I hope you can understand and forgive me one day."

"I wish I'd known he was alive."

"You never had a decent father. That's the only thing I'm sorry for."

Without makeup, she changed from a mysterious, glamorous goddess to a wise, ageless woman. The only negative force in her stable life was me and maybe the new, sleazy Jeffrey. I wished that I believed her and could move on, but something nagged at me. She'd kept her secrets out of guilt and the misguided rationale that what we didn't know couldn't hurt us.

I suspected that nothing had changed, which meant that she had a whole deck of cards I hadn't seen yet.

"Are you going to see him?" Mom asked.

"I think so."

"Thinking has nothing to do with it. If you thought about it, you'd spare yourself the anguish. I guess you need to touch the stove for yourself." She slathered on hand cream and rubbed the extra into mine.

I wanted to pull away, but I didn't. "I only have your word. Maybe there's another side to the story?"

"You seem hellbent on finding out for yourself, so what difference does it make what I say?" She let go of my slick fingers.

"You don't tell me anything. Fragments of information interspersed with lies don't make you the credibility oracle."

She shook her head, and I followed her pink fuzzy slippers to the living room. "I'm no victim, and neither are you. We make our own choices, live with the outcome, and move on."

"Do you think that this is about me wanting to play victim? Oh, poor me with the fucked-up childhood?"

"What did I tell you about swearing?"

"Sorry, I forgot the rules."

"You had so few rules. I never stood in the way of you doing anything."

"Can I have tea?" I asked and settled myself on her pristine couch.

"It's the middle of the night."

"Moon party?" I asked, tucking her furry throw around me. I wasn't going anywhere.

"I suppose you want a story?"

"Doesn't everyone?"

She gave me a long look, an exasperated sigh, and went to make us tea. With my feet tucked under me and a knot in my belly, I waited, thinking about David and wishing that I was curled up next to him, and the only stories being told were the ones that writers imagined out of thin air.

Chapter Twenty-Six

S hedding her Vivi heels, plain old Patricia closed the massive oak door. She hoped that her mother was upstairs putting the twins to bed, and she could sneak to her room. She'd climb under the covers, pretend she was sick, and get some sleep. Since the excitement had worn off, Patricia was exhausted. If she didn't have slight bruises on her thighs and a dull ache in her personal parts, she would have thought that the night had been a dream. He'd said she was made for him. He fed her strawberries in bed, traced whipped cream down her body, and kissed it off. He said he'd take her to Hollywood because she should sing in the movies. He knew people. He would make her a star.

Her mother entered the front hall with a spatula in her hand, a brown floral apron dusted with flour, and her dark hair in a merciless bun on the top of her head.

"Where have you been?"

"Out with Ginger."

"You're a common tramp. I know you've been holed up with a man all day."

"That's not true. Someone's lying to you or mistook me for someone else. I saw a double feature with Ginger and grabbed hamburgers right after. She paid for me. Wasn't that nice? Birthday money from her Aunt Grace."

Rosalind smacked Patricia with the back of her hand. Flour dusted Patricia's cheek as she reeled from the hard slap and staggered against the heavy hall tree. Hats and coats rained down. Her mother had choice words regularly, but she'd never taken a hand to Patricia before.

"I'm engaged." Patricia thrust out her fingers. Champagne haunted her veins and made her careless.

Rosalind picked up Patricia's hand and peered at the ring. She snorted and flung her daughter's hand away. "You're ruined."

"You think he's playing me? He's not like that."

"How would you know?" Rosalind wrinkled her nose and scowled at the ring, which she regarded as a dead, fetid thing attached to her daughter's finger.

"He loves me."

Her mother gave a guttural laugh and pointed at Patricia with a spatula. "If this con man loves you, why didn't he ask your father for your hand in marriage?"

"Because you and Daddy would say no."

"For a good reason. You're seventeen, Patricia Jane, and have no business whoring around or getting married."

"What about what I want?"

"Are you getting what you want? I suggest you take off that repulsive excuse for a ring, never tell a soul about your reprehensible lapse of judgment, and I'll pray for a miracle."

"I don't think anyone is listening to you, Mother."

"Is this what he's taught you so far? No respect for your parents?"

"I will be with Verin."

"Go to your room. I'll speak to your father about this transgression of yours. I suspect he will have something to say about it."

"No, he won't. He never says anything. You don't let him speak, let alone have his own thoughts. No wonder he's always working."

"Shut your mouth. You have no understanding of what you've done. That man got what he wanted for the price of a few dinners and made you a whore. I'll light an extra candle and pray St. Tarcisius will speak with Mary on your behalf and give you back your virginity."

"I'm happy I gave myself to Verin."

"You'll have to trade for something else. I'll look for signs." Rosalind walked, head high, into the parlor. She ate one of the sugar cookies at the saint's feet and rearranged the rest. "In the meantime, you will not see that man again, although I suspect he's moved on by now. That kind does."

Patricia followed her mother and stood behind her, hands on her hips. "What do you know about *that kind*? You never leave the house except for the market and church. Did you learn about that kind at the butcher's, or maybe at the holiday potluck? Did that kind touch your skinny ass in thanks for your potato salad recipe?"

Rosalind slammed her spatula against the wall, cookie crumbs flying. The slotted metal square flew off the handle and smacked St. Tarcisius in the face, breaking his nose, which dropped into the plate of cookies at his feet. Rosalind's nostrils flared like those of a hunted wild pig, and she put her hands over her mouth in horror at the desecration.

"Blasphemy! You will burn for this, Patricia Jane, and no fire extinguishers exist in hell. Ask your father. He'll confirm I'm right."

"You're the one who broke the spoon."

Rosalind, approaching hysteria, screamed at Patricia, "It's a spatula, ignorant child! How can you marry? You don't know the difference between cooking utensils."

"I know the difference between your empty life and the life that I want!" Patricia shrieked.

"You know nothing about my life, you self-centered creature. You've thwarted me since the day you were born. Verin is a sham. He's a shark in sheep's clothing. If you leave this family for him, you will come back over my dead body. Do you understand?"

"It's a wolf, Mother, not a shark. In case you forget, make a note on your Bible story notecards. I have no intention of returning to this house."

Sudden calm engulfed Patricia. She was getting what she wanted—no, needed—and couldn't wait to leave her crazy mother and this house. She ran upstairs to her room and stuffed her secret dresses, a few other clothes, and her makeup into a laundry bag as fast as she could. Something poked into the lock on her door. She went for the handle; it was jammed.

"I'm locking you in for the night, Patricia Jane. I'll give you one last chance to come to your senses. If you continue with this farce, you are dead to me."

Chapter Twenty-Seven

P atricia slid down against the door, overwhelmed, exhausted, and unable to understand why her mother tortured her. There was no way out of her room. Only last week, her dad had cut down the supposedly diseased Chestnut tree outside her window. She crawled into bed, wearing her pink dress infused with Verin's scent; cologne, tobacco, and booze. It lulled her frantic thoughts as she cried herself to sleep.

Awake with a plan before the sun streamed through her window, she shoved a nail file into the lock, jamming it inside until pieces of metal fell to the floor. She grabbed the laundry sack, tiptoed downstairs before anyone woke up, and slammed the front door shut.

She ran three blocks in her heels, took them off, and kept going until she couldn't breathe. No more chores, no more lectures, no more no—till she thought she'd die. Verin would give her all the yesses she could handle, if she could find him. She knew his late-night haunts but nothing about his morning routine. Maybe the pirate bar served breakfast. Patricia knew she should conserve her little bit of money, but a bus would take forever, and she didn't have that kind of time. She spied a taxi with the light off and hailed it.

"I've finished my shift. You'll have to wait for another cab."

"Please. I'm desperate for a ride."

"What's the hurry?" asked the driver, an older bald man with gentle brown eyes, as he leaned out the driver's side window.

"Do you know the name of the pirate bar downtown? It's called Captains, or Ships, or something like that."

"You mean Bluebeards?"

"Take me there, please?" Patricia looked at his name printed on a card stuck on the visor. "Buddy."

"What's in the bag?" He smiled at her and winked.

"Money from the bank I robbed last night."

"I don't take bank robbers or kids running away from home to bars this early in the morning."

"I'm twenty-five. I work there. I'm late for my shift. Please?"

"Yeah, okay, kid. Headed that way for breakfast anyhow. Get in."

"Thanks."

Patricia swung her bag in first and slid into the back seat. The coarse fabric scratched her stockings and tore a run. Damn. The cab stank of stale smoke, and the upholstery, once golden, had turned the color of dried-up mustard on a picnic plate. He spun the car onto the road, back where Patricia had run from. She ducked down as he passed her house.

"Is this the scenic route?"

"What are you? A comedian?" Buddy asked.

"No, I'm a singer."

"I had a daughter about your age. Worst day of my life when she ran off. Are you gonna do that to your family?"

"If I'd wanted a lecture, I would have seduced a priest."

Buddy made tutting sounds and looked at her in the rearview mirror. "You talk like that to your ma?"

Patricia looked out the window at the pavement whizzing past, taking her away from a house that stifled her. She couldn't breathe in between the small spaces her mother allowed her.

"Maybe, but it wouldn't matter anyhow. She hates everything I do."

She hates me. Patricia slumped down in the seat; her manic euphoria subdued by a stranger in a lumberjack shirt. She didn't have many friends. Ginger was too busy with her new boyfriend and going off to college. They no longer hung out like they used to. Other girls didn't like her, but then again, she was so focused on her career that she didn't care what they thought.

"Your meter isn't running," she pointed out.

"I told you, I'm getting breakfast. Holie's Diner near Bluebeards has the best jelly donuts you will ever taste."

"Why'd your daughter leave?"

"None of your business."

"You were plenty chatty asking me about my life. Now you don't want to talk?"

Buddy chuckled and looked into the rearview mirror again. "You're a pistol. What's your name?"

"Vivi."

"Well, Vivi, Becky said that her ma and I wanted a girl that she didn't want to be. Then, she meets this guy ..."

"Did you ask what she thought was best?"

"I'd do it differently if I had the chance," Buddy said.

"Did you hit her?"

Buddy braked hard at a red light and looked over his shoulder. "Why would you think that? Did someone hit you?"

"I wouldn't stay if someone hit me."

"You know what we didn't do, Vivi?"

Drained from the terrible night, Patricia looked out the window and shook her head. Suspicious of Buddy's motives, she didn't want to listen. She wished he would drive her somewhere where she could start over again, with no one to tell her what to do or how to think.

"We talked at her plenty and told her what she should be. I don't think she loved that boy, but I believe he listened to her and made her feel special."

"Are you making this story up to get me home?" Patricia said to the concerned brown eyes in the rearview mirror. "It won't work."

"I thought you were twenty-five and late for your shift?"

Patricia fumbled with the bag on her lap. Maybe she could sneak back later. She'd forgotten so many things that she wished she'd taken. Photos of the twins, Rose and Lily, the necklace that her bother Bob sent her from Paris. Sitting in the back of the old cab, she knew she'd rushed things. She didn't want to be engaged, she wanted a career, but somehow the two had switched. She had to find Verin and explain it to him. She could live with him while they worked on her career, but no marriage.

Buddy honked the horn at the slow driver in front of them. "What are you? Seventeen, maybe? Don't mess up your life for some man who tells you what you want to hear."

"Did you ever want something so bad you couldn't wait to start, and only one person believed in you? Shouldn't you trust that person, Buddy?"

"I'd trust your heart, but I'm not sure it's your heart that's thinking right about now." Buddy waited for the red light to turn green. "Does this believer of yours have a name?"

"Verin. He's the only person who understands me. He's getting me a record contract."

"Are you in love with him, or with what he says he can do for you?" Buddy asked.

"That's a stupid question."

"I wouldn't be so sure about that. Diner's ahead; so is Bluebeards—or I can take you home. No charge."

"I can't go back. My mom said so."

"I bet she'd change her mind if you apologized," Buddy said.

"I'm not sure I'd want to go back if I could. She thinks singing is one step away from being the devil's whore."

"Maybe you need to find a way to explain it without the smart mouth. I'll buy you breakfast; you can practice what you're gonna say."

"Why would you do that?"

Buddy pulled the taxi alongside the curb. "I don't like to eat alone."

"Oh my God, there's Verin across the street." She grabbed her purse and bag of clothes and scrambled out of the cab. She kissed Buddy on the cheek and tried to pay him, but he waved her money away. "Thank you for listening."

He handed her a grimy card. "You take my number, okay?"

"Thanks, but I won't need a getaway car again." She took the card, slipped it into her bag without looking, and it fell into the gutter. "Verin, wait for me!"

He probably couldn't hear above the noisy traffic and walked into the diner. Cars sped by while she waited to run across the street.

She checked her face in her compact, smoothed her hair, and wiped away the mascara ringing her eyes. She looked more like a baby raccoon than the sophisticated lady Verin had expected. She crossed the street and took a deep breath in front of the coffee shop. When she opened the door, she felt sick to her stomach. There was Verin in a booth, cozy as could be, his arms around the Mississippi.

Chapter Twenty-Eight

Patricia hid behind the diner's newspaper rack and peeked out from behind a *Good Housekeeping* magazine. She watched Verin in mute fascination and fury as he stirred Vanessa's coffee with his spoon then gave it to her to lick. Vanessa wore a violet wool pencil skirt with a black sweater, tight as tar on the road. Patricia would have recognized those boobs anywhere. Vanessa checked her delicate rhinestone watch, touched Verin's face, and headed to the door. The doorbell jingled while Vanessa sauntered past and out into the morning crowd.

A counter lady in a yellow-flowered dress with a white ruffled apron approached Verin's table. She looked like she'd been born with a coffee pot in her hand. He grinned at her, and she patted her gray-streaked bun under its hair net back into place. Verin said something and a slow blush appeared through thick layers of rouge that stained her wrinkled cheeks as she topped up his cup. He laughed, pushed the sweet roll across the table, and brushed a crumb off his navy suit. Did he flirt with anyone in a skirt? Heart pounding, Patricia slipped the magazine back on the rack and marched over to him.

"Baby! What a surprise." He stood up and pulled out a chair for her. Not the chair Vanessa had occupied—the chair across from him. "I'm glad you're here, Vivi. I've had a rough morning."

"Why were you talking to that woman?"

"I'll tell you if you get that scowl off your pretty face." He patted a passing waitress on the behind, much younger than the woman who'd filled his cup. "Get her coffee, will you?"

"It's self-serve, mister. You have to order at the counter first."

He flipped a ten-dollar bill on the table. "Now it's you-serve, baby. Coffee and a Danish."

She picked up the ten.

"Vanessa calls me this morning, says she's getting fired," he continued. "I know the owner of the joint. I tell her to meet me, give me the scoop, and I'll fix it for her. She's okay, but between you and me, I think she's drinking more than she's serving. You know what I mean?" Verin mimed guzzling from a bottle, head wobbling back and forth like a hula-girl dashboard doll.

"She didn't look like she had any troubles."

"You can't tell trouble by looking."

"I watched you."

"You spied on me? That's no way for a fiancée to act." He looked concerned—was he pained she could think him capable of being unfaithful? She knew what she'd seen.

"What's wrong with you?" Verin asked.

"She looks like more than a friend."

Verin took the coffee and pastry from the waitress and put it down in front of Patricia.

"Eat. You think so, huh? Shows what you don't know. Maybe you shouldn't open your trap about things you don't know shit about." He gestured to her food, stirred more sugar into his coffee, and waggled the wet spoon in Patricia's face. "I help people, Vivi. You got a problem with that? Want me all to yourself? I didn't peg you for the selfish type, but I've been wrong before."

He banged the spoon down on the table. Nearby diners looked up; a woman shook her head and whispered to her friend. Patricia's face burned right along with her gut. The fluttering of new love, the blissful butterflies, turned into angry wasps, stinging their way through her intestines.

"Why'd she lick your spoon?"

"Are you kidding me? I didn't think you were the paranoid type, either. Maybe this thing between us isn't such a good idea. You are a baby, after all. I'm sad you'd think such things, especially after yesterday."

He pulled her hand close and kissed her fingers. Her tears dripped on the table, the wetness turning spilled sugar into sticky puddles. She took her hand away from him and traced a heart in the clear sugar water; he wiped it away with a napkin.

"She acted like your girlfriend. Are you sure?"

"Sure? That you're overreacting? Yeah, I'm sure about that. I gave you a ring, baby." He took her face in his hands and leaned in close, kissed her nose.

"I don't know what to think."

"Then don't."

Patricia unwound the cinnamon roll and fed the wasps in her gut tiny pieces, hoping they would go away. Verin appeared upset and wounded. Had she betrayed him? Maybe adults licked each other's spoons. She'd shared plenty of straws with Ginger. When she listened to Verin, he sounded so logical. Ashamed of herself, she tore her paper napkin into pieces in the secrecy of her lap.

"Hey, baby. Stop that. Why are you crying?"

"I'm sorry, Verin. I've had a horrible morning, too, but I shouldn't have doubted you for a minute."

"I forgive you, baby. I forgot you're a kid. How could you know anything?" He leaned in close enough for her to smell Vanessa's jasmine perfume on his coat while he wiped her tears with his lipstick-stained napkin. The wasps hissed and stung, but she ignored them.

They spent the day arm in arm in the park, and she screamed with delight when he pushed her as hard as he could on the swing. He laughed when she told him to stop, that she couldn't take anymore. Popcorn-fat ducks clustered around while they sat thigh-to-thigh on a bench near the ornamental lake. She'd forgotten about Vanessa and how Verin had made her feel stupid. He'd asked her about the laundry bag, but she didn't want to break the spell and didn't know how to tell him she had nowhere to go. She lied and said it belonged to Ginger. Said they had plans for a movie, and she would take it to her tonight.

"It's getting late, baby. When do you have to see your friend?"

"I can see her anytime. I want to be with you."

He held her head and kissed her mouth. Heady with desire, she kissed him back, put her arms around his neck, and crawled onto his lap, the way she'd watched girls do at the Squirrel. He slid his hand up her skirt.

"Hey. Get a room!" a man yelled as he walked past, a basset hound on a jeweled leash, his wife pushing a baby carriage.

"Sounds like a damn good idea. What do you say—feel like room service?" Verin traced a finger up her leg. "Hey, you've got a run in your stocking. Kind of a mess today, aren't you?"

"I guess so."

"A lady should check these things. Didn't your mother teach you? I can't have people thinking you let yourself go."

"It's a run, Verin. I have another pair."

He smiled at her and lit a cigarette. "Why don't you fix that before we check in? It's a nice hotel."

Patricia took her bag and walked across the park, looking for somewhere to change. The ladies' room had an "out of order" sign plastered across the entrance, so she ducked behind a shed that stored small rental boats for the lake. She crouched in the dirt to avoid being seen and switched the offending stocking for a new one. She shuffled back to Verin, head down. He sat on the bench, cigarette smoke blowing away from him like he didn't have a care in the world. He gestured for her to turn around like a trainer ordering a seal to perform tricks.

"That's my girl. Perfect, just the way I like you."

"What happens if I'm not perfect?"

"I won't let that happen. Let's go, baby."

Chapter Twenty-Nine

P atricia lay on the bed, rolled up in a rumpled white sheet, legs in the air, her pink-painted toes tapping the ornate headboard in time with the radio. An embroidered, gold satin bedspread pooled on the floor along with her dress and underthings. She studied the embossed room service menu while Verin showered. She wanted one of everything.

"Verin, why doesn't the menu have prices?"

"Cause it's all free, baby!" he yelled from the steamy bathroom.

"Tell me why?"

With a white towel around his toned waist, he moved toward the bed, a gold watch strapped to his wrist. "Good places never put prices on the guest's menu. Only the guy with the wallet gets to see them."

"Can I see your menu?"

"No."

"I don't want to older something expensive."

"Don't worry about it, baby. I've got plenty of money. I like to see you eat."

Patricia tossed the menu aside and wrapped the sheet around her naked body. Verin grabbed her wrists and pushed her to the mattress with one hand. His towel slipped off and fell to the carpet. He reached for the second bottle of champagne. Ice dripped off the bottle and onto the bed. A smirk on his lips, Verin popped the cork with a flourish worthy of New Year's Eve while chilled bubbles cascaded over her.

"What are you doing? Stop it, Verin. I don't want to sleep on wet sheets."

He ripped the sheet away from her body, but she grabbed it back, a protective shield.

"You don't want the sheet wet? Take it off," he said, his voice cold like the wine.

"You're wasting champagne." She didn't care, but she didn't like how he grabbed her and didn't listen to her when she said no.

"I don't intend to let it go to waste."

Foamy drops rained while he trickled champagne down the length of her body, turning the sheet translucent, her body revealed against her will. Shamed into stillness, she looked into his face. No warmth shone from his eyes, his playful ways missing in action. Confusion and fear shared the fence that separated what she wanted from what she didn't. The wasps hissed and burned her gut.

Verin put the empty bottle upside down in the ice bucket and peeled the drenched sheet off her body. She watched him. He was like an actor in a silent movie, his coal-black hair slicked back and shiny from his shower. His eyes on hers, he licked her sweet, sticky flesh clean. Her body didn't respond to his smooth and practiced touch, and her mind ran wild with an unnamed fear. She pushed his head away from her breast, her voice a whisper, tears sliding down her cheeks.

"Why'd you have to do that?"

He stared at her; no words passed his mouth, his eyes focused with disdain. He lifted his shirt from the floor, shook it, and inspected it for imagined dust. He buttoned up like it was June and had time to wait for winter. His pants, jacket, and tie got the same treatment. He smoothed back his hair, lit a cigarette, and dragged a roomful of smoke into his lungs. He hummed and examined his gold lighter like he'd never seen it before. It joined the cigarette pack in his jacket pocket.

"Get something to eat, baby." He leaned over the bed. "You don't have to pay. Just give them the room number when you order."

"I don't want you to go." Patricia grabbed him.

He shook her off like she was a needy dog and walked to the door. He looked back at her.

She clutched a pillow in front of her nakedness, sobbing, her heart broken. "Please don't leave me. Where are you going?"

"Remember who loves you," Verin said, and walked out the door.

She ran after him and leaned as far as she could around the door without being seen as he strolled along the hall, checked his watch, and got into an elevator.

Patricia hopped around the room frenetically, zipping up her dress and sliding on stockings. She yanked at the delicate fabric and watched as a run made its way up her thigh. She wiped her eyes with the back of her hand. What was wrong with her? She loved his attentive ways, the warmth he kindled when he touched her. What difference did it make if the sheets were ruined? The hotel didn't care; they were probably used to it. Verin didn't want a nag like her mother—he wanted a woman who deserved him.

Cold and shaking with the fear that she'd blown it, she pulled off her clothes and gave up the notion that she'd find him. She lifted the bed-spread off the floor and wrapped herself in its heavy folds. She bundled up in a wingback chair and faced the window, peering out, hoping Verin would appear. She convinced herself that he went to buy cigarettes and that he would be right back. Hours later, hungry and with a terrible headache, she dialed room service and ordered roast beef, cherry pie à la mode, and a bottle of scotch. She charged it to the room and downed her first drink with a bite of pie. By three in the morning, she'd passed out, wrapped in the bedspread in the chair by the window.

Hours later, Verin slipped into the hotel room like a sly cat who'd spent the night outside causing havoc and made his way over to the bed. "Hey, save any for me?" He sat on the bed as he unlaced his shoes.

She sat up, startled by his voice, and rubbed her eyes. "Verin?"

"Expecting someone else? Jack, maybe?"

"I'd never cheat on you." She dragged the bedspread as she walked to the bed and stood before Verin. "I thought you'd be right back."

He ignored her, rose, and poked under the silver lids at the cold roast beef sitting in a pool of congealed fat, two pieces of pie drowning in melted ice cream. He lifted the bottle, appraised what remained, and poured out a double for himself.

"Looks like you drank your dinner."

"I wasn't hungry."

"Me neither," Verin said.

"I'm sorry."

"For what?"

"I let you down."

He held up the glass, examined the scotch, and sipped it gone. He carried her to the bed and laid her down like a precious doll. He smoothed her hair, ran his fingers down her face, and inhaled her innocence.

"It's okay, baby. I forgive you."

"I'm sorry, Verin. I won't do it again. I'll try to do what you want. I love you."

He stood up, removed his jacket, and reached for something next to the bed. "I know, baby. I got you these."

"They're beautiful." She inhaled the heady perfume of the roses, and while she buried her tear-streaked face in his neck, the smell of jasmine gagged her.

Chapter Thirty

Mom drew the furry white blanket to her like a second skin and rubbed her closed eyelids. At the other end of the couch, I reached out with my toes and touched her through the blanket. She leaned over and tucked my cold feet into the warmth, then gave me a tiny sad smile that didn't reach her eyes.

I wrestled with all she'd told me. I knew so little, but I couldn't reconcile the woman she claimed she'd been with the woman I knew. She poured another cup of tea and nibbled on a cold piece of toast. My heart ached with wanting to believe her. I hurt for Vivi, her naïve yet bright spark forced to lie in a horrendous bed of her own making. I decided to play along, but until I met Dad, I'd reserve the right to be skeptical.

"It's a relief to tell you about your father."

"Why didn't you tell me sooner?"

"Waiting for the right moment, I suppose."

"No offense, Mom, but the moment was forced upon you. Why would I believe that you were waiting for the right time to come clean?"

"Children should be spared the ugliness of the world. I let a monster be your father. You didn't need to know that."

"Did he do something else that you're not saying?"

"For God's sake, Leanne, you were a child. You don't tell children that their father is a drunken, philandering waste of space, among other things. If you thought he was a decent person, it would be like you had a good father."

"Except that you made him so perfect that no man could compare. I wonder if that's why I've been content with assholes." I set my teacup on its saucer and poured another cupful from the pot.

A look of horror passed over her face. "If I told you he drank, you could blame me for leaving a man who needed help, and I couldn't explain his sexcapades. If I told you the truth, you'd think you did something wrong, which you didn't. Kids take trauma on themselves. I've seen talk shows."

"Do you think it's your fault for not knowing any better at, what, seventeen?" I nibbled the edges of a waffle. "Way back when I knew something wasn't right—no one could be that perfect."

"You never had a clue. Neither you nor Jeffrey asked about him much."

"You made him into a fucking saint. We didn't want to upset you. I had a billion questions, but you got this look on your face—"

"What look, and don't swear."

"I don't remember."

"Leanne, it's my look. I want to know about it."

"You're such a control freak. Do you remember Father's Day when you caught us with a bonfire in the backyard?"

"Ah, yes. When you and Jeffrey made Father's Day cards in secret and burned them so the cards would reach him in heaven, you also lit a tree on fire and burned down the fence."

"Half the fence, and it was Jeffrey's fault for signing his name in lighter fluid. You willed yourself not to cry or throw things by pinching up your face like an apple doll. You did that a lot."

"I was upset about the fence."

"Choked up over an old fence that was about to fall anyway? Sure, I believe you. That's why we never asked you questions about Dad. We didn't want you to remember the pinnacle of perfection and be sad."

She grabbed the edge of the blanket and rolled the soft fluff between her fingers. She looked nervous, edgy, and steeled for unavoidable pain.

"I hated myself, Leanne. I had complete self-loathing for what I had done to both of you. The entire fire department, all with wedding bands, mind you, were asking questions, and Jeffrey piped up about how he didn't have a daddy."

"So, they felt sorry for you. What's wrong with that?"

"They shouldn't have. I didn't have a dead husband; I had a useless bastard who couldn't be bothered with his children or me." She sniffed, shook her head, and raised it, eyes straight to mine. "I'm no victim."

I handed her the box of tissues from the coffee table and swallowed down my guilt. She made me feel like shit for dragging her back to the past.

"Jeffrey sucked up to the firefighters so that he wouldn't get in trouble. Rascal."

We both laughed. I decided that even if her story wasn't true, as a single mother in the sixties, she'd had a more complex and challenging time than I would ever know.

"People say that you can't choose who you fall in love with, so stop blaming yourself."

"Where did you read that garbage? The next one's always a Band-Aid for the last one," Mom said.

"Is that why you never dated?"

"Something like that."

Fragile old threads wove themselves into the present as we sipped the last of the tea in silence. Damn. If each man was a bandage, I'd spent my life in triage.

"When did Dad leave?"

"I did the leaving," she said.

"Wouldn't a true bastard take off one day and never come back?"

"Shouldn't you be whisking or dipping something in chocolate?" She gave an unconvincing yawn and blinked at me. "I need to go to bed."

"Does he know he's dead?"

"Yes, he does, and Leanne, I love you, but I've had enough for tonight."

"One last question. Why would he agree to be dead?"

The cozy, close feeling evaporated with that crucial question. My chest constricted as I waited for the answer. If he'd been in on the death pact, he never wanted to see Jeffrey and me again. There had to be something else. He must have loved us.

Secrets that had crept forth under the quiet of night slunk back into their old hiding places, like keys lost where I couldn't find them. Familiar frustration, sticky with repetition, replaced the empathy of moments before. The Sphinx returned, her lips a sealed vault.

"That's it? You tell me he's a complete bastard, as bad as it gets, but you go quiet for the finale."

"I'm done."

"I'm begging."

"I'll leave you a letter. You can open it when I'm dead."

I closed my eyes, and rubbed my temples. I imagined Mom hooked up to a polygraph machine. "It's a Small World," interrupted my musing, and David's name blinked on my caller ID.

"Are you going to answer that?"

"Saved by just one moon and the golden sun," I whispered to her and reached for the phone. "Hello?"

"Is it too early? I know I should wait for the I'm-super-cool-not-that-into-you forty-eight hours, but I couldn't," David said.

"I think it's fifty-six hours."

"Funny, you don't look like a stickler for rules, or torture."

"Just when you think you know a person," I answered David, glaring at Mom as she folded up the would-be security blanket and hung it on the back of the couch.

"Since I've messed up the forty-eight- and fifty-six-hour rules, how do you feel about lunch?"

"I'm playing hard to get."

"I don't think it works when you tell me your evil plan. How about dinner? I can pick you up at your place. I'm still good for that bottle of Chianti," David said.

Mom looked at me and nodded. I threw a sofa pillow at her.

"We're skipping the hard-to-get thing?" I asked.

Mom dried her precious teapot and nodded enthusiastically. I waved her away like a seagull pestering for a handout on the beach.

"Say yes," she whispered to me.

"Looks that way," David said.

From the first phone call, I'd grasped he was light years beyond every man I'd taken home and pushed out the door before sunrise. How did the untrusting learn to trust? My mouth was as dry as sawdust on an old garage floor. I looked around for my tea, but like my mother's story, the tea things had been put away for another day. Insecurity and something else I couldn't shake, born of my mother's recent disclosure, found its way out.

"I'm telling you right out front that my trust issues are a headliner you might want to avoid."

"I'll take that under advisement," David said.

"You can change your mind. I would understand. Think of this as the chicken exit on a roller coaster."

My mother threw a damp dish towel at me and walked off in disgust.

"Noted and filed. I'll pick you up at seven."

He hung up, and I directed my attention to mom. "I'll see you later." I slid on my shoes and gathered my purse. "This isn't over."

She waved at me as I headed to the front door. "Get some rest before your date. You look like hell."

"I love you too. Let me know if you suddenly feel the urge to come clean. I know there's more."

"Are you going to see your father?"

"Yes."

She came toward me, kissed her fingertips, and placed a kiss on my forehead.

"Do what you need to do."

Chapter Thirty-One

I mages from my mother's past flickered through my mind like an old-school flipbook: the angst-filled teenager, the smitten siren without the wiles. I eased into stop-and-go morning traffic, much like the push-and-pull of destructive love. I'd known more than my share of charming, smooth-talking men, the skin-crawling sensation of being drawn into a monster's web. Was she any different? How could I not believe her?

With flawless brush strokes, she'd painted a not-so-pretty picture of the doting innocent and the player, but on the fringes of my awareness, something continued to warn me not to trust her. No one was as naïve as she made out. There were plenty of holes in her stories, and Vivi used Verin to make her a star. Damn. I was determined to hear him out with an open mind, and maybe an open heart.

Wired from a billion cups of Irish breakfast tea, I pulled up in front of Levi and Paulka's Victorian and found parking on the tree-lined street. The façade of the house was magnificent—black, gold, and turquoise. Inside, the décor was ever-changing, depending on the season, inspiration, and leftover set dressing from the last lavish wedding.

"Darling, what a surprise," Paulka said as he answered the door in an Egyptian-looking toga, circa Tutankhamun, the wild and crazy years. He gave me the usual three air kisses on my face. "Oh my God, you look haggard. Levi's taken Eloise and Elliot to school, so you must confide in me."

"I'm hungry, not haggard."

"I'll tell Levi to bring food on the way home." Paulka shut his eyes and made a teepee with his fingertips.

"What are you doing?"

"Telling Levi to pick up bagels. I'm taking telepathy classes at an online university. Susan's idea."

Oh, God.

"Okay, let's test you. Why am I here?"

Paulka assumed the closed-eyes tepee position. "You're stuffed with angst like a cabbage roll. Is it about your mother?"

"Impressive," I yawned through feigned enthusiasm.

Paulka looked insulted, but he led me to the living room and puffed the pillows. He returned with a demitasse of delicious coffee, and I drank without thought. Huge mistake. One of Prescott's recipes, no doubt. I'd ingested a potent concoction with organic honey and steamed elk milk. I could stay awake with no jitters until next week. How was I supposed to get a nap and refresh my haggard visage?

Paulka settled across from me, reclining like a pharaoh on a white settee with a cup of ordinary coffee. I arched to stretch my aching back, admired a fresco of Osiris and Isis overhead, and waited for Levi. The scent of fresh, warm bagels filled the air. Paulka arched his brows at me and rose to kiss Levi.

"Hey, Leanne. How crazy is this? A force came into my mind; it said bagels, so I got bagels," Levi said, his toffee-brown eyes sparkling with mischief.

Paulka threw both hands in the air. "Voilà." He took the bag from Levi. "I'll meet you two darlings in the dining room after I plate these."

"Let's be wild and crazy peasants and eat from the bag," I said.

"Are you insane?" Paulka said, and whisked the bagels off to the kitchen.

"He can't put ideas in your mind, can he?" I asked.

"He likes to think that he can," Levi said. "I always bring bagels after I take the kids to school."

"Ahhh, you pretend. I can't imagine any man I've known doing something so sweet."

"That's love." Levi shrugged and helped me up.

"Ready for therapizing?" Paulka joined us in the dining room, carrying a gorgeous terracotta tray with glorious food.

I helped myself to a sesame bagel, piling it high with cream cheese, sliced tomatoes, smoked salmon, and red onions. Before I bit into it, I had second thoughts, and took the onions off. It was bad enough that I would look like crap by seven tonight; I didn't want to smell like it too.

"Levi, do you have a sleeping pill handy?"

"Chinese food comes with fortune cookies. Levi, does Jewish food come with Xanax?" Paulka looked serious and shook out his napkin.

Levi gave him an air kiss. "Only in Beverly Hills and Palm Springs, my darling. Leanne, why do you want a sleeping pill?"

"I never went to bed last night, and I have a date with David tonight. I'm desperate for a nap. *Someone* thinks I look haggard." I shot Paulka a dirty look.

Paulka arranged the capers on his salmon into a heart shape. "You want me to lie to you?"

"Maybe you can read minds," I said. "Mom and I played the disclosure game until the wee hours of the morning. I'm not sure that she told the truth. She could've read the stuff in a cheesy novel."

Levi got up. "I'll get you a pill, and don't start without me. Paulka, no telepathy. I want to hear this for myself."

Paulka and I ate while we waited for Levi to return. He made strange movements with his lips and eyebrows. Telepathic messages to Levi? The mind boggled.

"There's three in here," Levi said and handed me the bottle. "Only take one at a time, or it's a thousand-year sleep. I'm not kidding."

Levi, über-conservative with pharmaceuticals, didn't realize that I needed to battle not only Paulka's coffee but also the caffeine from the tea I'd consumed by the gallon last night. I smiled, tipped out two pills without him seeing, and swallowed with passionfruit juice.

"What makes you think Patricia's lying?" Levi asked.

"She can't stop herself at this point. Once you board the falsehood express, there is no escape," Paulka said, and popped a caper between his pout.

"Paulka, my love, I asked Leanne."

"Until I talk to my dad, I'm reserving all judgment."

"What makes you think dear old Dad will be forthcoming?" Levi asked.

"Spies can't be trusted," Paulka said.

"My love, no one said he's a spy. Where do you get these wild ideas from?"

"Dad disappeared, and now he shows up? He's either a spy or a magician." Paulka topped off his juice with champagne and raised his glass. "Case closed."

"What did Patricia say?" Levi asked, and served himself coleslaw and a pickle.

I gave a substantial, theatrical sigh. Paulka was rubbing off on me. "The naïve and beautiful young woman fell for the dashing player to escape her batshit crazy mother."

"Is he in San Francisco?"

"I don't know, and I doubt she'd tell me if she knows, but he's alive, and that's something."

I didn't mention the psychological and physical abuse—assuming it was true. It would be difficult if I reconciled with my dad, since Levi might ditch me in favor of the tragic drama queen, AKA Mom. I pushed my plate to the side and laid my head on the table, allowing the medicinal effects to take over my body.

"I can't believe that Patricia would make anything up. She's no longer trying to protect you, so why wouldn't she be truthful?" Levi asked.

"I adore Patricia, you know I do, but I'm with Leanne," Paulka said. "Once a lemon, sour forever."

"I'm sure they have situational ethics in Romania," Levi said with his famous eyebrow raise.

"Of course we do, and people can change, but why would Patricia want to? She's fabulous the way she is," Paulka made even less sense than usual, and my eyes felt heavy like someone had coated my lashes in lead mascara. I could hear them, but couldn't make myself respond.

"Don't listen to him. Leanne?" Levi asked.

"She's out cold like a boxer on the mat. The angst has worn her out, poor little schnitzel."

"My fault. I should've told her to take a half."

"She's out for the counting of the sheep. What time is her date?" Paulka asked.

"How would I know?"

Paulka rummaged in my purse. What was he looking for? Levi carried me to the guest bedroom. I tried to tell them to set the alarm, but between a silky sea-green duvet and heavenly pillows, I slipped off into the bliss of a drug and bagel-induced dreamless sleep.

Chapter Thirty-Two

T he pungent scent of ginger tea floated in the air, but it seemed far away, like I would need a passport to drink it. My eyes adjusted to the light, and the buzz in my head subsided as I became coherent. Two little faces peered down, more intrigued than concerned. Both children were dressed in dark green tights and leotards, bows and arrows in hand—tiny warrior elves with matching trays.

"Daddy said to wake you up and be gentle." Elliot dropped his bow on the bed, the arrows on the floor. "We brought you dragon tea."

"You have to get ready for your date," Eloise said. The elves giggled, nibbling chocolate macaroons.

"Oh, shit! What time is it?" I asked.

"You shouldn't swear," Eloise said, pursing her tiny lips, her blond curls bouncing against pointy plastic ears.

"Don't tell, okay? Where are your dads?"

"Calling someone. You're late."

"Oh shit!" I swung my legs down toward the soft rug and stood up, only to plop back down on the bed.

"You have to put two dollars in the rudeness jar now," Eloise said.

"You're dizzy. Better drink the dragon tea," Elliot said, observing me through his black-rimmed Harry Potter glasses.

"Who made this? Is this a potion?" I asked, and sniffed the drink.

"It's plain old tea, Auntie Leanne," Eloise said, rolling her baby blues.

I fished two tens from my purse on the floor and put my finger to my lips. "Let's not mention the swearing."

The elves ran from the room, money in their clutches, Eloise shrieking that Auntie Leanne had paid them off. Levi popped his head around the door.

"Feeling better? Refreshed from your nap?" He sat next to me on the bed and straightened the pillows.

"You should give those pills to stressed-out brides."

"I don't think it's legal."

"Dear Miss Kitty says, if you wouldn't date yourself, you shouldn't be dating. It's true, you know. Maybe I shouldn't go."

"David made reservations at Henry for eight. Five stars and imported beeswax candlelight."

"Don't ignore me, and how do you know?"

"We used your phone and texted him. He thinks you had a crème brûlée emergency and moved dinner back an hour. You're meeting him there."

"Crap. Scott's favorite bar." I shook my head to clear away the unwanted image of Scott getting creepy on my couch. "What time is it?"

"Seven-fifteen, and forget about Scott."

"Why didn't you get me up sooner? I don't have time to get home and dressed."

"You can borrow something from Paulka."

I ran my hands through my hair and tried a few deep breaths, a hot mess as usual.

"I'm canceling."

"No, you are not. Paulka has a closet full of fabulous clothes. He loves you enough to lend you his new boots."

"Red, white, and blue with stars? No, thanks."

"Did you just meet him? Seriously? He's been buying and selling on high-end websites. It's his new excuse to shop. He's definitely got an eye for style."

Groggy and vacant, I crawled back under the covers. Paulka waltzed in with an armful of dresses, and Eloise and Elliot carried shoes and bags. They were fabulous- the accessory elves.

Paulka dragged me from the bed.

"Try the silver one, Auntie Leanne," Elliot said and smiled at me, nodding encouragement, his elf ears slipping.

"Can I do your makeup?" Eloise asked.

"Anything you want, sweetie," I said. "Dress me as fast as possible."

After a quick shower, Paulka and the elves swirled around, zipped up, zipped out, and threw dress after dress on the bed. The attention reminded me of Sleeping Beauty and her fairy godmothers, except that Sleeping Beauty had a sparkling pink dress, not supple, strapless, black Italian leather that either covered boobs or thighs but not both at the same time.

"I'm not wearing this. I look like a dominatrix."

"What's a domino-trick?" Elliot asked.

"It's another name for the pizza guy," Eloise said.

"You look more like Julia Roberts in *Pretty Woman* than a dom," Levi said, high-fiving the elves.

"Can we have pizza?" Elliot asked.

Paulka gave Elliot a quick kiss. "Of course, my sweetie. A Prada bag to complete the ensemble for the stunning Auntie Leanne."

"I look ridiculous," I said. "I'm wearing my jeans. He can deal with it."

"You're out of time and have no choice. Relax; you look sexy and gorgeous," Paulka said.

"I can't walk in these boots. I feel like a drunk hooker."

"Why change the habit of a lifetime?" Paulka waved me out the door, the elves beaming alongside him.

Levi mouthed, "You'll be fine."

Chapter Thirty-Three

I crept into Henry, a classic American upscale joint at the wharf, and tried to keep my boobs from popping out of the strapless, black lace bra that Paulka had pressed into my hands while the kids were out of the room. I listened to the sounds of ice clinking and bottles sloshing. I was dying for a drink, so I skipped the haughty-looking maître d' and went to find David alone.

Scott's cologne hit me in the loins before his arms wrapped around my waist, and his hands ran down the front of my thighs. "Someone's looking mighty hot. Never pegged you for the biker-chick type. If you'd dressed like this when we were dating, I wouldn't have cheated."

I slapped his hands away and spun around to face him. I swiped his drink off the bar since he'd had enough, desperate to calm the anxiety and hating the sexual need he'd conjured up.

"What's this?" I asked.

"French vodka. Goes down like water."

"Then why don't you drink water? They'll fill a bowl and put it on the floor for you."

"I've missed your sarcasm, and I love your new look. Angry baby seal meets sexy Puss in Boots."

I tossed back the entire martini. "Fuck off, Scott. I have a date who has manners and a meaningful job."

"I didn't know they let Hell's Angels in here."

"He's a doctor, you idiot."

I handed him back the empty glass, wished I'd never worn this damn dress, and motioned the bartender for a refill. Since the bar was at capacity, I leaned against the polished wood counter and waited for acute dizziness and slight nausea to stop before I resumed my search for David.

"Thanks," Scott said and reached for the icy cocktail.

"Get your own." I intercepted the drink, sipped with my eyes closed, and ate the caviar-stuffed olive.

I turned my head to look at the view; the moon was rising over the water, and the bay was restless, like my mood. I shut out the man-child's petulant whine. How had I put up with him? A warm palm on the small of my back produced instant calm. How did he do that? David leaned over and kissed my cheek. Pleasure flowed through me, reigniting last night's kiss.

"Sorry, I'm late. One of my patients ran away from home. Did you get my text?"

Scott rose from the barstool, straightened his jacket, and put his hand out to David. I swallowed my anger and pretended to be a grownup.

"David, this is Scott. Scott, this is David."

"Nice to meet you, Scott."

They sized each other up, and David won the gladiator toss. Scott swiveled back to the bar with a slight nod and a grunt.

The haughty maître d' glided over to David, all smiles. "Your table is ready, sir."

"Good thing that you showed up when you did. I thought the baby seal might bite if she wasn't fed." Scott never knew when to shut up.

David looked like he had a selection of choice comments, but he smiled at Scott, picked up my drink, took me by the arm, and led me into the dining room, composure intact. If his hand on my back calmed me, his dismissal of Scott made me ecstatic.

"I thought that you were the jeans or simple black dress type, but you are one smoking hot lady. You look a bit dangerous," he said, pulling out my chair, lips brushing my neck. "But I'm not afraid."

"Thank you." I sat and finished the last drop of my drink. "Smoking hot is better than an angry baby seal."

"By the way, we're adults. No need to tell me anything about the cave dweller back there."

"Cave? Scott hasn't made it out of the swamp. I'm sorry he was rude to you."

"I feel sorry for him. I get to have dinner with the beautiful baby seal, and he doesn't."

"I thought you'd forgotten."

"That was a little bit funny."

"You're easily amused."

A white-aproned server approached with a beaming face.

"My name is Jimmy, and I'll be handling all your needs this evening. Would we prefer another cocktail, or would we like to order something from the wine list? Our cellar is a marvel."

He passed David the wine list and both of us menus. I tried not to giggle at "all of your needs"—something about it struck me as funny. I worked to get a grip on myself. Jimmy hovered at full attention while I deliberated: cocktail or wine? The wine seemed like an excellent idea instead of another potent martini, but I waited to see what David would say.

Another server placed artisan rolls on the table, and a third filled glasses with mineral water, complete with minuscule slivers of cucumber and lime. As much as I disliked water, I picked up the glass, but the garnish looked so much like tiny green fish that I set it back down, slightly revolted. I took a roll, hoping that the bread would settle my stomach.

"Jimmy, perhaps you'd like to suggest something," David said and closed the wine list.

"I'm so glad you asked," Jimmy said. "Peruse the menu, and I'll be right back with a spectacular Pinot Noir."

The spectacular Pinot Noir arrived, and Jimmy poured a generous taste for David.

David handed me the glass. "I chose last night. Your turn."

I picked up the wine, swirled it, and put crimson lips to the glass. I prepared for the potion to amaze. I set the glass down, feeling shaky. I needed a minute.

Jimmy seemed concerned at my underwhelming reaction. "Madam doesn't appear wowed. I'll be back. A woman like you knows exceptional and shall have it.'

"No, Jimmy, it's fine, delicious," I said to the air as Jimmy rushed away. Damn. This wasn't good. I wasn't high maintenance, and David could get the wrong impression.

"I wonder if we could ask for another candle, or a miner's hat. I can barely make out the menu," David said.

"Susan and I dissected candlelit restaurants once, deemed them manipulative but lucrative."

"You don't need candlelight to look good." David toyed with the saltshaker. "Is that creepy? I'm being honest, but it sounds creepy, even to me."

Compliments usually made me uncomfortable, but he was so sincere, so beautifully transparent, that I let it drape around me like a velvet cloak and held it close.

"It's not creepy coming from you. I like candles. Candles are the equivalent of 'Let's Pet It On. You know, the Marvin Gaye classic?'" I caught myself slurring.

David nodded and flagged down the nearby Jimmy. "Jimmy, could we order? Been a long day."

David was perceptive. Considering that I hadn't eaten anything except half a bagel a million years ago, I needed more than a fancy bread roll and some herb-flecked butter to stave off the effects of sleeping pills chased with two double martinis.

"If I may, the sea bass is truly magnificent, and the Moroccan veal chop with apricots and olives is to die for."

"I don't eat anything cute," I said, making big eyes at David.

"How intriguing. I didn't see a picture of the sea bass, so I could be wrong, but generally, I don't find large fish all that attractive," Jimmy said.

"I'd like the sea bass, please."

"I'll have the unattractive fish as well," David said.

"The duck is splendid, finished in a red wine and fennel reduction. Tempted?" Jimmy asked, hands in the air.

"Ducks are cute," David said and winked at me.

"Poisson for two without delay. Oh, the sauce has lobster. I'm checking, but..."

"Lobster is not cute," I said, winking at David, wondering if I'd accidentally said 'lute.'

Jimmy bowed away from our table and into the crowded restaurant, only to return within seconds with half the cellar for my approval and two helpers in tow.

David whispered, "Does he know you're in the business?"

"It's the leather dress," I whispered, louder than intended.

"They say that doctors get special treatment."

"Ask Paulka to take you shopping."

"He has excellent taste," David said, his eyes appraising my bare shoulders.

My napkin slipped off my lap, and while I tried to retrieve it, the blond bread boy saved my woozy ass and brought me a fresh one. In an unprecedented effort to impress, Jimmy poured more than a taste into five wine glasses, and Jimmy's minion, with polished precision, slid chilled plates with a sublime butter lettuce salad with hazelnut glazed figs and creamy fontina in front of us.

The figs weren't the only glazed thing—David became blurry, and every bone in my body told me to get out of dodge while I still could. The last thing I needed was to get up close and personal with the salad.

Spectacular arrived in a Château Haut-Brion Bordeaux, too heavy for sea bass, but since Jimmy had gone to so much trouble, and David was gorgeous, sweet, and perfect, I nodded my approval.

David held up a hand, and Jimmy stopped mid-pour. "Call me crazy, but I'm suddenly in the mood for a little fresh air and a burger." He slipped Jimmy a handful of green, and Jimmy—a wistful smile on his charming face, pulled my chair out with gracious attention.

"Another time, Madam. Enjoy your evening."

David's arm was solid and warm around me. I leaned into him, each step measured and thoughtful. He couldn't see my face, which was a good thing. He should have taken my advice in the beginning. As much as I wanted this, him—I wasn't ready.

Chapter Thirty-Four

I forced my eyes open, and the morning-after slapped me in the face. The room was dark enough to delay the inevitable. Barely able to move, I started with my feet, which were cramped into birdlike claws. I tried to wiggle them and hit resistance. My boots were still on. So was my bra, wrapped around my wrist like a bracelet.

The last thing I remembered was leaning against the bar, insulting Scott. Something came back to me about Sea World. *Sea World?* Scott knows I hate zoos. At least he had the decency to leave my thong on. I took in crisp white sheets, a nautical print duvet, and matching curtains that shielded my shame from the daylight. This wasn't Scott's bed.

The relief I hadn't gone home with Scott became abject panic; I'd wined and dined my way into David's California King. I crept from the covers and hobbled to the bathroom, with as much stealth as possible, my toes in abject agony. The last thing I needed was to wake the warm, lightly snoring lump under the covers. Good. David snored. David wasn't perfect.

I searched through drawers and the medicine cabinet for something to clean off the heavy mascara smeared on my face and to defeat the intense pain pounding inside my brain. Surprisingly, the doctor had little in the way of conventional medicine. I took several pills from a blue bottle labeled "Mystical Headache Remedy", fished around for mouthwash, and if there was a God, a new toothbrush.

I found a sealed SpongeBob SquarePants toothbrush, which begged to be used, and questioned, assuming that David didn't send me packing if he woke up before I'd left. My mouth a definite improvement, I sat on the cold, yellow-tiled floor, backed up against the tub for leverage, and tugged at the boots. My elbow hit the tub's edge and knocked a vintage, cobalt blue bath salt jar to the floor as pain reverberated through my arm like a tuning fork. I rubbed my elbow and cringed at the breakage around me. With no broom or dustpan in sight, I carefully swept the mess up with my hands.

David tapped on the door. I dumped bath salts and broken glass into the bottom vanity drawer and pushed the drawer closed with my fingertips.

"I hope you like waffles. Are you okay in there?"

"I'm fine, thanks. Be right out."

"Take your time."

"Okay, great."

I yanked harder on the left boot, but it wouldn't budge. Hot and sweaty with the effort and the enormity of my most colossal fuck-up to date, I wiped away tears of frustration, only to feel the raw pain of bath salts on delicate eye tissue. Eyes shut and stinging, I fumbled for a towel, wet it, and pressed the cool on my eyes. I opened them to see thick black mascara streaks on a once pristine blue and white striped towel. I stuffed the towel in with the broken glass in the drawer and discovered a big bottle of Coconut Bliss body lotion. Paulka would kill me, but it was better than slicing the boots open with a razor, and I was desperate.

I poured lotion alongside my legs and into the boots, hoping I could ease my legs free. Three-quarters of a bottle later, they wouldn't budge. My legs and the beautiful couture boots were as slimy as the bottom of an old swimming pool. I imagined Paulka moaning, his hands clutching my shirt. "How could you? It's like putting the Mona Lisa in a dishwasher to clean a spider web." God damn it. I looked around for a razor. The boots had to die.

"Hey, Leanne, are you sure you're okay?"

I groaned with the effort of yanking the boot yet again.

"Let me help," David said.

"No."

"I'm a doctor. I've seen it all."

"You've seen enough."

"Are you sick?"

"Can you leave for a few hours?" I coughed for effect.

"What's wrong?"

"Do you have a drug for mortification? Slip it under the door, wait thirty minutes, and I'll come out."

"I may have underestimated whatever it is you're going through, but believe me, I want to know you, warts and all," David said.

"I don't have warts. Did you inspect me?"

"It's an expression. Tell me what's wrong."

Let's start with humiliated, and go from there. Oh, God, please let me wake up. This can't be happening.

"My boots are stuck."

"I'm not surprised. I couldn't get them off last night without disturbing you. Okay, this isn't a problem. I used to ride as a kid, and my boots got stuck all the time."

"You don't seem the horsey type."

There was a long silence. I wondered if he'd gone to get a crowbar.

"I'm not, but I wanted you to feel better."

"I'm wearing a thong."

"I know."

"I know you know, and that makes it worse."

I gave one last tug and collapsed on the floor. I pulled a stomach muscle I didn't know I had, and my left thigh cramped.

"Leanne, put on my robe and open the door."

"Are you laughing?"

"Only a little."

Both my feet were swollen and begging for release. I pulled myself up, holding the toilet for support. The lotion squished and slid further down while I reached for David's robe to tuck around my exposed ass. I unlocked the door and perched on the sink.

"Well, cowgirl, looks like you could use a little help."

I pressed my thighs together while he kneeled before me and prepared to yank off the boots. There wasn't going to be an encore from whatever happened last night. This was David. Nothing happened last night. I studied the vent in the ceiling. Something about the situation reminded me of my annual pap test.

He tried not to laugh, the nape of his neck bare and kissable. He looked up and caught me watching. The vent hadn't been that interesting.

"It's not funny."

"A little funny?" David said, smiling.

"I feel like a giant ass."

"Looks petite and perky from here."

I cemented my thighs together, closing the San Andreas fault.

"Focus."

David put one hand on my calf, and the other cradled my ankle. "Hold the sink. One, two, three."

He yanked hard and fell backward to the floor, his prize clutched in both hands over his head. I lost what little balance I had on the porcelain perch and fell forward, straight onto David.

"Good morning," David said.

"Hello."

His lashes were long, almost doll-like, with flecks of amber in the blue of his eyes. I swallowed. My breasts were smashed against his chest, my legs between his. Nervous, I licked my lips. Damn. I could get used to a David body pillow.

He dropped the boot and put his arms around me.

"Ready for the other boot?"

"That would be good."

David held me against him. I'd forgotten that my foot hadn't had circulation for hours. Was he contemplating a kiss? Checking if my pupils were functional? SpongeBob-brushed, I was ready and willing until my foot got wet.

"Edison. Leave her alone. Sorry about that. He likes coconut."

Edison continued to snuffle my foot, and the heavy breathing was all too familiar.

"Did he sleep with me?"

"The guest bed is surprisingly comfortable. First time I'd tried it."

Humiliation complete, I rested my now-scarlet face on his chest, turned my head to the side, and tried not to giggle.

Chapter Thirty-Five

With my wet hair wrapped in one of David's towels and my body scented with manly body wash, I followed the smell of breakfast into the sunny kitchen.

"What do you remember?" David asked. He pulled out a chair and set down a mug of much-needed coffee and a plate filled with steaming, crisp, flawless waffles.

"Are you asking as a physician or a friend?"

"Maybe a little of both."

"I don't do blackouts if that's what you think."

"Did I say anything about blackouts?"

David dished up fragrant strawberries and piled them on my plate.

"Do I smell nutmeg, bourbon vanilla paste, and brown sugar?"

"Impressive. You could give up your day job and sniff for drugs." David looked delighted with himself. "I spruced up my game. Actually, I have no game, but you inspired me."

I cut half a strawberry into quarters, then eighths, and dipped a dot of a berry in the light dusting of powdered sugar on my plate.

"Can we talk about last night?" David asked.

I cut into the crisp waffle, popped it in my mouth, and it disappeared like magic. Eating was better than talking. David refilled my coffee cup and waited with saint-like patience.

"This isn't going to sound adult and reasonable," I said.

"I figured that out for myself. Go ahead, I'm a doctor, not a judge."

"I was a little, umm ... restless after our Mobs date, so I called Susan and ..."

"Wow, you don't sleep."

"Then the pinball machine in my head wouldn't stop, so I went to my mom for another thrilling chapter of our secret family saga. I was there till the sun came up, and because I'd had a vat of tea during story time, like an idiot, I went to visit Levi and Paulka."

"Did Paulka make you the super coffee? Brett told me about that stuff."

"He did, and dumb like a bunny, I drank it. Once I realized my mistake, I took pills to get some beauty sleep for our date. Mistake number infinity plus one."

"Thoughtful—not smart, but considerate. Let me guess the rest. You drank a couple of cocktails as an antibacterial measure against Scott's hands."

"Yup, and then the wine tasting did me in. The last thing I remember thinking is that blackened peaches would be more interesting than figs."

"Nothing after the close inspection of your salad?'

"Nothing until I woke up with your dog."

David added peppered turkey bacon to my plate, and I noticed dimples flickering on his cheeks. More of the night returned. I'd confessed my cute animal dietary observance. David leaned over and refilled my cup with a splash of fresh coffee. French-pressed. Paulka would be so proud of him. I noticed a fresh hickey on David's neck, and although I'd be better off without the gory details, I couldn't resist.

"Did I do that?"

"Leanne, if you want to torture yourself, put the boots back on."

"I need to know."

"Why?"

"Because you will know something I don't, and I'll be haunted forever."

"You told me that you were a vampire princess and wanted me to tie your hands together so you couldn't hurt me. Happy?"

"I did? Are you sure? I have a thing about vampires, but I've never told a soul."

"I convinced you that the bra made a lovely bracelet, and you told me that jewelry had to be real, or it didn't count." He passed me a pitcher of cream.

I put my head on the table, hands over my ears, hiding from his laughter.

"You're a sweet, pliable drunk, and one day I will take you to Fiji, so we can swim naked and sing 'Come Away with Me' to purple-striped fish."

Edison laid his ginormous black and white head on David's lap and looked into his master's eyes. David fed Edison waffle crumbs and avoided my horrified gaze. They seemed to be having a mind-meld about what to tell me.

"I like you in my robe." He pushed Edison away and pulled his chair close to mine. "I'd love to spend all day like this, but I have to get to work."

"I should get home," I said.

"Relax here with Edison. I'll be home by four."

"Then what?"

"We'll order in Chinese with lots of garlic in case the vampire princess shows up."

I gathered our plates and put them in the sink, breathed in the sanity of eating breakfast with a man I could adore, and eased out of the embarrassment of a night that was declassified, and no big deal.

"What do you say?" David asked.

"Why me? I need to know, especially after last night."

"I buy the same groceries week after week, have season tickets to the same theater and ball games since college, and have had three dogs, all named Edison."

"What about middle names?"

"Dogs don't have middle names, and don't change the subject. I feel something with you that I've never felt with anyone else, and I can't begin to explain, let alone understand. I don't think I need to know."

The anyone else hovered around us like a ghost, just like last time he said it, perhaps an actual spirit, watching from the top of the refrigerator, pissed off that I'd used her lotion. The deeper I fell for David, the more an unnamed fear clutched my heart and warned me to steel myself against what could only be pain and loss. That fear, always with me, had nothing to do with the dead.

I turned on the water, soaped up a sponge, and wished that David would hold me. My skin twitched in need of some proof of his desire to be as real as he claimed. David must've been taking the same mind-reading class as Paulka, because at that instant, he pushed the old waffle iron, sifter, and mixing bowls aside, and lifted me onto the tile counter. The sticky batter, flour, and powdered sugar-coated my naked ass like a coffee cake ready for the oven. I swallowed the butterflies fluttering in my throat. My wise mind couldn't stop me in time.

"Did you make waffles for your wife?"

"She did all the cooking. I looked up recipes and went shopping while you slept."

He wasn't a player. David was the real-deal kind of guy I could let into the secret places of my heart where no one had been allowed. Terrifying.

His robe slipped off my shoulder, his eyes stared into mine, the distance between us closed, and the raw surge between us was enough to scorch the counter. If it got any hotter, the excess batter would cook on my ass.

"Are you sure you don't want the chicken exit?"

"If I wanted the chicken exit, I would have let the waiter pour that wine."

His fingers traced my jaw as tears fell, and anger swallowed me whole because I'd wasted so much of myself on men with limitations. This man wanted me, and I knew better than he could how much he risked. I wouldn't feel guilty. I vaguely remembered a cheeseburger, fries, and a huge Gatorade from last night. I slid soapy hands down his back, pulled his body between my legs, slipped my tongue into his mouth, and met sweet acceptance for whatever and whoever he believed me to be.

In between strawberry-flavored kisses, he stopped and nuzzled my nose, my cheeks, inhaled my neck, and returned to my lips.

Dizzy with possibilities, and delirious with lust, I wanted this man. I moaned into his neck, refusing to acknowledge any ghosts who waited to steal my happiness.

David picked me up. My thighs wrapped around his waist as he carried me into the bedroom, where we continued to kiss like naughty teenagers.

I let him peel his robe off me, but the knotted belt refused to loosen. David pulled his shirt off and paused, gazing at me. I became a golden pool of liquid butter.

"You are gorgeous."

"You are beautiful, insanely beautiful," David said.

"Do you have to mention insane?"

He held my face between his palms, and I'd never felt so safe; his soul warmed mine. For a mind-blowing second, I knew his thoughts. Our lips met, and I couldn't help but moan.

"I will remember this moment long past forever," David said.

I would, too.

The feeling was like fire to a caveman; mystical, scary, maybe too good to be true. David dragged the sheets up and over us, like a fort, and I laughed with relief. He was for real, and under the warmth and darkness, we shared pure abandonment. I stepped into a freedom he encouraged me to take. Our kisses slowed and deepened, and my desperate hold on an ordered world no longer mattered. We left the fort when we couldn't breathe, and David used his skilled doctor fingers to untie the robe.

The bed shook, a five-point six on the Richter scale, as Edison bounded up and dropped his drool-covered, king-size dog toy between my boobs. I sat straight up, desire quenched.

"It's a sign. We should stop."

"Signs aren't peanut-butter-scented. Edison, off the bed." David pushed at Edison and reached out to pull me down. "I love your hair. It's like liquid cinnamon. I've wanted to touch it since I saw how it shined in those pictures near the Duomo."

He stroked my hair, kissed my lips, and his mouth trailed down to the dangerous sweet spot on my neck. I pulled his head up to my mouth. The bed shook. A seven-point eight. Maybe a nine.

"Your dog doesn't want this to happen." I didn't mention my concern about the lurking spirit of his wife.

"He likes you. He's bringing you his favorite things."

"Last time I checked, black rubber wasn't on the list."

David traced a finger down my throat. "How about black leather?" He dropped his voice an octave and tossed the dog toy across the room.

"I deserved that."

"I'm teasing. This is unusual; he only brings toys to me."

"What about Crystal?"

"Crystal never came to my house. No one has." He moved his hand away and sat, leaning back against the wooden bedframe.

Insecurity unrolled a fresh batch of caution tape. I wished I didn't like him so much. David sat beside me, his glorious chest exposed and beckoning me to rest my soul-weary, insecure head, but I couldn't. Edison had no problem getting the love he wanted. He wedged between us, and David rubbed his buttery-soft ears. I'd give anything for an uncomplicated love. Edison pawed David for more attention and jumped off the bed when none came. The man was mine for the moment. He took both my hands, our eyes locked together.

"I haven't been with anyone since Jessica died."

Radical honesty made me sweat. I let go of his hands and whistled for Edison—better buttery, soft ears than my instantly cold and clammy palms.

Why didn't Susan interrogate Brett for this information? Sensitive intel should be included in the initial briefing. Widowed. Doctor. Will wait for sex. I clutched the sheet around me.

"You said you dated."

"I've gone out."

"But no sex?"

"Since when is dating sex?"

"They tend to go together."

"Okay ... I kissed a few women, but nothing like what happened between us. I told you that Twister was in the closet. Why is that so hard to believe?"

"Men aren't like that."

David's jaw dropped. "Wow. You didn't believe me."

He didn't know what kind of special he was. We watched Edison make circles on the bed and fall asleep, his toy between his giant paws.

"Leanne, my patients are old. It's possible someone will die before we finish this conversation, which is going to be a long one. Can we talk tonight?"

"You mean the later on today, kind of tonight?"

"Yes, the traditional dark following light, unless that doesn't apply to a vampire princess," David said. I detected a slight chill in the air. Did he regret his disclosure? Should I be flattered?

I gave him a soft punch on the arm. "Your confidence in me is a little unnerving. I'm not sure I want to be like Christmas morning for a five-year-old."

"Why not?"

"Can you say pressure?"

"Would you feel better if I took a test drive with someone else?"

"No."

"I'll get down the ornaments."

As my internal weather warmed to scorching, he grabbed me, and we snuggled under the covers. I put one hand on David's cheek, and he moved his hand atop mine. Together, in a safe place, with so much to lose, we held hands.

Chapter Thirty-Six

D avid drove me to Levi's to pick up my car, and after a scorching kiss, I flew home to change into jeans, then back out to Levi's office for an emergency meeting. The guys had left at least fifty texts, which constituted a culinary emergency. In the inner sanctum of their downtown office, modern and neutral, Levi and Paulka sat at either side of a glass table for a tasting. I stretched my neck, twisted it to get the kinks out, and plopped down in a gray silk-covered chair.

"We've left a thousand, maybe two thousand messages," Paulka said.

"Paulka stopped counting when he got to infinity," Levi said. "How was the date?"

A minion brought a pot of tea and set it on the table. Paulka passed me a cup of steaming orange-scented tea with rosemary biscotti on the side.

"Is this safe to drink?" I asked.

"Do I look like I poison late-morning beverages?" Paulka asked hands across his chest in mock offense. I took the tea.

"You're stalling. How was the date?" Levi asked.

I dug through my purse, hunted down a pen, and wrote Paulka a check for a thousand dollars.

"What on earth is this for?" he asked.

"The boots. I'm adopting them."

Paulka clapped his hands in triumph. "The penny has fallen from the darkness. Since when do you buy expensive footwear? Ha! She doesn't want the boots; she can't return them to their rightful owner, who would be me, because she left them at David's."

"Why can't you go back? What happened?" Levi asked.

"Who said I couldn't go back?" I asked.

"Forget the boots!" Paulka said. "How many fig leaves does it take to cover David?"

"Buy a ticket to Florence and pay for the deluxe art tour. I want to buy the boots."

The minion brought champagne over. I waved him away, but since lunch was pending, and God only knew what was in the tea, I took a flute and sipped—too fast, because the minion raised perfectly shaped eyebrows in subtle reprimand.

"Did you find some morals at the morals store? You've spilled grape-leaf status before." Paulka pouted.

"Stay for lunch." Levi waved down the minion. "Anthony, be an angel and bring another

place setting for Leanne."

"You always kiss and tell," Paulka said, and passed me lobster bisque.

"David is different," I said, and took a spoonful, concentrating on the flavor. "Too much cognac."

"Good different or bad different?" Levi tasted the lobster bisque and made notes on his tablet.

"She left the boots, which means she took them off. Foot massage? What about the sexy thong?" Paulka winked at me with both eyes multiple times, like a child's baby doll with a glitchy battery.

"Don't assume, my love. It could be bad-different. Leanne doesn't want to go back and get them," Levi said.

"Don't you people listen? I have the boots." In frustration, I poured myself another glass of bubbly.

After tasting the mushroom soup, Paulka said, "Maybe the chanterelle cream would be better than the lobster. It goes with the Western theme. What about a bison chili?"

"What Western theme?"

"That's why we called an emergency meeting. Phoebe and Sophia moved the date up and decided on a Western theme," Levi said.

"I'm booked with my usual deliveries, Mobs, and the Greenburg wedding. Can't do it."

"Make it happen, and the boots are a bonus. If not, I insist on their immediate return." Paulka tore up my check and sprinkled the bits of paper on the carpet. "As for your fashion knowledge, which is sketchy at best, those boots are more than five times your silly check of nothingness," he said, and popped a piece of baguette into his mouth.

Little did Paulka know that his pricey boots were inside out, drying in my bathroom. Who knew silk-lined leather didn't respond well to coconut lubrication?

"How soon?" I asked, spooning up the mushroom soup. "It needs shallots and Italian parsley. Why don't you use Zen Soup? You'll swoon with every spoonful. Ask Susan."

"We have two weeks. There's too much at stake for surprise chefs," Levi said. "Maybe next time."

"Did you say two weeks? It can't be done. Why did they move up the date and change the theme? It's over three hundred people, and we've been planning Cirque du Soleil for eight months."

"True love and a celebrity wedding. We don't say no to either," Levi said, all business.

"I'd have to find two assistants to pull this off."

"I thought Candy returned from Venice?"

"Oh, she's back and brought a supposed chef with her. She calls him La Tigre, but I'm not sure that's for his cooking skills."

Paulka pressed his palms together and peered over the top of his fingers like an evil movie villain. "The boots, Leanne. Do you want them or not?"

"We can't pull this off without you," Levi said.

"I would use my voodoo dolls to punish you both, but they formed a union and won't work without pay," I said.

"Isn't the work its own reward?" Levi giggled, trying to be serious, which he wasn't.

Anthony set down tiny plates of assorted salads and glass urns of dressing.

"I thought today was only soup?" I asked.

"Oh no, my love. We have a three-hour tasting blocked. Plenty of time to fill us in on David," Levi said, picking up one of six chilled salad forks and giving me an encouraging nod. Paulka took a fresh bottle of champagne, popped the cork, and filled Levi's glass.

"We have ways of making you talk."

* * *

A mountain of cookbooks and scraps of paper littered the surface of the butcher block, all useless. Damn. A beef jerky torte? A biscuit and gravy gâteau? Yum. Since Levi refused to give me more than one glass of champagne, I had a horrific headache, and nothing romantic and delicious came to mind.

I faced Neil, Candy, and La Tigre like a drill sergeant. "Okay, kids, what are we doing for this event? It's got to be original, Western, and travel well."

"Clint Eastwood?" Neil asked, thumbing through a beat-up nineteenth-century American cookbook.

"You're not helping."

"How about pastry ponies?" Candy pursed her lips, making a perfect Gina Lollobrigida pout.

"Spaghetti Western has taken on a whole new meaning," Neil said, twisting his earring.

"Ponies and profiterole tumbleweeds? Oh, this is fun." I shook my head and made notes. "Think, people."

"Leanne, you have to slow down," Candy said. "La Tigre speaks a tiny bit of English but no American."

"For the third time, he has to wear a real shirt in the kitchen. Health department rules." I peered through La Tigre's net shirt at his chest. "Is that a cannoli tattoo?"

"Si può fare pony pasticcio?" Candy stroked La Tigre's face and ran her hands over his hairy, netted chest. He shook his glorious, dark mane in confusion until she made neighing sounds and pranced around the room.

"Non posso fare."

"He doesn't understand what ponies have to do with weddings, and I agree." Candy sighed and batted long, fake lashes—another health department liability.

He gestured like a maestro, his enthusiasm most evident in the way he stabbed the air with a random whisk while whispering in her ear.

She straddled him and got lost in his espresso-brown eyes. "I told you he's brilliant."

"What did the half-naked wolfman in my kitchen say that's so brilliant?" I asked.

"Two pastry swans, their wings gently touching, forever on a white crème anglaise lake on individual silver plates."

I turned to La Tigre. "No swans, ponies, and put on a damn shirt. Pronto."

Candy and La Tigre both glared at me. My phone rang with the only link to the sane and drama-free life that I didn't deserve and yet craved.

"Kung pao or mushu?" David asked.

Oh, no! I cleared my throat. "I'm really sorry, but I can't tonight."

"The no-sex thing threw you?"

"No, of course not. Not a big deal." Liar. "I have a huge event; the date moved up, and you wouldn't believe who's getting married."

"Was it the waffle batter on your butt? Too much too soon?"

I took my cup and moved out to the alley for a bit of privacy from the inquiring minds listening to my conversation. I laughed, leaning up against the alley wall.

"It's the widower thing? You warned me, but I didn't listen."

"It makes me a little uncomfortable, but that's not why I have to cancel."

"Leanne, I had a wife, loved her dearly, and she died. I'm not going to hide that. I'd like to be married again. For that to happen, I have to date, and I'd like to date you. Exclusively."

"I've never been marriage material."

"I've been thinking about you all day."

"Oh, boy. You might have to come over with oxygen."

Previously inactive regions of my brain went off like the Lite-Brite I had as a kid. I could understand manufactured manipulations, but authentic emotions? They were restorative, but bizarre and hard to believe.

"Are you canceling dinner for work, or avoiding a potentially uncomfortable conversation?"

Was I freaked out over the weighty build-up with me as the featured baby Jesus in David's Nativity scene? Until he put it out there, I would have sworn it was all about swans, ponies, and half-naked Italians. Not to mention an impossible deadline. I had a sneaking suspicion he'd minored in psychology. I'd have to check with Susan.

"Why is everything so good and yet so complex with you?" I asked.

"I make you think?"

"I've spent a lifetime avoiding it, so knock it off."

"Where has this not-thinking approach gotten you?"

Candy leaned around the door, her ponytail undone and face flushed pink. "Three organic raspberries, halved to signify the journey of marriage, with a tart lemon glacé to show the pain of love?"

I put my hand over the phone and yelled at her, "No journeys! Please. I'll be back in five. Button up your shirt."

Candy flipped her bleach-blond hair at me and slammed the screen shut. Several of the local guys wandered up the alley. I pounded on the door. "Candy, bring out cookies."

"Perhaps I'm overreacting. It sounds like you have plenty on your plate," David said. "Maybe I need a session with Susan—is she still taking victims for practice therapy?"

I took the cookie plate from Candy with my free hand and passed it to Norman. "Can you taste the lavender?" I whispered.

"A subtle hint," Comb Over Norman said, and gave me a thumbs-up.

"David, under no circumstances let Susan play with your mind. Let me get through this wedding and I'll make it up to you."

"Weekend away, make it up to me?" David asked.

I'd been okay with the batter and had worked through the footwear humiliation, but something about being in his first relationship after the love of his life, had sent me back to bubble-wrap jail. I sank on my heels in the alley with the empty cookie plate in my hand. An old, familiar feeling that I was a horrible burden, unworthy, hit me, and I couldn't talk.

"Hey, Leanne. You still there?"

"Isn't that my line?"

"I'm sorry if I sound pushy."

Neil emerged from the kitchen door into the alley and lit a smoke. Even his laid-back braid looked agitated. "Man, that Italian dude is too much. He wants to make life-sized chocolate statues of Venus on horse-back."

"David, I have a situation in the kitchen," I said. "I'll call you back."

"I'll save you a fortune cookie," David said, and hung up.

Damn. I shouldn't have canceled. I had used work to avoid an uncomfortable but necessary conversation. I'd been right that fake wouldn't fly with him, and the juicy slap of stupid was an excellent reminder to do the right thing. The Wild West could wait; an apology couldn't.

"Neil, feel like a crash course on the pastry business?"

"No need. I aced all my Cordon Bleu classes."

"You never told me."

"Dessert is drama and ego, and I don't do either. Soup is simple."

"Help me out with Mobs order? You'll have my undying gratitude."

"Can't eat gratitude, Leanne."

"Five hundred cash."

"Deal."

Chapter Thirty-Seven

N eil put on wire-rimmed glasses and started a to-do list on the whiteboard.

"Listen up, you two, Neil is in charge."

"Why Neil? He makes liquid food. He's no artist," Candy said and lounged on La Tigre's lap, his hands stroking her tanned thighs. "Why can't I be in charge? I'm the assistant."

"Neil is dependable, unlike someone who ran off to Venice. He also knows how to focus and never wears shorts in the kitchen."

She pouted. "You underestimate what I picked up in Italy."

I pointed at La Tigre. "What was wrong with a Vatican snow globe?"

"Leannearisima, Mobs order. What else?" La Tigre stood beside him, arms crossed, until Neil mimed washing his hands. "La Tigre, I don't want self-tanner on the food."

"I donna take—how you say?—instruction from other men in the kitchen." Tigre flicked the hair net that Neil had tossed him onto the floor.

"You learned English already?" Candy kissed his face at least a hundred times and spoke slowly. "We will do the immigration papers tonight."

"Cook first, immigration papers second, and I don't want to know any more for my protection." I shook my head at Neil. "I knew he could understand."

"Leannearisima, I'm gonna, how you say, make you so proud."

It was impossible not to like the overgrown Italian G.I. Joe doll wearing a net shirt over the Brazilian rainforest, with its copious carpet of hair that feathered down into the tight, low-slung jeans he wore, not that I noticed.

"I appreciate you wearing the hair net," I said slowly.

"Es a no problem." He winked at me and patted Candy on the ass. "I love America. She's so hot for me."

"I'm so happy for you. Kids, I'll be back in an hour. Start on the panna cotta."

* * *

I boxed up a rum baba from the walk-in fridge, poured a shot of rum to freshen up the cake, and poured a second shot to freshen me up. I covered the telltale box with my hoodie and slunk out of the kitchen to make peace with David, but not without a bit of help first. I revved up my car and called Susan.

"You could have mentioned that David's wife-shopping."

"A widower's always hunting for wife number two, and kudos to David. I doubt most of them will share the obvious so soon. Did you give him points for honesty?"

"Points? The wife thing is ricocheting in my head like a baby otter in Springtime. What were you thinking? I pulled out of the alley into the busy street. "How could you neglect to mention that David hasn't had sex since Jessica died."

"What am I? His priest? He's Brett's buddy, not mine. How would I have known?"

"I've seen you cross-examine your husband."

"Leanne, men don't talk like we do. Hmmm, I wonder how long Brett would wait for sex if I died."

It was a good thing that my ass didn't grow like Pinocchio's nose when I put my foot in my mouth.

"Forget that I told you anything."

"No sex since Jessica? Amazing. She was sick for at least a year."

"I don't want to know."

"You should be grateful that he's waiting for the right one, and that, for some reason, he wants you."

"Thanks a lot."

"Oh my God, Leanne. This isn't about you. It's about him," Susan said.

"Do you drink the blood of small children?"

"You're nothing like Jessica, according to Brett."

"That blows out the replacement theory. He's trying to fix me. He's a doctor; it makes sense."

"That's ridiculous, Leanne. This guy is fabulous, the real deal. A charter member of the good-catch club. Why would he look for someone to fix?"

As usual, Susan had an excellent point. Maybe her online therapy school wasn't such a joke after all. "Why me?"

"Why not you? Both Levi and I agree that except for your need to overthink and sabotage a good thing, you're a member-in-training of the good-catch club."

"You make me sound like a trout, and don't you people have your own lives to worry about?"

"Levi's concerned, and don't yell at me."

"Hey! Watch where you're going!" I yelled at a bus driver who cut me off.

"I have a new thesis for class."

"Not now, please."

"It's called the Lone Ranger. It's what you should be working on right now."

"What I'm working on is trying to get to David's in one piece. Sometimes I hate the city."

"Why don't you buy your mom's house?"

"And live there alone, surrounded by ghosts?"

"Paulka's right. You are a pointy barnacle today."

I pulled up to a red light. A guy in a silver SUV held up his phone. I could make out a picture of his boy bits. I flipped the guy off and changed lanes.

"Susan, I'm scared to death of messing this up. What if Jessica's watching?"

"Do you want to read my paper, 'Haunted Mansions?'"

"No more theory, Susan. Help me like a normal person."

"The ghosts are all in your mind."

"Maybe he likes cake and doesn't want to be alone."

"You're impossible. He's cleared for takeoff, do you understand? You don't have to worry about sleazy motives; he has none."

"The reason matters because if he's looking for a replacement, David isn't as into me as he thinks he is."

"I've heard about Jessica. Blond, professional, almost preppy tennis player. You're no replacement."

"Exactly my point."

"To thine own torture be true."

"People don't trust a therapist that sounds like a pilgrim."

She chuckled. "That's why I'm a lawyer. Look, Leanne, your comfort level is self-torture whether you do it to yourself or hand the whip to some man. Figuratively speaking, of course, except for that English guy. What was his name? Adam?"

"Aren't you listening? I don't want to sabotage myself."

"My client's here. He's fifty-something bastard who left his wife of twenty-five years for a college girl. Sometimes I hate my job."

"Can you double-charge him and give the money to the wife?"

"I do my best to color inside the legal lines, but points for the thought. Gotta go. I love you, and use your bracelet beads."

"I think the woo woo jewelry can wait. Gotta go."

I parked under a magnificent willow and cut the engine. The two shades of blue siding with white gingerbread trim and a cherry-red door looked loved. I walked up the brick steps to the front door, my offering in both hands, a smile plastered over anxiety, and rang the doorbell.

A small, brown-haired, David-lookalike answered the door with Edison behind him. "Cake? Cool," he said. Not familiar with kids, I guessed him to be about ten. I looked past him into the front hall, hoping to see David and get an explanation for the mini him.

"I'm Leanne. Can I come in for a second?"

"I'm not supposed to let anyone in, but you can leave the cake." The boy patted Edison, who wouldn't look at me. Damn, dog pretended we hadn't spent the night together.

"It's a special cake."

"Do you want me to sign for it?"

"I'd like to give it to David in person."

"He's supposed to be here, but late as usual. Patient stuff. It used to make Mom mad, but I don't care."

It was a Mexican standoff, complete with a rum baba. He looked like David, talked like David, and, as Paulka would say, the penny from darkness fell and hit me on the head.

"David's your dad?"

The kid looked at me, the cake box, Edison, and back to me.

"Well? Is he?" I drummed on the box top, my heart speeding up and matching the rhythm.

"Why don't you ask him?"

"Because he's not here."

"My dad told me to be careful telling strangers personal information. You could be the government, and the cake could be a bomb."

"I'm not the government, and mandarin cream filling never explodes."

"Are you his girlfriend?"

"It's possible." I lifted the lid of my sugar-scented truth serum and held it toward the kid.

"He's my dad."

Afraid I'd vomit on the Welcome To Our Home doormat, I shoved the cake box at the kid and stumbled down the steps. Fuck my heart. I stabbed at the car door lock, scratched the paint, and jammed in my house key, screaming in my head. "To thine own *torture* be true."

I dropped the key, found the right one, and hopped in. Shaking, I drove a couple of blocks down the street, where the kid couldn't spy, and pulled into the park. David was shopping for wife number two—someone to replace the SpongeBob SquarePants toothbrush when worn out and make cookies on demand. Damn him. Kids were fine, but not when they popped out of a hat like a white rabbit in a magic show. He should have told me; I should've known better. Mom was right: men lied to get what they wanted. So did friends. I would kill Susan before the sun went down. Maybe she hadn't known about the sex thing, but she knew about the kid.

I pounded the steering wheel. So much for perfect. So much for "I'm new at this." Bastard. Liar. He had sincere down to a waffle-flavored science, and I'd fallen for it. Damn him. I whacked the steering wheel again and headed to my kitchen to plan for Phoebe and Sophia's wedding—something I understood and could always get right. The wedding of the year had the potential to elevate my business beyond my wildest dreams. If other people's happiness was all that I could trust, I'd forget about any personal life and lavish my attention on my favorite celebrity lesbians and their dreams. Besides, I had a soft spot for Sophia. We could be twins.

Chapter Thirty-Eight

A glass of Viognier called my name, his voice soft and chilled. I call him Vinny—something to loosen and ease the pressure of acute disappointment. I leaned against the cooler, cheek pressed to the cold glass, letting the wine soothe me. I twisted my hair into a bun and tied my apron on tight. I took another Galloping Gourmet-worthy slurp.

"Leannearisima, your purse is singing."

Candy sang along to "It's a Small World" and stirred an enormous copper cauldron full of heavy cream.

A row of giant meat hooks lined the white wall, and beneath them sat a worn wooden bench. My old jean jacket and black leather Versace bag, courtesy of Paulka, because I had horrendous taste in bags hung on the first hook. My purse vibrated along with the ringtone.

"I'm not interested," I said.

Candy lifted the spoon and checked the cream "Can I have some wine too?" Out of habit, I watched it coat the back of the spoon.

"Open your own bottle and take that off the heat." I headed for the couch and sprawled out.

"Hey, Leanne, how about some soup with the booze?" Neil stood over a bucket full of apricots. He quickly removed the pits, settling the succulent halves into a pan of anise-infused sugar water.

Candy brought Neil a glass of red. "No thanks, I'm good." He pulled the cooked fruit off the stove and put on full pan.

"Candy, bring the red wine over here." I was cheating on Vinny, but he didn't need to know.

Neil took the wine away and replaced it with a bowl of steaming soup and fresh bread on a tray.

"The Versace is singing again. I think you need to say hello. You won some contest, eh?" Tigre's face was flushed with the heat coming off a pan of blanching almonds instead of Candy's thighs.

"Contest winner? Trust me; I'm not the lucky type," I said.

I stared at the tomato bisque and the hunk of fresh bread with chunks of salt glistening on the crust. I tried not to cry.

"Eat up and slow down on the vino." Neil patted my shoulder and got back to work. I watched him layer chocolate foam with delicate slivers of candied apricots and a double-cream custard spiked with Tia Maria into tin trays. Later, he'd dust the tops with crushed amaretto cookies and shaved dark chocolate. My team had the Mobs order well in hand, which gave me faith they could pull off the wedding and I could continue drinking.

"It's singing again, Leannearisima."

I put the spoon down. "Candy, throw my bag in the freezer."

Tastebuds and heart rate pacified by the bisque, I pulled out an over-sized sketchbook, my favorite way to imagine—a barn with sky-high ceilings and bales of hay wrapped in white linen. I penciled in a long trestle table and what could be on that table to delight hopeful romantics. The cheerful innocence of possibilities, a dream of something pure and, if not for eternity, at least until a therapist, even a fake one, could no longer help and a divorce attorney could. My God. Susan was a genius.

"Wow, I didn't know that you could draw," Neil said, peering over my shoulder on his way to the freezer.

"I can't."

"You say that a lot," he said.

"Leave me alone."

My minions made their way through the Mobs order with precision. Tigre squeezed pounds of blood oranges for granita, Neil started on hundreds of Tartufo, homemade hazelnut gelato robed in dark chocolate, with a frozen liqueur-filled cherry in the center along with gallons of crème anglaise for the potent little bombs to sit on courtesy of Candy. No wonder I found solace in food: simple ingredients lurked behind the complicated illusion, and doing the right thing was all in the execution.

"Who's buzzing the door at this hour?" Candy said.

"Norman and friends," Neil said. "I'll take out vichyssoise and bread."

"Norman doesn't like cold soup," I mumbled. "Take the tomato, but skip the basil chiffonade garnish. He's allergic."

"Angelica from the heaven you are. I think I want to give a present of special zuppa to Norman. Be right there."

"Wait, La Tigre. It's the front door buzzer. Oh my God, it's an immigration guy." Candy paled beneath her fake tan, mesmerized by the security monitor.

"La Tigre, get in the freezer. I'll handle this." I dropped the sketchbook and readied myself to protect my own.

Neil nudged Candy out of the way, wiped his glasses on his sleeve, and peered at the monitor.

"Looks like he's wearing a lab coat," he said.

"I don't hide from anyone. I stand my ground."

I pushed all three out of the way. David, dressed in a white doctor's coat and navy slacks, gazed up at the camera. He held a bunch of pink roses, and had his Mini-Me in tow.

"Holy shit, he must have called Susan or Levi for the address. Traitors."

"Or Googled your business," Neil said.

"I'm not here."

Candy nudged me away from the monitor. "A doctor? Are you sick? Why didn't you tell us?"

"Do I look sick?" Candy reached out to touch my forehead. I batted her hand away. "Neil, tell him I'm not here."

La Tigre put a hand on Neil's chest. Neil shoved La Tigre and headed for the door. He barred the way.

"Is this the guy who sings in the Versace?"

"See why I only make soup?" Neil grabbed a glass of water and sat on the couch, an unlit cigarette between his lips.

"Yes, La Tigre," I said, "He's the this guy, and he's got doghouse flowers, which means he's a guilty."

"I will take care of him, Leannearisima." La Tigre straightened his shirt, handed his hair net to Candy, and stepped outside. I turned up the volume on the speaker.

"Buona sera. Bella rosa?"

"A gift for Leanne. Who are you?"

"First, you will say."

"I'm David. Can I come in for a second?"

"I'm not letting anyone in this a place. I take the flowers." La Tigre patted the child on the head.

"We need to deliver them personally," the kid said.

"Do you want me to sign a paper?"

"No, thanks. Michael, my nephew, wants to deliver them himself."

"She's not here. She's supposed to be, but sometimes she's late in the night. Maybe she's on a big, hot date."

"She's on a date?"

"She could be."

"Could you tell me? Please?"

"Why don't you ask?"

"Because you said that she's not here, and she's not answering her phone." David sounded frustrated. I almost felt sorry for him.

"Come on, Dad, let's go."

"Not funny, Michael. Ask her to call me as soon as possible, please. It's important." David put his hand on the kid's back, and I watched until they were both out of view.

La Tigre put his hands on his narrow hips. "I'll do that soon or later. Buena notte."

I flicked off the speaker, turned off the monitor, and uncorked another bottle of Vinny. Nephew, my ass. Looked just like him. There is nothing like lies from a guy to inspire romance for other people. I'd been sucked in by the slickest of them all; and David had seemed so genuine. I sketched horses, cows, and a few chickens, Old McDonald with white tulle. Damn. How could he skip the, oh, by the way, I have a kid, part?

"That guy is on the back. Banging on the door."

"Go Tony Soprano on him," I said through sips of my mind-numbing potion.

Neil flicked the monitor and speaker back on. "Popcorn, anyone?"

"The kid's gone," Candy said.

"Good," I said.

"It's a different guy. Immigration?" Candy asked.

"I wish," I said, taking a look at the monitor and a big slug of Vinny. "That's my brother, Jeffrey."

Chapter Thirty-Nine

"Let him in, La Tigre."

"I'm most happy to send him to his camper car and snap the other leg like a breadstick."

"It's an SUV, and Jeffrey isn't dangerous."

"He looks dangerous." Candy crossed her arms over her chest. Neil laughed at her and returned to filling cherries with booze.

"He's an orthodontist," I said. "He only tortures children and his wife."

Jeffrey hobbled over to me, his sanctimonious smile embracing full-on righteousness. He pulled out a chair and plopped down at the butcher block, his crutches balanced against the side. "I've never been in your kitchen."

"I've noticed. What do you think?"

"Smells amazing. How do you not get fat?"

"Why don't you have little colored bands on your teeth? Wine?"

"No, thanks. I'm not drinking anymore."

Neil set a cup of steaming coffee in front of Jeffrey and gave him a nod. "I'm going to turn up the music. Helps me think."

"Thanks, bro."

Bro? "Do you know Neil?"

"I've seen him around."

"Interesting—you notice men, too, not only women."

Like curious cats, Candy and La Tigre moved closer than necessary, eyes on sugarcoating violets but ears trained in the direction of my conversation. Neil cranked some extra loud Van Halen to distract the nosy pair.

"Still ordering off the internet?" I asked.

"Nope. I'm in a program, two programs, actually, so Marie let me move home. What about you?"

"I'm signed up for pilates and yoga but never go."

"I meant, what about your drinking?"

I motioned to my glass. "Wine when I cook, the occasional cocktail, and I've never been so drunk that I ordered sex on the internet. I'm good."

"What's your problem? What did I do to you?"

"You're a man."

"I want to help."

"Well, don't."

"This isn't about you, anyway. Mom got an offer on the house. She wants you to look it over." Jeffrey picked up the hot coffee and wrapped his hands around the cup. He gave me a Bambi stare and put a folder on the table. "I know that selling the house is hard for you."

Fuck them both. God, this hurt more than expected. I glanced at the paperwork, and profound grief settled between my ribs and gut, but the lucky charm eating man-boy didn't need to know that.

"Things change," I said.

Mom had measured us against her bedroom door, the night before school started for the year, making a deep notch in the frame along with the date. How would she remember those moments without the house? I thought that she'd be there forever. Did memories mean nothing?

I pushed the folder away, my chest impersonating a wheezy accordion. "I don't want to know anything."

"Are you sure?"

"It's not my house."

"Mom wants your okay," Jeffrey said.

"She never asked my opinion before she put it on the market, so she can't have it now." I reached for the wine. Jeffrey put his hand over mine and stopped me.

"Do you want to come to a meeting?"

"I fucking do not, and don't preach to me. My only problem is the invisible sign on my back that says, 'Lie to me; I'm too stupid to know any better.'" I knocked Jeffrey's hand away and overfilled my glass in defiance. "You and Mom deal with the house. Sell it to Elvis. I don't fucking care."

"I'm seeing a therapist."

"Do you want a paper award or something more substantial?" I took a fortifying gulp of wine and exhaled like a sailor on a bender after fifty-two weeks at sea. Do you want to come to a meeting? Fuck you, Jeffrey.

"I'm uncomfortable about Mom lying to us, too."

"Well, you act like it's no big deal."

"Not having a dad is a big deal. I imagine it's the same for you."

"Jesus, Jeffrey. Stop with the junior therapy routine. I get enough of this shit from Susan."

"Let me help you."

"No thanks, and I'm fine. I have a lot of disappointment in my life right now, but I'm fine."

"You said 'I'm fine' twice."

"Don't count my 'fines.'" I slurped down half my glass. "You better go. Marie's probably tracked your phone."

I was an ass, and being mean to Jeffrey. He was trying to help. My stomach twisted like a hot pretzel, and I wiped away tears. I didn't need his sympathy. I didn't need anything from anyone.

Jeffrey swallowed a few times. "Mom said you want to see Dad. She asked—no, begged—me to stop you."

"It's my mistake to make." I pointed to my chest in case Jeffrey didn't understand. "I'm sick of being the victim of everyone's mistakes. I'll be the victim of my own stupid choices."

"How is that better?"

"Shut up, Jeffrey. Why don't you take your soapbox, some goodies for the kids, and go home to your too-good-for-you wife?"

I stood to pack some cookies, but the room moved, and sitting became the better option.

"I'm going to catch a meeting on the way home. You could come with me."

"Just shut the fuck up, Jeffrey."

I didn't believe for a second that Jeffrey was as even-keeled as he appeared. I recognized a bullshitter when I heard one, as long as they weren't buying me dinner in a fancy place with beeswax candles. Speaking of bullshit, how dare Mom tell me to "do whatever you need to do," then turn around and make Jeffrey stop me.

"Candy? Pack up something chocolate for the kids."

"Why don't you do it?" Candy asked.

"Because devils have glued my ass to the chair."

Neil set down a cup of coffee before me, poured in heavy cream and a spoonful of sugar, and stirred, his eyes never leaving mine. "I'll give you a ride home. La Tigre, pack the van, and we'll take Leanne home, then drop off the Mobs order."

Jeffrey reached out for my hand. "I'll take her home."

"Oh, no, Jeffrey," I said. "I've had enough lecturing for one night, and you better get home before the drawbridge is closed and you have to spend the night outside the city gates with the filth and vermin. Oh, I forgot you like filth." I ignored the coffee, poured another glass of wine, and decided to stop when I couldn't remember what number glass I was on.

"Don't let her drive," Jeffrey said, heading to the door.

"Jeff, wait up. I'll walk you to your car," Neil said.

"You wanna go home, Leannearisima?" Tigre said. "No problems to finish for us."

"Neil is giving her a ride," Candy said.

"Don't you people listen? I don't need anyone to give me a fucking ride."

"Your brother thinks that you need someone to give you a ride." Candy stood before me, arms crossed, her minuscule nose in the air. "So do I."

"Thousand-dollar bonuses all around, except for Candy." I downed the wine and strolled with woozy confidence to the freezer to get my purse. "Sees you guys tomorrow at ten." I fished in my bag for my keys.

"I have the key, Leannearisima. I'm gonna speed you home right now."

Chapter Forty

"I 'm a fancy driver from Roma. I get you home, run back, no problema."

"It's a few blocks, and I'm, how do you say? Fina!"

"I take you pronto. So fast, like a miracle of the speed."

Tigre removed one of his net vests. Overdressed for driver duty? He and Candy shared a lingering kiss, which made me want to vomit.

"Guys, I could be home by now."

"Ciao, il mio amore."

"You could be getting a UTI," Candy said, wagging her finger at me. "And remember, I'm the amore."

"That's DUI, and don't worry. I love the accent, but Sasquatch has never been my thinga." Tigre opened my car door and fastened my seatbelt. His chest hair poked my face. If he got any closer, I'd cough up a furball.

"I can walk."

"Si."

"I'm not drunk. I had a bad day. Amore problema."

"Si."

La Tigre was an exceptionally cautious driver, especially for an Italian.

"I should've let him explain."

"Es good. He forgives you for the evil witch in your spleen."

We drove along in silence. So what if David had a kid? So what if he didn't tell me? I'd put up with cheaters and a guy who took me for thousands of dollars and a damn nice car. Self-loathing crept into my evil spleen like mistletoe smothering a defenseless oak.

"Thank you for the ride," I said, drunk tears threatening again. La Tigre pressed my keys into my palm and looked at me with velvety chocolate eyes. Did he expect more? A tip? An espresso con panna before heading into the beauty of the night?

"Wait, uno memento. I get you out."

"Oh, no thanks. I've had enough armpit for one night." I swung my door open, tripped on the curb, and tumbled face down on the street, my purse a busted piñata.

"Holy shit, Leanne! Are you okay?"

I scooped up lipsticks, receipts, the crap of the every day. "Hey, what happened to your accent? I heard Jersey Boy. Spill, paisan." I sat on the steps and patted the spot next to me.

"Es a miracle. My Inglesa is perfecto."

"I'm-a waiting."

La Tigre sat, his back against the iron railing. He rubbed his GQ stubble, and his eyes were wide open and terrified. If eyes were the window to the soul, he was at bullshit overload and wanted out.

"I've got a confession."

"You think-o?"

He took a deep breath, and then removed a flower from the planter box and yanked the petals off.

"I'm not from Italy."

"That's been established, and leave my flowers alone."

Between the intimate, up-close-and-personal moment with the sidewalk, and La Tigre's ridiculous deception, the haze in my brain somewhat cleared.

"It's not a total lie. My great-great-grandparents came from Italy, but I'm from New York."

"Un-fucking-believable. You lied to Candy, and to me. Immigration terror? Health code violations?"

"It's not my fault," La Tigre said.

"Are you kidding me? How could it not be your fault?"

"I'm shy, a cooking nerd, not a bad guy."

"We'll see about that."

"I met Candy on vacation and thought she'd like me better if I was a sexy Italian. I have body hair and took Italian in school. She liked me so much that I never got around to the truth."

"Where'd you go to cooking school?"

"The CIA, Culinary Institute of America. Not the spy guys."

"I know what CIA means and you a one lucky amico that I need help right now."

"Don't tell Candy. She'll be upset, and you'll be shorthanded."

"You won't give up the net shirts and gold chains in the kitchen?"

"Tight jeans, either. I've compromised my ability to father children, but for now, I need tight pants."

"That's the only good thing you've got going."

"Tight pants?"

"No, you idiot. The culinary chops. Then again, the tight pants are a good idea. Liars shouldn't have children."

By allowing the ruse to continue, I'd rack up a million lousy karma points, but I desperately needed his culinary skills, and damn it, I liked the poor hairy bastard.

"Italian until after the wedding, and then you'll fess up, promise? I have enough drama in my life, and you're right; I can't afford to lose anyone."

"Thank you, Leanne. You won't regret this. I'll work my ass off for you."

"What's your real name?"

"Tony."

Damn. A glimmer of truth lurks beyond every lie. Palms stinging, I stood up and unlocked my front door.

"Buona sera, Tony la Tigre."

I dumped slices of cheese, crackers and a jar of olives on a plate, poured a glass of mineral water, and stripped off for a soak. The plate was balanced on my boobs, the sustenance close to submersion. A green olive rolled off the side of the plate and plunged into the depths; the *Titanic*, stuffed with pimento.

I checked my phone for a text from David, but there was nothing. I should've let David and the kid in. The ghost wife might be looking for a drunken slut of a mom for Michael. I fit the bill and liked the idea of having a kid. They lived longer than dogs or cats. You could get close, and they moved away if you got lucky.

I chewed a soggy cracker and washed it down with water, then I dropped the remaining olives in my glass. *See, Jeffrey? I don't have a problem.* The loss of the house sat like a hundred-pound wheel of Parmigiano-Reggiano on my evil witch spleen.

We could've lived in the house with his bratty kid and his wheezy dog, but the high priestess of lies had sold my childhood home, and heartless bastards would dig up the Vincent Price landscaping to put in a pool. I should have bought the house myself before it was too late. I needed my forever home, a comforting illusion to continue to surround me. La Tigre? Fuck.

I grabbed the phone off the bathroom floor, but it slipped from my wet, drunken grasp to join the lone olive on the bottom of the tub. Gratified and more than a smidge smug, my wise mind enticed me with my favorite old blue sleep shirt and cozy covers. I had other ideas.

— ell —

"Open up, Mom." I leaned against the bell and hammered on her door.

"What happened to your phone?" Mom asked.

"It's drying out."

"I hear that's not the only thing that should be drying out. You smell like your father. Did you drive here?"

"Did your favorite child report back and win a cookie?"

"I don't have a favorite sweater, let alone a child. Why are you being ridiculous and scaring your brother?"

"Can I come in?"

"I don't know, Leanne. Can you walk, or is your butt still glued to devils?" She didn't move, so I hiked past and lay on the white leather couch with my feet on a pillow.

"He didn't get his facts straight. He never does. My butt was glued to a chair, not to devils. Duh."

"Take your shoes off my couch."

"Why are you dressed up again?" I didn't move.

"It's my new thing: wearing silver sequins after midnight. I pretend I'm Marilyn Monroe and have a cocktail party with invisible friends."

"You like pretending, don't you? Like my invisible Dad."

"Don't be rude, Leanne, to Jeffrey or to me. What do you want, anyway?"

"Would you like to make me tea?"

"No, I would not. I'm tired and not in the mood for one of your interrogations, especially when you're drunk. Go to the guest room and sleep it off."

"If you didn't lie, I wouldn't have to be the FBI, would I?"

"What did I lie about this time?"

"Can't you keep track? Maybe this will ring a bell: 'Go ahead, do whatever you want?'"

"Oh, you should have known I didn't mean it."

"How could I possibly know?"

"I'll make you tea."

"Sure, and use loose leaf, something that steeps for a year. That will give you extra time to fabricate your next ruse."

"You are ridiculous. No one's out to get you."

"Then why does it fucking feel like it?" I yelled.

I slipped off my shoes because *I* wanted to take them off, wrapped the white, furry throw over my head, and tucked it around me. Like a Russian fairy tale princess off for a walk on the tundra, I stalked around the living room, pissed at the world, but mostly at myself.

Three new black-and-white photographs in silver frames graced the wall. One of Jeffrey, Marie, and the kids on a beach; my graduation from college with my arm around Susan; and an eight-by-ten of Mom pregnant with Jeffrey or myself, or maybe some other kid she'd never mentioned. They must be special to have made the decorator cut. Equally fascinating was a grand piano that I'd swear hadn't been there the other day.

"Hey, Liberace? Do you want candlesticks for Christmas?"

Mom had changed into a pink velour tracksuit. It was possible that this woman wasn't my mother at all, or that Paulka had taken her shopping blindfolded. I'd never seen her in pink. She set a black lacquered tray on the coffee table. A stream of amber-colored liquid made its way into jade green porcelain cups with delicate gold rims. More pirate plunder, no doubt. She took her tea and settled across from me in a new white leather chair.

"When did you decide to leave your lucrative cooking career and become the high holy inquisitor on a permanent basis?" She slipped a lemon slice into her cup. "I don't have to tell you anything."

I added a splash of brandy from the decanter on the coffee table. "Did you tell Jeffrey not to let me talk to Dad?"

She scowled and put the decanter on the floor between her feet. "Maybe yes, maybe no. I might have said such a thing, but I can't remember."

"Try? For me."

She sipped her tea, put the cup down, picked it up, and took a second sip, swallowing what little concern she had for my needs. "I said, 'Jeffrey, she's going to dig up something so ugly and twisted, she will never undo the damage.'"

"Then why the fuck did you tell me to do whatever I wanted?"

"Who am I to stop you from a world of hurt? So be it if you won't let me protect you anymore."

"Protect me from what?"

She twisted and turned her bracelet. Ha! That was probably her liar's tell. I'd ask Susan later if I remembered.

"It's late, and you're yelling and swearing and drunk."

"Is Beethoven coming by to give you lessons by moonlight?"

"I have a private teacher coming by early tomorrow, not that it's any of your concern."

"Jeffrey's already cornered the market on midlife crises and no offense, but you're a little old."

Mom snatched my tea cup and gathered the rest of the tea things onto her tray. They rattled like the skeletons in her closet. "Don't you dare be so mean to your brother. He's trying to change."

"You always come to his rescue."

"I've always come to yours. I am not the enemy, Leanne."

I grabbed my half-full cup off the tray and swallowed all of it, to her evident annoyance. "Oh, yes. Tell me more about my evil bastard of a father, and I'll think about not talking to him."

"Promise me you won't."

"I can't."

"Promise me you'll slow down the drinking."

"How about you promise me that you'll stop lying."

"I have nothing to tell you, " Mom said, sinking back into her chair, the tea tray on the coffee table.

I wouldn't be a great mother, but at least I'd never lie. I'd answer any question at any time of the day or night.

I gathered my shoes and shoved my feet into them. Fuck the laces. The furry blanket hung from my shoulders like a superhero cape. "I have some apologizing to do if you're not talking."

"It's about time. Your behavior is outrageous, and your brother has enough going on without you adding to the drama."

"Why is everything about Jeffrey?" She tried to stop me from leaving, but even tipsy, I was fast on my feet. I had no web of lies to slow me down.

Chapter Forty-One

I sat in my car outside Mom's building, not ready to face David. I wasn't completely stupid; I shouldn't be driving. I leaned back in my seat, a full moon flirting behind the clouds. All those parties had trained me for deep thoughts in the middle of the night. A normal mother would have forced me back to bed, not fed me caffeine-laden chocolate. I took my phone out of the bag of rice I'd buried it in and called Susan. I could listen through the crackling noises how to apologize for being a horrible bitch to a sweet guy who didn't deserve it.

"Hey, a quick question about David?"

"Go ahead."

"Why wouldn't he tell me he had a kid?"

"Because he doesn't have one. Anything else?"

"There was a kid at his house, and he said David is his dad."

Susan laughed. "Michael? That's his nephew. He comes over once a week to hang out. Michael is very protective of David since the death. It's a trauma response. Gotta go."

A reasonable person would have asked questions before she hung the accused. An intelligent person would apologize and leave the country. *Fuck my life.* Between the constant feeling that men can't be trusted and the ultimate liar's lies, was it any wonder I had issues?

It was over. Why would David forgive a relationship-phobic, untrusting person who didn't understand the first thing about intimacy, whose mother never had a good word to say about men, except for the phony gold standard in a borrowed coffin? I called David, but he didn't answer. I left a genuinely pathetic, please call me, and hunted for a napkin to clean the steamed-up window. My phone rang, the excitement lasting only for a moment—Paulka, not David.

"Hello, Paulka."

"Darling, I have exciting news from the rose-colored telescope of the future. The ladies decided to move the wedding to this Saturday. They couldn't wait another minute to hitch the horsey wagon. Isn't that romantic?"

"Paulka, please put Levi on."

"So snippy. Are you in one of those hormonal things?" Paulka asked.

"No, sweetie. This is my new normal. Where's Levi?"

"He's talking to Sophia. Working out details. He says they've reduced the guest list to only close friends and family."

"Good, how many?"

"One hundred and nineteen."

"I'm getting a one-way ticket to Vegas."

"You hate Vegas, all those trashy dessert buffets, so I know you're joking. Let me tempt you back from your craziness. *Vanity Fair* is covering the wedding."

"Do I get a trip to Tahiti as a bonus?"

"Levi, she says ..."

"Bye, Paulka. Hanging up to book my trip."

I tossed the phone in the back seat. *Vanity Fair*? It's a good thing I loved Levi. I trusted him to make this work, and the publicity would be spectacular. Imagine that. I did believe someone.

I rummaged through the mess and found an old notebook and pen. It didn't matter that the pad was tiny; the list of people I trusted would fit on a Post-it. Why did I trust Levi? He had no agenda, loved me as I was, and he'd never leave me.

Someone rapped on the glass, and a nose scrunched and distorted pushed against the steamed-up window. I screamed.

"You've terrorized me enough. Can't you leave me alone?" I said after recovering my wits from the backseat.

"If you'd look up, I wouldn't have pounded on your window," Mom said. "Come back upstairs."

"I'm going home, after I drive a stake through my frozen and useless heart."

"Leanne, either come upstairs or let me in the car. People will think I'm picking up a hooker or doing a drug deal."

I unlocked the passenger door. She fingered the breathing bracelet hanging from my rearview mirror. "I thought that I was doing the right thing."

"This isn't about judging you. I want to understand what happened so I can fix what's wrong with me."

"You were a judgmental child."

"You made me that way."

"I made a terrible mistake, and when I thought it couldn't haunt me anymore, it rose from the dead."

"Dad?"

"No, not Dad. I made my peace with that rat bastard recently. You and Jeffrey both ..."

"Me and Jeffrey, what? What do you mean?"

"I thought I'd cushioned you both from my mistakes, but look at you. Both of you drinking like a fish, Jeffrey ruined his marriage, you with terrible men because you think that's what you deserve—both of you are victims of my choices. There, I admit it. It's all my fault. Is that what you wanted?"

Once the careful camouflage fell away, she revealed a woman, wracked with decades of guilt and remorse. We sat together, connected by the chains of culpability. I wished I'd stopped the questions, the relentless desire to know. I turned away, traced a D on the window, furious at myself for ruining my chance with David.

"It's getting cold. Let's go upstairs," Mom said.

"You sure? I don't want to push you anymore." I grabbed the blue breathing beads and pushed them over my hand.

She wiped her eyes on her sleeve. "You wouldn't be my daughter if you didn't push for the truth."

Chapter Forty-Two

M y mother gave me a mint-green tracksuit to put on. The soft velour was soothing, like hiding inside the Easter bunny. The rhinestone "Sexy Babe" on my ass I could do without.

"You don't wear this out of the house, do you?"

"It's my farmers' market staple. I get a discount from the tomato man. He calls me Miss Sassy Pants."

"You're kidding."

"His name is Gerald. He owns an organic hydro-something farm."

"And?"

"We've been dating for six months."

"Is he why you moved?"

"Gerald knows about real estate, among other things, and this apartment was a steal."

"I thought you moved because Dad showed up."

"Let's say that his arrival expedited things a bit."

"Ha! Trick question. So, you did leave in a big hurry. Are you scared of Dad?"

"I wanted to be closer to Gerald."

Was it cruel to drag her back into a past she'd chosen to bury? Not my fault. She forced me to squeeze it out, drop by painstaking drop. She'd always had the option to tell the truth. I could have worked my issues out years ago. I rechecked my phone: nothing from David. I sat on her couch and tore at my cuticles.

"I'm happy for you, Mom. You should have someone to spend time with."

"What about love?"

"Since when do you, of all people, trust men?"

"I've changed my mind."

"Well, aren't you a miracle."

"Gerald says that I shouldn't brand myself a mistake."

"Too bad it took you forever to figure it out."

We sat in silence, like sugared almonds in our pink and green outfits. Neither of us were willing to dive deep into our flaws nor in the mood to stir the absolute bottom of the reality pot.

"I've chased security by avoiding love." Mom said.

"Are you taking an online therapist class by any chance?"

"Don't be ridiculous. Gerald is extremely perceptive, and we talk about these things. I'm ready. Ask me anything."

The blue bead bracelet came with instructions. Breathe out stress with the old air; breathe in peace with the new. I tried a few rounds of bracelet breathing, but anxiety had a better sales pitch, and I hyperventilated. "Did you love Dad?"

"Initially, he made me feel like I could reach my dreams. I'd never had anyone who believed in me. Who doesn't want that?"

"Did he love you?"

"Our first Valentine's Day, he bought me a bouquet tied with a Rest In Peace Beloved ribbon and was livid when I complained. I should have been grateful since he'd been working; it had gotten late, and not a single florist was open."

"That sounds like something Scott would do. Surprised by a day that shows up every single year? Imagine that. What made you leave him?"

Mom fussed with a vase of exquisite, out-of-season lilacs on the coffee table. It was a telltale sign that she was stalling. Wondering which version of the truth would do the least damage.

"I'm going to make us more tea." Mom said and disappeared into the kitchen. She returned, surprisingly quickly, with two simple white mugs and a look on her face that I didn't recognize.

——— *ell* ———

Jeffrey swung the hard plastic cowboy toy straight into Patricia's face as she stopped him from falling. Stars danced before her eyes, and tears of pain blinded her. She sat down hard on the worn red floral carpet and patted her cheekbone and eye socket.

"Damn it, Jeffrey."

Baby Jeffrey looked wide-eyed at her; his rosebud of a mouth trembled, but he didn't cry.

"Mommy? Are you all right? Did Jeffrey poke your eye out?" Leanne asked.

"It's fine. It was an accident."

"He's bad like Daddy."

"No, Jeffrey's a baby. He didn't mean it, and your daddy's not bad." Patricia pried the cowboy from Jeffrey's grip. She gave him a soft teddy bear, which he smacked into the carpet.

"Does Daddy mean it?"

Patricia took Leanne's hand in her own and forced an animated smile—anything to avoid the question. You didn't tell a child her father was a rat bastard.

"Let's make a cake as a surprise for Daddy when he comes back."

"When's he coming back, Mommy?"

"When he finishes work. He's a hard worker."

"You always say that."

"Then it must be true."

Patricia dug through the few pots and pans and looked for the one cake pan that she owned. The kitchen was nothing but a wall of cupboards with missing doors and cracked shelves. A pathetic assortment of cooking things sat in a milk crate high on the counter, out of reach of inquisitive little hands. The yellow and gray checkered vinyl floor peeled up at the corners. Patricia taped it down, and when it wouldn't stay put, she put cans of peaches over the worst spots.

She should have seen the place before moving in, before they married, but Verin had only taken her to fancy hotels. When she first saw the apartment, he said the place would be fine with a lick of paint and complained about her shallow concerns. It was horrible, near the train tracks, and falling apart. It should have been condemned. What had happened to the money that he used to flash around? Tipping piano guys ten bucks a pop, drinking the best scotch, and all those hotel rooms? He barely gave her enough money for groceries, let alone something nice for the kids.

"Why didn't you get the stove fixed, Verin?"

"I didn't need a stove, baby; I go out to eat. I bet you want to make me gourmet dinners, so I'll get my baby a brand-new stove."

"Could you get the landlord to fix the cabinets and the floor?"

"Sure, baby. Anything you want."

"I'd really like it painted. It's run-down, Verin."

He put his hands on her shoulders, slid them down to her hips, and pulled her close to him. She could feel his arousal. Not again, she thought. She was three months along, and sick throughout the day, but that didn't stop Verin. With the moves of a generic lover, he kissed her mouth fast and moved to her neck, her breasts. He slapped her hard on the rear and walked her to the bedroom.

"Come on, baby. Let's see if you can earn yourself a new kitchen."

She never got a new kitchen nor new wiring for the old one. She'd been shocked by the stove several times, but Verin only laughed and told her to make a salad or use the toaster. Patricia found the cake pan and slapped it down hard. Tears stung her eyes while her face throbbed, her eye starting to bruise from Jeffrey's toy. She hated Verin for disappearing, smelling like another woman's perfume, and bringing home doghouse flowers. To show her how good she had it. Bastard. He said that she nagged. She would have stopped if he didn't give her plenty to nag about.

"Do you want a nap?" Leanne asked.

Patricia looked down into worried, green-gold eyes. Her baby girl was right, she didn't want to bake; she was exhausted. She hadn't slept for days. Besides, Verin would be livid if they weren't here when he returned.

"Why would we want to sleep when we can make a beautiful cake?" She patted the seat of a chair. "Climb up here, baby girl, and help me."

Thank God Leanne didn't know the difference as they mixed an egg with leftover rice, the last breakfast cereal, water, and an overripe banana. Patricia could barely see out of the swelling eye. She crushed a half-empty bag of frozen peas to her cheek bone while Leanne stirred the lumpy batter.

Leanne put a finger in the batter and licked it off. "I saved my Easter bunny. We could melt it and make a chocolate cake."

"That's a good idea, or you could put it on the top."

"I ate the ears."

"The bunny can go upside down. Daddy will think the rabbit is hiding."

Patricia kissed the top of Leanne's head so the child couldn't see her tears. She had a keg of tears, always on tap. No wonder he stayed away. Verin hadn't been home for three days. She had no idea where he'd gone or when he'd return. Part of her wished he'd never come back. She'd told him that before he left her with no money, no car, and a bridge so burned that she could never go home.

She scraped bits of rice off her engagement ring with a fork. The yellow stone Verin had claimed was a rare kind of diamond, a canary since she sang like one. She'd since found out singing like a canary wasn't a good thing, and neither was the worthless piece of yellow glass. She rested her head on her arms, the peas melting. Maybe she should throw them into the cake batter. It wouldn't matter. She remembered that first night with Verin. What a naïve fool she had been. Desperation made a fool of anyone. It was her mother's fault. Damn her to hell for pushing an innocent girl into a snake's bed.

Mom picked up her mug, cradled it against her cheek. "Leanne, you have to understand something. There were two kinds of men in those days: good guys and bad guys. There was one kind of woman. The kind that looked the other way when she had to." She sipped her tea and shuddered. "Your dad was one of the bad kinds. He'd disappear, drunk for days at a time. No shame, no remorse—he didn't bother hiding anything."

"Did you get married because you were knocked up?"

"We weren't married."

"The lies roll right off you like Twinkies on a conveyor belt. You wore a ring. Why didn't you tell me?"

"Deep, painful shame, Leanne. Why would I advertise such stupidity?" She tore the lemon slice from her tea into tiny triangles. "I bought the wedding band after he died."

"He tricked you? You thought you were married?"

"Would you want your kid, of all people, to think you're a class-A idiot?"

"Mom, I wouldn't have cared."

"Do you want to know more? It's not a pretty story."

"Yes. All of it."

It was after midnight, and the kids were fast asleep. Patricia lugged a basket of Verin's laundry into the bedroom, set up the ironing board, and heated the iron. She sprayed starch onto Verin's shirts, then ironed and folded the way he'd shown her. He wanted the shirts to look brand new from the department store, so they must be folded, never hung.

She took the finished shirts to his dresser and attempted to open the drawer, but it wouldn't budge. She set the shirts on the bed and pulled hard with both hands on the drawer. It wrenched out of the dresser, and in the back was a photo of Verin and the priest who married them. Both were dressed in brown cassocks with wooden crosses around their necks. She didn't understand until she saw paper cutouts of pumpkins, witches, and black cats overhead and recognized the bar at Bluebeards. "Halloween 1955" written on the back of the photo.

The wasps stung so hard that they made her breathless; she dug through her bottom drawer where she kept the kids' birth certificates and her wedding license. She ripped open the sealed envelope. Verin and Duke had signed their names; she'd signed it too, after several glasses of champagne. She held up a Sears appliance service contract with glued gold seals over the washing machine picture, screamed, and ripped it into oblivion.

"Are you making this up?" I asked.

Mom poured another cup of tea. "I couldn't believe it, either."

"Assuming it's true, why didn't you go home?"

"Leanne, I'd fallen for a fake marriage. That was worse than a real one."

"Did you at least try to talk with your mom?"

"I met her in a coffee shop down near the wharf when I was eight months pregnant with you. She bought me a tuna melt and a glass of milk. She ordered clam chowder and dumped bag after bag of oyster crackers in her soup. She said she'd told people I'd been on my way to a choir audition in Fresno, got hit by a truck, and burned to a crisp on the interstate. Nobody to bring home for burial. Better a dead daughter than a family embarrassment. Pour me one of those, will you?"

She finished her tea, and I filled her cup with brandy, a few drops spilling onto the glass table. I wiped them with my finger and put them in my mouth.

"Coincidental that she died by fire. Anyway, now you know where I got the idea to kill your father," Mom said. "Pretend he'd gone to Heaven."

"Your mother did that? You know how horrendous this story is, right?"

"That's why I chose to keep it on a need-to-know basis and figured you never needed to know."

"Didn't Ginger help when Jeffrey broke his arm? Someone knew what was going on."

She tilted her chin and squared her shoulders. "Ginger figured it out, but I couldn't bring myself to call her. She never said so, but she hated Verin, and I didn't feel I had options. I gave the hospital a bad check."

With both hands over my eyes, I had no words for the insanity that filled my ears. Could the whole crazy story be true?

"I'm sure she was convincing ... lots of crying, praying, and extra cookies for St. Tarcisius. I've never understood why she hated me so much." Mom took a long swallow of brandy. "You look a lot like her, except for her height. She was crazy but beautiful."

Truth or lies, this was the most I'd ever heard at one time. I stayed quiet, listening and learning.

"If she hadn't been dead, she would've been livid, because a lawyer found me years later, and I got my share from the fire settlement. Dad made sure they were well covered."

"It's hard to believe that your dad or your brother Bob didn't look for you."

"They believed her or didn't want to question her. Until that lawyer showed up, no one that I know of looked for me. Anyway, it's not all bad. I bought our house from the owners and paid for Jeffrey's education—yours, too."

"Why didn't you contact your brother and the twins?"

"I made the same mistake that I made with you. I didn't want to ruin how they felt about Mom. How can anyone have a chance at happiness if they suffer as a child? I wanted you and Jeffrey to have a chance, so I kept a few things to myself."

"More than a few things ..."

"Does what you know change anything?"

A lifetime of information poured down and drenched all reasonable thoughts. I wanted David's calmness to wrap around me and make all this craziness go away. I checked my phone—still nothing.

Mom stood and kissed the top of my head. "I'm not counting, but you've had at least three teacups of brandy. There's a new bed in the guest room. Why don't you try it out?"

"I need to go home."

"I'll get you a nightgown and a toothbrush."

Aching sadness took me to my dark place. I'd ruined it with David, my one chance at a good guy, and Dad might be a rat bastard after all. I looked around for the decanter, but it was gone.

Chapter Forty-Three

D epressed and drunk, I let Mom tuck me into bed. She switched
off the bedside lamp and settled into a cozy armchair.

"I'll stay until you fall asleep."

"Can I have a bedtime story? A true one?"

"The truth won't help you sleep."

"Does Gerald know everything?"

She sighed into the darkness. "No one does."

I yawned and nestled deep into the buttery softness of mom's million
thread count sheets. "I'm listening."

Verin tossed his keys, wallet, and hat onto a wooden table by the front
door. He staggered into the small living room, crowded with an ugly red
three-piece couch set he'd bought without telling Patricia. He flipped on
the television, lit up a smoke, put his feet on the coffee table. The stench
of bourbon rose from him like a humid, sweaty swamp.

"Where have you been? It's been days."

"What's it to you? You don't want to be in my bed. It's not good enough for you? Beautiful girls are a dime a dozen, Vivi. You better watch yourself."

"Can you turn that down? You'll wake the kids."

He ignored her request and patted the cushion next to him. The stench of booze mixed with another woman's scent wafted off him. Patricia held her ground.

"It's too loud," she said from the kitchen, arms folded across her breasts.

"I deserve a little relaxing."

"Didn't you hear me? The kids are asleep."

"Tell you what, Vivi. Stop your bitching. Do something useful for a change and mix me a drink."

She didn't want to fight. Before he disappeared, they'd taken the kids to Golden Gate Park. Money rained from his pockets for caramel apples, saltwater taffy, and a boat ride on the fake lake. They'd bundled up the kids when it got chilly and held hands on a plaid blanket, watching the fireworks. He told her she looked like summer, that he needed her sweetness, and that he'd always love her. She'd pressed against him and wished it was true.

Days later, the familiar mixture of tobacco, booze, and yet another mystery woman swirled off him. She'd been a fool to believe it would be different.

"I'm going to bed." She handed him a scotch on the rocks. He took it with one hand and pulled her down with the other.

"Stay up with me. Get yourself a drink—loosen up, for Christ's sake."

"I'm tired, Verin. Jeffrey will be up before six, then Leanne."

"I'm up now," he said, and rubbed his crotch. His whiskey-soaked breath suffocated her as he leaned in close to kiss her. She turned her face away, her stomach clenched with fear and loathing. He laughed and moved to her shoulder, his wet mouth sliding over her skin, fingers fumbling with the tiny pink buttons on her nightgown.

"Stop it, Verin. I told you I'm going to bed."

"What's wrong, Viv? Getting it someplace else?"

"Oh, sure, in between diaper changes, I dance naked for the mailman."

"I bet you fucking do." He pinned her arms above her head and leaned down to smell her crotch.

"What the hell are you doing?"

"Checking for mail."

She wrenched both hands from his grasp and pushed his head away. "Stop it, Verin." He sat up and stroked his stubble. Never a good sign, but tonight she was fed up, didn't feel like letting him have his way.

"I'm not like you, Verin. I would never cheat. I have principles and morals. You wouldn't know anything about those, would you?"

"Getting mighty upset for a girl claiming innocence."

"I am innocent."

"Prove it."

"No."

"Show me, Viv, or I'll know you're getting it somewhere else. I'll get you watched. Maybe I already have." He pinned her down, his muscled thighs alongside her body to hold her still.

"Let go; you're hurting me."

"Do you like it when he hurts you?"

"What him? What the hell are you talking about? Are you crazy?"

"Crazy for you, baby. What happened to my sweet girl?" Verin captured her wrist with one hand and used the other to stroke her cheek. "Why's my baby a bitch?" His voice had dropped to a whisper.

"Maybe if you didn't leave for days at a time. If you cared about the kids and me."

"Didn't I take you to the park? Don't I make sure you have enough money?"

Patricia didn't answer. Staring up into his eyes, she considered how to keep him quiet without giving in.

"I appreciate what you do. I'm sorry. I don't mean to nag."

"Good girl. Kiss me, Viv."

"Give me a moment to brush my teeth. I'll be right back."

He smacked her hard on the rear as she got up. "You better be."

Patricia locked herself in the bathroom, turned on the sink faucet, and sat on the edge of the tub, exhausted. It was like living with Jekyll and Hyde. She couldn't go to him when he was like this, not when she knew he would hurt her.

Last time, Leanne asked if a wild dog had bitten Mommy's neck. Good thing her baby girl hadn't seen the rest of her body. Patricia brushed her teeth and stared at herself, haggard at twenty. She'd questioned him after the first few times. He said that he couldn't remember; she knew he did. In the beginning, he brought flowers the next day, took her out to dinner if they could find a sitter, brought home takeout if they couldn't. A gentle knock on the door and she opened it to a miniature version of herself.

"Mommy?"

"Hey, baby girl. What are you doing up?"

"Can't sleep. Jeffrey's crying."

"Go and sing to him, Leanne. He likes that."

"He's wet and stinky."

"Oh, no!" Patricia held her nose, and Leanne giggled. "Okay, let's go change him. Shhhh, now. Daddy's asleep in the living room."

Patricia lifted Jeffrey from his crib, wiped his runny nose, and looked for a fresh diaper. One left out of seven. Would this child ever be potty trained? Verin wouldn't buy anymore, said she had plenty since she had nothing else to do but laundry.

"All right, little man, try not to pee anymore tonight."

Jeffrey looked at her. Wide eyes and smiles. He was an easy toddler, not like Leanne, who hated going to bed. She claimed a smelly monster came into her room when she fell asleep. Patricia knew all about monsters, so the light stayed on until Verin came home, turned it off, and claimed that no one would waste his money.

"Sleepy time, sweet ones."

"Jeffrey's thirsty. Me too."

She hoped Verin had passed out on the couch. Patricia didn't want to risk waking him by going to the kitchen.

"You had enough milk at dinner."

"Please, Mommy?"

Her baby girl was thirsty. Couldn't she get some damn milk from the kitchen? In her own house? The wasps stung.

"Go to bed. I'll bring milk."

"Juice, please?"

"Sure, baby girl. Sing to your brother."

Patricia slipped past Verin into the kitchen. He'd turned off all the lights, and his cigarette glowed in the dark. No light meant he was dangerous. She filled a bottle with milk and Leanne's kiddy cup with the last of the apple juice. His shoes tapped the floor behind her. Cold sweat trickled between her shoulder blades as she topped up the juice with water.

"I'll be right back. The kids need milk."

"They can wait."

"I'll be a minute."

"Viv, I said they could wait."

"I don't have much. At least give me a goddamn minute to take milk to my kids."

He knocked the bottle and the cup from her hands, and they fell to the floor. The last of the milk swirled around sharp fragments of broken glass.

"You don't have much? How is that? Here, let me give you something."

Verin dragged her to the couch, pressed her face down into the scratchy red upholstery, lifted her gown to her neck, and trailed half-melted ice cubes down her back. The kids stirred, and she willed them to stay put—there was no telling what Verin would do if they came out. Without warning, without a sound, he entered her. Hard, sharp, painful thrusts, all the while biting at her neck, her shoulders, anywhere he could reach. She lay stiff and silent as a corpse. Verin could be the gentlest, the sweetest of lovers. He could also be as evil as they came.

"You're a whore, Vivi. My little girl who likes it rough. Bet your mailman can't give it to you like I can."

Done, he flipped her over. Tears spilled down the sides of her face and soaked the couch cushions.

"I'll give you something to cry about."

"I'm crying because you're such a lousy lay. You're right. The mailman is better."

He slapped her hard across the face. She tasted blood in her mouth, and knew that she should have kept quiet, but all the anger, frustration, and hurt boiled up and canceled all thoughts of self-preservation. She wanted to hurt him the best way that she could. He traded hostile lust for fury and smacked her across the face again, shook her by the shoulders, the force knocking over a heavy glass table lamp.

"Mommy?"

"Go back to bed, little girl, and take Jeffrey. Now!"

"Mommy, are you okay?"

"Leanne, go to bed!" Patricia said, yelling at her daughter for the first time. Jeffrey hid behind his sister.

"Goddamn it, Vivi. Get them out of here."

Patricia pulled herself up from the couch and pulled her gown to cover her body. Bruises behind her eyes began to swell. She needed ice, and needed the kids to get to bed. She needed a new life.

"Come on, baby girl. I'm so sorry. Mommy didn't mean to yell. Let's get that juice."

What had the kids seen? Her mind raced with the wretched possibilities. Did children remember? Jeffrey was too little, but what about Leanne, her smart baby girl?

"Can't you do anything right? I'll put them to bed," Verin said.

"No, Verin. I'll do it."

"I said I would. Go clean yourself up. You're a mess." Verin reached down and swooped Jeffrey under his arm like a package. The little boy lifted his arms out to Patricia and began crying. "Silly Mommy. She hit herself with the lamp," Verin said to Jeffrey.

"Give him to me."

"No, he's my son, or so you tell me."

"You put him down, Daddy," Leanne said.

"Look what she's learned, Viv. How to be a bitch like Mommy."

Jeffrey cried louder as Verin manhandled him. Leanne tugged at his pants, which were falling off. He swatted her away with the back of his hand. Leanne made a fist and hit the only part of him she could reach: his groin. He dropped Jeffrey like a sack of garbage; the baby screamed. Verin stumbled down the hall after Leanne, belt in hand. She shut herself in the bathroom and locked the door. Jeffrey howled on the floor, his arm at an impossible angle. Verin stumbled back to Patricia trying in vain to fasten his belt around his waist.

"You broke his arm." Patricia cradled Jeffrey against her chest, smoothing his head and making soft noises to calm him down. Her heart pounded so hard that she thought she might break in half.

"I didn't do anything. Leanne made me drop him."

"He needs to go to the hospital."

"You're overreacting. Get some ice. He'll be fine."

"I swear to God, you drive me there or I'll kill you one day."

"Good luck with that."

Verin grabbed his keys and hat and headed for the door.

"Where in the hell do you think you're going?"

"Out."

Chapter Forty-Four

F ace planted into a soft pillow, I woke up and snuggled back under the yielding covers, unwilling to move. Fragments of Mom's story came back: Jeffrey's arm, terrible yelling and fighting. Why hadn't I remembered before now? More pieces came back to me, images fading as I tried to grab them tighter. Did I imagine them to fit her story? What was real?

We spend most of our lives avoiding what is accurate, and as I snuggled into her thousand-thread-count brave new world, I wanted to believe her more than I'd ever wanted a dad. Women left men who cheated, wanting something better for themselves and for their children. I'd confided many a man-mess to Mom, but she didn't know all the details.

She didn't know about the guy who took secret naked pictures and blackmailed me into getting them back. She didn't know about the guy who had a thing for dime bag hookers, who after morning coffee and a quickie, said I should get tested. Maybe I understood her reluctance to disclose—after all, I did the same thing for the same damn reason.

A huge weight lifted from my soul as I swung my legs over the bed and embraced the idea that, in believing her stories, I could have a new world, too. I didn't have to like what she'd done, but I understood it and I could let it go. I checked my phone—still nothing from David.

I walked into the kitchen. "Good morning," I said. "Your new bed is heaven."

"Coffee?" Mom asked.

"How long have you known me?" I kissed her on the cheek and planted myself at the breakfast bar. Her apartment looked pretty in the morning light.

"You look lovely in pink. Keep the nightie."

"It's too innocent for me." I sipped my coffee, well rested for the first time in ages.

"Thanks for talking last night."

"Do you still want to meet him?" Mom slipped a slice of sourdough into the toaster, poured grapefruit juice into glasses, and passed me one.

"I don't know what I want."

"Gerald says the truth, however painful, is better than temporary happiness." She tried not to smile.

"One of these days, I'd like to meet Gerald. I'd also like to hear 'Chopsticks' on a grand piano."

She laughed, a deep, throaty purr. "I can play. My mother taught me. Hymns to baby Jesus and St. Tarcisius. I think she made up 'Where Art Thou Crumbs of Confession.'" She sipped her coffee, calmer than I'd seen since Jeffrey's accident.

"You're like a box of Cracker Jacks, aren't you? It's always a surprise along with the treat. I'd love to stay for the recital, but I'm going to swing past David's and see if it's too late for triage."

"I'll drink to that," Mom said. We clinked coffee cups. I smeared a piece of toast with peach and ginger jam from an embossed jar with a fancy label.

"Can I take a shower and borrow the green tracksuit?"

"I thought you hated it."

"Seems to work for you."

"Okay, but I need it back. Sentimental reasons."

Mom actually blushed. I needed to meet this Gerald, and soon. I blew her a kiss and went to shower, and to put on mint-green confidence with rhinestones.

I pulled up in front of his house and checked for a text from David. Nothing. His car was in the driveway, and enthusiasm for a heartfelt apology began to stick in my throat. I kept the engine running in case a quick getaway became necessary. Craving reassurance from the king of calm, I called Levi.

"You don't call, you don't write, you don't text. Where have you been?" Levi asked.

"You're a helicopter parent."

He didn't laugh. "You're a diva."

"What is that supposed to mean?"

"I emailed you the final wedding details. Radio silence isn't a good look. Leanne, this is the second time this week."

I bowed my head against the steering wheel. I'd seen the email, and the texts, but for the first time in my career, I'd blown Levi off. Terrible, horrible person.

"This wedding could put us all on the map. I need your focused, laser-like perfection. Leanne, I won't sugarcoat this; you're making me as nervous as Marie Antoinette in a guillotine showroom."

"Levi. I'm on it."

"Fabulous. Are you at Kook? Ready to work?"

"Not exactly. I'm at David's. I'm going to throw myself at his mercy, and then I'm all yours."

"How old are you again?"

"Why?"

"You're behaving as though you've never had a boyfriend."

"He's the first one worth counting."

"Make it quick and get your gorgeous ass to work before Paulka needs smelling salts and a Xanax."

"Where's your faith in me?"

"In the witness protection plan until this wedding is over."

"One mistake and this is what I get?"

"You've been slipping."

"Since when?"

"Ask the olives in your next martini. Paulka is hyperventilating. The Dutch tulips arrived frozen with mold, and the tumbleweeds wouldn't hold still for gilding. Ciao."

I turned off the engine as guilt and shame set up camp together in my chest. Levi, my forever cheerleader, had retired his glittered pompoms? I couldn't blame him. My wise mind nudged me—whatever happened with David, I could live with it. I nudged her back, but I'd never forgive myself for losing him.

I walked up to David's front steps. A paint-speckled drop cloth covered the porch. A painter brushed by me as David walked out, backpack over one shoulder. I prepared myself to take whatever he dished out. I deserved it, but I'd start with small talk. Transparency was hard, and I was a beginner, after all.

"What's with the painters?"

"I needed to freshen the place up."

"Oh." Paragraphs of possibilities ran through my brain, none of them positive. He stood in the doorway, smiles for the painters that came in and out with brushes and ladders, but nothing for me.

"Did you need something?"

"To talk?"

"I'm late for work."

"My mom's boyfriend says truth is better than temporary happiness."

"Wise man."

"I shouldn't have assumed that you lied to me." I talked to a handsome slab of concrete. This silent, brooding man was a side of David I hadn't seen before. Angry? Sad? Disenchanted? All of the above, no doubt. "I'm so sorry."

David folded his arms. "I don't get it. You believed a kid you've never met was telling the truth but assumed I would lie to you?"

"Michael told me that you were his dad. Why wouldn't I believe him?"

"You think I'd hide a child from you? Why would I do that?"

"It made sense at the time."

"You expect men to lie, don't you?"

"I warned you, flawed is my middle name."

"You did, indeed," David said.

"I know I've been unfair."

"You didn't give me a chance to explain. I made Michael buy those flowers with his own money to apologize for lying to you. That's how strongly I feel about truth."

"Can you forgive me?"

"Would it make any difference? Would you believe me the next time your insecurities get the better of you?"

"You're not making this easy."

"There's no point in having a relationship if you can't trust me." He sat down on the steps, rested his head on his knees, and looked up at me. "You're the first person that has ever doubted me, and I don't like it."

My heart fell out of my chest and landed next to David, cracked in half.

"Relationship?"

"I had hoped that we were headed in that direction," David said.

"What about now?"

"Damn it, Leanne, you're making me feel like an idiot. I have women being thrown at me by every medical department known to man, and yet I wonder what kind of Christmas trees you like."

"Douglas fir."

"Can you handle radical honesty?"

"Define radical."

"You drink too much, live in a world of hurt you won't deal with, and a baby bat has better communication skills."

I'd heard enough. I turned away, left my broken heart on the steps, and walked to my car. Disappointment roared through my veins, into my head, making it hard to hear, see, and walk without crying.

His hand gently grasped my arm and turned me around. "Why are you leaving?"

"You gave me a Dear Jane face-to-face. I don't need or want an autopsy of our short yet amazing relationship that showed promise until I fucked it up." I knew I was ugly crying, but I couldn't stop it. "If nothing else, please believe how awful I feel. You deserve so much better, and I have no business expecting you to put up with me." I took his hand off my arm and continued to the curb. My nose dripped, but Mom's tracksuit didn't have pockets for tissues. People with sparkly words on their ass must never cry. I wiped my eyes with my sleeve and fumbled with my keys.

"I don't give up easily," David said.

"Just because you can, doesn't mean you should."

He wiped away a tear that slipped down my cheek.

"I'm giving the booze a rest."

"Your liver thanks you."

"I'm working on my hurts, too."

"Glad to hear that."

"My communication skills may never be better than a baby bat."

"I'm willing to take my chances."

"I can guarantee you'll have an easier time with someone else. I wouldn't blame you if you walked."

"Just because you can doesn't mean you should," David said and pulled me close.

I laid my head on his chest, remembering the best kiss of my life, the one where I knew his thoughts like they were my own. I lifted my head, and my lips found his. Relief surrounded me like a protective orb. We made up for the time already missed and promises already broken. If I wanted to make this work, the bubble wrap had to come off for good. I'd have to take the same risks that he took. He pulled away to look into my eyes.

"What are you thinking?" David asked.

"About taking off my bubble wrap."

"I love it when you talk dirty."

"I've got a plus-one for a celebrity wedding. I hear the desserts will be spectacular."

"Are you going to trust me?"

"Yes."

"I believe you."

Chapter Forty-Five

My heart back in one piece, I let Madeleine Peyroux's "Don't Wait Too Long" swell from the speakers. I waved goodbye to David and got a breath-stopping-hand-over-his-heart and a wink for my trouble. My wise mind sang along, thrilled that I'd stabilized my dark and desperate ways. My minions were hard at work when I walked in, bright-eyed, and exuberant. Neil handed me a cup of coffee, his eyes positively starry. He'd listed possible dessert options on the whiteboard, leaving out a wedding cake. The ladies didn't want to be conventional. Imagine that.

"A crêperie in a barn stall would be a first," Neil said.

"Tell me more."

"Stone-fruit fillings have a western feel—think old-school canning—but we do it high-end. Nectarine coulis, brandied plums, poached white peaches and cream." Neil sipped his coffee and watched me.

"With a sprinkle of edible gold dust, you guys might have given me a reason to live," I said. "The wedding's in two days."

"I'm gonna make flaming clouds of gold," La Tigre swung Candy around the kitchen.

"Oh, Paulka left a message," Neil said. "The guest list changed again. I think he said four hundred, but it could have been forty. It's hard to tell with all the rambling. Does Paulka run?"

"Only after Brazilian men when Levi's not looking," I said. "Why?"

"There was lots of heavy breathing and panting."

"Maybe a heart attack," Candy suggested.

"Panting means the headcount is four hundred, not forty," I said. "I can't believe this. Kill me now."

"This breathing sounded like a sexy time to me."

Knowing the truth about Tony, his faux-Italian sounded ridiculous. How could Candy not realize? Amazing what someone could miss when they didn't want to see the truth. I put a hand over my lips to hide my smirk, and reined in the desire to spill all I knew.

"The best dessert of my life was in a tiny pâtisserie in Reuil-Malmaison," I said. "It was a layered peach and almond blancmange with raspberry purée, and heart-shaped cookies edged with dark chocolate worth dying for on the side."

"I'm gonna sculpt a tiny edible gold horse for the top." Tony flexed his arms.

"Okay, but no stallions," I said in an exaggerated Italian accent and gave him a tiny smile and a wink.

The door buzzed, and Candy peered at the front-door monitor. "Hey, your brother's here, and he's got donuts."

Jeffrey showing up uninvited with donuts couldn't mean anything good. Donuts, like kids' cereal, meant Jeffrey was depressed. If he had bear claws, he'd done triplets in a cheesy motel.

Candy opened the door, peaked in the box and squealed. "Thanks, Jeffrey. Buttermilk bars. I love these."

"Hey, Jeffrey, can this wait?" I asked. "We're super busy right now."

Jeffrey stood still, head hung low, a gym bag slung over his shoulder, leaning on his crutches.

"I'm gonna make espresso for the, how you say, the American ring-a-dings," La Tigre said. "I want the jelly sprinkle princess one."

Neil took the donut box and dug out a chocolate covered one smothered in crushed peanuts.

"Ten-minute break, compliments of my brother, then hit it," I said. "No more screwing around. Save me the coconut one. La Tigre, I'd kill for an espresso."

"Can I stay with you for a few days?" Jeffrey asked.

"She kicked you out again? What did you do this time?"

All three chefs watched us with sugar-covered mouths. Candy licked jelly off La Tigre's net shirt. He smiled at me and shrugged.

"Not in front of the children," Jeffrey said.

"Ten minutes, guys. I mean it." I took Jeffrey's gym bag from him and led him to the walk-in.

"In here?" Jeffrey said. "It's freezing."

"It's private."

"Haven't you seen the movies where they lie down in the snow—"

"I don't have time for this today. Give me the nutshell version."

"The kids found a browser window I forgot to close."

"Not good."

"Marie says they are scarred for life, and this time I'm not coming back."

I was frustrated with Jeffrey, but I understood. Change is hard, and it doesn't happen just because you want it. "Anything else?"

"Can I have one of these beers?"

"You're not making this worse by drinking. What happened to your special meetings? Can't you call someone?"

Jeffrey grabbed a head of butter lettuce and threw it at the metal wall. Neil walked in, interrupting the assault on his produce.

"Neil, give me five."

"You better come now," he said. "I can talk to Jeffrey."

Jeffrey hurled another lettuce.

"Candy left."

"What? Why?"

"She heard La Tigre on the phone with his American mother."

Oh, no. Not today. "Jeffrey, stop with the produce. Where'd she go?"

"Leanne, I'm freezing," Jeffrey said. "I've been in my car all night. Can I go to your place? Please?"

"Go to Mom's abandoned house."

"It's tented for termites."

"I don't need this, Jeffrey."

"I'll take Jeff to your place and look for Candy," Neil said.

"Hell no," I said. "You have to work."

"I'll look for her," Jeffrey said. "Cute blonde, right?"

I sighed, shut my eyes, and prayed to Julia Child. "Go straight to my place. No drinking. No internet. Promise?"

"Leanne, I want to make this right. I'll do anything."

"That's what I'm afraid of."

Chapter Forty-Six

Around midnight, I sent Tony and Neil home. I had no idea where Candy had gone, and although I felt her pain, I couldn't spare anyone to look for her. On my way home, I stopped for necessary non-booze supplies and planned a long soak in my tub. When I arrived at my place, Jeffrey lay face down on my couch, his phone clutched in his hand.

"I've got rum raisin, mint chip, and double chocolate cherry fudge," I said.

"Marie won't pick up her phone, and three cars are in my driveway."

I tossed Jeffrey a coloring book and crayons. "Don't stalk your own house. It's creepy. She's entitled to comfort, you know."

"I don't want her to tell anyone. It's humiliating."

I put the mint chip and a spoon on his back, settled myself in a chair, and ripped open a family-sized bag of sour cream and onion potato chips.

"You cheated, you lied, and you've made her question her entire life with you. Leave her alone."

"Could you go? I'm worried about her."

"Snoop for you?" I dug out an extra-large chip and bit it hard. "Hell no."

"You look like crap," Jeffrey said, rolling over and pulling the lid off the ice cream.

My back was killing me, and my fingers resembled bird claws from cutting out hundreds of horses in edible gold leaf with a tiny blade. I wanted a drink. A small one to help me relax. Besides, no one eats potato chips without a drink. A white Russian wasn't a real drink. More like a dessert. Almost like chocolate milk. I dusted potato particles off my lap, headed for the kitchen, eyed the vodka, and grabbed the rum raisin. Jeffrey nodded toward the ice cream in my hand.

"David said you stopped drinking."

"He told you? When did you talk to him? Today?"

"I shouldn't have said anything."

Jeffery put a massive spoonful of ice cream in his mouth, grabbed the Baby Animals at Easter coloring book, and drew a yellow bikini on a bunny. I stroked my breathing beads and counted down from infinity.

I left Jeffrey to further desecration and spooned the hectic day away, one faux-boozy raisin at a time, in my bubbly bathroom temple. My phone rang, interrupting communion with my last vice: high-fat dairy products. I draped a towel around my dripping body, hoped it was David, and rushed to the kitchen where I'd left my phone,

"Brett hasn't come home," Susan said.

"That's not like him. It's one a.m. Did you call the police?"

I detoured by the freezer and returned to my tub with the dark chocolate cherry fudge.

"I need to talk to Jeffrey," Susan said.

"Jeffrey? My Jeffrey? Why? How do you know he's here?"

"I can't tell you." Susan's voice cracked.

"Are you crying? Susan, answer me. I can't help if you won't tell me what's wrong."

"Have you forgotten that I'm a lawyer?"

"Just because you eat children for breakfast doesn't mean you can't bare your soul once in a while." She didn't laugh. This was serious. "What's going on?"

"I can't get a divorce. I know what happens. Please get Jeffrey."

"Don't make me figure this out."

"Leanne, not now. I'm begging. I need Jeffrey."

I wrapped the damp towel around me, unlocked the bathroom door, and padded into the living room. Jeffrey had his back toward me, his laptop open, and his earbuds in, oblivious to all potential consequences. He basked in the glow of a highly fake orgasm. I snapped the laptop closed, then plucked his earbuds out. The coloring book slid onto the carpet along with whatever shred of dignity he had left.

"How long have you been standing there?"

"Long enough. Susan's on the phone for you. How does she know you're here? Does she know about this issue of yours?"

"Yes, she does. Give me the phone."

"Leanne, give him the damn phone," Susan said.

"I'll take it in your bedroom if that's okay," Jeffrey said.

Was Susan counseling Jeffrey for sex addiction? Did Marie hire her for the divorce, and she was giving Jeffrey a heads-up? Are Brett and David out on a double date with Crystal and a neurosurgeon? Oh, my fucking God. Was Susan Jeffrey's most recent option?

"Don't touch my stuff." I turned my back on him. "I'll be on the couch. Thinking."

—ell—

At four a.m., right on schedule, the wolf howled, not that I'd gotten a minute of sleep. I headed to Kook to finish the wedding order and tossed my phone into the walk-in fridge for peace. I put on a little Chris Isaak to lower my blood pressure. I'd bang out everything except the choux pastry. I was baffled over the Susan and Jeffrey thing, and quite frankly, I didn't want to know.

Something rustled behind the couch. I grabbed a slotted spoon and a ladle and snuck toward the suspect sound. The rustling stopped; the sofa moved. My heart pounded. I lifted the spoon and crept closer.

"Don't hit me." Great. The fake Italian popped up, Candy right next to him.

"Don't whack him, Leanne."

"Ouch, that hurt," Tigre added.

"I should stab you both."

"With the slotted spoon?" Candy asked.

They both giggled.

"I'll explain," Tony said, the fake Italian back on.

"No more Italian, or I'll hit you again."

"I love his Italian. Makes me feel special." Candy threw her arms around him. Tigre grabbed her and pulled her close.

"Do you want a glass of prosecco?" Candy asked.

"I'm not drinking," I said, flopping down on the couch, heart returning to its usual stressed-out beat. "You forgave him?"

"Of course I did. Why would I have a problem with a hot Italian guy I can't keep my hands off of?"

"He's a Jersey boy with a bad accent who's with you under false*tto* pretenses."

"He loves me."

La Tigre, a.k.a. Tony, nodded. He put his arm around Candy, his face nothing but serious.

"We plead the young and stupid defense," she said. "We want to finish the wedding."

"No more drama? No leaving? No matter what?"

"I'll make you an 'I'm sorry' omelet to prove it," Candy said.

"She makes a magnificent omelet." Tony ran a whisk up Candy's leg. She squealed like a piglet.

First David, then Candy. This forgiveness thing was getting interesting, and I was hungry.

"Fine, but use a clean whisko."

Chapter Forty-Seven

M ollified by a sublime crab, gruyère, and spinach omelet smothered in lemony hollandaise with a pinch of Cajun spice, I relaxed in the security that the wedding of the decade would go off without a hitch. I headed home to apologize to Jeffrey and to get some much-needed rest, but he'd left. Hopefully, he'd gone home to Marie, where he belonged, and not to an all-night massage and pizza parlor. Exhausted but edgy, I forced myself to bed with Julia Child's *Mastering the Art of French Cooking* and dozed off in the middle of Pâtes and Terrines.

When the no-longer-soothing notes of Pachelbel interrupted my tenuous rest for the third time, I tied my robe on and figured that Jeffrey was back in the doghouse. Damn it. Susan graced my doorstep, her eyes devil red from crying, two medium paper coffee cups in her hands.

"Latte?" she asked.

My world was officially rocked off its axis. Susan didn't cry. Susan had nothing to cry about. She followed me into the living room, and we sipped in silence, a poignant ten minutes, each with a personal vat of excellent coffee.

"I'm sorry that I thought you and Jeffrey might be cheating."

"I would never cheat, not with your brother, God knows." Susan sipped her latte. "You're kidding, right?"

"Of course, I'm kidding." Kind of. "Why did you need Jeffrey?"

Susan lowered herself to the floor into the lotus position, filled the moment with as much serenity as she could muster, took a massive breath, and blew it out, along with enough tears to fill in the Sea of Galilee.

"Brett's a sex addict. Strip clubs and massage parlors," Susan said, leaving the lotus position for a flat on the back-starfish impersonation, breathing in and crying out.

"Brett, the wonder husband?"

She nodded and sniffed. She rose, went to my bathroom, and returned with a roll of toilet paper. She unrolled most of it and blew her nose. "He's two years sober, that means no acting out but last night, when he didn't come home? I guessed where he was and called Jeffrey to get him from the club. Brett is Jeffrey's sponsor. Isn't that ironic?"

It was no wonder that she was taking online therapy classes and studying psychology with a vengeance. I should have guessed, and not been so self-absorbed. No one could be as perfect as she'd made Brett out to be.

"Whoa. I had no idea. When did you find out?" I pulled pillows off the couch and made a nest on the floor.

"I suspected when we were dating and I busted him after our honeymoon when he didn't want to do the couples massage at the hotel but had a business card in his swim trunks from Happy Day and Night massage that he hadn't thought to mention." She unrolled the rest of the toilet paper and blew her nose again. "I made as many excuses for him as he did. I thought I would be enough ..."

"You could have told me."

"You wouldn't understand."

"How can you say that? I'd be there for you."

"You have a black-and-white view of the world when it comes to men. Think about it, Leanne. He's a professor at a major university. He could lose his job, and except for his addiction, he's a good husband." Susan pulled her make-up bag out of her purse and fixed her face. She put in eyedrops without looking. Obviously, this wasn't her first rodeo.

"What do you expect from me? Mom told Santa to keep his hands where she could see them at all times. According to her, all men were dickheads."

"You are not your mom."

"Don't make this about me. You didn't tell me because you can't stand anyone, including me, to see you as less than perfect."

We went back to our sides of the boxing ring. Imaginary trainers wiped imaginary sweat from our brows, and we rinsed our mouths and spat into our buckets—ding! Ding!

"You date dickheads to confirm that all men are dickheads. It's not rocket science."

"It's early. Why don't you see what Pavlov and Jung think about dickheads after lunch to confirm your diagnosis? You could be wrong."

"You blame David for things that don't exist except in your screwed-up psyche. That's the dumbest thing you've ever done. He's one of the good guys!" Susan yelled at me, which was bizarre, since she never lost her cool.

I sipped my latte and smothered the urge to yell. She needed to vent. Like the good friend I am, I continued to provide content. "I had probable cause, and get off my case."

"Leanne, you can't trick me with your pseudo-lawyer-speak. I invented it. You're so terrified to accept that a man can be decent that you fuck it up for yourself the first time—"

"Brett gawks at naked women on tabletops. Probably likes the homey kind, the complete opposite of his fabulous wife. Heather Hee-Haw, glues saltines on her nipples with Velveeta."

Susan slapped her thighs and stood over me, hands on slender yoga toned hips.

"See? It's not funny, and I knew you wouldn't get it. Brett's a good guy with a problem, like Jeffrey, like a lot of men, like your dad. How do you *know* he's a monster?"

"What's that supposed to mean?"

"He loved your mother, but he had a problem. It was a different time, so she couldn't deal with it, and he didn't know what to do. The world's changed; he could have changed."

"It turns out Dad's a definite dickhead." I headed to the kitchen, popped bread in the toaster, and pulled down two plates. "Eggs?"

Susan shook her head. "I'm fasting, except for coffee. It doesn't count."

"You said not to meet him. Would you please make up your mind?"

"Are you sure, or is this another reason to convince yourself that the good ones are one lie away from screwing you over, and now you have someone to blame?" Susan said.

"It took years to understand that Brett's addiction has nothing to do with me."

"Not everything's about you?" I smiled.

"Bitch." She smiled back and took a handful of shortbread Scottie dogs from the cookie jar.

"Maybe my dad's not a total dickhead?"

"We aren't our behavior, which means that we always have the ability to change. You don't know for sure that your mom's telling the truth.

Maybe there's another version out there, but you'll never know. That's two possibilities he's not a dickhead."

"You're pretty optimistic for a lawyer. Don't they teach that right out of you in school?"

"Everyone has a story, Leanne. Everyone."

Chapter Forty-Eight

Susan left after I'd promised that in the future I'd listen without judgment, keep the Brett the Wonder Husband mocking to a minimum, and she'd eaten all my cookies. Everyone has a story, indeed. Still bleary, I made a pot of coffee, and took a cup back to bed. A dozen options ran through my mind, none of them worthy. I gave up crafting the perfect blast from the past monologue and called Dad, with no plan. I'd winged my way through worse. I put the phone on speaker, set it on my dresser, out of my trembling and suddenly sweaty reach, and perched on the edge of my bed.

"Hello?"

"Hi, I'm Leanne, your daughter. I got your number from Jeffrey, your son."

There was silence. He cleared his throat—there was more silence. My heartbeat thudded like a Highland drum just before a gory battle scene.

"I know Jeffrey's name. Are you okay? You sound a little nervous. Why don't we meet in person? It might be easier, and I don't like phones. I've got to see someone's eyes—you know what I mean?"

His voice was smooth and deep, a soulful tone somewhere between Mufasa and Tom Jones. I wanted to get this over with as soon as possible.

I'd meet him for lunch, ask him about the marriage certificate, and watch his face for the truth.

"Good idea. How about today?"

He didn't answer, which made me nervous. After all these years, how could he wait another minute? I should have let him call the shots. Did I sound too needy?

"I have plans, but nothing I wouldn't change for you. How about La Folie the day after tomorrow? I'll need to make reservations. Eight?"

Couldn't he meet me sooner? I plugged in my newfound ability to reserve judgment—this was a big deal, and he wanted to make an impression. I couldn't begrudge him, and after so long, what difference did a few days make?

"Sounds great. I've been dying to taste their desserts."

He chuckled, and I couldn't help but smile. I was having dinner with my dad, and he didn't sound like a monster.

"It's a date. I'm glad you called, Leanne."

"Me too."

I pulled into the alley, in time to watch Candy and La Tigre slide the last trays of delectable goodies into the van.

"Hi guys, take a kissy break, and we'll head out," I said, unrolling my car window.

Neil leaned against the van door, an unlit cigarette dangling from his mouth.

"Tell me how you know Jeffrey," I said.

"He's your brother," Neil said.

"And?"

"Met him in AA."

"Why didn't you tell me?"

"Unless you know the whole story, there isn't any point in sharing a chapter. To be honest, I thought you'd judge me."

"You can tell me now if you want to; I promise I won't judge. I'm in the will-not-judge program."

Neil laughed and put his cigarette back in the pack. "Thanks. I might do that someday."

Neil, Candy, and La Tigre went ahead in the van. I followed them in my car, over the Golden Gate Bridge, and out toward Napa. The long ride meant more time to reflect on my apparent deficiencies as a human being. Was I as black and white as Susan said? My best friend didn't trust me enough to confide a substantial reality of her life. It was pathetic, but eye-opening too. Who knew that my trust issues were more about myself than them?

Ancient oaks wound up the long, gravel-strewn driveway leading to a fairytale French country estate. Dozens of paparazzi greeted me at the high stone wall, just before Snow White's cottage, which had at least seven security guards. I flashed the security brooch Levi gave me, rolled through, and parked.

Paulka met me with a half-ass double cheek kiss and a head-to-toe gaze while taking in my dark glasses, and a somewhat fake let's-do-this-thing grin. I looked like crap, but since the desserts were ravishing, he'd forgive me and chastise me later, but I knew that he was disappointed.

"Well, look what the goat dragged in? At least the barn looks fabulous. It came from Provence. They assembled it like an Ikea bookcase. Come, I'll show you."

"This place doesn't have a western theme and where's Levi?"

"Use your imagination! It's the best we could do at the last minute, and he's in the dressing suite with Phoebe. She's having a moment."

"Have you lost your touch? The brides cry on your shoulder."

"Are you in a mood again?"

"No."

I followed Paulka to the barn, where my crew unloaded a miracle. Neil had met all my expectations and then some. He would be an excellent business partner if expansion became a reality. My team made me proud with their crisp chef whites and determined faces, and the presentation was beyond compare. I looked forward to growing my business since it was the only thing I could get right, with a little help from my very own minions. Maybe a lot of help.

"Paulka, I need to find Levi, and get someone to move these goats."

White ribbon and tulle twisted around upright wooden posts, with honeysuckle, roses, and peonies cascading from the rafters. The air was glorious, minus the earthy tang of the animals.

"Darling, the miniature goats are accessories and lend a credible note."

The herd, complete with floral head wreaths, were hardly authentic, but maybe I was as black and white about live decorations as I was about men. I said nothing.

"Paulka, your friends are eating the flowers," Candy said, holding her nose.

Horrified, Paulka scurried out—no doubt on the hunt for a wrangler dressed like Heidi.

"I kinda like the goat thing," Tony said, kissing Candy's cheek. She entangled herself in his arms and leaned in for something hot and heavy.

"You two, focus, please. This is a simple wedding. Two people who love each other, making a forever commitment. Can't you tell? Now put on your cowboy costumes."

Who was I to judge two detail-crazed women wanting to make soul binding vows in a luxurious, faux Wild West setting. Not my wedding, not my goats. The dining and dancing area was canopied by night sky painted on silk with tiny lights spread over ancient oak trees. The usual dedicated minions, this time dressed in leather chaps and Stetsons, arranged golden tumbleweeds and silver grass around whitewashed tables. Strategically scattered flowers and silver sheriff badges announced a Who's Who of Hollywood. Levi and Paulka had outdone themselves, except for the goats, which had Paulka's brand of crazy written all over them. It was some childhood fantasy, no doubt. I bet Mom told him the singing goats story.

Two horses, one white and one black, stomped and swished while a team brushed and braided manes and tails with fragrant blossoms and silky ribbons. I usually deliver and leave the actual serving to Levi and Paulka's minions, but the behind-the-scenes was fascinating, and Phoebe was only a stroll away.

A deputy came by with a tray of tempting mimosas and offered me a refreshment. I may be a shitty friend, but I like to believe I have one redeeming feature: I keep a promise. Further along the tree-lined path, "When You Say Nothing at All" by Allison Krause filled the air as the band rehearsed. It was the perfect choice for a wedding. Relationships are easier when everyone keeps quiet. My wise mind shushed me, and I stilled my inner bitch, but the song got to me. I'd never been sentimental—correction—exposed enough of myself to have a song with anyone, but if I did, this would be the one.

The heaping pile of romance lured me into wondering pensively what could be with David if I could keep it together. Lost in thought, I walked smack into long white robes covered with glittery stars and moons. Rays of palpable calm radiated off this woman like a mirage and pulled me into what felt like authentic serenity.

"I'm so sorry. I should look where I'm going."

"Not a problem. I'm Mona. I'll be presiding over the nuptials." She appraised me with wide-set hazel eyes and luminous mahogany skin. "You are?" she said, offering her hand.

Whoa. My wise mind would love this woman—serious good vibes.

"I'm Leanne, with catering. Do you know where the brides are dressing?"

"I'm heading over there now. Levi texted me. Sophia hasn't shown up, and Phoebe is beside herself."

"Oh, don't worry, she'll be fine. Happens all the time."

She patted my arm and smiled at me. "Not with my weddings, it doesn't."

"Some people think getting married is terrifying."

She looked down at my hand and back up to my face. "Never been married?"

"Never found the right guy."

"Refreshing to hear you have standards and don't settle."

Did she mean it, or did she feel sorry for me? I glanced down at Jeffrey's name, blinking on my phone.

"Excuse me. I need to take this, my brother. Family comes first." Even if they act like animals.

Mona nodded and walked ahead, her robes billowing in the warm breeze.

"Hey, Jeffrey. How are the hookers in your life treating you?"

"I prepaid for a year and gave them David's address," Jeffrey said.

"Always thinking of others. I'm kind of busy. Did you need something?"

"Marie let me move back in. Separate bedrooms, but it's a start."

"Don't screw it up again. Sometimes you don't get another chance."

"I'm doing hypnosis with Susan. Trying to stay on a good path."

He sounded so perky that I couldn't confide that Susan was using him as a guinea pig or share about my talk with Dad. He'd worry, tell Mom, and she'd get difficult and might even lock me up in Alcatraz. As the song said, it was better to say nothing at all.

Chapter Forty-Nine

I found the bridal suite and beheld what looked like a wake in progress. Heavy drapes blocked out the brilliant day. Empty bottles of booze crowded the tops of tables, jockeying for space with magnificent bouquets of peonies, roses, and lilies—the scent suffocating in the closed room. Phoebe wailed and moaned, her head against Mona's magnificent bosom, sobbing like her heart was broken for eternity.

A tall, imposing brunette dressed in business formal stopped me at the door, handed me a nondisclosure agreement and an expensive-looking pen, and plucked my cell phone from my grasp. I signed my name on the document and put my palm out. Without a word, she and my phone left the building. Levi sat on the edge of the bed, arms and legs crossed. He rose and gestured for me to be quiet and follow him.

"Levi, Wonder Woman stole my phone."

"Don't worry, she'll give it back. Tempers are a bit frayed. Come with me."

I looked back toward the distraught Phoebe, her pain touching a place I chose never to visit. Nothing was worth that kind of torture. Levi hustled me into the connecting room which had a single vase of flowers and better air. He sank onto a white chaise and put his feet up. I lay back on the brass bed, wishing to share the heavenly softness with David.

Arms behind my head, I stared up at a bronze chandelier hung with chunks of real quartz.

"Levi, I'm not stupid. This is more than a bride having a moment. What the hell is going on?"

"I love it when you're soft, girly, and sensitive."

"I'm a cynical bitch, a terrible friend, and an ungrateful child. Shall I go on?"

"None of that is true, and you know it."

"What's happened? Where's Sophia?"

"We don't know, but we do know that she's been cheating for two months with a country singing penis."

"Been there. It's brutal, but one lives on. What was the name of that guy? Skylar or Sam? Slinky! That's it. So many jerks. I can't keep them straight."

"Leanne, for a smart cookie, you do not see the magnitude of the impending crisis. Hollywood marriages are like royal weddings. You don't send four hundred guests and the paparazzi home without the wedding they came for."

Levi lifted himself out of the chaise and pulled out a confection of a gown from an armoire. Josephine Bonaparte and Paulka would have mud-wrestled over it. It featured an empire waist, ivory silk georgette, thousands of tiny seed pearls covering the bodice, and a matching veil. It was breathtaking if you liked that kind of thing.

"Hold the dress in front of you. I want to see something," Levi said.

"No."

"Can you ride a horse?"

"I said no."

"You look enough like Sophia to pull this off. Leanne, you're our only hope."

"I said no, Princess Leia. Hey, why don't you call Mom? She looks like me and enjoys lying on a grand scale."

"I'm desperate and begging."

"Try Paulka; we're the same size."

"He doesn't look like Sophia."

"He loves cowboys."

"He's scared of anything bigger than a goat. Leanne, I promise that no one will ever find out."

"I need a drink," I said out of habit and rolled the blue beads up and down my wrist.

Unaware of my latest resolution, Levi poured me an eighty-proof bribe on ice. I wanted to drain it, flip it over crystal ball style, and harness its powers of mystical observation. Should I fake a wedding in front of hundreds of people? How many karma points would be sacrificed? I put the drink on the nightstand, took a calming breath, and mentally thanked the bracelet.

"I can't."

"Please, Leanne."

"I invited David to the wedding. He's all about truth, honor, and the full good-guy Boy Scout pledge. Lying will not compute."

Levi gave me sad puppy eyes.

"I'm sorry, really, but there's no way he'd understand, and I'm on thin ice as it is."

Phoebe wailed, and we rushed in to find her in the dark recesses of a massive armoire. Mona sat on the floor, peering into the void, white robes surrounding her like a biblical cloud. I'd had a serious girl crush on Phoebe for years. She was gorgeous and damn funny, her characters heartbreakingly real, and her raw magnetism impossible to resist—nothing like this devastated shell of a woman on the supposed happiest day of her life.

"Pass me something. I'm going to vomit," Phoebe said.

I dumped out the only thing handy, a silver ice bucket, passed it into the dark closet, and crouched next to Mona.

"Phoebe, come out. I've fixed the wedding. Leanne's going to stand in for Sophia," Levi said, using his sweetest voice, the one reserved for small animals, children, and me, when a man-mess reached its natural consequence. Its magic was powerful; I was caving.

Mona got face-to-face with Levi, down on the ground, way past the ropes of personal space. "I will not mock the sanctity of marriage." Love you, Mona.

"I'm not doing any mocking either," I said and gave Mona a thumbs-up.

"Madam, with all due respect, I don't think we have a choice," Levi said, helping Mona to her feet.

Did he call her Madam? This was serious.

"I'm not about to officiate a fake wedding."

A weak voice came from the closet. "Mona, please. Oh, I'm going to puke again. The pills didn't mix with the tequila."

"Leanne, could you call David? She needs medical attention that's discreet and fast."

"Levi, can I talk to you in private?" I asked, pulling him back into the small room.

"What happened to the girl that can't say no?" he asked. "Think about the paparazzi at the gates. Don't you want to protect Phoebe?"

"How do you know David won't spill the beans?"

"My intuition's never wrong. He's Abraham Lincoln, Gandhi, and Atticus Finch sprinkled on a red velvet cupcake."

"I can't ask him for anything out of the ordinary. I made good over the daddy mistake. Can't you call some Hollywood doctor?"

Coyote-like yips and long, drawn-out wolf howls came from the closet. Levi crossed his arms, gave me a long look reminiscent of my mother's zombie stares, and pulled me back into the main room.

"Watch her. I'll be right back," Levi said and headed onto the porch, clutching his phone.

Phoebe crawled out from the closet and rolled on her back, clutching a delicate lace veil speckled with vomit. Her sapphire-blue eyes looked up at me. This shattered creature, broken down, vomiting up her dreams, was the most beautiful woman I'd ever seen.

"You do look like Sophia. Would you cheat on me? Oh my God, I want to die," Phoebe said.

"Are you planning on throwing up again?" I asked.

"Are you a doctor?"

"No, pastry chef, but I know about drinking."

She put her weak, nymph-like arms out to me, incapable of moving. Her eyes closed, long lashes fanning on her ashen cheeks. I'd kill for lashes like hers; they were even longer than Jeffrey's. I leaned down to roll her over when, like a mummy awoken from a thousand-year curse, her eyes flew open, and she gripped my wrists and held me fast.

"I'm begging you. I'll give you anything you want. Please, I need you to be Sophia."

I pulled my wrists from her grasp, sat on the carpet, and traced the flowers in the pattern. "I understand how you're feeling, but a fake marriage isn't going to help. Get a couple of pints of ice cream and watch a movie, one of yours. It hurts, but not for long."

I sounded like a bad women's magazine handing out prepackaged crappy advice. She cried harder. I went for the namaste angle, hoping she'd stop sobbing.

"Truth is better than temporary happiness." I put my hands together in what I hoped was the serene cat pose.

She choked on sobs. "You think this is about me? I love Sophia. I want to fake this wedding to protect her. The public will crucify her for cheating on me with him."

"I don't want to be rude, but are you acting right now? You're terrific; and according to legend, I'm extremely gullible."

"Leanne, right?"

I nodded, though I was wary like Wile E. Coyote coming around a blind bend, the Roadrunner high above a ledge with a boulder.

"Can't you understand the life-or-death necessity of protecting someone you love?"

She was using my mother's rationale against me. It was amazing. She was making me question more than a wedding ceremony. My wise mind wanted an autograph, and I wanted to be sure I wasn't being worked.

"You sure this isn't about your career?"

Phoebe pulled herself up to a sitting position, tears like a river. She held her hands out and nodded for me to take them. "Leanne, I swear to you, I'm telling the truth."

Sobbing came from above—it was Mona. Great, gushing blubbering redirected my vacillating conscience. She floated down, kneeled in front of Phoebe, and held her. Levi returned and sat on the bed, amused with the happy ending and thrilled he'd saved the day.

"Please forgive me; I didn't understand. I'm honored to protect what you deem sacred," Mona said.

"Leanne?" Phoebe asked. "Please?"

All three of them watched me. I trusted Levi, respected Mona, and couldn't let Phoebe down.

"I need to cancel my plus-one and I'll only stand in for the ceremony. Levi, figure something else out for the reception."

"Not a problem. You can ride off into the sunset and stay there," Levi said.

Phoebe crawled onto the chaise and shut her eyes. "Someone get hair and makeup. And hand me the ice bucket."

Chapter Fifty

"Levi, give me a minute," I said. "I need my phone to call David and cancel."

"He's already on his way, and why would you cancel?" Levi said. "Explain the lovely thing you're doing. He'll understand."

"Damn it, Levi. He's a geriatric doctor, not a puke specialist."

"We know him, and he's better than discreet. He's kind."

"Behind my back? How could you do that?"

The bad juju had started already. You could burn in hell for less than faking a wedding.

Levi took my hand and pulled me into the smaller room. "David understood the situation and was happy to help."

"He isn't like us. He's normal, nice—he doesn't understand. Nice people don't do things out of desperation."

"That's what you think," Levi said.

The bedroom door flew open, and Paulka waltzed in singing "Here Comes the Bride." A three-person makeup and hair team trotted behind him and set up glam camp.

"Paulka, stop singing this minute," I said, turning to Levi. "No offense, but since when can hair, make-up, and The Model keep the scandal of the century classified?"

"Stop complaining, or I'll wear the glorious dress and ride a goat." Paulka held up the gown and posed in front of the floor-length mirror, eyes closed in romantic bridal bliss.

A fake deputy came through the door with a magnum of Dom Perignon and tri-tip sandwiches. Waves of nausea ripped through me. Sweat, like the beads on the bottle, broke out on my neck and dripped down my spine. I wanted to change my mind and get out of dodge. Normally, I'm the head honcho of the it's-just-a-piece-of-paper posse regarding marriage. What did I care that I was part of this façade? This wasn't real; it didn't matter, and I'd have another thing in common with Mom.

I reached for a crystal flute tied with a white satin ribbon and filled with bubbly. With the last golden drop, my conscience returned, and deep remorse showed up for the reckoning. I put the flute on a table and backed away. I'd broken my promise to David. I was a useless idiot. I blinked back tears and made my nose run.

"The faux bride's emotional, how darling," Paulka said, handing me a tissue. He clapped his hands, and his beauty team transformed me into a reluctant bride desperate for a refill. I didn't ask for one.

Muffled voices came from the other bedroom, and a bed creaked. I made out David's voice as he whispered soothing words to Phoebe. A spark of jealousy pricked my gut. I knew Phoebe was half-naked on the chaise except for a vomit-speckled veil, her waist-length blond hair floating around her like a fairy princess, and she was on a serious bender.

David would carry her to the four-poster bed and put an IV in her fragile arm to inject a bag of fluid into her gorgeous body—all with chivalrous calm and a two-year long lack of sex.

"Leanne, snap out of it. Rebecca can't apply eyelashes while you're making banshee faces," Paulka said.

"I don't see why makeup is necessary," I said. "Wrap me in tulle like a mummy, put me on the damn horse, and let's get this over with."

"Because," Levi said, walking back into the room, "although we've moved the ceremony another twenty feet away from the audience and banned all cameras, you need to look like Sophia, and thank God she likes heavy makeup."

"Don't let David in here."

"He'll calm you down. I'll get him."

Paulka swatted Levi's arm. "What are you thinking? It's horrendously bad luck. Have a minion put a blindfold on Dr. David until the charade is complete. On second thought, I'll blindfold him myself."

"You're both silly," Levi said. "How's it bad luck? She's not a real bride."

Tears flooded my eyes, and Rebecca had to fix my lashes—twice. Two hours later, a sad Sophia lookalike in a fabulous dress looked back from the mirror.

"Pass me an ice bucket."

High on my borrowed mount, a gentle breeze teased my gauzy veil. Dizzy with fear, I stroked General Lee's sweaty neck, baffled by the poised Phoebe. She was exquisitely calm, not showing a single sign of the hot mess she'd been only hours before. I bet she'd begged David for sedation, and how could he refuse? Atop a high, flower-strewn pedestal, Mona nodded to us, her composure intact. I nodded back and wiped sweaty palms on the beautiful dress.

"Dear friends, we gather today to celebrate Sophia and Phoebe acknowledging the forever commitment student of love honor. Marriage, like all worthy relationships, is equal in its gifts and sacrifices. This is the path you have bravely chosen, and we bless those who walk this commitment in grace, for the learning of love is a force beyond all others.

Marriage tests what it means to be human, what it means to be fearless, what it means to let go of our weary and wounded egos. The gifts of patience, faith, and the never-ending search for our best selves are opportunities that test us. The opportunity to be your best possible self is what you offer your beloved as you join each other in the spiritual journey of this lifetime and perhaps the next."

I sunk into Phoebe's wide-eyed gaze and allowed the depth of Mona's words to sink into the deepest part of me, my Mariana's Trench, where fish without eyes lurked. Phoebe honored what Mona said. She'd told the truth and done the right thing by Sophia regardless of her heartbreak. Humbled by her example, I took her hand, hoping to learn to do the right thing, regardless.

"In the depths of their feminine powers, Phoebe and Sophia accept the divine and generous gifts of the goddess, the blessings from the holiest of realms to honor their cherished union. I speak for the goddess and ask for this exchange of rings to symbolize your commitment.

"Phoebe and Sophia, you do not join to be one but remain separate, a loving witness to each other's magnificence, as it should be, never to hinder the divine spirit in which you emulate the goddess. Do you agree to this in the name of all things sacred?"

With her head held high, Phoebe reached for my other hand and slid an engraved gold band onto my ring finger as her horse softly neighed.

"I do," Phoebe said in a clear, lucid, and loving voice.

I took a mental step back in horror as hypocrisy pricked my skin like ten thousand mosquitoes. I indulged in everything I'd recently railed against, even if it was for a noble cause. I panicked and couldn't speak. Phoebe mouthed, "please," General Lee stomped, and my wise mind gave me a gentle squeeze around my silk-clad shoulders. I swallowed back a storm of tears and adorned Phoebe's trembling hand with a matching gold band.

"I do."

"By the powers vested in me by the great state of California, and with the deepest of respect and love, I pronounce you wives."

Phoebe reached out and lifted my veil, leaned in closer, and kissed me. I touched my lips to my partner in crime. Mona winked and launched into a surprisingly good rendition of "Desperado," allowing us to canter off and make our escape to thunderous applause. My stomach galloped ahead of both of us.

Chapter Fifty-One

P hoebe passed through the meadow and kept on riding. She wanted to be alone, and who could blame her? I walked General Lee around the pasture till the coast was clear and then returned to the dressing rooms where a grass-chewing cowboy waited on the whitewashed porch, whistling "My Way."

I couldn't make eye contact with him. I leaned forward and hid my face on the General's silky neck until I could master my emotions. Once my ivory cowboy boots touched the ground, I murmured a thank you to the wrangler and walked into the quiet of the empty room.

It took an army to get me ready, but I peeled off the beautiful gown alone, unpinned the veil, and let my hair fall around my face. Standing in a borrowed white lacy bra and panties, I washed off layers of contour, pulled off fake lashes, and became horrid old me.

After I'd dug my jeans and a T-shirt out from my backpack, called by the music of water cascading over rocks, I made my way to the creek. Climbing atop a smallish boulder and, on emotional empty, I pondered nothing more complicated than the clear water flowing by.

"Where's your pretty dress?" David asked as he walked toward me.

The man I was in love with had watched me marry a woman I barely knew to cover the sins of another. A little light conversation was all I could handle. "I've had enough of dresses for today."

I took the glass of lemonade he offered and extended my other hand to help him over the rocks to my sturdy boulder for two.

"I didn't want you to see me."

"I heard, but I can't resist a beautiful bride. Can you forgive me?"

David settled beside me; my denim-clad thigh pressed against his dress pants. I closed my eyes and lay back, the connection to nature soothing and welcoming. "How'd you know I was here?"

"I followed the smell of meaningful sacrifice. It's a little like pesto, only better."

I had to laugh. "What's that noise? Sounds like clapping."

"That would be Phoebe and Sophia showing up at the reception after signing the official paperwork. Lovely wedding, all things considered."

"Sophia? Seriously?"

"According to Paulka, Sophia realized that she couldn't live without Phoebe, but couldn't call, since Phoebe had thrown her phone at a wall. Sophia called Paulka, who snuck her into the grounds dressed as a cowboy with a zillion-gallon hat. Paulka said 'a zillion,' not me."

"I figured that. You don't seem the embellishing type."

David put his finger on his chest and shook his head. He slid down the boulder, took off his dress shoes and socks, and stood with the trickling water running over his toes.

"Sophia and I watched you and Phoebe tie the knot, then Sophia snuck off to wait for her in the woods." David gave me a big theatrical wink. "'Desperado' is their song."

"Are you making this up?"

David grinned. "No one could make this up. I'm hoping that Mona will do an encore later tonight."

"Do I have to give the gifts back?"

"Only the ring. Sophia's going to want that."

I rolled the heavy gold band up and down my finger. How could Sophia expect Phoebe to welcome her with open arms? Could she forgive and forget? I needed a little forgiveness myself.

"I had a glass of champagne today, and I swear it's the only drink I've had since I told you that I would stop."

"Leanne, I didn't ask you to stop drinking for me."

"Sounds like you care."

"I do."

"I happen to know that those two words can be faked."

"Not by me."

David climbed beside me and reached for my hand. I held my breath. He slid Phoebe's ring off, put it in his pocket, and kissed my bare finger. "I'll get this back to its rightful owner."

My heart swelled with the pure goodness of this man, and instant regret for the crap I'd put him through. The water tumbled over the rocks and leaves danced in the warm air.

"Funny how a wedding makes you remember what marriage means," David said, climbing up and lying next to me.

"When You Say Nothing at All" floated on the breeze.

"She sounds like Alison Krauss," I said.

"Could be—one of my favorite songs. Want to dance?"

"I can't. Someone might put two and two together."

"Dance with me here. I like it better anyway," David said.

We slow-danced until long after sunset. It was a brilliant night, far away from the city lights, full of stars to wish upon. We danced and kissed by the creek until Neil came looking for me. David helped load what little was left, and I headed back to the real world.

Exhausted but peaceful, soaking in creamy peach bubbles with nothing but peppermint tea in my cup, I wiggled my toes out of the water and called Susan.

"I ordered you a do-it-yourself home strip-club kit. Should show up in five to seven days. The saltine pasties might be delayed due to high demand," I said.

Susan laughed. "Thank you. Your thoughtfulness knows no bounds. Your breathalyzer and juice boxes should arrive any day now."

"How're you doing?"

"Employing all healthy coping methods available, but the florist is thrilled. Brett's ordered daily flowers, oh, and a pair of vintage emerald earrings showed up on my pillow. In other words, back to normal."

"Now I understand why you have the jewelry of a queen."

"I'd be happy with a chia pet, tin foil, and a sober husband. Anyway, enough about me, I hear *you* make a stunning bride."

So much for taking it-to-the-grave secrecy.

"Who told you? Levi? Paulka?"

"David. He brought phenomenal leftovers on his way home. You outdid yourself."

"Thanks. Speaking of secrets, can you keep one?"

"Sure, what's up?"

"I'm meeting my dad tomorrow night. I don't want anyone else to know in case it doesn't go well."

"Bad timing. Levi and Paulka are throwing you and David a thank-you dinner tomorrow night. It's supposed to be a surprise."

"Crap, I can't cancel on my dad."

"Meet him for mocktails and come to dinner or reschedule your dad for breakfast. It's the safest meal of the day. No one starts anything heavy over eggs."

"I can't reschedule. Oh my God, I'm having a pre-panic attack."

"Pretend it's a blind date."

"That's disgusting—he's my dad—but you sound so caring; I could almost believe you're a real therapist."

"What about Levi's dinner?" Susan asked.

"I'll make something up to get out of it gracefully."

The warm water and emotional day took their toll. I grabbed a towel, wrapped up, and stifled a yawn.

"If you can't make it, let me know. There's only so much I'm willing to fake."

"Very funny. Hey, you're invited too?"

"Are you kidding? They have highly coveted reservations at Sorcière."

Chapter Fifty-Two

A motorcycle engine revved below my apartment. I crawled from bed and closed the window. Nerves strung like a new guitar, I dug through my closet. What did one wear for a reunion with a not dead yet Dad? My phone beeped once. He'd left a message. Something had come up tonight, but he could meet me this morning, at eleven. My stomach churned, and acid rose along with appropriately timed panic. I'd planned on a whole day to calm myself. I listened to the message again. An old diner? Great. I could wear jeans and make it for Levi's secret dinner.

After a quick shower, and a smidge of makeup, I set off for Al's Pancake Paradise. I dodged traffic in a part of downtown that I didn't often visit. I'd wanted—no, needed—more time to prepare. Mom's stories bounced around my brain, images that I didn't want to be true.

I found a space in an alley that smelled of garbage, and I parked between two delivery trucks. I checked myself in the rearview mirror and rubbed away a smudge of mascara under my eye. My gut churned as I forced myself out of the car, sidestepping a broken bottle and a discarded sleeping bag. I ran fingers over my blue beads, but mindful breathing was useless as I swung the old glass and metal diner door open, and my heart stopped. There was only one guy present, and he was sitting in a booth with a cup of coffee and a bunch of red roses in waxed paper.

His dark hair looked dyed, with only a couple renegade silver strands to give away his secret. His blue eyes were surrounded by thick lines from too much sun, or he'd skimped on the moisturizer. He cut a decent figure in his gray suit and crisp white shirt without a tie, an older gent for the GQ special edition of "seventy is the new sixty." His shoes were polished, a vintage gold watch anchored him to the past, and Polo oozed from his pores.

"Looks like you're waiting for someone special," I said, remembering what he'd said when he met Mom. A not-so-subtle way to let him know I wasn't anyone's fool.

"You look special to me," he said and rose from his seat. He came around the table and helped me into the booth. Was he old-school sweet, or controlling? "Sorry about dinner. We'll go there next time."

A wall of crushing disappointment hit me hard and unleashed a surprising gust of anger. Fear felt like anger, didn't it? I'd ask Susan in the ultimate debriefing.

"I've never been special. My daddy ditched me."

"If all you want to do is give me a hard time, maybe we should skip this, and I'll get myself back to the cemetery."

"I'm sorry, but this isn't easy for me."

"Looks like we have something in common."

He reached out and smoothed my cheek. I couldn't think or breathe. I was like a prehistoric animal stuck in a tar pit. I excused myself from the table and rushed to the ladies' room, where I splashed water on my face. I could hear the roar of blood in my ears; red waves crashed on a desolate beach. Stop. He was an old guy making amends and deserved a chance. People can change. The rusted towel dispenser held one sheet of scratchy brown paper. I patted my face dry to buy time and went back to the table.

A pretty server in a red-flowered dress with a ruffled white apron was chatting with Dad. She set a brown mug with a tiny chip in front of me and filled it with coffee. I added creamer from the cold metal pot, the condensation leaving a ring on the glass-topped table. I ripped open two sugar packets and stirred, coaxing my heartbeat to match the steady rhythm of the spoon. My gut had been wrong about men before, plenty of times. I smiled and drank the coffee. My heart raced like a caged animal.

"You're prettier in person, like your mother. I bet she's still a looker."

"Yeah, she looks fantastic."

"I bet that she never told you, but she had to beat them off with a stick. I kept a candle burning even after she left me."

He reached over the table to take my hand in his, but I pulled my hand back and hid it, safe on the paper napkin on my lap. I didn't feel comfortable playing the doting daughter in the 'My Dad Came Back from the Dead' movie of the week.

"Are you always so jumpy?"

I picked up my mug with both hands. It was the worst coffee I'd ever tasted. I added more sugar and stirred, and stared at the chip on the rim. She'd had a lot of admirers? Was he implying that she'd cheated?

"What does she say about your old man?"

I dropped both hands to my lap, covered my tummy. "Not much."

"Do you lie like your mother?"

The knots in my stomach floated like buoys in the burning acid of my gut. He didn't know me. He hadn't made any effort to be a father. He had no business saying shit about Mom. I wanted information, but pissing him off wouldn't help me get it. I waved the server over and ordered a ginger ale.

"I was trying to spare your feelings," I said.

"No need."

"She says you're a bastard."

He snickered. "Loves her little dramas. She's a better actress than a singer, that's for sure." He waved the server back over, and she got a wink for her trouble. I tried to read him, but I couldn't. Was he lying? Man, he was suave. If the bastard remark had affected him, he appeared to take it in stride. The server set my soda down and offered me a small roll of TUMS.

"Thanks."

"No problem. We give them out with the chili burger." The server smiled at me and held out a glittery purple pen over a pad.

"Ready?"

"I'll take the blue-plate special. My daughter would like your famous buttermilk waffles, the whipped cream and strawberry ones, and a side of bacon."

My dad gave the server what could have been a hundred-watt smile but had dimmed it to forty. I was generous. Make it twenty watts. He'd sprung from a time capsule, his ways too much a part of him to change, including ordering without consulting me.

"Sure thing, Grandpa. I'll put the order in right away." She winked back at him.

The plastered-on grin became a thin-lipped line, and he stroked his chin. He appeared to be as full of himself as Mom had said. Neil had said that there was no point in discussing a chapter unless you had time for the whole book. I had no right to judge him. I wanted to know how the story began and how it ended, then he'd damn well better believe I'd judge. He'd agreed to breakfast. He could have stayed dead. I silenced Mom's voice in my head and chewed on a Tums.

"I hear the waffles are the best in the city, but being a fancy chef, you'd know better."

"How do you know about me?"

"You think I don't know what my daughter's doing?" He smiled, and took a sip of coffee.

"I'm surprised that you're interested."

"Why wouldn't a father be interested in his kids?"

"When someone ditches you, it's hard to believe that they care."

"I didn't ditch you."

I'd read enough books on how to spot a liar, and surprise—he appeared to be telling the truth. Interesting. My wise mind pulled up a chair, and my stomach settled down, no thanks to the gut-rot coffee. "It's not like she held a gun to your head."

His tan reversed a few shades; there was something that he didn't like about my comment. Maybe I should back off a little. Be kind, be gentle, be patient. Hadn't I done that my whole life? I'd given every bastard more free passes than a ski resort with shitty snow, and for what?

"There's a lot that you don't know, Leanne."

I gave him my best big-girl smile. "Are you willing to fill in the blanks?"

"If I did, would it make a difference? From the way you spoke from the get-go, it seems like your mind is made up to hate me."

The server brought my breakfast. I slid the bacon onto his plate alongside his two over-easy eggs, greasy sausages, and rye toast. Eyebrows raised, he picked up the bacon and took a big bite.

"Enjoy your breakfast," she said. "Anyone need a warmup?"

"I'd love a warmup." He slid his hand around the server's waist, squeezed her, and held up his empty cup.

"Aren't you spry for a grandpa." She filled his cup with steaming coffee, and I could see the disgust hidden behind her fake smile. Good for her.

I played with the whipped topping and slightly frozen strawberries on my plate. My dad groping a server young enough to be his granddaughter tipped the scales to Mom's side. Sad and disappointed didn't begin to cut it. I didn't realize how much I'd wanted her to be wrong. Finished with kind and patient, I pushed my plate aside, and grabbed my purse. I needed David. His waffles, and his loving arms wrapped around me. It was a mistake to resurrect the past.

"Not good enough, huh? I guess you're used to better things," Dad said.

"I guess I am."

"You're as judgmental and insecure as your mother. Let me guess, I was too friendly with the waitress."

"Server, not waitress, and if you must know, yes."

"Sit down and hear me out. How are we going to get to know each other if you judge me before you understand me?"

"I can't see any reason for you to grab her."

"I don't know who's been grabbing you, but that wasn't a grab. It's a friendly gesture."

"She makes a living from tips. She can't afford to piss off a customer by telling him to keep his hands to himself."

He laughed and took his time spreading a paper napkin on his lap. "Don't get your panties in a bunch. Did the girl have a problem? She laughed, in case you didn't notice. If she had a problem, she'd have told me. Contrary to popular opinion, I'm a nice guy. Your mother never understood me; she couldn't be bothered. That's a damn shame. We were good together most of the time."

He poured syrup on his eggs and ate with lusty joy and questionable manners. If he was guilty as charged, how could he be so calm and content?

"Eat your waffles, baby, before they get cold." He poured red syrup on the steaming square and gave me a hopeful smile.

The need to please him, like a little girl out with her daddy for a special breakfast, unnerved me. Where had my boundaries gone? I choked down a tiny piece.

"Sometimes, people misunderstand innocent intentions. They get confused and don't stop to ask questions. That was the problem with your mother. She'd get an idea in her head and make it real. I always wondered if she was crazy like that fucking loon Rosalind. Crazy is genetic. I hope that you're not like that."

"I'm working on it."

"You've got a lot going for you. Don't fuck it up with crap that you can't fix."

Hurt that I didn't want him to see filled my eyes. I picked up the soda and drank it while I blinked the tears away. He hadn't noticed anything but the bacon on his plate.

"I never heard that you were a thinker."

"Now you know." He spread grape jelly on his toast from one of those little plastic squares like he didn't have a care in the world. Maybe he didn't. "Tell me about your business. You make a decent paycheck for some fancy brownies." Did he eat his toast with a con man's savvy gleaming in his eyes? No, Mom had poisoned me against him.

He didn't look like a man beaten down by life or dragged down by the past. He looked like a winner, like someone who'd made mistakes, but pulled himself up and years later wanted to make amends. It seemed reasonable and fair to give him a chance. Someone had to, and shouldn't that someone be me?

"You said that you follow me, so you've seen the hype."

"Is it real?" He asked.

"Yeah, it's the one thing I'm good at."

He pushed his plate aside, wiped his mouth, and threw the eggy napkin on the table.

"I've come into a little money and was thinking about opening a small restaurant. Would you be interested?" He looked sincere, ready to step into the shoes that Mom had denied him.

There was nothing that he could have sprung on me that would have shocked me more. He didn't want to take—he wanted to give? I'd had plenty of experience with players and shakers, and all they do is take. This guy was rough around the edges for sure, but sincere. There was the possibility Mom was kookoo for coconuts. If nothing else, I would trust but verify until I knew otherwise.

"One question, for now."

"Shoot. I'm an open book," he said.

"Did you physically hurt her?"

"I loved her like I'd never loved anyone else. After a few years of therapy—don't look so shocked—I realized that she had to live in a make-believe world so she could avoid looking at herself. Narcissists do that. Anyway, I'm not going to bad mouth your mother. She was a shitty wife but a good mom." He took a long swallow of coffee. His eyes watered, he coughed, and he cleared his throat. "I did what she asked until

I couldn't. I'm not getting any younger, and as far as I know—you're my girl."

"I don't know what to say."

"Say you'll give the restaurant some thought and do me a favor?"

"Sure. What?"

"Don't tell your mom. Trust me, she won't understand."

Chapter Fifty-Three

Dad might have been on his best behavior, but he seemed like a decent guy. I suspected that some of what Mom said was real, but, as he said, she tended to embellish the truth for her own agenda. I'd take it slow and keep a little distance until I really knew him, but after all this time, I'd be damned if I wasn't going to have my dad in my life. I stopped off at a trendy salon, dropped Paulka's name and had my hair cut to my shoulders. Then, with my sassy glistening hair, I grabbed a fancy bottle of non-alcoholic sparkler on the way home. I couldn't wait to share the news with David. It was time for new beginnings—lots of them.

After all the stress leading up to the enlightening breakfast, I crashed on my couch for a bit of beauty sleep, careful not to mess up my new hair. Visions of Dad and I working in our restaurant played in my head. I'd hire Neil, Candy, and Tony. Paulka would design the interior, and Susan would draw up the deal. Levi would hold my hand and David would be so proud of me.

Pachelbel woke me, and I swung the door open to Paulka's favorite minion holding a drool-worthy vintage aqua gown. Aqua is not a color I'd choose, but when I held the gown close and spun around, the diaphanous chiffon swirled around me like ocean mist. I gave credit to the master and a twenty to the minion.

In the dress, I looked like a mermaid, fresh from the deep. I pinned my hair back to show off the aquamarine earrings that came with the outfit, then down again. I looked like I felt—deliriously happy, my heart on the outside for the first time.

At seven sharp, my new hair, dress, and I were rewarded with an awe-struck David in a stunning vintage tuxedo.

"If I said that you are the most beautiful woman in the world, would you believe me?"

I threw myself into his arms, nothing I'd usually do, but I was a mermaid, the normal rules didn't apply and I couldn't resist.

"How could I not? You always tell the truth."

David took my hand and slowly spun me around. The dress showed off its magic.

"I feel like a kid on his first date. I can't think straight."

I led him to my couch and handed him a flute filled with the non-alcoholic champagne garnished with strawberries cut into roses.

"Don't think."

"One question?" David smiled at the roses and patted the couch. I sat next to him, and he pulled me even closer.

"Sure."

He traced a soft finger across my cheek, bent to my neck, and nuzzled that tender spot two inches below my ear. I squirmed in my seafoam. "Why are Levi and Paulka going to such trouble? They had someone drop off the tux."

"They're grateful. I don't think Phoebe would have married me if you hadn't brought her back from the dead."

"You don't consider yourself married, do you?" He laughed.

"Just a little bit." I gave his quizzical face a soft kiss and popped a strawberry in his mouth. "Don't worry about Levi and Paulka; you'll get used to the lavish displays of appreciation." I gestured at the eclectic mix of luxury items around my living room. David caught my hands mid-gesture.

"I could get used to you."

Should I tell him about my date with Dad and the restaurant? Not now. We had plenty of time. He held my hands in what was now—if I got really lucky—my forever safe place. He lifted one hand and kissed it, and then the other. Pepe Le Pew could take lessons from him. He raised my chin and leaned in. My eyes closed and my mouth found his. I slipped without hesitation or reservation into the mystical place of cherished love I'd never believed would happen to me. A haven made me dangerously hot. Who knew? My wise mind coughed and stepped out of the room.

"We could be late, you know," I said, my breath shallow and measured.

"Tempting, but I think a romantic weekend away is more my style." He kissed me again. It was debilitating.

David came up for air. "I don't think your beautiful hair will appreciate my convertible tonight, and the top's stuck in the overly wind-blown position. Could we take your car?"

"Whatever makes you happy."

I'd have promised him anything.

The six of us sat in comfortable black velvet chairs around a big circular table covered in snowy-white linens. Levi and Paulka had spared no expense for a special dinner to honor our contribution to the wedding ruse of the century. David leaned back in his chair, a glass of red wine in one hand, his other arm around me.

"The chocolate mousse is divine," Paulka said and kissed his empty spoon.

"It's not orgasmic like Leanne's," Susan said. Her low-cut black dress set her new emerald earrings off to perfection.

"Did you read that in a review?" I asked her and snuck a taste from Paulka.

"Everything's orgasmic with Susan these days," Brett said and ate a large bite of apple tatin.

"Trying to keep up, my love. Last night you sexualized a toothpaste commercial," Susan said.

"Sorcière has an excellent pastry chef," Levi said, smoothly leading us away from the dangerous road of sexualized personal products. He cracked the top of a mocha crème brûlée and spooned it into his mouth.

"Susan, tell us about the toothpaste commercial. How exciting. Was it a sexy naked Belgian production?" Paulka asked.

Levi stuffed a considerable spoonful of crème brûlée into Paulka's mouth and gave Susan a stern look, telling her to simmer down. She didn't.

"Paulka, is enamel protection hot to you?" Susan asked and sipped on her dirty martini. "I'd like to know."

"How about a round of cognac?" Levi said. "Paulka, my love, can you find out when the show starts?"

Paulka gave Levi a noisy kiss and sashayed off into the crowded room.

An eclectic collection of chandeliers sparkled above us. I caught a vision of David and myself in the mirrored ceiling as the lights dimmed. David ran his fingers down my back, and we giggled until the room was cloaked in the inky darkness.

The stage lights came up on sheer crimson curtains that parted to reveal a six-piece jazz combo wearing white dinner jackets and black ties. My heart swelled as glorious music swirled around us. David kept his arm wrapped around my bare shoulders.

"The maître d' gave us magic wands." Paulka whispered and passed them around with glee.

David kissed my cheek and squeezed my hand under the table. I glowed like the dark red candles that flickered and waved my glittery star-topped wand at him.

"Did you cast a spell on me?" David asked, his wand resting on the table, eyes locked on mine.

"If I tell you, the spell won't work."

Paulka shushed us both, and we settled down to watch the show. In a long, sequined, black gown, Mom walked to center stage. Sleek cinnamon hair surrounded her face. I held my breath; goosebumps rose up and down my arms. She took the mic off the stand and slipped into "I Put a Spell on You." Our table was right below her, as close to the stage as possible. She found me in the dark and sent a "now you're mine" straight to me with a wicked smile. She was ridiculously good, but I didn't like surprises, and Levi knew it.

I leaned over toward Levi. "You could have warned me."

"We wanted her to be a surprise," he whispered.

David put a hand on my knee. "Levi, how did you know that she was performing?"

"Paulka brought me here for Rat Pack Tuesday."

"She was singing with Sinatra, or was it Dean Martin? I mix them up. Isn't she marvelous?" Paulka stared up at her like a child watching fireworks on the 4th of July.

"She told you that she was singing?"

"Yes, and she made us promise not to tell you," Levi said. "Until she was ready."

I sipped my virgin daiquiri, pensive at best. My wise mind suggested that I give up the illusion of control. I considered, then Mom blew away all my annoyance with her sultry voice, not to mention her magnetic presence. No wonder she has a grand piano in her living room. No wonder she'd moved into the city and wore fabulous dresses in the wee hours of the morning. I'd forgotten about the old forty-five hidden under my bed. I couldn't wait to listen to it.

Except for the wand-waving, we sat still as altar boys at church, entranced by the magic playing out before us. Susan stopped baiting Brett, and Levi and Paulka listened with a reverence that bordered on the spiritual. When I could drag my attention away from Mom, I noticed a well-dressed older man sitting at a table to the left of the stage. He sat alone, his eyes never leaving Mom. He placed a pink peony on the stage, and she picked it up halfway through "Come Rain or Come Shine." She touched the flower to her cheek, kissed it, and tossed it back to him. Gerald must have felt me looking because he turned and smiled at me.

At the end of her act, she took a graceful bow, acknowledged her band, and the curtain fell. The applause and wand-waving went on and on, but she didn't come back. Sly devil. Keep them wanting more. A burlesque revue began, very Moulin Rouge, a sexy number with dancers in black witch hats and silver brooms. I stole a look at Susan; she twisted her emerald earrings. She'd ordered a bottle of champagne, her glass on permanent refill status from an attentive Brett, whom she tapped, or whacked, depending on her mood, with her wand when she wanted a refill.

I leaned into David's neck and breathed in his goodness. "I have to go and see her. Do you mind if I go alone?"

"As long as you tell her that I'm her latest adoring fan," David said.

I kissed his lips, whispered thank you, and found my way backstage. A sudden shyness came over me, but I saw her dressing room and walked in. It was small but movie-star fabulous, with a makeup vanity complete with light bulbs all around, a cozy couch with a white fur spread, like the one at her house, and a coffee table covered with fashion magazines. The older man who I presumed to be Gerald was already with her.

"Leanne! Gerald, this is my fascinating and talented daughter," Mom said.

"Pleased to meet you, Leanne." Gerald put out a hand for me to shake.

"I'm pleased to meet you," I said. "And you, Vivi."

Mom laughed, high from her performance. "Gerald, honey, I'm famished. Would you mind ordering dinner before the kitchen closes?"

"She never eats before a show," Gerald said. "Don't know how she does it." They looked like an old married couple if the wife was a glamorous singer and the husband was a sharp man about the town without the edges. "The usual?"

"I'd like the steak au poivre tonight. I'm starving."

"Here?"

"I'll break tradition and join Leanne's table if they have room."

He gave her the cutest smile and left to order her dinner. There was something steady, dependable, and charming about him. He looked like he lived to take care of her. I liked him already.

"Paulka will drink champagne from your shoes if you sit with us," I said.

"Only if I let him wear them." She laughed. I'd never seen her so happy.

"I'm in awe and maybe a tiny bit jealous."

"Gerald got the ball rolling. He's the man I wish that I'd met all those years ago. Don't say anything, but I'm sure you'll have a family wedding to cater sometime next year."

"How wonderful. Congratulations."

"Too early for those, so shh, don't say anything to anyone. Especially your brother."

Keep something from my baby brother? Not a problem.

Mom powdered off a little shine, smoothed her hair in the mirror, and fixed her lipstick.

"I have some good news too. I met Dad."

I watched her face pale in the mirror. The lipstick dropped to the floor.

"When?"

"Today for breakfast. It went surprisingly well."

I was about to tell her about the restaurant offer, but she whirled around on her chair, breath coming fast. I could see a flutter at the base of her throat. My stomach hurt.

"Why did you see him?"

"I told you that I wanted to make up my mind, maybe it'd be nice to have a father in my life."

"Why did I bother telling you anything?"

"He's harmless, and he's mellowed with age. He seemed impressed with my career, and he bought me breakfast."

"Leanne, you didn't hear the last story, did you? Leanne? Answer me."

I didn't want to confess that I'd passed out and missed the all-important season finale. I'd pretended over breakfast that I'd heard more than I did. Now, I wondered what the hell I'd missed.

"I thought it would be safe to fall asleep! If you wanted to tell me the ultimate revelation you should have made me coffee, and not offered a cozy bed!"

Mom twisted her hands like she didn't know what to do with them. She played with the rings on her fingers, and smoothed her hair again. She reached for a bottle of water and knocked over a vase of tall blue delphiniums. She didn't move to clean it up. This wasn't the time or place to discuss her part in all of this. I was sure that he would be willing to talk with her, to clean up the past once and for all. She'd been so young, and as he said, it was easy to read something the wrong way. It was also possible that she was crazy like her mother, and she'd made everything up. I loved her anyway.

I picked up a hand towel, mopped up the mess, and stuffed the flowers back in the vase willy-nilly.

"Goddamn it, Leanne. How can you bring that sordid piece of shit into my life again? Do you have any idea how much pain that man caused me? How much I lost? Now you come in here, of all places, acting like a five-year-old who had a happy meal with Daddy?"

"I thought you'd be pleased. He was nice to me."

"Nice? He asked you about your career for one reason. He's after money."

"You don't know that."

I wanted to tell her about the restaurant, to prove he'd changed, but she didn't let me get in a word.

"Did he discuss the merits of white chocolate versus dark or mention your celebrity clients and big paydays?"

Gerald knocked and poked his head around the door. Mom and I both froze.

"Sweetheart, your dinner's almost ready. Are you two okay in here?"

"No, Gerald. Far from it." Mom trembled with anger, at Dad or me, I didn't know which.

"I'll leave," I said. "I didn't mean to upset you. Nice to meet you, Gerald."

Mom pulled Gerald in and locked the door. "Stay, both of you. I want this out for good."

"Mom, I don't think this is the time."

"I've held the truth, buried it, ate it, slept with it, so you didn't have to know, but Leanne, I'm not holding this pain anymore. If you met with him, then I'm done protecting you, and Leanne? You need to know the devil that you're dealing with!"

She was yelling. She threw things, but she never yelled, and I hoped that she would stop, because the fact that she yelled unsettled me far more than any of the words that flowed like a runaway train out of her mouth.

"I don't want to know any more, not like this." I put my hands over my ears. What the hell did I miss when I fell asleep?

"You met with him. He made you like him. He will worm his way into your life, take you down a filth-filled path, and you won't come back."

"Sweetheart, do you want to sit down?" Gerald asked. "I'll get your dinner."

"Don't leave, Gerald. I've spent a lifetime wondering if I did the right thing by my kids. I'd love for someone else to judge for me for a change."

Chapter Fifty-Four

Patricia and Ginger sat at their favorite table at Luigi's. A red-checked cloth, two glasses of cheap red wine, and a basket of Luigi's famous garlic bread to share. Nothing had changed in the restaurant or between them. Patricia was filled with a warmth, a relaxation that she'd forgotten how to feel.

"It's been ages since I've been out," Patricia said.

"Well, that's what happens when you shack up and pop out babies." Ginger passed the garlic bread.

"Ginger, we're married." Patricia took a piece of the fragrant bread with the most garlic. Verin would leave her alone tonight.

"Viv. You are the last girl I would judge, you know that."

"Have you been talking to my mother?" Patricia finished her wine.

"Oh, hell no. I wouldn't go near her. Mom and Dad had to change to St. Luke's after you 'died.' I think they were afraid she would curse them or something. Oh, that reminds me. Mom said to give you this for your kids."

Ginger handed Patricia an envelope stuffed with cash.

"She didn't have to do that."

"Mom said you didn't get a wedding, so this is her way of giving you a little gift."

Patricia felt the weight of the envelope. "This is a lot of money. I can't take it." She tucked it back in Ginger's purse.

"She wants you to have it. Viv. She's known you since you were a little girl. It broke her heart when I told her what your mom had done. Take it. Five hundred dollars could change your life." Ginger tucked the envelope in Patricia's purse. "Subject closed. Want another glass of wine?"

"I better get back. I don't like leaving Verin alone with the kids. Leanne is crazy clingy for days after he watches them, not that he does it often. I think he ignores her."

"Let's not make it so long next time. I miss you."

"I miss you, too. Are you still seeing Jason?"

"College is full of cute guys, and I like to keep my options open."

The women giggled and grabbed their coats and purses. They hugged each other goodbye outside the cozy restaurant. Patricia decided to walk, even though, for a change, she had money for a cab. She couldn't believe that they'd given her five hundred dollars, money that Verin would never know about. Since she hardly ever got out at night without Verin's possessive eyes on her, she took her time, enjoyed the misty night air, and watched the couples strolling along the street, sharing a secret joke, and laughing because they enjoyed being together.

She remembered when she'd been Verin's sun and moon, when she had lived for pleasing him and it had seemed that he lived for her. Now, he claimed that she'd forced herself on him, tried to trick him so that she could get into the music business. She'd wanted his help, but she'd also loved him. He said that she was old, and no one would like her, and she was lucky that he didn't kick her out. Was it true? She did feel old, exhausted, and used up. She passed a bar. A bass lit up the place with a smoking solo. She wanted to go inside and show the room what she could do. But she'd blown it. Dreams were as useless as sequins on a broom.

Patricia didn't know if it was safe to make noise, so she stood in front of her apartment door. If she woke the kids, Verin would yell at her. If he were asleep and didn't know when she'd come in, he'd accuse her of being out all-night whoring around, and she'd be sore and bruised for days. He'd have his way and whisper that she was lucky to have him.

"Rebranding," he called it. The wasps burned. She took off her heels in the hall, not wanting to wake Leanne and Jeffrey. They needed their sleep, and Verin could go to hell.

She felt for the light switch. The living room was empty; he must be dead drunk and in bed. She would wake him up, show him the time. If he'd drunk enough, he'd go right back to sleep. She padded down the short hall to check on the kids. Thank God, Verin left had left Leanne's night light on so that she wouldn't worry about monsters.

That hint of light illuminated Verin in the darkness, so drunk that he didn't notice Patricia standing in the doorway. He had Leanne on his lap, his pants around his ankles.

A primal scream erupted in Patricia's mind but didn't reach her lips. Without a second thought, she grabbed the ceramic teddy bear lamp on the dresser and smashed it on Verin's head.

He stood, and Leanne slid to the floor, her nightie up around her waist. "Fucking idiot woman. What the hell did you do to me?"

Patricia picked Leanne up, and the child hid her face in her mother's shoulder, softly crying.

"It's okay, baby girl. You're fine. Nothing happened." Holding Leanne, Patricia placed herself between an enraged, bloody Verin, and Jeffrey's crib. "You get out of here, and don't you come back."

"Look what you did to me." He touched his head and stared at the blood on his hand. "I should call the police for husband battering, you fucking crazy bitch."

"I said to get out before I kill you."

Eyes red like a bull and his breath labored, Verin pulled up his pants, fastened his belt, and used a fluffy toy elephant to wipe the blood that dripped from his head. Leanne stopped crying and clung to Patricia, her little face smeared with pink rouge and lipstick that Verin had let her put on. Jeffrey stood in his crib, his blanket clutched in his hand, his blue eyes big as he stared at the bloody toy on the floor.

"Goddamn, woman, you've split my head open. I'm gonna need stitches. I'll be back. Don't you go, Vivi. You leave and take my kids; I'll find you and kill you on the spot." Verin grabbed his keys and slammed the door.

"Leanne, I need you to be Mommy's big girl," Patricia said, and held out an empty pillow case. "Put your favorite toys in this sack. Some for Jeffrey, too."

"Is Daddy coming back?" Leanne said. "Will he kill you?"

"No, baby girl, we're leaving right now. You have to hurry."

"Daddy will be mad. He says we're getting ice cream after I'm good."

Sick from the horror that she'd witnessed and all she didn't know but guessed, Patricia thanked God for the money in her purse. The wedding present would buy her and the kids a couple of months in a new place, where Verin would never find them. She threw baby supplies and clothes for herself and the kids into a big brown suitcase. She searched for her record and her green dress. She could get work. Make money. She grabbed the photo, the one that could exonerate her from being a complete idiot, and tossed it in the case. Confusion flooded her brain.

Did she see what she'd thought she saw? Would he do that? How could she even wonder? She wasn't crazy, not like Verin said.

"Daddy's back." Leanne stopped packing toys and hid behind her mother. Patricia pushed the suitcase under the crib.

"Shhh, don't say anything."

Leanne nodded. "I won't even whisper."

Verin slammed the door behind him, struggled with the lock, and put his hands over his face. "Jesus fucking Christ, I killed a man. The red light changed too fast. He ran out in front of the car. I couldn't stop. There's blood on the headlights. It was an accident, I swear, Vivi."

"Oh my God, Verin. They'll know you were drinking."

As soon as she opened her mouth, she witnessed his terror turn to fury. She backed away from him. He was dangerous. She had to think of something, fast.

"This is your fault, you stupid bitch." He staggered toward her, the shock already wearing off. "If you hadn't hit me, I wouldn't have been on the road."

"I'll go and see what happened. We can figure something out. I'll clean up the car, too."

"Don't let anyone see you or do anything stupid—the corner, by the Chinese restaurant. The bastard had no business walking on the road. It's his fucking fault, and I'm not going to jail for it."

"Take a shower and sober up. I'll take the kids, so they don't bother you."

As soon as Verin shut the bathroom door, Patricia made the let's-be-quiet-for-Daddy face the kids were used to, held Jeffrey close with one arm and the suitcase with the other. Leanne gripped the back of Patricia's coat as they left the apartment.

Patricia put the kids in the back seat and the suitcase in the trunk and thanked her lucky stars that Verin hadn't wanted the kids to stay. She didn't believe in her mother's God, but something powerful had helped her, and she knew in her soul that it was a gift not to be wasted.

She drove, shaking until she got to the restaurant. The street was deserted and quiet, Wing Foo's sign said closed. She got out of the car and walked to the side of the road, where a dark, lifeless shape lay. As soon as she'd confirmed he'd killed a man, she'd go to the police and Verin would rot in jail, and he'd never hurt Leanne again. Patricia had never seen a dead person before and continued to shake, but she moved closer, and knelt beside a large, black dog, the ground wet beneath him.

She sobbed like she didn't know a person could. She ran her hand over the dog's head, down his back, tears soaking the soft black fur. She blessed the dog for saving them, for giving her and the kids a chance to escape.

When her tears slowed enough to see her way to the car, she grabbed the old plaid picnic blanket from the trunk and dragged the dog to her car. She'd take the dog with her and give him a proper burial so Verin wouldn't know the truth, and because the dog deserved one. He weighed at least a hundred pounds; she struggled but, fueled by necessity, lifted him into the trunk. She pressed the lid closed and wiped her eyes.

"Leanne, Mommy has to use the phone booth across the street. Be my big girl and take care of Jeffrey. I'll be right back, and don't get out of the car, okay?"

"Yes, Mommy."

"Good girl. Then we'll go and get that ice cream you were talking about."

Leanne nodded to her mother, her eyes big and serious. She held Jeffrey's hand with one hand and the bloody elephant with the other. Patricia fought the urge to rip the toy from Leanne's hands, toss it as far away as she could. Across the street, she put a dime in the payphone slot and waited, her heart thumping hard in her chest. Verin answered.

"You were right. He's dead."

"Are the police there?"

"Yes, lots of them. One's taking pictures, a doctor's examining the body, and a couple of cops are talking to some guy. There are chalk lines in the street. It looks like they got a witness, maybe two."

"Did anyone see you?"

"I'm hiding up the street. They've got big spotlights on the scene. Oh, no. A woman's here. She's trying to get to the body, but the police are holding her back. She's crying and has a child with her. A little boy. Should I go to her?"

"You fucking idiot. Stay where you are. I can't go to jail, Vivi. We'll go back East. I've got family there—a clean start. I'll stop drinking, no more cheating. Viv, I swear it."

Patricia wished things were different, but she'd never forgive him now. The phone made a noise, and she fed it a few more dimes.

"I'm not coming back, Verin, not ever. If you don't want me to go to the friendly officer who's asking questions and tell him what you did, and where to find you, you will do as I say."

"You're fucking stupid, Viv, if you think a cop would listen to you."

"You are dead to the kids and me. You will never try to find us, and if you do, I will tell the police that you killed this poor soul out for a walk in the moonlight."

"You'd go to jail, too, for hiding the truth."

"You know what? You're right. I'll tell them where to find you right now or you can take my advice and get as far away as you can and don't come back."

Patricia stopped talking. She knew to say more would be to lose the fish she had on her hook. Seconds ticked by. His heavy breathing made her jumpy, and something crashed to the floor in the apartment. She closed her eyes and laid her head against the phone, heart thumping so loud that she was sure he could hear it. She waited for either a life sentence or a pardon.

"I love you, Vivi."

Patricia hung up and exhaled the stale, dirty air in her lungs. She walked to the car and, shaking, shut the door with a firm clunk.

"Who wants to get an ice cream cone?"

Chapter Fifty-Five

I couldn't move or speak. Everything slowed around me. It was like nothing was real. I slid to the floor and grasped the carpet under me with both hands. I tried to pull myself back into this world long enough to understand one thing. My mouth was so dry that I could scarcely get the words out.

"How could you not tell me?"

"And make you live with that the rest of your life? Let that bastard make you suffer more than he already did?"

"You knew that I would see him. I told you. Mom, how could you?"

Mom trembled in Gerald's arms. He stroked her hair. He held her hands between his larger ones.

"Leanne, I thought that you heard me, but didn't want to talk about it. In a million years I never thought you'd see him." She continued to cry, her false eyelashes like wet caterpillars on her contoured cheeks, like a cartoon character. Nothing looked or felt real. I ached to bury myself in her arms and let her soothe away the abject horror that smothered all that was good in me. I couldn't. I could only hurt the ones I loved. At what point was her story, my story?

"I understand not telling me as a child, but did you ever consider what my life could have been if I'd known? I drink like a fish for a reason that

I didn't know about. How fair is that? All the rat bastards that I attract like flies to shit. I have no issue with you protecting a child, but an adult should have been given the god damn fucking chance to heal!"

"Please, don't take this out on your mother. Can't you see what it cost her to protect you, and how much she suffered to keep you safe?"

Not his fault, but shut the fuck up, Gerald. You can't understand. You don't know me. "Does Jeffrey know any of this? Because it sure as shit explains his recent fuck-ups."

"I've never told anyone until tonight," Mom said. "I wanted to tell you, but it seemed safer, kinder to wait until you asked."

"How in the hell could I ask about something I didn't know about? All I see is someone who tried to control the truth so she didn't have to feel guilty. Why didn't you get help? Why didn't you tell someone? It was easier to lie, wasn't it? You didn't have to face it if I didn't know what he did. You could pretend my father didn't—"

I couldn't go there.

"Leanne, you have every right in the world to be upset, but place your anger where it belongs, when you're ready. You have his number," Gerald said.

My gut flipped upside down; my flesh crawled. I wanted to get away from her, from everyone, from myself. I wanted to sleep forever, and if that wasn't possible, I wanted to drive far away, where the sordid truth couldn't find me. I remembered the feel of his hand on mine at breakfast, and stumbled around the room, looking for somewhere to throw up. Fathomless horror held me in its grip while I heaved my dinner into a pretty pink trash can, my body shaking, icy sweat soaking the mermaid dress.

"Baby girl, Leanne. Please hear me out."

Blinded by tears, not willing to listen to her, I stumbled toward the dining room. The table was littered with glasses, all shapes and flavors of glorious, mind-numbing liquid. They sparkled in the candlelight. I grabbed my clutch from the table, waved away my confused friends, and headed for the valet. I needed to drive, alone, to make sense of the mass of pain infesting my body, like a demon eating me alive, soul first.

The valet brought my car, and I slid in. David caught up to me and held the driver's door open.

"Leanne, let me drive. Anywhere you want to go."

"I'm driving, and don't ask me anything. Please."

David walked around the car and sat in silence, his hands flat on his thighs, his eyes on the road. I screamed inside my head, wanting to tell him, but too ashamed. The little girl inside me was horrified I'd heard her secret. She begged me not to tell David or anyone else. Shame smothered us both into silence.

I drove out of the city, across the bridge. I needed the roads of my childhood under the wheels, to help me to find my way to what I didn't know I needed. David sat still, with an occasional glance at me. He swallowed with the effort not to speak.

"Leanne, I'm not asking what happened, but you need to slow down. Let me drive so that you can think."

"I don't want to think. That's why I'm driving."

"I imagine you're in an awful place—"

"Please ... don't."

"Leanne, I love you. I want to help, whatever it is."

I sobbed harder, I hated that our first "I love you" was on the worst night of my life. What else could they take away from me? Long-buried visions swam before me. Yelling, fighting. The bloody elephant. Oh,

God. That night came flooding back. My body clenched, the smell of waxy lipstick, his hand between my legs, a rough beard hurting my face, and his whispering. He called me Baby. I couldn't go there. If I did, I would run the car right off the road.

"Leanne, please, slow down."

"Do you want me to stop? I can let you out so that you can get away from me, from this? I wouldn't blame you."

Tires screeching, I pulled over to the side of the road, where the gravel met the dirt.

"Here, I'll get out," I said, shaking and sobbing, I slammed the car door. "Take my car."

"I'm not leaving you."

"After tonight, I'm further away from being Christmas than ever."

"Did you hear me say I love you?"

A car flashed by, faster than I'd been driving. A screech of tires came from down the road, then nothing. The car sped off again.

David helped me into the passenger seat. He buckled me in.

"Leanne, you are stronger than you know. Whatever it is, you will be okay. Please believe me."

I sat, freezing, shaking, eyes unblinking and fixed on the ground passing by. I caught myself rocking back and forth, holding in a scream that if I gave an inch would never stop. I desperately wanted to reach out and tell David, let him hold me against his chest and soothe away my pain with his magic voice, but I couldn't, and I didn't know why.

"Hey, there's something in the road," I said.

"Where?"

"Over there."

"It's a dog. Those assholes hit it."

A dog? You've got to be fucking kidding me. David pulled the car over, ran to the dog.

"She's alive, barely," he said, looking up at me.

"It's not moving, David. I've seen a lot of this. It's dead or will be soon." Tears ran down my face, and I wiped my nose. The horrible rocking started again. I couldn't stop.

He put his head on the dog's chest. "She's breathing. Shallow, but she's breathing. Do you know a vet around here?"

I nodded. David wrapped his dinner jacket around the pup and tossed me the keys.

"Hold on, little one," David whispered to the dog.

I held the passenger door open while he slid in, the dog cradled in his arms.

I shut his door and walked around to the driver's side, tears streaming down my face so thick that I didn't know how I'd see to drive. I started the car and glanced over at David. His eyes were closed, his lips squeezed tight. He cleared his throat and wiped at his face.

"Don't get your hopes up," I said.

"Goddamn it, Leanne. I will hope if that's alright with you. I lost Jessica, but you know what? I never stopped hoping that there would be a happy ending. Neither did she, and sometimes, all you get is hope, and that has to be enough, because that's all you're going to get."

Shocked by David's outburst, I stopped crying, sped up, and pulled into the only twenty-four-hour emergency clinic in the area. I ran ahead of David and banged on the reception bell.

"Hey, help. We've got a dying dog here."

David ran up behind me, the dog in his arms.

"You don't know that," David said, his voice slow and measured.

"You don't know that she isn't dying."

"I know I'll do anything to save her."

"Maybe she'll die anyway, and you've wasted your time."

"Nothing's a waste when you love someone!" David said, his face red, his eyes watery, threatening to spill. "Why is that so goddamn hard for you to understand?"

The receptionist didn't seem rattled by David's outburst. She attached a pile of papers to a clipboard and handed it to me with genuine concern in her eyes. I picked up a pen and stared at the long list of questions until they blurred on the page. My tears dripped faster than I could guess anything the papers demanded I know. I gave David the clipboard, my hands shaking.

"I can't do this right now."

The dog opened her eyes and looked at me from David's lap. The amount of blood dripping from his jacket told me that things would not go well. A man and a woman, both in scrubs, ran through double doors and took the dog from David, his white shirt and hands crimson.

"There's a restroom if you'd like to wash up. Help yourself to some coffee while you wait. Dr. Kendra's examining your dog. It will be a while." The receptionist gestured to a do-it-yourself coffee station. "You could be here all night."

"We're not waiting." I slapped a credit card on the counter. "Can you copy this?"

"We don't know what the treatment plan is yet," the woman said.

"It doesn't matter. I'll pay."

"It's variable depending on what's wrong or if—"

"I get it."

"The paperwork says you found the dog on the road?"

"Please, take the goddamn fucking card. I need to leave!" Fuck. I was yelling and bawling in front of a stranger just doing her job. Fuck. Fuck. Fuck.

I blew out a breath, refilled my lungs, and looked deep into David's eyes, memorizing his gorgeous, old-soul face. I'd make him miserable. I loved him too much to hurt him until death us do part, and he'd said that he wanted a wife. My hands were over my mouth, trying to stuff back the words I didn't want to say.

"I'm so sorry, David. I can't be who you think I can be. Maybe there was a chance before, but not after tonight."

I ran out of the clinic and slid into my car. The mermaid dress clung to my cold, wet, and muddy legs. I wanted to peel it off, along with the skin from my bones. I needed my bath. Oh God. Fresh tears spilled and flooded my face as I realized ... the baths. The forever need to soak away the filth I'd felt on me but didn't know why. I screamed my way back to the city.

Chapter Fifty-Six

Jeffrey and I watched a cowboy show in our pajamas. He had the foot kind because he was a baby. I had on a new pink nightie that Mommy got that when we went out. She had to get a dress because she had nothing to wear to the only god damn fun she'd had in too long.

"Oh, for God's sake, Verin. I'm getting dinner with Ginger, not Attila the Hun. There's nothing to be concerned about," Mommy said, picking up her purse from the kitchen table.

"Not unless Attila likes a tight blue dress." Jeffrey squirmed like a worm in Daddy's arms, reaching out for Mommy.

"Be nice. Ginger is my best friend, and I don't remember the last time I saw her. Are you sure that you can take care of the kids?" Mommy took Jeffrey from Daddy and put him in the highchair, with his squeaky mouse. "You go out all the time, and you don't hear me complaining."

Daddy made himself a cold tea in the biggest glass we have and sat down next to Jeffrey. He gave me a sip of tea once when Mommy wasn't home. I don't like tea. He pulled me onto his knee and gave me a smoochy smooch. His face was butter smooth today, so I smooched him back. He likes that.

"I can feed my own kids dinner, Vivi. You go along and don't get into any trouble."

He swatted her on the rumpus kinda hard. She blew me and Jeffrey a *Saturday Rose* pink lipstick kiss. *So pretty.*

"Be good for Daddy. I'll be back before you know it."

"Can we eat on the couch and watch TV?" I asked when the door closed.

"Sure thing, whatever my baby wants, but don't tell Mommy."

Daddy scooped Jeffrey from the high chair, and he crawled after us. Daddy brought sandwiches on a tray, and the cowboy noise hurt my ears. Mom doesn't like the TV so loud, but Jeffrey and Daddy love cowboys, and Daddy doesn't care a goddamn about the noise the neighbors can hear.

"Come on baby, eat your sandwich." I didn't like my sandwich. It was ham. Yuck. I like Porky Pig, so I don't like ham. I gave it to Jeffrey.

Daddy took another drink of his tea, put his fingers into the tall glass, plopped an ice cube in my apple juice and smooched my face again.

"To the prettiest princess in the whole kingdom." He clinked his glass to my special cup, and we laughed. Daddy said that we could get ice cream if we were good. I'm going to be double good in case Jeffrey acts up again.

Daddy gave me a big wink and looked at his watch. His watch is so shiny that no one can look at it in the sun or they will be blind. It has magic powers too. The watch keeps me safe from all bad guys. Mommy doesn't know our secrets. Daddy got more tea, gave me two ice cubes, and watched the door.

"Are you missing Mommy?"

"Why would I miss Mommy when I can have a special night with my princess? Finish your sandwich and we can get that ice cream before Mommy gets home."

Over and over, I slipped under the water, and when I couldn't hold my breath any longer, I surfaced, and slipped under again. For nine days, I cried in the tub, no bubbles wanted or necessary, until a deathlike calm claimed me and, naked, I crawled into bed. I slept more profoundly than I'd ever known without dreams, until my flesh woke me with remembering and I'd fill the tub once again.

Like beloved friends, I let the stages of grief take me where I needed to go. They held me in a firm but loving grasp while I sunk into what was and what I could do nothing about. I skipped denial because there would be no return to blissful ignorance ever again. Within the warmth of the water, I allowed everything that I'd buried in sturdy little boxes to surface. It was ugly and shameful. Anger, bargaining, depression, and acceptance – no words could capture the tumultuous and torturous ride I had chosen to take. I wanted to heal. I wanted to accept, but that's the hardest of all—the one I'd spend years working on if I wanted a good life, and I did.

I dried prune-like hands and turned my phone on. Multiple messages from Mom, Levi, Susan, Paulka, Jeffrey, Marie, Neil, Tony, and Candy—even one from Phoebe and Sophia—but nothing from David. I let the phone fall to the floor and added more hot water to the tub. I nibbled on the toast I'd made until it was gone. The plate joined the phone on the floor. For the first time, the deathlike exhaustion didn't come. My mind was alert, sorting through the recent damage that I had caused.

I'd thrown a credit card at shame and self-loathing. David said that nothing is a waste when you love someone. We both knew I was the dog.

I'd been run over by a bastard, and David would do anything to save me. *Why is that so hard for you to understand?* A lifetime of repressed guilt and shame and the worst part was that I'd lost David over something that never was my fault.

I rinsed the conditioner from my hair and let the last bath swirl down the drain. I got out before the water was gone. I wrapped a clean towel around my body, and while I put my hair up in another towel, I knew the reason that David had taken a chance on me and why Mom had spared me as long as she could. Faith in doing the right thing. Did they have any faith left in me? Mom possibly, David ... absolutely not.

I tore the tag off a new pair of jeans, dug for my favorite buttery-soft sweater and padded to the kitchen, dressed for the first time in days. My kitchen counter looked like the after-effects of a wild party—empty booze bottles everywhere. That terrible night, every last bottle went down the drain. I wouldn't replace it with a binge buy at the corner liquor store. I'd get help, and never drink my shame again.

Mom used to tell us that the best things you do, you may never know that you did. She'd done so many best things, and so had David, Susan, Levi, and everyone who cared about me—more than they would ever know. On day number nine of my self-imposed exile from those who loved me despite my flaws, I picked up my phone and started with Jeffrey.

"Did you use penis enhancement drugs with your internet hook-ups?" I asked.

Funny. Yay me. I didn't lose everything.

"You must be feeling better," Jeffrey said, chuckling.

"Yeah." Ravenous, I foraged in my bare fridge, the almost empty cupboard. I settled on an open jar of peanut butter, grabbed a spoon, and headed for the couch.

"Mom told me what happened at the club."

I pulled one of Paulka's cashmere blankets around my body and made myself small in the couch cushions.

"My appalling behavior in front of Gerald?"

"She told me about Dad," Jeffrey said. "I never knew."

Fresh tears filled my eyes. *How can there be any left?* I swapped out the peanut butter for what was left of a toilet paper roll tucked into the cushions and blew my nose.

"You don't have to talk about it," Jeffrey said.

I breathed deeply, evenly. *Hello, pain.*

"I'm sorry that I wasn't there for you," I said through a handful of damp paper. "I've been hiding ..." *For too long.*

"You have nothing to apologize for, you never did."

"Thanks."

I shut my eyes tight, forcing the tears back, until the ache in my chest let go of its iron grip. Breathe. It took several long minutes before I trusted my voice. New and improved Jeffrey didn't badger me to speak until I was ready. *Change is good.*

"Can I go to a meeting with you this week?" I asked.

"Let's start with Wednesday morning. They have donuts. Leanne?"

"Yeah?"

"You should call Susan. She's worried sick."

"I'll stop by on my way to Mom's."

"Leanne?"

"Yeah?"

"I love you."

A hot gush of tears soaked my face, and after a few minutes of pain-wracked silence, Jeffrey hung up. *Would this ever stop? I love you too little brother, but I can't speak without losing my shit and there isn't much shit left to lose.*

After dumping all the bottles in the recycling bin, I got in my car. I hadn't been anywhere since *that* night. The empty passenger seat was covered with dried blood, dried mud, and tuffs of jet-black fur. I started crying again, swallowed hard, then let the tears fall unchecked. *The sadness will stop.* Had David named the dog before they died? I bet he did—something old fashioned-like Fred or Maryanne. *I missed him.* I found my way to Susan's and parked under leafy trees, and a bright blue sky. *Funny how the world doesn't stop, not for birth, death, or those sucky places in between.* With dark glasses on and a black baseball cap pulled so low I could barely see, I let myself in through the kitchen door.

"Take off the awful hat and let me see your damaged psyche." Paulka had tears in his eyes.

Susan, Levi, and Brett the wonder husband sat with pink champagne in flutes and a yellow legal notepad in front of each and every one. Traitors. I wasn't in the mood for an intervention. Surprise, kids, this drunk already promised to attend donut mornings. Levi crushed me in his arms.

"I've been worried; we've all been so worried about you. You didn't call—"

"I know, and I didn't write. I'm sorry."

"Shirley Temple?" Brett asked, springing into wonder husband action, a pretty glass magically appearing in his hand.

"Apparently, the Leanne Spencer spy network is still up and running efficiently. Did Jeffrey use smoke signals or morse code?" I asked, pulling up a chair. "Coffee, if you wouldn't mind. I haven't had a decent cup in days."

"Right on it."

Brett didn't give me one of his incandescent smiles. He looked wounded and caring, and when he landed a soft kiss on my cheek, I reached out and took his hand. He wasn't Brett the wonder husband anymore. He was Brett, the truly nice guy married to my pushy best friend who was doing the best he could. I kissed him back.

"Thank you." I slapped my hand on the table and called the meeting to order. "Now let the intervention begin. Hmm. This is strange. Don't you know I'm already signed up to kick booze for good with Jeffrey? Didn't my brother, your chief spy, inform the counsel? Oh, I get it. You don't believe it's true. Expect me to gain ten pounds and consider smoking."

Susan sat stick straight in her chair, her pouty lips a thin line, but she couldn't trick me. Her psychoanalyst wanna-be brain rotated at warp speed behind that soft, pensive gaze. She wouldn't back down without a fight.

"It's not an intervention, silly. Jeffrey told us he'd take care of that part."

I didn't like the sound of this, or the multiple strands of breathing beads hanging from her neck and wrists, gently jangling as she moved toward me, a serene smile now curling her lips to the heavens. *What they hell is she doing now?*

"We are composing letters to your father," Susan said and gave me a hug. *Everyone knows. Jeffrey told them. I'm gonna puke.*

Paulka let out a small shriek. "Father? More like the pubic hairs of a rotting hamster. Oh, I better write that down."

The frightened little girl living inside my body shut her eyes, drew her arms and legs into a ball, and hid somewhere between my ribs and my heart. Susan wrapped her arms around me. I soaked in her misguided but loving goodness.

"Please don't," I whispered to Susan.

I'd happily played client to her shrink when shitty relationships fueled her fancy, but not this. *Too raw, too real.* Brett placed a mug of fresh coffee in front of me, and sat behind his legal pad, picked up his pen.

"We hurt for you, and it's the only thing we can do," she said.

Susan slid a pad of paper and a bright green gel pen to me. *Did the green mean something? A new beginning? The grass over a grave when no one is home.* Poor Jeffrey. It wasn't just an adult drink at a tender young age that fucked him up. *That mother fucking bastard. I want to write this in blood.*

"Levi, can I trade green for red?"

Levi passed me the red pen, and no one said as word as I gathered my mug and notepad and padded off to Susan's living room. I swathed the silvery cashmere blanket around my shoulders, and the little girl stirred. She was anxious. *We can do this.* I swallowed the biggest lump I'd ever known. *We have to do this.* I stabbed the paper a few times, made a couple of scribbles, and the pen took off on its own.

> *Dear Dad,*
>
> *I thought that I missed having you in my life. I believed that the gaping hole in my heart was where you would be—if you had lived. I pretended about what it would be like if*

you had cheered on my first Baked Alaska, the acceptance on your face when I'd show you a report card with B's and C's (mostly C's). I'd imagine how I'd grudgingly respect your sage advice about men before my first dance, and how worried you'd be when I came home past my curfew.

I'm glad I had those dreams for as long as I did. My imaginary dad, the one that Mom created, was the best dad that I could ever have had. I'm so lucky that, armed with my extraordinary friends and a relentlessly loving mother, I can face who you really are—and not let what you did destroy me. I'm going to find a real therapist and heal. I'm going to do whatever it takes for as long as it takes to put you back in your grave where you belong. I will never forget or forgive you and you better believe that I am not your victim.

Leanne.

The sweet scent of burning wood drifted in through the French doors leading out to the garden. *Of course.* The drama queen in Paulka and the faux therapist in Susan would settle for nothing less than a ritualistic burning. *Let the games begin.* I took my soggy letter, so wet with tears that I didn't think it would burn, let alone fly off to some magical goddess who would send me rays of healing love in return.

"Why'd you get the fire pit? Planning a luau? I bet Paulka has several grass skirts and knows the hula," I said, tweaking Susan on the arm.

"Brett made it. We've been burning our feelings all week."

"That explains the half cord of wood by the gazebo."

Brett blushed, and I understood without judgement. Levi came around behind me and let me lean into his warmth. He stroked my hair and confirmed my belief in all things good. *I'm good.* My wise mind nodded and smiled.

One by one in deep reflection and great solemnity they pitched *Dear Leanne's Asshole of a Dad* into the flames, except Paulka. His ritualistic dance came first. Then he plunged his letter into the heart of the fire, and lightly burnt a pinky. Levi kissed it better. Fragrant smoke played around my head, my friends gave me space and yet again held my pain, sharing it between them. *You have taken nothing from me, and you never will again.* I tossed my letter into the fire. The damp paper smoked, and the edge where I'd torn it from the pad burst into flame and fell as ashes onto the stones below. *It isn't over. Not even close.*

"How do you feel?" Susan placed one of the breathing bead necklaces around my neck. Levi tucked a tissue into my palm. Paulka gave me the sweetest little bow. I smiled. How could I not? The truth was that I didn't feel any better in regards to the asshole of the universe, but the crazy over the top fire pit ceremony? Priceless.

"Much better. Thank you."

"It's only a start, and you'll need more work. I signed up for *Chasing Trauma and Bringing it Down.* Only twelve lessons." She shoved a pamphlet of some kind into my hand, I shoved it in my pocket.

Oh, God. Bringing it down, like Bob the wildebeest in his final moments. Please no.

"I can't wait." My lips touched her cheek. "I need to go to Mom's now."

Chapter Fifty-Seven

I parked in front of Mom's building, tossed my keys with attitude to the valet, and for the first time, really took in the handsome façade of her building. *An old bank.* The penny from darkness fell and I knew why she'd moved in such a hurry. He'd shown up at the house, and she needed a fortress where she'd be safe forever.

Mom was outside the elevator, and we were in each other's arms, like two trees grown from the same small patch of earth. She took my hand and walked me into her home as the afternoon filled the living room. I smiled. She had known that I would come and trusted me to do the right thing.

"Why does your hair smell like a campfire? It doesn't matter, go to the living room," she said. "I'll be there in a sec."

From the kitchen came the familiar sounds of the fridge opening and closing, Mom slapping a saucepan on the stove, and the subtle scrape of a wooden spoon mixing real cocoa and milk together. It was the one thing that she made better than I did. She set two mugs with cat tails for handles on the coffee table and put a box of Kleenex in between them. I took the orange cat mug, blew on the frothy top, and sipped chocolate-flavored love. When I put the mug down, I couldn't look her in the eye. Wretched sweeping shame kept my head bowed. She put a hand on either side of my face and tilted my head to face hers.

"I love you."

That was all it took for the words to tumble out, along with another river of tears. I grabbed a handful of tissues, and after the first handful was soaked, I gave up and let her see my heart.

"I'm so sorry. I should have listened to you. I thought if you were wrong, he could be right." I feel so ashamed. "I believed your stories, but I wanted so badly for him to be good."

I sobbed, great guttural sobs, and began rocking again. I drenched her pretty dress in snotty tears and still couldn't stop crying. With her arms, her whole body, as close as it could be, and I clutched her until the tears slowed enough to see her face—raw red eyes with dark circles. She wasn't wearing any make-up. Her cheekbones were sharp angles in a thin face. She looked like she'd seen a ghost.

"I should have told you sooner," she said. "I should have taken you to a child psychologist when you were little. I didn't know exactly what he'd done, and I was scared that if you'd forgotten it, it would traumatize you to remember before you were ready."

"You don't know what he did? You've suffered all this time, not knowing?"

Mom trembled and sipped from a glass of water on the coffee table.

"I was scared to know, and based on what he'd done to me, I expected the worst."

She sobbed with a suffering that engulfed me and kindled a torch for justice. *Fuck the letter. I'm not done with you yet.* Mom untangled herself from my embrace, wiped her eyes, and blew a big breath through pursed lips. "I'm sorry, Leanne, I am so sorry. I will spend the rest of my life making up for what I did and didn't do."

My face scrunched up, and nails dug into my palms. Memories swirled, and my skin crawled. Long, slow breaths, Susan's beads in my hand—*do it for her.* She'd suffered long enough.

"Do you want to know?"

She steeled herself and nodded, her eyes lit with fear. *We can do this.*

"He'd get in my bed and smell of cigarettes, and toothpaste, and soap, and perfume and booze. He'd cuddle me, and shhh me, don't wake Mommy. I remember worrying about you being tired all the time, and it seemed kind to be quiet."

She didn't interrupt. I felt like an ass.

"What if I'm remembering it wrong?" I asked.

"I suspect what you remember is close to the truth, even if it's not exact. You've always had an excellent memory."

"He'd have PJ bottoms on, take off my nightie, spoon me, and whisper I was so pretty. He'd call me princess and baby, and that part was—nice." *Oh, Shame.* "Other times, he'd get naked and rub himself against me—and he'd hurt my arms because I'd try and get away from him." My mouth wouldn't move, I couldn't get out the rest. *This is for her.* "My bed would be sticky when he left." Mom's face couldn't get any whiter, her eyes any bigger. She nodded for me to continue. "*That* night, he said that you didn't love him anymore. I let him put make-up on me because he was sad. He was dead drunk and crying. Then Jeffrey's screaming made him mad, and he ripped my panties off and looked right through me like I wasn't there.

Mom gasped, her face even whiter than before. She shook like a person in the movies who had just received a terrible shock.

"Mom! He couldn't—" *I can't say it.* "He didn't enter me. He'd tried but was too drunk, and then you came in."

She picked up the cocoa, her hands still trembling, and stared into the drink, tears plopping into the mug.

"You did the right thing, Mom, not telling me. I wouldn't accept it; I couldn't hear it. I didn't realize how much I remembered until the glass cracked."

"I always wondered what you knew. Over the years, I'd tested the waters, but you'd shut me down. I figured that when you were ready, you'd let me know."

"I wish I could take away what he did to you, and what I did to you."

She set her cup down and stroked my hair away from my sticky face. "You didn't do anything, Leanne."

"He doesn't deserve any more of us."

"No, he doesn't, and he never did."

I leaned up against her and let myself feel the pain. We'd be okay, and Susan would have plenty of material. *David.* Too bad I'd be alone.

"Oh, I forgot to tell you; David called to check on you."

Of course, he did. He's a sweet, caring, lovely man, and you blew the best thing you'll ever have. "I owe him the apology of the decade. I think it's his late day for work, so if we're good, I want to go to him."

"Leanne, just because you do the right thing doesn't mean it's easy or you will get what you want."

"I know. He called because that's the right thing to do, but I have no illusions that he wants me anymore." *I'm apologizing because I am an ass and hurt him.*

Mom stroked my hair and wiped another tear from my face. Then she took both my hands and smiled through her tears. "Would you do me a favor?"

"Anything."

"I'd like to have the four-leaf clover over the front door. Would you go and get it for me?"

"I thought you didn't want anything from the past?"

"That clover isn't the past. It's the future." She kissed me and pressed my keys and a bottle of water into my palm. "Drink; you look dehydrated."

I took the water.

Chapter Fifty-Eight

I'd been horrible from the beginning. I was an insecure, untrusting, hot mess he didn't deserve. I had had no business grilling him about Crystal. He'd been nothing but understanding. I mentally slapped myself for the situation with Michael. David at the hospital, David by the creek, David kissing me with such passion that I forgot to beat myself up, David and the boots. *Well, cowgirl, it looks like you could use a little help.* Oh my god, I'd been so stupid, so cruel, and yet he'd called Mom to check on me. *What else did they talk about?* I didn't want to know.

I parked and ran up the stairs to his door, my heart beating hard and fast. No answer. No car in the driveway. *Damn.* I'd have to come back later. In the meantime, I'd dissect my sins and improve my apology as I drove out to the old house to get Mom's clover and say goodbye.

Across the bridge, I reached for the bottle of water. If Dad was an evil son of a bitch, then water wasn't Caesar's pee. I preferred Diet Coke, but I'd cried so many tears, and the water wasn't really so bad. *Poor Mom.* She had not only been living a lie but living in enough fear to leave her beloved home at a moment's notice and take nothing. *Poor Vivi.* What she'd endured for over forty years. Unbelievable. The bastard had thought nothing of a cozy breakfast to win me over, and for what? To take advantage of me again because *he knew I didn't know. How did he guess that?* Mom had run for a second time and never confronted him. *Fuck that shit.*

The car screeched as I pulled onto the side of the road where the gravel meets the highway. A lonely stretch of road, where a woman and two small children made amends to the dog that saved them. Sleep in peace? *Not yet.* Fresh, angry tears ripped through my throat as I stalked from the car and paced the dirt. Truth-fueled rage pulsed through me, enough pure hate to quench any fear. You can't hurt me now; narcissistic prick and judgment has a name. *Fuck you, Verin!* I screamed at the phone that I pulled from my jeans. *Fuck you, forever.* It wasn't enough, so I called him for the last time.

"Hey there, baby. Have you thought about my offer? I'm heading out to sign the papers."

"You are a lying piece of shit, Verin."

"Verin? What happened to Daddy?"

"You choose to forfeit *Daddy* when you fucked your daughter, fucked up her brother, and tortured an innocent, trusting, good as gold soul of a young woman."

"Wait a second—"

"It's all true. You're the bastard fucking liar, not Mom. I'm not scared of you. There's no dead dog to save your sorry ass, and you won't be chasing me from my home."

"Leanne, baby—please listen. I'm not lying."

"Shut the fuck up, Verin. You are a sad piece of work, and there is no statute of limitations for what you did."

The bastard laughed. He actually laughed. I wiped the spit from my lips with the back of my other hand and pulled the pamphlet Susan had slipped me from my jeans. For the second time that day, I held it like a prayer book. I already knew it by heart.

"Do you think anyone will believe you? There's a reason they don't put children on the witness stand, baby."

"My best friend is a top lawyer in San Francesco. She's got a very sympathetic buddy in the DA's office. Guess what her specialty is?"

I held the phone away from my ear and up to the sky. The wind could listen to the excuses and ravings of the sick fuck. I was done. I tapped the red end-call button.

Chapter Fifty-Nine

An old pick-up truck filled with tools, a ladder, and moving boxes, was parked in the driveway at Mom's house. I sat in my car and scanned for people. The coast clear, I carefully stood on Sandy Shitridge's planter and took the clover down. I rubbed the dust off with my T-shirt—a few cracks shone through the old gold paint. Standing on the porch, I took one last look at the oak tree and the sold sign. Tears flowed down my cheeks. Why hadn't I bought the house? I never thought that she would actually sell it. I slid my dark glasses off my head and headed to my car.

A black dog with a pink bandage and matching collar limped out from the garage. Another dog, like a baby cow, ambled over, licked my hand, and waited at my feet. A tense, worn-out, and insanely handsome David trudged toward me with a moving box.

I stared at the three of them. "You bought the house?"

"Love at first sight," David said, his voice subdued, eyes on Edison.

I petted the smaller dog. "She made it." My dark glasses were on. I didn't need David to see any more tears, even happy ones.

"No collar, no chip. Eddie convinced me that he needed a wife. He doesn't like dating. Her name is Lola."

I leaned down and inhaled the scent of warm sun on Lola's fur and inspected the cast. She licked my tears.

"Why'd you buy the house?"

David put the box down and patted the grass beside him. Eddie and Lola stretched out, and Lola rolled on her back. I sat down and rubbed her tummy.

"I'd been looking to move before we met. Too many memories, too much pain, and it didn't feel like my home. I didn't feel attached to it, or anything in it. I thought that I should stick it out, but I couldn't. Once I met you, it didn't seem right making a life with someone else there. I suspect that your mom came to the same conclusion."

Mom? The clover! Sly minx. She knew exactly where David would be. She'd talked with him. Did I have a chance? David lay back on the grass, his arms behind his head, looking into the sky. I couldn't read his eyes. Was he wounded? Resolved? Angry? My stomach balled into a knot. I took my glasses off and scooted closer to him. My hands itched to touch him.

"David, I'm sorry that I left you at the vet. That's the worst thing I've ever done. I have no excuse. I'm ... so sorry. I have never treated you like you deserve to be, and I'm sorry about that, too."

His face stiffened like I'd made the reality worse by talking. A sharp pain shot through my gut. This was torture.

"Jeffrey filled me in on what happened backstage at the club. You could've told me."

I buried my face in Lola's thick neck. "I didn't know how."

What had cracked open that night at the club wouldn't be closed up again. I came up for air, looked at David with watery eyes, and sniffed like the sad little girl I'd hidden for years. He reached out and pulled me down against his warm body, and I held onto this man who understood that I had done the right thing regardless of the outcome that I most feared. He smiled at me. He wasn't going anywhere?

"What would make you happy right now?" David said.

I looked over at the box he'd set in the grass. It was marked fragile and filled to the top with bubble-wrapped treasures.

"I'd like to order a pizza, help you unpack, and once it's dark, make a fire."

"Unpack? You can't trick me, Leanne. I know you're after my bubble wrap."

He pulled me tighter and settled warm, soft lips on mine. He wasn't going anywhere. A pack of kids on bicycles rode by and yelled at us to get a room. Eddie licked my leg.

"I'll forgive you on one condition."

"Anything."

"You won't get mad?"

"Never."

"Your Mom and I have become pretty good friends in the last nine days. She said that I could have anything in the house you didn't want." He kissed me again. *Delicious.* The kids swarmed by again beeping horns and declaring the utter grossness of kissing.

"I want everything. You'll have to live here and share with me. Are you okay with that?" David said.

I took his hand, walked to the porch, and handed him the clover, my heart in my throat. We both kissed the scratched token of eternal hope, and David hung it back where it belonged—where it would live forever. He opened the front door, and as I walked through, breathing in the scent of a thousand baths of lemon oil, I knew where peace would always find me.

THE END

Acknowledgments

Alexandria Brown and Tina Beier of Rising Action Publishing Collective, thank you for trusting me with the words, all the words. You opened your ears and your hearts to Leanne's story, and I am forever grateful. Your kick assness knows no bounds, and for what it's worth I am so damn proud to be one of your writers.

Cathie Hedrick Armstong of the Purcell Agency, literary champion and my friend, thank you for taking a chance on a baby writer and believing with the faith of the ages.

Miss Nat Mack. Book Designer. It takes nothing short of alchemy to bring the soul of a character to the light. Thank you for giving Leanne and Patricia the chance to been seen. That's all they ever wanted.

Early eyes. Ara Grigorian, Lauren Alsten, Lindsay Guzzardo, and Angela Knight. Thank you for pulling forth what needed to shine and letting go what didn't. Your guidance was a welcome and gentle push in the perfect direction.

Thank you to The Santa Barbara Writers Conference, and especially to Grace Rachow, Matthew Pallamary, and Melodie Johnson Howe.

I have a special place in my heart for writers, and a whole peony pink room just for Camille Pagán. Your dedication to share and inspire others is beautiful. Both within the stories you craft and in the real world. Neil Gaiman, your signed 8 Rules for Writing are a beckon of light and my mirror. If rule number 8 wasn't so long I'd tattoo it on my ass.

The First Readers. Karen Grant, Elia Escobar, Dani Burckhardt, Judy Roll, Dierdre Locke, Jennifer Matarese, Lois Brown Klein, Ronald Doctors and Sonia Gordon, thank you for sharing what made you laugh, made you cry and kept you reading past bedtime. This is what my writing soul lives for; the ability to drop a stone in a pond and hear about the ripple in the night. For those that now watch from the other realms, I hope you are proud. We did it.

The Witches aka the critique partners: Toni Guy (the bathroom witch), Suze Gray Williams (the blender witch) and Mikko Cook (the kitchen witch). As much as I treasure our magical world of words, the best gift is finding the sisters of my heart. Thank you for the infinite encouragement, inspiration in the most unlikely of places and for your continued pursuit to make me drink water. Love, The Bedroom Witch.

A special thank you to my mom, Rachael Doctors. Who knew that grounding me (for nothing) and making me write get-out-of- jail essays would lead to a writing career. I hope my love finds you in the mists of Cleopatra's bath.

Lewis, Taylor and Miranda. For you, the manners Olympics, wisps of us, forever in print. Thank you for growing into the grace and kindness of wise adults.

Mike Shumann, you show me that love can be simple, good and well within my world. Thank you for sharing your musical gifts, your heart and your oh-so-beautiful mind with me. Love is indeed the in-be-tween's.

A special thank you to Anastasia Poland aka the garden witch. Everyone should have a wise mama bear like you.

And, dear readers, thank you for letting Leanne and Patricia into your world. May your hand open the gates that you need most, and may you have the courage to believe you deserve a healthy love, and to let it find you when the time is right.

And finally, thank you to the rat bastards of the world. You provide a service, the hard lessons. The worst lessons. Your welcome.

About the Author

Melanie Doctors is an English-born American author who likes nothing better than crafting stories that need a box of tissues on standby. Her debut novel, Sleep in Peace, is no exception. She describes her process best, saying, "I write the stories that won't leave me alone. I hope they won't leave other people alone either." When she's not diving deep into what it means to be human, she's writing music with the acoustic duo, Witches and Beer. Playing music in her adopted city of Boise, Idaho, is the perfect companion to crafting the next page-turning wild ride.